Night of the Revel

RACHEL HAWK

Book Cover by James at Go On Write:

http://www.goonwrite.com

To my fabulous writing tribe, for without their encouragement this book would still be collecting dust.

To my wonderful husband, for his continuous support and his 'listening ear' when I'd ramble on about fairies, sprites, and monsters.

This book is for my children, my biggest fans, who constantly ask for Mommy's stories and inherited my love for reading and magic.

And to all of you who believe in magic, this book is for you.

PROLOGUE

Hemlock Cottage lived on 55 Piccolo Ln. And it was lonely.

Houses are unique...they have a specific signature, a fingerprint if you will. Houses produce heightened levels of emotions. Some radiate happiness, others make people jaded. Some can be scary, some create envy. Most administer a sense of safety and security. However, there is one type of house that is extraordinarily special. Those exceptional abodes are a rare gem, highly sought after, but rarely discovered. And what is it that makes them so spectacularly special you may ask? Well...these dwellings excel in the preservation and safeguarding of secrets. But not just any old secrets, goodness no. The particularly peculiar and unexpected sort of secret is their bread and butter.

Hemlock Cottage, concealed by plush foliage, steady oaks, weeping willows, and a hint of perfumed roses, was such a house.

The scent of honeysuckle, lilac, and clover danced in the air, quite unlike the stale burning fog that hovered across the river. The Cottage was a hidden escape within the dried concrete and bustling noise that most residents found themselves living in New Jersey. A jeweled secret that not many knew about...and even fewer were privy to its secrets that were so jealously guarded.

The Cottage loved flowers, specifically cascading morning glories and climbing roses that it boasted on its sunny side. This twisting tangle of red and blue flowers reached upwards toward the stars. A small stable lay adjacent to the main house where a freshwater spring bubbled in the backyard, surrounded by clover and wildflowers. Just beyond the spring, a weathered stone bridge stood over a twisting creek, where the backyard vanished into a deep forest at the edge of the property.

Hemlock Cottage had been abandoned for nearly four decades. No one wanted it. Quite out of the way from the supermarket or restaurants. It was inconvenient to the modern connoisseur. Well, regardless, the Cottage was over 30 minutes from a major highway. Highly impractical. The real estate agent didn't even want to mention the Cottage wasn't near any cell towers. What? No cell reception? Ridiculous! No neighbors for miles around, a feat so close to New York City. What if someone broke in? Poor Hemlock Cottage was truly an enigma, sandwiched within a world of blacktops and buzzing mobility. Or...maybe the modern eye couldn't see beyond the surface appearance.

The Cottage was not always like this, alone and forgotten. It was previously owned by the Loricks; a substantial family of eight. Sadly, it has been said most of the children moved far away once their parents passed on. Those children had children of their own. And those children have had grandchildren. The quaint Hemlock Cottage was remembered in many stories, tucked away in warm and loving memories. Always told by a campfire or at dinner because everyone knows comforting stories should be told comfortably. But no one came to visit the little Cottage. So, it sat patiently. And waited. It was this patience that caught the eye of Professor Ambrosino.

Now the dear professor had fallen in love only five times in his life. First, listening to the haunting melodies of Jethro Tull. Second, his discovery of the world of anthropology. Third, the birth of his only daughter. Fourth, his newly wedded wife Tabby. And fifth? It was looking at the weather-beaten, two-story, brown, and white cottage. He was taken with Hemlock's quaint, quiet, and earthy appeal. The professor could have been described simi-larly... well . . . if you excluded the quiet part and the quaint. But Ambrosino was certainly very earthy. There wasn't a moment where he wasn't covered in mud, soil, dust, or muck.

Hemlock swayed slightly and creaked ever so softly in the perfumed breeze. The little weather-beaten, two-story, brown, and white secret keeper was thrilled to finally have life back in her walls. Hemlock Cottage welcomed the Ambrosinos. It was quite unknown at the time, but the Hemlock Cottage took a particular shine to the professor's daughter, Lily Ambrosino. As the southern breeze sang through the trees around the weathered cottage, announcing the end of tedious learning and the beginning of dreamy summer days, Hemlock Cottage creaked with anticipa-tion. It could not wait for Lily's story to begin.

CHAPTER
ONE

L ily sat on her new windowsill, overlooking the backyard, as the warm breeze wafted in to ruffle her neck-length black hair. Taking a deep breath, she tucked a few stray curls behind her ear as she inhaled a cornucopia of sparkling flowers and warm musk.

She smiled, the feeling of contentment seeping into her bones. Now, this...this was perfectly perfect. Lily found herself gazing out towards the woods again, for almost the tenth time that day. It had quickly become her favorite viewing spot as she loved to see the sunlight dance across the creek and sparkle throughout the green leaves.

Lily brought her knees up to her chest, quietly sipping her steaming cup of jasmine tea. As the warm cup permeated her hands, she continued to watch the dense forest, feeling the rare moment of contentment stretching out from a moment to a minute. A lively Kenyan beat steadily pumped through a set of custom-designed speakers she built with her father.

Lily's room was a motley assortment of relics from all over the globe that was in various stages of unpacking. Having a professor of anthropology for a father tended to mean they acquired all sorts of things such as a didgeridoo which was a gift from an Australian aborigine, a fertility idol given to Lily by Kanika, princess of a tribe deep within the Congo, dreamcatchers given to her by a Mexican shaman, and Buddhist statues from Tibet. Just to name a few. Strewn all over the floor were piles of books, and teetering stacks of papers right on the edge of falling over. Some may have called it a textbook pack rat or hoarder. To Lily, it was organized chaos at its finest.

Turning away from the window, she placed her cup down and began to rummage between sheets of *Plants, Ants, and Quadrupeds*.

"Now where is that application?" she murmured to herself, tucking a strand of curly hair behind her ear.

She blew away another stray curl that tickled her upper lip. The stubborn strand came back once more, covering her eye. She wrinkled her nose, annoyed, as she smoothed it behind her ear again. She kneeled back towards the pile. Lily paused her search as a rustling squeak interrupted her train of thought.

Lily rolled her eyes. "I suppose you think this is funny don't you Rox?"

She smiled over towards the small atrium in the corner of her room. Rox darted out, chirping excitedly. Rox was Lily's pet sugar glider. She found him abandoned on her father's dig in Australia. He was the runt of his family, left alone to survive. Her father and the locals on the dig offered to take Rox to a sanctuary, but Lily refused. Rox had her the moment he looked at her with his hugely adorable eyes. Those same big eyes blinked at her now, acting innocent. He spoke a series of clicks, almost as if he was laughing and went back behind his drape.

Lily pursed her lips as she gazed at the pile of papers. Her eyes widened as she caught sight of a familiar form. *Ah ha, found it*, she thought triumphantly. Slowly, she began to pull the piece of paper from the bottom of one of the large piles. The tall tower teetered from side to side. Holding her breath, that annoying hair strand still swaying in her face, Lily closed her eyes and tugged. The tower lurched as her hand froze.

Just like Jenga, keep it steady. Slowly, Lil.

Keeping her eyes closed, she tugged again and the paper freed itself from the stack. Cautiously, Lily cracked one of her eyes. The papers didn't move. She smiled, pumping her hands in the air not once but twice in victory. Yes! For once her clumsy self didn't cause another disaster.

She was still gleeful over her small victory against inanimate papers and started to smooth out the crumpled application when her dad yelled.

"Lil! *Dove sei?*"

"Upstairs in my room!" she yelled back.

"*Che fai?!*"

Before she could reply, Professor Ambrosino burst through the door, all the while hastily attempting to put on an ink-splattered tie, his eyes glued to his chest. His fingers fumbled with the knots as he called out frantically.

"Lil! What are you doing? Tabby, Arianna, and Brandon will be here any minute! Are you ready?!"

What he didn't notice was that he was missing his right shoe and the shoe he did manage to put on was lacking a sock. In his haste, he also failed to notice the stack of books that Lily had 'organized' near the door. She could only stare as her father hit his elbow on her copy of the *Egyptian Book of the Dead* while he wrestled with his wrinkled tie. This action caused an unequal opposite reaction. Do you know those domino games? The ones where they're placed in a precise order, but one wrong move causes a chain of events where all the dominos fall over. Well, Lily's books became large dominos as they tumbled one after another, knocking Rox's atrium on the floor, the cage door swinging open as the sugar glider hissed in protest. Her father lay in a pile of books with a highly agitated Rox sitting on his head. His curly black hair stuck out at all angles, his glasses askew as he blinked in confusion.

Lily chuckled, quickly covering her mouth to hide her smile so her father wouldn't be embarrassed. He was trying so desperately to make everything go smoothly tonight. But if there was one thing she knew about her dad, it was that if something was supposed to go smoothly, some type of speed bump inevitably surfaced. In spades.

As the professor tried to gently remove a clinging Rox from his head, Lily tried to put the focus back on the subject at hand.

"Dad, relax. I'll be ready in a minute. I was looking for my Cornell application." She waved said application in emphasis.

Lily walked to her grandmother's oak dresser to grab her hairbrush. Her father only had a few personal belongings in their possession. Most of their stuff was stuck in a storage unit while they were off on digs all over the world. It was at least four years and they still didn't take out anything from the storage locker, save for her grandmother's dresser. The dresser had been passed down to the women in her family for years. Each had to carve a symbol that was important to them. Lily was practicing carving a stargazer lily. Practicing being the loose term, Lily thought ruefully. More like struggling. She was frustrated she couldn't even carve a simple leaf. But she knew this was too important to give up on. Her father always told her that unless you understand the past, you cannot understand the present. Every life is a story and every person is a storyteller. *Never stop asking*, Dr. Ambrosino always told her from the time she could remember. There were no right or wrong questions, as long as you kept asking.

As Lily sat on her grandmother's embroidered stool, Rox jumped off her father's head and climbed onto her shoulder. He chirped affectionately as he nuzzled into her neck, Lily absently rubbing his head. She gazed at her reflection in an ornate silver mirror that she discovered in the attic the day before. It was intricately carved with vines and flowers that crept into the silvery glass. Her father thought it was made out of a type of pewter, but the silvery glow it cast made Lily question her father's logic. She kept scratching Rox, admiring the expertly crafted work. She wondered why it was left behind, collecting dust in some quiet attic. It looked too valuable to be tucked away in a corner. She stared hard at the smooth surface, contemplating taking a small sample of the metal to see what it was made of. She blinked. Was it her imagination or did the mirror's face ripple as if a stone was plopped silently in a still lake? Lily reached forward, her hand outstretched....

Her dad coughed loudly as he brushed imaginary dust off his shoulder, breaking her unfocused gaze. She dropped her hand to turn around to see her father awkwardly trying to stand up, his arms teetered outwards to keep balance.

He coughed again. "Lily? Maybe...if you have some time...you can pick up some of these books." Her dad struggled to walk over the sea of fallen books and tripped again, falling into another pile with an "Ooomph".

Lily mentally rolled her eyes, suppressing the urge to bring up her father's study which was laden with tomes and books up to the ceiling.

"I'll be ready in two minutes."

With expert movements she fixed her hair in a loose bun, a few curls falling out here and there. Hazel eyes stared back through her mirror as she checked the clock; finished with 30 seconds to spare. Lily took a second look in the mirror, wondering briefly if she should do something more. Maybe she should curl her hair? Maybe some blush? *Nah, why bother*, she sighed ruefully. Besides, no matter how hard she tried, her stepsister would outshine everyone. Ari, her stepsister, was a beauty.

Even at sixteen, she was like one of those golden princesses Lily used to read about when she was younger. Ari was one for the spotlight while Lily preferred to be in the background, observing. She frowned slightly. Even if she tried, Ari would probably comment on her 'trying too hard'. Lily looked away and closed her small makeup bag with a forceful snap.

Rox jumped off her shoulder with an excited chirp. Her father had finally removed himself from the books, still fumbling with his tie. Lily raised her eyebrow.

"Don't worry Dad, we're still unpacking everything. I'm sure Tabby will not mind the mess. After all, I seem to recall it wasn't me that knocked the books over." She looked pointedly as her father tried to put the books upright, only to have them fall again.

Her father put his hands out in surrender, his tie half done. "*Bene!* Okay sweetie, forget about the books. It's just," he paused, his brow furrowed as he ran his hand through his already messed-up hair. "I want this to go well. They haven't seen the house yet. I want Tabby to be happily surprised."

Lily's eyes softened, her annoyance disappearing as quickly as it came. Bless her father; he really loved her stepmom. He seemed even more nervous if that could be possible, than the time he asked Tabitha Greene to marry him. This ranked up to the time when he tripped up the church steps and managed to knock over the father of the bride, which caused Tabby's father to shuffle her down the aisle with a twisted ankle. In the end, her dad got married in a suit with a ripped leg. She smiled; her father was her father. What did it matter that he couldn't tie a tie?

Lily got up and batted her father's hands away and, with expert moves, fixed his tie. "Tabby will love the cottage. How could anyone not fall in love with this place?" Professor Ambrosino smiled in relief, his glasses tilted askew.

"Don't worry Dad." She tried to reassure her father, bending to clean up the book mess. "The pasta's cooked, the salad is in the fridge, and the bread is keeping warm in the oven. And your surprise for Tabby is all set. Though that took some effort let me tell you. That basement is really dark."

Lily shivered. She vividly recalled the feeling of being watched from the shadows when she was setting up Tabby's new dark-room for photography. Lily shook herself. It was only her imagination running wild. It was a dark basement that needed a good cleaning. Everyone was scared of dark basements. It was like people being scared of clowns, or spiders, or heights. Nothing special.

Her dad smiled, squeezing her shoulder. "You're a lifesaver sweetie. I was a little preoccupied with the new lecture on copper weapons. I completely lost track of time."

Lily wasn't surprised. Her dad was always in a book and forgot things often. She was used to taking care of little details like that. She didn't particularly mind. *Though...a break would be nice once in a while*, she thought. She looked up to see her dad had opened his arms to give her a warm hug.

"Thanks *Fiore*, I couldn't do this without you." He smiled warmly. Lily leaned into the hug, slightly embarrassed he still called her flower.

Her dad stepped back, his hands resting on her shoulders. "I really appreciate you getting the surprise ready. I hope Tabby likes her new darkroom. Speaking of... *Ho dimenticato!* I forgot! Did you get everything settled for your college visits?"

Lily grimaced. She was used to her dad changing subjects randomly in the middle of a conversation, but she didn't want to talk about college. "I'm getting there. I have an interview on Friday." She toyed with her scarf, refusing to look her dad in the eye.

"Dad...what if I say something wrong?" Already scenarios were playing in her mind about her botching up the interview.

Her dad smiled reassuringly. "*Fiore*, you'll be fine. You're always so hard on yourself. You get that from me ya know." His eyes crinkled warmly.

Lily gave an exasperated pout. "But everyone's already in college at my age. And what can I have conversations about huh? Ancient Egyptian rituals? Come on! I'll be a laughingstock." She tried to be sarcastic, but all she felt was insecure. Her shoulders drooped as she tucked her hair behind her ear.

Her dad laughed, a deep-throated, full-bodied laugh that she couldn't help smiling along as well.

"Dad it's not funny!"

"Oh!! *Il mio piccolo fiore.* Believe me when I say there is no one in this world like you. And you'll see it for yourself soon enough. Soon I'm gonna have to get used to you bringing friends around the house. Maybe even a *ragazzo*?" He winked.

"Oh please." Lily snorted. She never really dated. A cup of tea/coffee or a movie didn't count, and those were extremely few and far between. When the average guy on her father's digs was a decade older than you, there wasn't much to choose from in the dating pool.

Her dad chuckled. "Well, don't immerse yourself in your studies. Try to live a little. I'd love to see you make more friends."

Lily protested. "I have Charlotte!"

"Who you haven't seen in two years." He gently reminded her. "Charlotte is great sweetie, but she's in Sorrento."

"We talk all the time, with email," mumbled Lily.Her dad sighed. "I'm talking about making friends in the same time zone. Someone you can call up a moment's notice if you need to vent about something."

Lily's ears grew hot. Granted she hadn't spoken on the phone with Charlotte in a few months. But that didn't matter. Their friendship was the kind that no matter how much time passed, they'd jump right in as if nothing changed. But, if she was honest with herself, she could see her dad's point.

"Just try for me sweetie. *Promettimi?*"

She reluctantly looked up and sighed loudly. "Fiiiine. I promise."Her dad nodded, a satisfied smile plastered on his face. As he hurriedly fixed his glasses, she noticed the conversation took a hard-left turn as his eyes suddenly grew serious. He coughed awkwardly. "Eh em! Um...Lil, for tonight, could you also promise me that you'll be nice to Arianna."

Lily refrained from smacking her forehead in exasperation. *Here we go*, she inwardly groaned. She silently tried to pray to every deity, god, entity...you name it...to keep her eyes from rolling toward the ceiling in a blatant show of frustration.

She unclenched her jaw and calmly spoke. "Dad, like I told you the day I met Arianna, and on Tabitha's birthday, and the ballet, and the rehearsal dinner, and the wedding, AND the wedding reception, I am doing the best I can."

Her emotions clogged her throat. What she said was true. She was doing the best she could. And every time, no matter how hard she tried, it felt like she kept hitting an emotional brick wall. Her stepsister was rude, vindictive, petty, and manipulative. Just to name a few traits, they always seemed to be directed at her. For the life of her, Lily couldn't understand why and try as she might, she could never get her new stepsister to even smile.

Her dad gave her a pleading look. "Give her another chance. She is still young and still needs time to get used to the idea her mother and I are married. And remember...*familia.*"

"Family isn't perfect." Lily sighed, rubbing her temples. Her father only saw a young girl who was still coming to grips with her mother remarrying after years of being a widow. He believed her stepsister was the type of young girl who simply needed time, understanding, and love and suddenly it would be all sunshine and roses. But Lily knew this wasn't some romantic family comedy. Arianna was spoiled and selfish, to put it bluntly. But, ever the responsible one, Lily always had to be calm and collected. It was her responsibility to keep trying to cross the never-ending bridge between them.

Lily looked up. It was getting close to dinner. She headed towards the door to make one last check on the food, sure her dad forgot something. *He probably hasn't even set up the table yet.* Rubbing her chest, the familiar suffocating weight of responsibility closed in around her. She glanced back, her father looking at her like a sad puppy. What would it be like to run away from it all?

She mentally smacked herself. *No! Stop thinking like that.*

Lily sighed. "Alright, alright, fine. Brandon and I get along okay. I'll do my best with Arianna. I'm sure we'll get along... eventually."

Yeah, she thought to herself sarcastically. *I think she'd prefer if I took a swan dive off the Brooklyn Bridge.*

Her dad tugged his tie, which messed up everything she had done, and gave a goofy relieved grin. "*Fantastico*! You watch sweetie, you two will be the best of friends soon enough."

If Professor Ambrosino really knew the relationship between the stepsisters, he probably would run to the high hills. But of course, being clueless and naïve, he only thought the best of his daughter and new stepdaughter.

At least he can live in a happy fantasy land, Lily mused to herself.

"Sure Dad, but if that girl complains about counting calories tonight, I can't guarantee how the evening will go. And Dad?" Lily paused as she walked out the door, a quirky grin on her face. "You're missing a sock."

TWO

A few hours earlier

RIIIING

Ursa Academy's bell rang loudly in the hallways, signaling the beginning of summer. Arianna Greene flipped her long strawberry blonde hair over her shoulder as she hoisted her backpack casually and stood up to leave chemistry class. Another year had come and gone. She sighed, walking out into the bustling hallway.

"Hey, Ari! You ready?" Ari turned to her best friend, Samantha.

Sam's curly blonde bob bounced as she sauntered over to Ari, weaving in the crowd of kids exiting the front doors.

Ari groaned. She was not looking forward to the school's end-of-the-year trip to the Met. "I guess. But this is going to be soooo boring."

Sam twirled her curly strands around her finger, her black

high heels tapping on the stone tiles. "Yeah, it'll be lame, but at least we're done for the year. And we can totally have privacy to plan the party once your mom and stepdad go on their honeymoon." Sam raised her eyebrow. "They are still going, right?"

"Yeah yeah, they'll be gone in three days." Ari waved her hand dismissively.

"Great that's one problem down. And your weird stepsister, what's her name?"

Ari sighed. "Lily, her name is Lily."

"Yeah whatever – what's the plan to make sure she doesn't ruin the party?"

Ari jumped, startled when a large warm hand landed on her shoulder.

"Party? Did someone say party?!"

The hand was attached to a handsome brown hair, brown-eyed senior boy. Matt Broker was, by far, the most popular boy in school. He checked all the boxes. Senior, popular, the quarterback for the academy's football team, captain of the lacrosse team, and all-around flirt. Ari couldn't believe he was talking to them. While she was ranked high in the popular group amongst the sophomore class, she wasn't at Matt's level. At least not yet if Ari or Sam had any say about it.

Speaking of her best friend, Sam smiled coyly at Matt. Ari knew that behind that smile Sam was going to make sure the most popular guy at the academy was going to come to their party. Come hell or high water, Samantha Clarion always got what she wanted. "Yeah, we're going to have the party at Ari's new house. We'll have more details soon. You're, of course, invited Matt."

Matt squeezed Ari's shoulder and gave the girls a playful smile. "I'll tell the guys. Here's my number, keep me posted will ya?" He reached down and grabbed Ari's phone, punching his digits in. Ari stared in shock when he handed the phone back to her, looking at the ten digits on the screen.

Matt turned when the other guys from the football team yelled at him to hurry up. "Talk soon girls!" He called out as he jogged away.

Ari's smile grew. She couldn't believe it! She carefully slipped her phone back into her backpack, making sure not to lose the precious number. Sam grabbed her hands tightly.

"Did you hear that Ari? This is going to be the best party EVER if Matt is coming! Oh, my, God, we have so much to plan. Think we'll have enough time at the museum? Let me see the guest list!" Sam perused her phone, scrolling through a list of names.

"We'll have to invite Adam and Derek of course. Maybe Alyssa and Celeste, but definitely not Jaime she's annoying and maybe -" Before Sam could finish her sentence, something knocked into her.

"What the - "

"Move move MOVE!" A familiar male voice yelled out.

Ari's eyes widened. "Brandon! What are you doing?!"

Wisps of blonde hair peeked out from behind a black ski cap. Sky blue eyes glinted at hers as her brother raced down the hallway, fast as humanly possible. Her brother was never one for taking his time. Between motocross and skateboarding, he was always knocking (actually crashing) into something or someone. He looked back over his shoulder, still running.

"Sorry sis, can't talk! Gotta go!"

Sam rubbed her shoulder and muttered. "What's he running away from this time?"

Ari looked back to where Brandon had come from, and her eyes widened. She tugged Sam's shoulder urgently, motioning to the bus.

"Umm, let's get on the bus. Now!"

The doors slid shut behind them, the bus beginning to move, when the academy's least favorite teacher, Ms. Johnson, threw the school doors open and stomped outside. Ms. Johnson, the freshman and sophomore chemistry teacher, was a stern woman whose face reminded Ari of one of those hairless cats. She had pinkish skin with folded wrinkles that were more pronounced when she frowned, which was all the time since she donned a perpetual scowl from morning until evening. Ari couldn't see those wrinkles now because Ms. Johnson was sopping wet with chunks of white goop that covered not only her face, but her normally frizzy black hair looked like cement. The strange substance was drying and flaking in pieces onto the sidewalk. Bright patches of yellow paste were plastered down her standard brown slacks and blue blouse. The students stared at her while she screamed and waved toward the bus.

"Brandon Greene!!! You get back here THIS INSTANT!"

However, it was unfortunately too late. The bus had picked up speed and the driver did not hear Ms. Johnson above the loud music he was playing. Ari watched as Ms. Johnson stopped in the middle of the road, still yelling in anger. Laughter rang at the back of the bus. Her brother was smiling, the other students clapping him on the back.

Ari rolled her eyes. Her brother's pranks were too juvenile in her opinion. She knew he was considered popular in his group, but only as the class prankster and daredevil. Nothing to brag about in her opinion. She sighed and looked out the window, her face leaning against her palm. At least the school year was over, and she could focus on what really mattered. She pulled out her phone, looking at Matt's number again. Yes, hosting the party of a lifetime is what matters. This was going to be a piece of cake.

THIS DEFINITELY IS *NOT GOING to be a piece of cake,* Ari thought as she sat on a stone bench in the latest exhibit at the Met. The new exhibit was titled, "The Emerald Isle, the Celts and the Druid Influence" She mindlessly stared at the artifacts while Sam listed off what was needed to pull off the party. They chose this space because no one was around to bother them. Ari barely heard Sam's rattling off one issue after another.

"– and we'd need a DJ. Maybe Jared's brother can help, he performs at The *Rose.* And the food, geez, think we should hire La Fontaine to cater? I can put it on Daddy's black card. And – Ari? Hellllooo...earth to Ari."

Ari shook her head and turned to see Sam's raised eyebrow.

"Am I boring you?" Sam asked sarcastically.

"Sorry, it's just a lot." Ari glanced down, feeling bad. Sam was putting so much effort into this. She wondered why she wasn't as excited as she should be about this. This was supposed to be the best thing ever, but all Ari could feel was annoyance. But she wouldn't ruin this, especially for Sam.

Sam sighed. "Yeah, I hear you. But this will be the party of the year girl! Just wait." Sam clapped her hands together. "You know what? Don't worry I really got this covered."

Ari looked up with big eyes. "Are you sure?"

Sam waved her hand dismissively. "Absolutely! I'll take care of everything. You make sure the parents are well on their honeymoon and your stepsister is out of the way."

Ari groaned. That was probably the hardest task Sam could give her. Her mom and new stepdad leaving weren't difficult, though you would think that making sure adults were gone would be the hardest part of throwing a party. But no, it was her boring by-the-book stepsister. Ari was drawing up a blank on how to make it so Lily would not be at the house.

"Sam? I'm not sure how I can get Lil to leave," Ari was wracking her brain. Lily didn't have any friends in the area, she didn't party, and she didn't go out. *Geez, she's like an old cat lady without the cats*, she thought bitterly.

Sam stood up and put her hands on her hips, glaring down at Ari. "Well, you'd better find a way. There is NO way we're having her there."

Ari closed her eyes. "I know Sam. Lil would ruin the party. Don't worry I'll get her out of the -"

"Woaaaah! Did I hear party?"

Ari moaned as Brandon flopped down with a thud on the

bench. He stretched his legs out, looking down at her with a lazy grin. Brandon was already taller than Ari even though he was only fourteen. He leaned back on the bench, waiting.

"Look, you can't say a word about this got it?"

Brandon's grin widened. "Wait! Is this going to be at Tony's new house?"

Ari knew she made a mistake. Now that Brandon knew about the party, she had to figure out a way that, 1) he wouldn't tell mom and 2) ....he wouldn't tell mom.

Ari sighed in defeat. "Okay Brandon what do you want?"

He rubbed his hands together eagerly. His eyes got a twinkle in them that usually occurred when he made a particularly difficult stunt on his board.

"Do my chores for a month AND I want a KPC pro skateboard."

Ari gaped at him. "What?! You're kidding, no way!" That was almost all the money she had saved for the latest Gucci purse she was eying up. There was no way! It was her money and she intended to keep it.

Her brother looked at his fingernails and shrugged. "Well then, I guess I'm going to be having a conversation with Mom later tonight. I think in the middle of dinner with everyone would be good, might as well involve Tony and Lil." He peeked through his wavy blonde bangs and smirked at her. Ari's shoulders tensed as she bit back a growl. She was stuck and he knew it. *The little brat!*

Ari blew out through her nose in frustration. "Deal. But if I'm getting you that skateboard then I do your chores for one week."

"Three!"

"Two weeks and I won't complain about blaring your loud music for an additional week."

Brandon pursed his lips, thinking. "I'll take that. Including not complaining about me playing my drums for that week."

Ari rolled her eyes, "Ugh! Okay fine." Sam elbowed her in her rib sharply. Ari yelped. "What?"

Sam whispered in her ear. "How about Lil? Maybe you can use him to get rid of her."

Ari's eyes widened in understanding. Of course, Brandon could take Lily out of the house. It was perfect. Plus, then Ari wouldn't have to worry about Brandon pulling any pranks like dosing anyone with water or slime.

"Brandon, actually I'll do your chores for the month along with the music AND the skateboard."

His grin split, but she interrupted him. "But, in addition to not telling Mom, I need you to keep Lil occupied."

Brandon's face flushed. "What do you mean?"

"Keep her away from the party. I don't care how, but make sure she doesn't know about the party." Ari folded her arms across her chest. "You know she'll ruin everything if she's there."

Her brother nervously tugged his sleeve, his shoulder-length hair hiding his face. Ari pressed him.

"Well? Do we have a deal?" She asked impatiently.

Brandon sighed, clearly uncomfortable. "Look, I don't like the idea of lying to Lil. She's a nice person."

"I don't care how 'nice' she is. She's embarrassing. Keep her away and I promise to hold up my end of the deal. If not, well, I'm sure there are other ways." She was bluffing, but Brandon didn't have to know that.

Brandon stood up, glaring. His hands clenched at his sides. Gone was her carefree brother, the one who always had a joke. The one who let things slide. Ari's eyes widened, surprised to see such anger in his blue eyes.

"We have a deal, but whatever mean thing you and your side-kick clone," he waved his arm towards Sam, "may have in mind for Lil just forget it. If not, the deal is off and I'll make sure Mom knows. Got it?"

Ari blankly stared at him. Quickly, she put on a cold smile. "Yeah yeah, sure Brandon. Deal." She stuck out her hand. Brandon looked down at it, sighed, and shook her hand.

"See you at the car Ari." He ground out, walking out of the exhibit, leaving Ari and Sam alone again.

Sam shook her arm excitedly. "You did it, girl!! That was awesome!"

Ari wasn't so sure, but at least she had the two most important things checked off the list. "Now we can get down to the fun stuff." She began searching on her phone for party drink ideas.

Sam whistled low. "Speaking of fun, check out what just came in?"

Ari looked up and found herself staring at the most handsome guy she had ever seen. That was putting it mildly. The guy was something out of this world. His hair was like a burnished rose gold, like pale sunsets in the Caribbean where the sun would cause the blue sky to blush to a rosy hue. He even had a golden tan as if he had been living by a beach his whole life, which made his eyes and hair glow even more in the dim light. He was tall and slender, but toned muscles strained against his aquamarine shirt. He was looking at the newest exhibit with interest, particularly focusing on some of the ancient books and goblets that were lined in a display case. His movements were smooth with an air of confidence. Suddenly, he tensed and turned around, staring right at her. Ari sat frozen under his stare. His eyes were like molten gold. He had to be wearing contacts.

At some point, she realized her mouth was slightly gaping open and quickly shut it with a snap. While she had hoped it had gone unnoticed, she was wrong. Her mystery guy smirked at her with those intense eyes mocking her, much to her embarrassment. He had a small dimple on his cheek. *How is that even fair?* Ari blushed and tried to avert her eyes, but she kept looking at him through her peripheral vision. She saw he was still looking at her and she could feel the coldness of his gaze wash over her. He put a finger to his chin and tapped it in thought, all the while looking at her.

"I'm gonna say hi-"

Ari jolted at Sam's announcement. Panic flooded her as Sam started to stand up. Grasping at Sam's purse, Ari desperately tried to distract her. "Why would you do that? It looks like he's busy."

Sam scrunched her eyebrows together. "Umm, with what? The old relics over there? Pu-lease."

"You don't even know him, Sam." Ari hissed. She shouldn't care if Sam talked to him. What was the big deal anyways? Still, Ari found herself holding onto Sam's purse. She kept tugging, trying to get Sam to sit back down.

"Does it matter? He's hot as a cup of espresso. He looks our age too. I want to invite him to the party. Have you ever seen such gorgeous brown eyes, Ari?"

Ari looked up at Sam in confusion. Brown eyes? She glanced back and found the guy was gone. *That's weird*, she thought.

Sam followed her gaze and pouted. "Oh darn, now he's gone. Well, at least Matt and the football team are coming."

With that she sat back down, promptly opening up her phone again to run through the checklist one more time, acting as if the guy had never shown up. Ari, on the other hand, was still reeling from the encounter. He definitely did not have brown eyes, but maybe it was the light. No, she shook her head. She never saw eyes like that. They were like fire diamonds. Ari forcefully shook her head again, dismissing the fanciful thought. What did it matter, he was gone and he'd be another distant memory. Though she couldn't help the nagging feeling that pricked the back of her mind.

THREE

The summer breeze softly brushed Arianna's face as she sat in her mother's sage green Ford Escort. The car smoothed yet another turn while Brandon played the latest game on his smartphone, his headphones blaring some punk song that Ari couldn't remember. Grinding her teeth at the distraction, she laid her head back on her hand with a "humpf".

Looking through her rearview mirror, Tabitha Greene's, now last name Ambrosino, deep blue eyes turned to see her eldest child's pout. Ari still had a hard time understanding why her mother looked twice at the goofy anthropologist, let alone marry him. Her mother was a knockout. Curly short hair, like a sophisticated Shirley Temple, with blinding blue eyes that Ari's dad always would say reminded him of the Aegean Sea. But it was her mom's smile that made was truly beautiful. Her mom's smile had pronounced dimples, no bigger than a pea. You couldn't not smile in return; it was like magic. Her father used to say her mom was kissed by an angel.

But angel or not, her mom was no stranger to the working world. She might have looked like a beauty queen, but she was tough. Because of this trait, Tabby was one of the top photographers in the fashion industry. Ari knew the ins and outs of the fashion industry by the time she was six. She went to fashion week every year. Some of the top designers had her mother's personal phone number. But her mother decided to retire from that lifestyle when she married Tony. Instead of high fashion, her mother was excited to branch out into nature photography with a new job at National Geographic. Arianna cringed thinking about her mom trading Louis Vuitton for national parks.

"A dime for one of your thoughts?" Mrs. Ambrosino asked, the question accompanied by her warm dimpled smile. Ari refused to smile back. Her mom would always tell Ari and Brandon that a penny can be for tons of thoughts, but a dime, well that was reserved for a special secret thought. Even though Ari thought it was cheesy, it still brought up images of more pleasant times. Times when her father was with them, laughing and joking together as a family.

Ari kept staring out the window. "Nothing." She mumbled into her hand.

Her mom raised an eyebrow. "Oh really? What did you and Samantha do today at the Met? Were there any new exhibits?"

Ari's thoughts went back to the mysterious guy. *Who was he?* And better yet, why in the world was she so anxious when she thought of him. The last time she had that type of feeling was the day her father went to work and never came home.

Definitely not something she wanted to tell her mom. "There's a new Irish exhibit. Something about the people who lived there or something. You may have liked it since you're going there soon," she grumbled.

Mrs. Ambrosino ran her fingers through her curly hair, leaving wisps falling over her face, and sighed. "I thought we were past this."

Ari rolled her eyes and crossed her arms, slouching even more in her seat. "Whatever," she muttered.

Mrs. Ambrosino glanced back at her daughter, who looked so much like her first husband and sighed, disappointment coloring her tone.

"Listen Ari, please give it a chance. Give *them* a chance. Tony is trying so hard."

Ari winced inwardly, feeling a tiny sliver of guilt creep in. She hated seeing her mom looking so disappointed.

"He isn't so bad." That was the closest she'd come to an apology.

Ari continued with a grimace. "He's just goofy...and messy. I mean, can't he be cooler? Or I dunno, put on a shirt that doesn't have a stain on it."

Mrs. Ambrosino chuckled, steering another turn without missing a beat. "That's one of the many things I love about him. Tony is unique. He doesn't care about appearances or what people think." She added softly. "Lil is special too."

Ari snorted. "If by special you mean weird then sure. Lil's a freak." She put her nose in the air and tried not to notice Brandon giving her a side glare.

Mrs. Ambrosino's eyes widened. "Why on earth would you say such a horrible thing?"Ari turned her face away from the window to glare at her mother through the rear-view mirror.

"It's true! Have you seen her stuff? And how she dresses? All those flowing shirts and wraps? Not cool at all!"

Mrs. Ambrosino changed gears, making the car jerk. She remarked firmly. "Now you listen to me Arianna Hope-Margaret Greene. Lily is *not* a freak. She happens to be a wonderful spirit. You can learn a lot from her."

Ari glared. *Why is she standing up for HER?*

"YES!! Top score!" Brandon kicked the passenger's seat and whipped his arms out, almost smacking Ari in the shoulder. Slowly, the tension evaporated. Ari's shoulders relaxed. But, Ari knew her mother must be wrong. There was nothing to learn from Lily other than becoming an outcast and becoming some old cat lady. It was as simple as that.

Brandon pulled one earbud out, music blaring. "Hey, Ma! Are we there yet?"

"Almost. We're on the road to the house." Mrs. Ambrosino replied.

Ari stared at the fields and trees. "Um, Mom. There's nothing here." All Ari and Brandon could see was a dirt road, surrounded by forest illuminated by a setting sun.

Brandon's brow furrowed. "Ma, I don't see any other houses. Where are the neighbors?"

"And where is the phone service? I can't call Sam!" Ari stared blankly as the No Service icon flashed at her.

"No cell service and no neighbors. It was a steal from what Tony has told me," Tabby replied.

Brandon blinked and muttered under his breath. "No kidding it's a steal, who in the world would want it? It's like children of the corn or some other backdrop for a horror movie."

Dust from the dirt road was falling softly around the car as Brandon and Ari could faintly see a small object in the distance. There, in the reddish glow of the setting sun, was a tiny little cottage surrounded by...

Ari gaped. *Nothing! There is absolutely NOTHING here!* Nothing but fields, a cottage, and trees. Tons of trees. What in the world was her mother thinking, taking them to a place like this?

Mrs. Ambrosino eagerly craned her neck over the steering wheel, her gaze squinting. "I can't wait to show you guys! I know you'll love it."

Ari stared in disbelief. She knew when her mom told her that Tony bought a house outside the city, but it was even worse than she thought. It was in the middle of nowhere New Jersey!

Brandon, recovering from the initial shock, attempted a peace offering. "It doesn't look too bad. Maybe there's a space to build a ramp?" His mother's eyes flashed in gratitude in the reflecting mirror.

Ari wasn't ready to be as forgiving as her brother. She put her face in her trembling hands, anger surging. *Great! As if this day could get any worse.* As the car kept digging up the dirt road, Ari picked up her phone, staring at her blank screen wondering. *Could it?*

CHAPTER
FOUR

Lily was outside when the little Escort turned into the driveway. Her new stepmother practically jumped out of the car as she rushed towards the door, curly hair bouncing behind her. Lily smiled. Tabby was so bubbly it was adorable. She didn't remember much of her mother; actually, she couldn't remember anything. When her father introduced her to Tabitha Greene, she didn't know how to react. She never had a mother before so how was she to know what one was like? Would she like having a mother? And, more importantly, would Tabby like her? But in the end, it was Tabby's smile that erased all of Lily's fears. It was so genuine and full of warmth. Lily wondered if her mother had a smile like that.

"Hello Lily! Is your father inside?" Mrs. Ambrosino shouted excitedly. Her smile was wide, the sun illuminating behind her.

Lily cupped her hands around her mouth as she yelled back, "He's inside. Go right in, he'll give you the tour!"

From inside Lily heard an equally excited voice. "Is that my Tabby?!" Ambrosino tripped over the first cobblestone at the same moment his new bride hugged him hard, keeping him upright. It was a warm reunion for the newlyweds.

Too bad the same couldn't be said for Lily's new stepsiblings. Ari practically dragged herself out of the car. Brandon tried to look nonchalant, but he glanced around the vast acreage of woodlands with a nervousness only a city boy who never saw more than a few acres of green without being surrounded by pavement would have. They definitely were out of their element.

Lily squared her shoulders. *Alright Lil, time to mingle.*

She waved, keeping a bright smile plastered on her face. "Hi, Brandon! Hey Arianna!"

Brandon smiled back with his answering wave. "Hey, Lil!"

Ari raised her eyebrow at him. His face reddened slightly, quickly stuffing his hand back into his pocket. Lily pretended not to notice. Instead, she opened her arms to hug them.

"It's good to see you," she said, moving forward.

Ari backed away, scrunching her eyes. "Yeah sure," she mumbled. Brandon started to move but paused. Eventually, he stuck out his hand.

Lily's smile faltered. *So that's how it is.* She awkwardly brought her arms down. Keeping her smile in place, she took his hand in an embarrassing shake. "So uh, how was your last week of school?" She mentally smacked herself in the head. *Geez smart,* she thought, *lamest question ever.*

Ari's brow furrowed, clearly annoyed. "Fine."

What followed was an inevitable weird silence with Ari refusing to look at her. Brandon looked between the girls before he spoke up loudly. "Oh it was great, last day Walt got his butt kicked by that new kid Drew. Got it all on tape. Wanna see Lil?"

Lily laughed, grateful for the save. "Hmmm, do I want to see a kid get his butt kicked? Maybe later."

Brandon shrugged his shoulder, smirking.

Mr. Ambrosino, still hugging his wife, came out of the cottage. "Hey Arianna, Brandon! How about Lil shows you around the place."

Lily wanted to walk away and leave her new siblings to fend for themselves. However, her dad's hopeful face focusing on her, she caved faster than a sandcastle at high tide. "Ah... sure. How about it guys? Want a tour?"

Brandon started walking, a spring in his step. "Sure why not?"

He looked back at Ari, who remained suspiciously quiet. He inclined his head. "Ari? You coming?"

Ari glanced at her mother, who was looking at her with a similarly hopeful expression. The small pain in her heart quickly subsided to a rush of hard anger. "Why would I want a tour of this stupid old house. It's so tacky." She glared back, her hands fisted at her side.

Mrs. Ambrosino's smile faltered. "Don't be rude Ari. Just take a look around. Please?"

Ari pouted, her shoulders slumping. "Ugh! Fine, whatever." Her mom gave a grateful smile, then went inside with Tony.

As soon as the parents were out of sight, Ari turned back and glared at Lily. "But I don't have to see it with you two." She roughly pushed past them to walk ahead toward the stables.

Lily watched Ari walk away, grateful she didn't have to spend time with the sourpuss brat. She whispered to Brandon, hoping Ari couldn't hear her. "Well, that went well huh? Think she can walk in those heels on the grass?"

Brandon sputtered out a laugh. "If you look at her closely, she's trying reeeaaally hard not to stumble."

Lily and Brandon shared a look before they doubled over in laughter. She wiped a tear from her eye, grateful to have at least one of her new siblings treating her like she wasn't a dung beetle. She glanced over where Ari disappeared, her mouth tense.

Brandon stopped laughing and frowned when he saw the strained look in Lily's eyes. He nudged her arm. "Hey, don't worry Lil. It's gonna take time for her to warm up to everything. Especially now since we're staying here."

Lily winced. "Ari didn't seem happy about it."

Brandon sighed, folding his arms behind his head. "She hasn't been thrilled. Especially when we finally got to see the place. We both were kinda in shock but hey it's cool." He shrugged. "Place doesn't look half bad. Once you get over the quiet. Think Tony would mind a ramp over there on the green?"

Lily's lip quirked upward. "Not at all! But don't let Dad try the ramp, he'll fall on his face."

"Maybe Tony wouldn't be that bad." Brandon glanced at Lily, a mischievous look in his eyes. They both paused before they laughed again as a shared image of the professor falling on his butt played in their minds.

Lily, feeling better, grabbed Brandon's hand. He looked down in shock, but she didn't notice. She was too busy looking again at the sunset. "Come on, let's take a look around." She tugged his arm towards the stables.

While Brandon and Lil took their tour, Arianna walked towards the brook. Or rather, she tried to walk. Her heels sank so far into the grass she stumbled at every step. Frustrated, she took off her shoes and threw them behind her with a thud. Ignoring the filthy stable, she walked along the stream where the wild-flowers were in full bloom, emanating the sweet smell of honey-suckle and roses. Crickets chirped in a tinkling symphony. Ari paused to listen, the sound strangely pleasant but unnerving. She was used to the blaring sounds of honking horns from the city. *It is a pretty place*, she thought reluctantly. *But it's not New York.*

She picked up a stone by the creek bed. Smooth and round, it fit perfectly in her palm. A small cobblestone bridge crossed the stream into the woods. Thick green ivy surrounded the base of the weathered stone, which dipped into a forest of water lilies that gathered underneath the bridge. Ari stood on the bridge and looked out towards the woods. *Dad would have liked this spot,* she thought sadly. Her eyes teared up. Her dad had been gone six years now. Shot in the line of duty. He was a hero within the police department, they were told. Ari frowned, anger welling up. What did that matter he was a hero, he was dead. *Gone and never coming back,* she thought bitterly. The tears kept coming, splashing on the small stone in her hands. Ari closed her eyes tightly, the salty tears biting. *Didn't fairy tales say you make a wish and throw coins in the water?* She clutched the stone so hard her fingers turned white. She wished with all her heart to be away from here, from everyone. She tossed her stone, and it sank with a "plop" into the water, scattering small fish and water lilies in every direction.

Startled, Ari peered over the bridge, looking for her stone. While she was searching for it, her eyes caught some pictures that were carved into the side of the bridge. Touching the cold wet stone, images appeared, spiny creatures with wings, humanoid figures sporting animal bodies. They ranged from piercingly beautiful to intensely horrifying. It was a mix of macabre and angelic, so much so that Ari was transfixed and she couldn't turn her gaze away. The more she stared, the more the figures appeared to move on their own. When she thought she saw a particularly scary-looking owl woman lifted it eyes to her, she yanked her hand back with a jolt, her fingers still stinging from the cold.

A tree limb snapped somewhere in the forest, its echo resounding across the background. Ari jumped. Her gaze roamed, finding nothing. As she kept staring at the densely packed forest, somehow, it beckoned her to enter. The branches swayed invitingly, the red-gold rays of the setting sun burnishing the trunks from ordinary brown to a lustrous copper. Her feet moved on their own. One step, two steps. As she neared the edge of the little bridge, heat rose from under her heel. Her foot hovered at the end of the bridge, a footstep away from the woods before her mind cleared.

What am I doing, she thought, shaking her head. Her blonde hair fell over her face, the cobwebs clearing away but still grazing the outer corners of her mind. She hugged herself closer, uneasy. What made her want to go into those woods? She hated the woods. They were icky and dirty, and not to mention she had no cell phone reception. Suddenly cold even though the summer air was dry and hot, she turned and quickly walked back towards the cottage as far away from the bridge as she could.

AT THAT SAME MOMENT, Brandon and Lily arrived at the stables, still laughing as Brandon continued telling the most ridiculous jokes. Even though the jokes were awful, Lily enjoyed Brandon's enthusiasm and tenacity when he delivered the punch line. Lily didn't find many things she could laugh about lately, so she genuinely appreciated Brandon's effort.

The stable was a miniature replica of the Hemlock Cottage, almost to the exact detail, save for one thing. Above the stable door, there was a carving. A series of intertwining ribbons that resembled an entwined circle. It resembled Celtic origin, but Lily couldn't place it precisely. To their right, the creek gently flowed at the edge of the wood, creating a natural property line. As she stared at the woods, something tugged her – ever so softly – like a gentle string - towards the swaying branches glistening within the effervescent light.

"Hey Lil-"

Lily jumped out of her thoughts, the weird feeling vanishing, and looked over to see Brandon watching her with an anxious expression.

"Yeah?" she asked.

Brandon stuck his hands in his pockets and briefly looked down at his shoes as he mumbled. "I was thinkin' since Ma and Tony are headed to Ireland for their honeymoon on Saturday-"

A lump rose in Brandon's throat, cutting his voice off. He was usually good at lying, typically it was no big deal. So why was a pit growing in his stomach? He didn't want to lie to Lily, but a deal was a deal. He tried to clear his throat with a resounding cough.

"Um...You think we could go into the city on Saturday? I really wanna see this extreme sports convention and I know Ma wouldn't let me go alone." He gave his best "puppy dog" look, forcing his eyes to widen, adding a few dramatic blinks.

Lily paused, looking at Brandon's big blue eyes suspiciously. She hoped this was a sign he was trying to get along, but she still had concerns.

"Let's talk to Tabby," she replied.

Brandon's face fell a little. Lil felt a pang in her chest. *Dang it,* she thought. *Way to go Lil, already you're screwing this up.*

She put her hands up in a placating gesture as she rushed to explain. "But, I'd love to go!"

Brandon's face turned upward again. Her rambling continued. "And I've always been a little curious about dirt bikes. I bet she'll say yes. Honestly, I'm sure she won't mind."

Brandon beamed. "Thanks Lil, that means a lot!"

He paused a moment when something moved out of the corner of his eye. He frowned.

"Hey, do you see that?"

"Where?" Lily lifted her hand to cover her eyes from the

blinding sun. She squinted as best as she could but could barely see anything through the glare.

"There!" Brandon pointed towards the clump of oak trees directly behind the stables. The lower brush moved faintly in the waning light. A shadow moved towards them. Her heart slowly pounded as the shadow, gradually but gracefully, cut through the brushes and stopped at the creek.

Lily's gaze centered and focused, her confusion dissipating in a wash of unsteady relief. Laughing at her silliness, Lily softly smacked Brandon's arm. Brandon whirled around, eyes big.

"Brandon you can relax. It's only a horse."

Brandon peered back towards the creek and, sure enough, the scary shadow was nothing more than a horse. Well...it was a big horse. Never had they seen a horse so big, except for those monsters that pulled plows in the movies. But this horse wasn't nearly as burly, and not shaggy. Its coat was pitch black, its luxurious mane sporting the same color. But in all honesty, the horse wasn't simply black. Its coat glistened with warm ruby tints as the sun illuminated the stallion in a blood-red halo. With the sunlight at its back, the horse's piercing eyes seemed to glow eerily in the setting sun.

"Oh yeah. Stupid me." Brandon laughed awkwardly. "Look at that thing. It's kinda dirty and he's way too-" He stopped mid-insult as the horse's eyes locked onto him.

Cautiously, the horse took another step toward them, but halted. Its hoof hovered over the creek, almost but not quite touching the water.

The poor thing must be scared, Lily thought as the horse remained motionless, staring down at the water.

She moved towards the creek, calling out to Brandon behind her. "Come on Brandon we should help him!"

Brandon stared at her, dumbfounded, before jumping after her. "Wait what? Are you crazy Lil? That thing could kill you with one hoof clonk to the head."

Lily craned her neck upwards as she reached the edge of the creek, standing across the water from the massive stallion. The horse was huge. She had to admit to herself that Brandon did have a point. Just one of those large hoofs could hurt her if the stallion decided he didn't want her help. Tendrils of unease swirled through her as the stallion pawed at the ground, its hooves digging into the soil. *Maybe Brandon's right. Perhaps he can find his way home.*

She was about to turn away, but the horse held her gaze. It stared at her, unblinking, its eyes dark and bottomless, almost hypnotic. Unable to turn away, a weird warmth surrounded her. It was a cocooning blanket that reminded her of the days she spent in the desert with her father where she enjoyed juicy figs and the smell of saffron and spices in the air. She blinked, losing sight of the horse for a moment. The scene vanished. Lily rubbed her head as if she woke from a dream.

She muttered. "I guess you're right Brandon. It looks like he might belong to someone. Which means someone is probably looking for him. We should at least give him a place to stay and give him some food. I can ask Dad to make some calls."

The stallion pawed his hoof on the ground with a neigh, seemingly in agreement. He nudged his head forward toward Lily. She reached out her hand at the horse's facial crest.

"Lil..." Brandon warned.

Lily ignored him, keeping very still. She knew that she could be seconds away from one of her fingers being bitten off by the gleaming bicuspids. She smiled warmly at the horse as she spoke, with what she hoped, was a comforting tone.

"Would you like to come across the creek with us?" She lightly brushed the horse's muzzle with her fingertips. She kept going in a coaxing voice. "The stable isn't that bad. It's nice and warm for the night and we can give find you some fresh food. You like carrots?"

She waited, her hand trembling slightly.

After what seemed like an eternity, the horse finally stepped forward, Lily's hand fully resting on the soft fur.

Brandon, flabbergasted, watched as Lily cautiously rubbed her hand on the horse's neck.

"Wow Lil. You a horse whisperer or something?" he asked.

Lily kept one hand on the stallion's glossy coat as she guided him across the creek. The horse trotted across the creek with no hesitation. With how easily he moved in the water, Lily wondered why he seemed so put off by it earlier. She let out a breath she didn't realize she had been holding.

Lily grinned at the horse, elated. "There, that wasn't so bad now was it?" She patted his shoulder affectionately, turning back to Brandon.

Brandon covered himself from gaping again and he rolled his eyes. "Seriously Lil, you do understand you're talking to a horse now. What's next? You going to teach a gopher sign language?" The horse snorted at Brandon, clearly agitated.

Lily raised her eyebrow, ignoring him. "A little help please?"

Brandon, startled, ran quickly to open the stable door. When Lily reached the stable, the horse's muscles tensed. Abruptly, he stopped in front of the doorway, refusing to go in. It swayed side to side as if deciding.

"Don't worry, I told you we'll bring you some food." Lily coaxed again. "Carrots still good?" The horse snorted with a shake of his head.

"Shouldn't we give him a name?" Brandon asked. While he was still reeling from the fact that 1) Lily was talking to a horse and 2) the horse seemed to be listening. He figured he might as well go along with the whole idea.

"Maybe he already has a name." Lily mused, absently stroking the horse's shoulder. The horse peered at her from the corner of his eye, moving slightly closer toward her hand.

"Aw come on. Like he'd really know the difference. At least we'd have something to call him other than 'Hey you horse'!" Brandon grumpily put his hands in his pockets.

Lily laughed. "Alright, let's see. What would you like to be called black beauty?" The horse looked at her again, directly in her eyes. Lily frowned. That strange feeling crept up again – like a blanket engulfing her, making things hazy. Then she heard something in a wispy tone,

"...*Cabyll*..."

The whisper faded away as a chill engulfed her, like she got dosed with a cold bucket. Goosebumps rose on her arms. "Did you hear that?"

Brandon stared at her, confused. "What? I didn't hear anything."

She scanned around and saw a boatload of nothing; only miles and miles of trees. "Just my mind then I guess," she mumbled.

Brandon frowned, seeming to question her sanity. "So...the name?"

Lily glanced back with a sheepish smile. "Sorry. How about Cabyll?"

Brandon crinkled his nose. "Cabyll? Hmmm...Kinda weird, is that a name from one of your dad's digs?"

"Ummm-" Lily stared, slightly panicking. Would he believe her if she mentioned she 'heard' it inside her head? Probably not.

Lily tugged on her arm nervously. "It just sounds like a neat name." She turned to the horse. "You like that name?"

The horse gave a sharp whinny, moving his head up and down.

"Yeah whatever, sure." Brandon stepped back towards the house, eyeing the horse warily. "How about we go back, think dinner's ready?"

"Sure, let's go." She turned her gaze back to their new house guest. "Cabyll." The name dripped so easily off her lips that it was slightly unnerving. "We'll be back soon. You take care alright?"

The horse stared at her with those beautiful eyes, and she couldn't resist running her hands through his soft mane one more time. He nickered at her before pulling away and stepping into the stable.

With that, Lily and Brandon headed back. Lily's gaze returned to the horse. Where did he come from? The stallion stared back, his eyes never leaving her. She shivered.

It's only a horse Lil – it can't understand you. Get a grip!

She rubbed her arms, an unnatural chill ran over her skin, even during a warm summer evening. Funny thing, as the screen door slammed behind her, the scent of saffron lingered in the air.

CHAPTER
FIVE

The next two days passed uneventfully. Brandon started putting together a makeshift skating ramp next to the stables. The horse, curious, watched him skateboard up and down the ramp trying new stunts. Lily kept an eye on the horse, feeding and brushing him. Her dad called around the neighborhood, but with no luck finding the owner. He said the horse could stay until the local shelter could find a place for it. Meanwhile, the newlyweds were packing, unpacking, and repacking. Professor Ambrosino kept packing too much and forgetting the important things, like underwear. Thank goodness for Tabby or else he would have only had toothpaste and a bunch of books. But, as he cheerfully pointed out, he'd at least have been packing light.

Lily and her father worked on getting the house in order while the newlyweds would be gone. They opted out of a babysitter.

Tabby insisted Lily could handle the household while they were gone. She was eighteen after all, and Tabby believed Lily was responsible and mature enough. It still didn't mean Dr. Ambrosino was comfortable leaving them alone. Just to be sure, he had a list of over fifty numbers Lily could call in any type of emergency. If the children managed to be infested with an unlikely swarm of African honeybees, they had a number to call.

While the rest of the household was keeping busy, Ari secluded herself away from the chaotic environment. Today, she was sitting on the bridge, staring out into the woods when a voice called out.

"Ari! Where are you?!"

Ari didn't answer, refusing to turn around. She figured if she didn't say anything, they would go away. But that wasn't the case. It wasn't until a gentle hand landed on her shoulder that she finally turned around. Her mother stared down at her with concern.

Ari ran a hand through her golden hair, letting it fall back in her face. "Hey Mom, what's up?"

Her mother sighed. "Honey, I wanted to let you know that we're set. We're leaving."

Ari blinked at her mom, keeping her face neutral. "Okay mom."

Tabby's brows furrowed. "Remember, Lil's in charge while we're gone."

Ari sighed loudly. "Yeah, I get it."

Her mom's forehead knitted with concern. "And you'll be okay tomorrow when Lily and Brandon go to the city?"

Ari stared down at her nails, refusing to look up. "I'll be fine."

"Are you sure? Do you need us to wait one more day? I mean it's not a big deal we can wait another day."

Ari held up her hands frantically. "NO! I mean...mom I'll be okay."

Her mom stared at her, unconvinced.

"Really Mom. Sam's coming over remember?"

Her mom gave a thoughtful look. "That's right, I almost forgot. Maybe the both of you could go with Lil and Brandon. You all could hang out. Bond. Get to know each other."

Ari pouted, turning her gaze away. "Mom I don't wanna go with them."

Her mom sighed, rubbing her temples. "Please Ari. Please try to give Lil a chance, will you? She'll be a great big sister to you if you let her."

"She will never be my sister!" She gritted through her teeth. Frustrated, she jumped up, marching away.

"Ari -" Her mom took a few steps towards her, reaching out.

Ari backed up, glaring. "No! Seriously, Mom, I know you're trying but still, give it a rest! I'll be civil but don't expect anything else from me in this backward place. I can't even find a mall around here! You think this will make us close?! Are you crazy? That girl is a freak! And there's no way would I ever, EVER, associate with her in public."

Mrs. Ambrosino shook her head, disappointed. "Listen sweetheart I know you still haven't accepted my marriage, but -"

Ari put up her hand. "Really mom, stop. Lil and I just don't mesh. Alright?"

Her mom's shoulders slumped. "Fine. We'll be leaving in an hour. We'll be back next Sunday." Her mom looked at Ari, her eyes pleading. "Honey, I know you're better than this. I love you."

Ari refused to meet her gaze and gritted out. "Anything else mom?"

Her mother sighed, her disappointment evident on her face. "Behave for Lil while we're gone. And please, for goodness sake, stop calling her a freak."

Ari walked away, barely glancing back. She tossed her hair as she spoke over her shoulder. "Whatever, have a great trip. It's not like you'll be gone forever."

"Ari this party is spectacular!"

Sam was breathless as she moved away from the makeshift dance floor and made her way over to Ari. Sam tugged Ari's arm so hard she grimaced.

"Ari? Ari did you hear me?!" Sam yelled into her ear.

Ari winced, her ears ringing. She leaned over to yell back in Sam's ear. "I heard you! Think everyone else feels the same?"

Sam grinned, her smile wide. "Of course! Look around!"

The dance floor was basically a small spot smack in the middle of the living room. Sam and Ari moved the couch and tossed the Egyptian cotton rug in the closet earlier. This made just enough space for at least a dozen teenagers to jump around. Which, as Ari could guess, was packed three times that much. Like sardines in a can.

The cottage's poor oak floors were taking quite a beating as the night progressed with dozens upon dozens of feet trampling all over it. The poor Hemlock Cottage was filled to the brim with high school students pouring out from its doors. Even the walls were trembling, the shutters shaking, due to the booming bass music and the stomping feet.

Ari couldn't help jumping up and down, a combination of nervousness and excitement. She didn't expect so many people to come (half of the sophomore and junior classes). This really would put her and Sam in the teen history books. *This is the best!*

She flinched as the familiar sound of smashing glass resounded from the kitchen. She grimaced. *Oh man, when Lily sees this...* Wait a minute. Ari frowned. Why did she care about what Lily thought? Who cares if there was a mess? She smoothed her hair and checked her nails. Tonight, tonight was all about fun.

Ari flinched when Sam's fingers gripped her arm tightly, shaking her. "Oh oh oh! Matt's coming this way! Ari! Quick! Fix your hair. It's a mess."

Ari embarrassed, smoothed her hair again. She was confident her hair was perfect. But that didn't stop her from checking under Sam's scrutiny.

"Hey Sammy, Ari, great party," drawled Matt as he sauntered over. His muscled frame towered over them. He gazed down at Ari with a grin. "You guys must have worked hard to set this up."

Sam flashed him a brilliant smile. "It was no problem, Matt. But...like seriously...it was all Ari's doing. If it wasn't for this new place of hers we'd never have been able to have this party."

Matt's eyebrows rose, and his eyes grazed over the cottage. "Really? This your new place Ari?"

A slight blush warmed her cheeks.

Matt nodded, impressed. "This place is pretty cool, so much space. The backyard alone is as big as our practice area." Matt mimicked throwing a football with a grin.

Sammy nudged Ari at her side, giving her a nod over to Matt. Ari smiled sheepishly, twisting a strand of hair with her fingers. "Oh, uh, yeah thanks Matt." Ari inwardly screamed with glee but tried her best to appear calm and cool.

As the bouncy pop music transitioned over to the calming melody of a familiar slow dance, she saw Matt's smile grow wider. He took a step forward and held out his hand.

"Ah hey, wanna dance?" he asked.

Ari's eyes widened. This really was happening! The most popular guy in school was asking her to dance. Ari stared at his hand, unmoving. She knew she needed to take his hand. Why wasn't she moving?

Sam looked between the two of them, blinking, before answering for her. "Of course she will!" In one millisecond Sam practically threw Ari into Matt's arms. Ari looked back to see Sam giving her a thumbs up mouthing, *You go girl!*

Ari whirled into the dance, the lights making her dizzy. Uneasiness trickled through her. It was similar to what she felt at the museum. Someone, or something, was watching her. She was so focused on it, she forgot she was dancing with Matt until he cleared his throat loudly. Surprised, she looked up at him.

Matt glanced down, concerned. "Hey Ari you okay? You're

shivering a little." His thumbs rubbed her arms softly while they swayed back and forth.

Ari's cheeks warmed. He was just trying to be nice. And here she was ignoring him. What was she an idiot? This was the most popular guy in school. She forced herself to smile.

"I'm fine. I'm not used to being the center of attention."

Matt laughed. "Somehow I doubt that. Ari...you're the kind of girl everyone notices."

As he stared at her, discomfort made her skin prickle. It wasn't so much Matt, but that weird sense of being watched. She struggled to keep the grin on her face as they swayed side to side.

"I guess you're right," she said.

Ari wished for the song to end. Matt's hands made her itch and she wanted nothing more than to pull them off and walk away.

While she was thinking of an excuse to leave the dance floor, an icy air blasted Ari's skin. She shivered as the cottage creaked and groaned. The wind picked up to howl softly while the shutters clapped lightly in the breeze. Maybe it was her imagination, but she could swear the horse was faintly neighing, but if she was honest with herself, it sounded more like a chilling laugh. The hair stood up on her arm, goosebumps prickling, as a familiar presence seared her flesh as if in ice.

Ari turned, slowly, afraid of what she would see.

His red-gold curls glowed in the light, but it was his eyes that managed to outshine everything. Sure enough, it was the boy from the museum. But...how? How had he known about the party?

He wasn't from their school. Did he know someone? What would bring him here to the middle of nowhere in New Jersey?

Those familiar red eyes bore into hers, seemingly more intense than the first time she met him. They simply glowed in the dim light, reminding Ari of a glowing sunset. He was dressed simply in jeans and a black t-shirt, but he still managed to command attention as all the kids stared at him with curiosity. He slowly walked closer, never taking his gaze from hers. *What is he doing?!* Helplessly, she watched him stalk through the crowd like a panther.

Her eyes widened as he stopped right behind Matt in the middle of the dance floor. He didn't seem to care that he was causing a scene as the crowd watched in silence. His eyes lingered on Ari for a moment, his lips turned upward in a smirk.

The boy tapped Matt on the shoulder. "Eh em. May I cut in?"

His voice was deep, and melodic, hinting at an accent, but she couldn't quite place it. Wherever he was from, his voice carried an air of importance with a slightly lethal edge to it.

"Yeah wha -" Matt paused and looked back and craned his neck upward. This was a feat since Matt was easily the tallest kid in school.

The boy's gaze drifted away from Matt, ignoring him. Ari felt his gaze on her, but she refused to look up. As if on cue, Ari heard the music change.

The boy extended his hand towards her with a slight bow as he smoothly asked. "May I have this dance?"

Ari's gaze latched onto his, stunned, her cheeks flaming.

Matt sputtered, glaring. "Now just a min -".

"Was I speaking to you?" The boy said coldly, not bothering to glance over. His eyes remained on Ari's, arm still outstretched.

Silence ensued; Matt was too startled to respond. The boy gave a huff, annoyed. "Now...as I was saying. Young lady, may I have this dance?"

He gave a dashing crooked grin, which set off golden sparkles in his eyes. Ari stared, not speaking, hoping her mouth wasn't gaping open like a fish. She hesitated before slowly moving her hand towards his golden one. Right before her fingers touched his palm, she was about to pull back when he grinned at her.

"One dance?" He persisted in a playful tone.

Ari tentatively took his hand and was struck by a combined sense of biting cold and intense heat. A tingling sensation traveled up her arm as if she was being shocked by a million sparks. She attempted to pull her hand back, but it was futile since the boy held her firmly, spinning her into a dance.

The music pounded through Ari's ears as she was swept up in a sea of noise. Unknown scents tickled her nose, reminding her of the warm sun being cooled by a crisp morning breeze. Ari's head swam while the lights danced around her eyes. Her partner twirled, he dipped; so gracefully that Ari felt embarrassed and gangly next to him. Her cheeks flamed even higher when she noticed they were alone on the dance floor. Everyone stared at them in silence. As if reading her thoughts, the boy leaned down towards her to whisper in her ear.

"Relax Arianna." He pulled her closer, his hand warm on the small of her back. "Listen to the music, I won't let you stumble."

Ari looked up, caught in his golden gaze. "Promise?" It didn't even register that he knew her name.

Instead of answering, he dipped her one-handed. She clenched her eyes shut, waiting to fall. But nothing happened. His cold hand speared through her hair as he cupped her head.

"Don't close your eyes, we're just getting started," he said with a confident smirk. The music picked up, the bass blaring and soaring into her.

Desperate to keep the conversation going she asked, "I never got to ask, what's your name?"

He shrugged as he spun her around again. "Why do you want to know it? Names are quite pointless, don't you think?" He winked with a devilish grin, but his eyes were icy.

Ari's head was becoming fuzzy. She tried to focus, to clear her head. "Pointless?"

He sighed, slightly annoyed because his pace slowed down a fraction.

"Why are people insistent with naming things? As if naming things gives you comfort." He shook his head in pity. "People think that suddenly everything will become clear if you give something a name. As if it'll answer whatever questions you have."

His hand reached up to cup her cheek. "It's not in the naming of the moment, but the moment itself. Moments are tangled. You remember a feeling of joy when you smell your favorite meal. Not the name of the meal. Only the smell." He looked at her, a determined air surrounding him. "You're holding yourself back Ari when you limit yourself. This moment, this very small moment, there is only you, me, and the music. You can live a lifetime in that moment. So...live and let the wildness take you petit oiseau."

He grabbed her around the waist and lifted her in a twirl. Ari closed her eyes and gave in. He was right. Why was she holding herself back? Just because of what others thought about her? She should be happy. Yes, she deserved to be happy, to do what she wanted to do. And right now, it was to dance.

Ari opened her eyes. Faint iridescence sparks floated around her, like butterflies. She felt effervescent, a bubble, and that feeling was unlike anything she ever experienced. She was light, so light that she knew she belonged in the air. And most of all, this boy, this wild kid, made her feel free. That she could be anything. Do anything. And at that moment, she knew without a doubt that she would go anywhere with him.

"Do you mean that Arianna?" He whispered, his nose almost touching hers as he slowed down the dance.

"What?" She batted her eyes to clear them. Why was his hand so cold?

"Did you mean it?" He asked her again, his gaze resting heavily on her.

Ari blinked, trying to clear her head. "Umm...yeah – sure." She was still hazy to recall what she mumbled out loud, but she wanted to please him.

He smiled, and holy moly was it a blindingly white smile. Ari did a double take. Did his teeth seem slightly sharper than normal? They were unnaturally white and straight. Her eyes shot up when his eyes warmed to molten gold.

"I'm glad you said that Arianna. I'll see you soon." With that, he gave her a slight bow, his head hovering over the back of her hand. Ari could feel an emptiness as his hand dropped from hers. He began to pull away.

"But -" She didn't even know she moved towards him, reaching out. She never got his name.

Then, as if he read her mind, he turned back. He reached out and gently grasped her hand once more. He placed a brief kiss on the back of her palm as he whispered. "By the way my curious little bird," he said coyly, "my name is Dain."

With a parting wink, he walked out of the room. A sharp icy prick lanced her palm. She opened it up and found a tiny necklace. Hanging from a silver chain was a delicate crystal shaped like a snowflake. Ari never saw anything like it before. Was he a magician as well? How did he get that in her hand without her noticing? Quickly, she tucked the necklace away from prying eyes and went to grab a cool drink.

Sam's grin stretched from ear to ear as she approached Ari. "Ari that was amazing! I didn't know you had those moves. I think we can safely say this party has cemented my name and yours in the cool book forever! Did you ask for his number?"

Ari blinked, confused. "What? Oh, no I didn't." She rubbed the snowflake absently in her pocket, reminding herself it wasn't a dream.

Sam pouted as she twirled her hair around her finger. "Aww too bad. But the night is still young. Oh, random change of topic, but did you see that room of your stepsisters? Talk about lame."

Ari frowned. "You went into her room?"

Sam shrugged, her hair flipping behind her shoulders. "Uh, yeah! I was bored. And what is with that ugly rat in her room?"

"Rox is not a rat, he's a sugar glider." Even though Ari didn't like Lily, she always had a soft spot for the little sugar glider.

Sam rolled her eyes. "Whatever, it sure looks like a rat. Doesn't matter anyways. Did you know she has all this old antique stuff in her room?"

Ari sighed. "Yes, her dad is an archeologist."

"Well, it's creepy. It needed a facelift." Sam had a deviously small smile playing across her face.

Ari shook her head slightly. By this point, she tuned out what Sam talking about. Her gaze drifted back toward where Dain left.

"Hey Sam, where do you think he went?"

Sam stared at Ari, puzzled. "Who Matt? He's right over there." She gestured towards the kitchen island. "He's been staring at you this entire time you know. I mean he seems totally interested. It's not too late to get his number."

Ari looked over. Matt was indeed staring at her. She shook her head. "No, not Matt. The other guy. The one I danced with."

"Ari...you didn't dance with anyone but Matt." Sam's voice rose with excitement. "Wait! Did you dance with someone else?! Who who?!"

Ari frowned, growing uncomfortable. She shuffled her feet, confused. "What do you mean who? That guy from the museum! How could you not see us?" A small pit hardened in her stomach. There was no way that guy was a dream. She couldn't have made it up! Could she? She shoved her hand in her pocket and flinched. The pendant dug into her flesh, a reminder she was not crazy.

Sam looked at Ari, worried. "Are you sure you're feeling okay? Believe me, if that cute guy showed up, I would have raced over to ask him to dance with me." Sam placed her hands on Ari's shoulders and looked at her with, what Ari deemed, was sympathy. "You haven't been on the dance floor since you told Matt you felt a little lightheaded. Maybe you should sit down and have some more water. You're looking a little pale."

Ari rubbed her forehead, wishing the fog would clear. "I guess I am feeling slightly lightheaded." She covered Sam's hand with her own, giving a slight squeeze. "I'm okay Sam. You sure you didn't see me with anyone else?"

Sam sighed, frustrated. "Sweetie, I told you already-" She looked towards the front door, frowning. "Hey, anyone else coming?"

Ari followed her gaze. "Everyone should already be here." *Except the one that nobody saw me with,* she thought glumly.

"Then why is the door open?" asked Sam, heading towards the door.

Ari's legs were like jelly as she raced across the room to catch up with Sam. They reached the front door, staring out into the darkness, seeing no one. Ari tilted her head, confused. Why was the door open with no one around?

Ari put her hand on Sam's elbow, trying to reassure her. "Sam no one is here. Maybe the wind simply blew the door open."

Suddenly, and all too suddenly, as Ari would think back on it, all she could see was a blaze of orange and red. Uncomfortable warmth spread throughout her body, fanning her until she was

61

sweating through her clothes. *Oh no!* Ari closed her eyes, holding in her panic.

Ari yelled out, lights dancing behind her eyelids. "Sam! It's -" Before she could get the word out Sam supplied the answer in a scream.

"Fire!!!"

CHAPTER
SIX

"Hey Lil, think we can have ice cream before we head back?" Brandon asked anxiously as Lily's dying Jetta weaved down the narrow road.

Brandon looked at the clock on the dashboard. It blinked at him: 9:45 pm. He frowned. The party would still be in full swing and there was no telling what Sam had planned if Lily showed up smack in the middle of it. Ari explicitly told him not to be back until 11:30 pm.

Brandon sighed. He thought it'd be a cakewalk to keep Lily away. He had the entire day mapped out. He brought Lily to Chelsea Piers so he could get some skating practice in. He took her into Brooklyn for some rock climbing (which Brandon found out she wasn't the greatest at, but A for effort). He even dragged her across Central Park to the other side of the city for dinner. It was all timed out perfectly so when Lily drove home, they would hit bumper-to-bumper traffic.

To Brandon's delight, luck was on his side all day. The fact he enjoyed spending time with Lily was a bonus. However, luck failed to mention to him that Lily, Miss Goodie-Two-Shoes always did things by the book Lily, happened to have a lead foot. Brandon grimaced when he realized he was pushing his foot on the car floor again as if he could slow down the car. At the rate they were going, they'd be back home in about ten minutes. Brandon threw out the ice cream request as a last-ditch Hail Mary. He remembered that Lily had a soft spot for good gelato, and the nearest one was a good thirty minutes away.

Lily looked at the dashboard, reading the time. She frowned slightly. "I dunno Brandon. I have to finish writing that letter for Cornell."

Brandon picked his nails, his nerves rising. "Well, you have some time for that right? Besides, you can't end the day without ice cream! And we only have cookie dough and mint chip at the house, which is super boring. There's a killer gelato place I know." He gave her a side smirk. "It has your favorite Stracciatella..."

Lily blinked. "How did you know that's my favorite?"

Brandon shrugged, refusing to look at her. "Ah – Tony might've mentioned it before. Come on please Lil!" He glanced up at her pleadingly.

She narrowed her eyes as she stared at him, hard. His hands were clasped together; his lower lip pushed out in a dramatic pout. Her own lip quirked up. He was so persistent and extreme, it was hard to say no.

Lily chewed her lip, debating. "It's getting late. Why don't we have ice cream at the house while I'll finish the letter? Cookie dough isn't *that* boring."

Brandon desperately glanced out the window. They were almost in the lane.

"I...I don't think I can wait Lil. I really want chocolate!" His voice rose, strained.

Lily laughed. "Okay okay, I surrender. Let's get some gelato."

Brandon breathed a sigh of relief as he slumped back into his seat.

"But -" Lily began. Brandon's eyes widened, his smile fading away.

She continued, not noticing his mood change. "Let's stop at the house first. Ari and Samantha may want to come along."

Lily turned into the long driveway to the cottage, hope blooming inside her. Brandon was right. They had a great day today. Maybe taking them to ice cream would be the first step towards a peace treaty of some sort between her and Ari. Out of the corner of her eye, Brandon shuffled nervously in his seat.

"What's going on Brandon?" she asked.

He mumbled, refusing to look at her. "Ah, um, they probably don't wanna come."

"Well let's ask them." Her Jetta sputtered and bounced along the dirt road.

Brandon silently panicked. The cottage would be in sight soon. He had to think fast. A smoke bomb? No...too dangerous. Itching powder? No, he didn't want Lily to get hurt. His frantic mind was drawing blanks. Then, his eyes widened as a light bulb went off. He cringed thinking about what he was about to do. *Well,* he thought with a resigned grimace, *might as well go for broke.*

He bent forward as he clutched his stomach. "Oh...oh nooooo!"

Lily frowned. "You okay?"

Brandon doubled over. Quickly, Lily reached out to rest her hand on his back, struggling to clasp the wheel with her other hand. The car hit another large bump causing them both to gasp.

"We're almost home." Her face knotting in concern. "I'll go faster."

Brandon's eyes widened, dismayed. "Noooooo," he moaned. "You need to stop now. Right now! I'm going to throw up!"

Lily's mouth opened, shocked. She twisted the wheel, causing the car to jerk drastically into the grass. The Jetta bounced over a ditch and lurched Lily and Brandon forward in their seats. Brandon put a hand over his mouth, his face slightly green. As the car came to an abrupt stop, Lily jumped out and raced to the passenger door ready to hold Brandon's head in case he didn't make it in time.

Brandon tried to hide his surprise, also while trying to hold down his dinner. He may have acted in the beginning, but Lily's Evil Knievel driving assisted in making his performance look more realistic. He bent over the side, breathing deep through his nose. His hat was off, his messy hair had fallen over his face. Reaching out, Lily gently smoothed his hair back.

She spoke in a comforting tone. "Here let me hold your head. I may have some medicine in the car."

Brandon briefly looked up at her in shock before putting his head back between his knees. Lily frowned. He didn't seem as sick as she thought. Before she could ask him, a strange light out of the corner of her eye. *Strange.* She turned, her eyes squinting in the distance. A pit formed in her stomach as her eyes widened in growing horror. The weird glow was coming from the cottage, enveloping her new home in a crimson, orange tint. *Oh! The cottage! Is it on fire?*

Keeping her eyes on the cottage, she frantically yelled back to Brandon. "Brandon! Brandon the cottage!!" Brandon didn't reply. He couldn't hear her. The blood was rushing through his ears since his head was still between his legs.

Lily looked back and forth, torn between rushing towards the cottage and staying to make sure Brandon was okay. Before Lily could decide, the fiery glow burst from the cottage, then disappeared.

Lily furrowed her brows and rubbed her temple. She didn't make that up, did she? A fire wouldn't have disappeared in a few seconds. The cottage looked completely normal. No fiery flames to be seen. She shook her head.

Lily turned back to Brandon, the frown still on her face. "Hey did you see -"

A car whizzed by them, the wind whipping her hair around, the bright headlights momentarily blinding her. She blinked her eyes, rubbing the sting away. Another car drove past. Soon, at least ten cars raced past them at an alarming rate, each one packed with teenagers donning panicked faces.

Lily stared in disbelief when the final rear lights of the passing entourage faded away down the lane. "Uh...Brandon. What's going on?"

Brandon stood frozen solid, staring. His face was in complete shock. While he didn't hear her, she observed he seemed to have made a complete recovery. *Probably wasn't sick at all*, she thought grimly.

"Brandon!" Lily yelled louder. Still no response. Disgusted, she hit him in the shoulder with a good *thwack*. He yelped and jumped back with surprising agility. *Sick my butt!* She glared.

"Wha -" Brandon swung his head towards her, rubbing his shoulder. He jumped too fast, the blood rushing to his head from looking at the ground so long.

Lily frowned as she demanded. "Tell me what's going on here."

Brandon groggily looked around. "Well, that's a good question Lil."

Lily stared aghast. "You're telling me you don't have ANY idea as to why there are at least a dozen cars that flew past us?"

Brandon raked his hand through his hair, his lips in a grimace. "Okay, now that I do know. Um...Sam and Ari decided to throw a party." He shrugged his shoulders, refusing to look at her.

Lily stared at him for a minute, processing what he said. Bitterness welled up. *Of course! How stupid am I?*

Lily brought her hand to her forehead and sighed. "How long did you know about this?"

He shuffled his feet, kicking a few stones onto the road. "Well...a few days now."

Lily noticed his reluctance to look at her. A cold chink entered her lungs, making it hard to breathe.

"They paid you to get me out of the way so they could have their party. That's the reason you wanted me to hang out with me. Am I right?" she asked, her eyes expressionless.

Brandon looked up, alarmed, and started to protest. "At first but that's not-"

Lily shook her head sadly, cutting him off. "Enough Brandon. Please get in the car. Let's go back and see what happened." She jumped into the car, slamming the door with a decisive thud. She clenched the steering wheel, completely dejected. There wasn't enough ice cream in the world that could make this better.

"But Lil -" Brandon stopped when he saw her face. He looked at the ground again, getting into the car without a word as he shut the door with a reluctant click. He botched this up. He wracked his brain trying to find a way to make this up to her. He would, somehow. Then something she said earlier finally registered in his foggy brain.

"Wait, what did you say before? What about a fire?" He risked glancing over at Lily.

Lily frowned, biting her lip. "I don't know. But, we're going to find out."

Refusing to look at Brandon, Lily took a deep breath and stepped on the gas.

CHAPTER
SEVEN

Lily closed her gaping jaw with an audible snap. She couldn't believe her eyes. Trash was strewn about, a motley assortment of plastic cups, plates, napkins, cans, and bottles. The cottage was like a scene straight out of one of those apocalyptic zombie movies. Scratch that. Make that a teenage zombie movie to be more accurate. She clenched her hands at her sides as her shock gave way to a wave of mounting anger.

She took a step forward and stumbled. Something wet wrapped around her foot. Lily looked down. A dirtied mass of colorful streamers entangled her calves. Lily closed her eyes and groaned.

"Arianna!!" She yelled, shaking her foot, the streamers slapping the floor with a wet thwack. "Ari! Get out here!"

A familiar voice called back, complaining. "Yeah yeah we hear you." Ari sauntered out from the kitchen, Sam in tow. The girls looked unconcerned, which irked Lily.

Lily rubbed her temples. "Ari, what happened? Wait," she put her hand up, "I think I got that figured out. What I want to know first is what caused the fire."

Sam and Ari both looked at each other silently, their eyes wide. Ari opened her mouth, but Sam interjected.

"What fire? We had the strobe lights on."

Brandon walked into the living room, poking through the mess. He gingerly toed a few empty cups with his shoe, looking around the messy room. "Umm...you sure? It looked like folks ran out of here pretty fast."

Ari glared at Brandon. "It was the lights. As if you have anything to say you snitch." Her scowl deepened as she continued. "You do know our agreement is over since you couldn't keep HER away." She gestured her thumb at Lily rudely.

Brandon's ears got red. He sheepishly looked down at his feet. He discreetly peeked up at Lily, who refused to look at him.

Lily stared at Ari, trying to remain calm. "Just so you know Ari, your brother did his best to keep me away. Guess I'm too stubborn," she said with a small smile.

Ari rolled her eyes. "Whatever. Well, as you can see everything's fine. Sam, call everyone back."

Sam reached for her phone, the dial tone blaring in the silence. Lily blinked, confused. How could they have reception? At a closer glance, she noticed the phone was a top-of-the-line model.

Figures, she thought, *only the most expensive thing for these girls. Can't go two minutes without a phone, can they?*

Lily crossed her arms over her chest. "Oh no you don't. Unless you're calling them to help you guys clean up. Otherwise, you both better start getting garbage bags and brooms."

Ari scowled. "Lil you aren't my mom. I don't have to listen to you! Do it, Sam!"

Sam smirked as she walked out of the room, the phone to her ear.

Ari kept glaring at them from across the destroyed living room. The weight of that anger hit Lily with the force of a steel pipe. She cringed. She wanted nothing more than to hide. Maybe she should yell back. No, it was pointless. Ari wouldn't listen to her. Lily's shoulders slumped. She was supposed to be responsible for her new siblings. She was supposed to be in charge. But she couldn't even manage to keep control of the house for one day. Resigned, she turned away, heading up the stairs with a sigh.

Put your headphones on and lose yourself in a good book. Maybe when I wake up in the morning this will be nothing but a bad dream.

Ari coldly laughed after Lily's retreating frame. "Yeah that's right! Just walk away. You couldn't win a fight even if you tried."

Brandon moved towards the hallway as Lily slowly walked up the steps. Lily refused to look at him. She didn't want to see that same callous expression on his face. But as she grasped the banister, she couldn't help but see him out of the corner of her eye. Maybe it was her imagination, but he looked sad. He leaned forward, looking as if he wanted to talk. Ignoring him, Lily closed her eyes and raced up the steps. Some things don't need to be said.

~

Lily couldn't run to her room fast enough. She quietly closed the door, resting her back against the cold wooden frame. She closed her eyes, blowing out a frustrated breath. What would it take for Ari to give her the slightest amount of respect? If she could place a bet, she was sure Sam called half the school by now. Soon the cottage would be neck-deep in plastic cups and rotting food.

Lily pinched the bridge of her nose, the telltale pounding of an oncoming headache swelled. She was at a loss. A complete and utter loss. Maybe being immersed in Bronte would drown out everyone. She grimaced. That would be selfish. She couldn't in good conscience "pretend" it didn't exist. Besides, if she just 'let it go', who knows what would happen. Her mind was already going through scenarios she would be responsible for; ambulance calls, explanations to parents, police reports. Well, that may be extreme, but with Sam and Ari at the helm who knew. She gulped, her imagination spiraling down past the town of Trepidation and straight into Anxietyville. Do not pass go, do not collect any reassurance. Rox made a few clicks, rattling the cage a little. Lily blinked, the noise jarring her out of her mental undertow.

"What's up with you bud? Too loud?"

Rox made some more, louder agitated sounds. He kept staring in one direction, pacing side to side. Her gaze fell on where Rox was fixated on. It was her grandmother's vanity. Her brush had fallen off, laying on the floor.

"Sheesh Rox, you're getting a little paranoid," she grumbled.

Paranoid? Pot calling kettle.

It was then, while Lily was kneeling on the ground, eye level with her vanity, that something caught her eye. Something new was etched into the soft glossy wood where generations of her family carved designs. Lily followed the curvature with her hand, feeling the rough grain dig into the soft pad of her finger. She drew her hand back, a slight bead of blood welled up from where the wood had split. Crudely etched haphazardly were letters spelling F-R-E-A-K.

Warmth rushed to her face. Her head pounded, blood boiling in her veins. It was as if a pot boiled over. It all came rushing back, the times Ari made fun of her, and yelled at her. And despite all that, she always turned the other cheek. She always kept quiet and did it with a "grin and bear it" attitude. Lily was shaking, her body trembling as hot anger coursed through her. She tried so hard to be patient. She's having a rough time, her father would say. Or, give her some time she'll love you, her stepmother would say. *I'm DONE being patient!* She threw open the door, storming out.

Before she knew it, she found herself at the bottom of the steps. Brando stared back at her in shock. The mirror in the hallway stared back at her and she could see why. Her normally composed face was replaced by wild eyes and red blotchy patches spreading over her cheeks. She glared at Brandon fiercely, her lip curling. His eyes widened and he slowly took a step back.

"Where is she?" She ground out, unclenching her fingers from her palms.

"I...in...the kitchen." Brandon sputtered, pointing behind him. He moved warily towards the wall, keeping still when Lily stormed past him. Next thing, Lily threw the kitchen door open with a bang. Startled, Ari and Sam looked up from their phones. Their eyes widened.

Ari recovered quickly and started to laugh. "Get out of here will ya? We're getting the guests back and we don't want them to see you." She gestured towards Sam who was speaking to someone on the phone.

"Who did it?" asked Lily. Brandon quietly walked in behind her.

Ari looked at Lily in confusion. "Who did what?"

Lily's dark eyes burned as she stepped towards Ari. "Which one of you carved into my grandmother's vanity?"

"Hold on a sec, will you?" Sam put her hand over the phone. "Oh please, that old thing -" She began, rolling her eyes. Suddenly, Sam's phone was yanked out of her ear.

"I SAID," Lil shouted, gripping Sam's phone tightly, "which one of you brats carved into my vanity?!" She slammed the phone down onto the kitchen table with a resounding THUMP, effectively cutting off the call. Ari and Sam looked at each other in shock.

Sam recovered, trying to not let her voice waiver. "It needed a new look, it was old and stupid."

Lily walked right up to Sam until they were nose to nose. She looked down at Sam not moving. Sam's chair flew backward, Sam still sitting on it. Sam looked up from the floor in surprise and horror. Lily bent down over her, scowling.

"Here's how this goes." Lily's voice got softer with an eerie calmness. Her foot rested on the arm of the chair, her elbow casually resting on her knee.

"You will *never* go in my room again. You will call everyone back you spoke with and tell them the party is over. I want no more excuses, no more attitude. And if I even hear you say the word freak again, I will gladly give you a demonstration of what I learned from one of my dad's interns who used to be a Navy Seal. Got it?" Her eyes bore into Sam's a moment before quickly lifted to pierce Ari's gaze.

Ari, Sam, and Brandon stared at Lily in silence. Sam's mouth opened like a fish gasping for air, but nothing came out. She stared and weakly nodded in agreement.

Sam, trembling, got up and glanced at Ari. Before Ari could say a word, Sam gathered her phone and dashed out the door not saying a word.

"You better call everyone Sam because if I see ONE person at this house, I'm calling your father!"

Ari stared at the dust trail Sam left behind her, blinking in confusion. Turning back to Lily, Ari shook her head, eyes wild.

"What's with you?! All this over a stupid piece of furniture that's tacky anyways?!" Ari clenched her teeth, her hands balled at her sides.

Lily's eyes narrowed. She yelled back. "That 'tacky' furniture is the ONLY thing I have from my mother!"

Everyone was silent. Lily never mentioned her mother. She didn't know much about her mother. Her father could tell her a twenty-minute story about how ancient Romans irrigated crops, but he had never spoken more than five sentences about her mom.

Brandon's eyes widened. Ari, at first, seemed like she was going to say something. Maybe apologize, but –

"Why do you think I'd care about that?" Ari's nose wrinkled.

Brandon's mouth dropped. "Ari that's enough. Quit it!"

Lily pointed her finger at Ari. "I've had it with your attitude! You are nothing but a spoiled brat. Why don't you get over yourself? Dad married your mom, we're family now...even if you may not like it."

Ari's eyes went wide, her lip trembling. "Don't you *dare* say he's my dad!"

Lily paused, confused. She looked to Brandon, who shrugged, then back to Ari. "I never said he was your dad."

Ari trembled in rage. "He'll NEVER be my dad! God, I'm so sick of this!" She stomped her foot. "How my mom married that mistake you call your dad I have no idea. But get one thing straight Lil. We are NOT family. We'll never be family. And I would never wish you on my worst enemy for a sister 'cause you're just horrible! You and your dad are an embarrassment and I hope that my mom realizes this on her honeymoon, so we leave this rag dump as soon as humanly possible. I'm outa here!" And with that, she stomped off into the yard.

"Ari-" Lily started after her. Brandon put his hand on her arm, stopping her.

He shook his head sadly. "Let her go Lil. She needs to go off and fume alone." He paused, looking down at his hand. He quickly lifted it to rub the back of his head nervously. "She really didn't mean that you know. About you being a horrible person. And about your dad too. Actually, I'm quite happy to have you around." He sheepishly attempted a half smile.

Lily couldn't find it in her to smile back. She sighed. "Thanks,

Brandon. We'll give her some time." *Like always,* she thought bitterly. Lily looked outside, following Ari's shadow disappearing towards the creek.

Tears streamed down Ari's cheeks as she stomped towards the bridge, the soft sound of crickets chirping around her feet. Her angry thoughts quickly drowned out the peaceful melody. That crazy Lily. Who made her the boss? How dare she even think of them as a family? What was she? Stupid? Couldn't she tell they would never be friends? Ari sat down on the bridge with a loud thump.

"Stupid Lil. Stupid party. Stupid cottage! Stupid stupid stupid!" Ari screamed into the stillness of the night. Her hands pounded against the rough stone, the carvings scraping her skin. She covered her face.

"If dad was here this wouldn't have happened. I want to go away from here! Oh, dad..." She sobbed. Her tears coated her scratches, the sting making her wince. If her dad was around, he would have gathered her up into his arms. *Don't worry princess,* he'd say, *things will be just fine.* But Ari hadn't felt a hug from her dad in six years. Her throat began to hurt as she cried harder, her stomach churning until her sobs became broken gasps. She couldn't breathe, her head starting to spin.

The wind began to pick up, its loud moan rolling over her. The breeze dried the tears from her face. She pried her swollen eyes open. A white mist started rolling in from the forest. It crept across the stream. Ari's nose wrinkled. It wasn't the familiar damp, salty smell. Instead, it smelled sickeningly sweet, like honeysuckles and lavender.

Ari took a deep breath, the sweet fragrance entering her lungs. The mist curled around her legs and a blissful calmness spread throughout her bones. She sighed, eyes closing. If only she could feel this pure contentment forever.

"*Ari -*" A soft voice floated through the wind, catching her ears.

What in the world? She listened again but heard nothing. Even the crickets were silent now, the air taking on a death-like stillness.

"I guess it wasn't anything." Her voice drifted into the mist.

"*Ari -* " The floating voice whispered again.

Ari turned full circle, trying to locate the disembodied voice. Her brain was foggy, but it was a warm feeling that made her smile. She looked out towards the forest, the familiar tug to go over the bridge crept in.

"*Just a little step over the bridge -*" The mist curled into her hair, whispering across her cheek.

She peered into the darkness of the trees. What was back there? Ari winced, a stinging prick on her hand. Warmth spread between her fingers. There, nestled in her palm, was the snowflake necklace. *I know it was real!* She clutched the pendant tightly, anchoring herself as the cloying mist surrounded her. *What harm could come from taking a quick peek in the woods?* A few short steps.

The woods beckoned. They swayed lazily in the sweetly

scented air, their limbs weaving and bending in a hypnotic dance that was eerily familiar. Ari found herself swaying in tandem, a tenuous pause.

"That's it Arianna, be with me, you promised -"

Ari slowly put on the glittering necklace, the snowflake burning an icy warmth throughout her chest. Without a backward glance at the cottage and her family, Ari disappeared into the inky blackness of the woods.

CHAPTER

EIGHT

L ily woke up to a crispy, mouthwatering scent. She rubbed
the sleep from her eyes. What was that delicious aroma?
Burrowing her face into the pillow, she managed to sneak
a glance at the clock. *Ah geez*! She threw the pillow on top of her
head, groaning. Even on the worst night imaginable she wasn't
able to hide in bed for another hour. Then she blinked. It was
morning! Hopefully that meant Ari had come back inside. She had
stayed up to clean but found herself being woken up by Brandon
who forced her to bed. Ari still hadn't returned. Brandon promised
he'd wait for Ari and they'd finish cleaning up. Lily took a breath,
the inevitable dread of what she'd find downstairs seeping into
her consciousness.

Lily pulled the sheets back over her head. *Maybe if I stay here, I
can pretend nothing happened. Yes, I'll stay here for the next five days
until dad and Tabby come back.*

Rox jumped around noisily in the cage, refusing to let her burrow her troubles. "Little traitor," she muttered into the sheets.

Lily stretched, kicking off the covers regretfully. *Okay, one step at a time. Remember, the tiniest action eventually adds up to large accomplishments.* Bed made, clothes on, teeth brushed, open door, walk down steps. Simple right? *Yeah...not really.*

Her feet took her to the kitchen. She rubbed her eyes, wondering if she was still dreaming. The kitchen was spotless. On the table, there were plates piled full of crispy bacon, buttery hot biscuits, fluffy scrambled eggs, and fresh fruit. She stared in amazement, the disaster that was last night's revelry was now picture-perfect. Not even one shred of paper was on the floor, the leather furniture neatly arranged and shiny.

Lily blinked, making sure it wasn't a mirage. Slowly, her shoulders relaxed. She smiled. "Boy, they must have really cleaned. I won't wake them yet," she chuckled to herself.

She fixed herself a plate of bacon and fruit when Brandon flew down the steps.

He sniffed the air like a dog and his stomach growled in answer. "Ah man what smells so good?"

"You mean you didn't do this?" asked Lily, confused.

Brandon raised his eyebrow. "You think I could cook this stuff?" He gestured towards the plates of food. "No way Lil. Mom banned me from the kitchen after the toaster fire of 2017." He heaped a healthy portion of eggs and biscuits for himself while cramming a few slices of bacon into his eager mouth.

Lily glanced at her food, still unsure. "Did Ari make this?" She poked at the fruit with her fork warily. Somehow the bright red strawberries and perfectly baked biscuits that were recently viewed as appetizing suddenly seemed disturbing. Which was quite a shame since her stomach was growling in protest.

Brandon spoke with mouthfuls of egg and bacon in his mouth. "I 'oubt it. She can 'ook a' all. Can't even nuke s'uff."

Lily pushed her plate away regretfully, trying not to look disgusted at Brandon who kept shoveling food in his mouth. "So, if neither of you cooked this, and I certainly didn't, who did?"

Brandon looked up, his fork halfway to his mouth. For a brief moment he looked concerned, but it was gone in a blink as he shrugged, taking another large bite. "Who knows? Maybe Ari catered this as a peace offering."

Lily's ears perked up. "Did you see her last night?" She didn't want to admit she was worried when no one woke her up.

Brandon continued to stare down at his plate. His cheeks were filled like a chipmunk, the bacon peeking out. "Mmmmh-mmm. I went 'ooking for 'er. S'e com bick bu we barewe twalked."

"Huh?" asked Lily.

Brandon swallowed with a large gulp. "I said she came back but we barely talked." He grabbed another large biscuit off the plate.

While Brandon continued to eat voraciously, Lily sat thinking. Something wasn't adding up. "Where did you find her?"

Brandon burped loudly. "Oh...sorry," he apologized sheep-ishly. "She was over the bridge out near the woods. She was just kinda standing there. Like completely out of it ya know? So, I went over to bring her back." He looked around and whispered conspiratorially. "Weird thing was she asked me if I was inviting her in. What a weirdo." He laughed, tucking in more food.

Lily gagged a little, holding her hand over her mouth. She couldn't believe how much food he was packing away. "Okay. I'll go up to see how she's doing."

Lily got up, still leaving her plate untouched, and headed back upstairs.

When Lily got to Ari's room, she tried not to notice how dark the hallway was or how eerily quiet it seemed to be. She wrapped her knuckles lightly on the door, unsure whether she'd be waking a grizzly bear with blonde hair.

"Hey Ari, it's Lil. Can you open the door a sec?" No response. Lily put her ear to the door. Nothing. She knocked again, louder. "Hey Ari, you awake?"

The door creaked open slightly, leaving a slim crack. The room was pitch black. Lily slowly pushed the door open and stepped into the darkness. Lily tried to find the windows but discovered they were covered with sheets. The sheets were painted black, with little white paisley flowers peeking through the paint. Well, if that wasn't a red flag flapping in the nonexistent wind Lily didn't know what else to call it. Ari was the type who liked to have every window open and all the lights on. Lily's skin crawled. Something did not feel right.

"Umm...Ari?" Lily kept close to the door; her hand rested lightly on the doorknob. Her legs tensed slightly. Instinct told her not to go further into the room. Call her silly, but she wanted to keep herself within the light emanating from the hallway.

A slightly hushed voice came out from the darkness. "I'm here..."

Lily squinted into the shadows. "Hey – I wanted to – ah say I appreciated that you cleaned up last night and for ordering the food." She frowned at a weird, unnatural tug on her jeans, which caused her leg to move back. She fumbled to keep her balance. A shadowy form moved slowly around the bed, or what Lily assumed was the bed.

"The wha – oh yessss. No problem Lil, no problem at all." Ari's voice whispered coyly. "Oh Lil, since you're here, could you come in for a second? I want to show you something."

Lily's leg jerked again. This time it was stronger and more urgent. *Boy, what a time for a muscle spasm.* She shook her foot, taking another cautious step backward toward the hallway. "Thanks Ari. Actually, I'm gonna head down and have some breakfast. You should eat something before Brandon gobbles it all."

Ari chuckled softly. "Oh I will eat. In a second..." The shadowy form slinked faster toward the door.

She gripped the doorknob tightly. "Okay, umm...I'll see you down there."

Quickly she backpedaled into the hallway and closed the door with a snap. She stood there a moment, her shaking hand clutching the handle tightly, keeping the door shut. After a minute, she pried her hand off the door, her shoulders sagging in relief. She stared down, puzzled. Her hands shook. Why was she so frazzled? It was as if her rational thought had fled. It was her stepsisters' bedroom for goodness' sake. She took a deep breath.

Calm down girl, it was only Ari. She rubbed her fingers together, willing warmth back into them.

On shaky legs, Lily found herself back in the kitchen. She managed to flop onto the bar stool. Almost half the breakfast was devoured.

Brandon beamed, oblivious as he spread some butter over the fluffy biscuits. "Lil, have you tried the biscuits yet? Sooo good! Oh man, this food is amazing! I can't remember mom making breakfast this good. Hey, did you talk to Ari? Is she coming down?"

Lily glanced down at her hands, hoping Brandon couldn't see the remaining tremors. She tapped her finger erratically on the cold granite slab. "Yeah. She said she'd be down."

Lily looked over at Brandon, her eyes glancing up the steps to make sure they were alone. She lowered her voice. "She seems a little off - " Before Lily could finish, Ari appeared behind Brandon. Her eyes widened. *How did she get down here so quickly? Wait...is she smelling his hair?*

The hairs on Lily's arm rose as the flight response swelled in her chest. As silly as it sounded, Lily knew she was staring at something, not someone. More accurately, one of those apex predators on the many digs she accompanied her father on.

Brandon saw her stunned face and turned around. He almost fell out of his chair. Ari was practically nose to nose with him. Brandon gave out a small yelp, the grape he had in his mouth bursting out with POP.

Ari stood there, dressed in baggy sweats, splotched with mud patches and paint stains. Her hair was dulled and frazzled. It wreathed around her head like a rusted copper nest and was so natty Lily doubted a comb could untangle it. Her feet were bare and grimy as if she had walked through miles of dirt, the toenails black and chipped. Her lip curled upward, her eyes sharp and hungry. After a beat of silence, Ari scratched her armpits with chipped pink nails.

Lily and Brandon stood in shock. Lily covered her mouth to cough discreetly. "Eh em. Morning Ari, do you want some fruit?" She gestured towards the large bowl of ripe berries on the table.

Ari didn't respond. Instead, she looked around the kitchen, sniffing the air. Then she shuffled over to the refrigerator. Jerking the door open, she grabbed a gallon of milk and slammed it onto the counter. Cabinets were thrown open as food went flying all over the floor until Ari found a sack of sugar and a large jar of honey. Ari tucked into the chair, hunched over as her wild hair covered her face.

They watched in fascinated horror as Ari poured a heaping amount of sugar into a big glass of milk. She tilted the glass and, without breathing, chugged the entire contents. Lily cringed as milk ran down Ari's chin onto her stained sweatshirt. She rubbed her mouth with her sleeve and grabbed a biscuit, pouring honey over it. Brandon audibly gagged at the honey that ran down Ari's arm to her elbow.

Brandon finally snapped out of his stupor. "Ah geez, Ari did you just-"

Ari laughed, a deep and throaty laugh. She shoved the entire biscuit (including her fingers) into her mouth. The honey coated a dirty sleeve, which had ants crawling over the wrist. Ari stared at them and licked her sleeve.

Lily tried not to throw up, but the acid taste of bile rose in the back of her throat. "Um, you want anything else with your sugar?"

Ari grunted and poured another glass of sugary milk.

Lily continued to stare at Ari's detestable new dining etiquette. Her eye's widened, fearful. Brandon reached out for the honey. How he still had an appetite amazed her.

"Hey, can I have some of that?" Brandon asked.

As his fingertips grazed the jar, Ari's lip curled up with a snarl. A low growl rumbled from her. Her shoulders were hunched together as if coiled to strike. Lily quickly grabbed Brandon's arm, putting herself between the two.

She squeezed Brandon's arm in warning. "Hey Brandon, could you help me feed the horse? I need an extra hand." Lily turned to Ari with a forced smile. "Ari, why don't you take your time and finish your breakfast, sound good?"

Ari gradually sat back down with a grunt. Lily and Brandon slowly walked backward toward the backdoor. Ari's eyes followed them, unblinking, as she continued to lick honey from her grimy sleeve. They managed to get outside, shutting the door with a snap. Brandon exploded.

"What is that thing?!" He pointed towards the door.

Lily put her finger to her lips. "Shhhsssh. She might hear you." With a glance, Lilly motioned for him to follow her.

Brandon scrambled beside her as they walked. "That *thing* in there is not a 'she'!" He gestured frantically towards the house. "I don't know what IT is, but it's not my sister." His eyes were wide and unfocused.

Lily frowned. "Come on Brandon. Of course, it's Ari, who else would it be?"

"I dunno. A pod person? You tell me!"

"It's Ari that's who it is. Just...a very dirty, bad-mannered, ill-tempered, disgusting Ari. But Ari nonetheless," she muttered. But it was rather odd. She shook her head. No. That had to be Ari. It was the only rational, logical thought. What other answer could there be?

Brandon raised his eyebrow, skeptical. "Sounds like you're trying to convince yourself more than me."

A tiny, disembodied voice echoed around them, startling Brandon and Lily. "Ah, but there is a simple answer! Well, not quite so simple, but an answer there is my dear lady and sir."

Lily and Brandon looked around, but they didn't see anyone. They looked up, down, left and right, and there was not a single soul in sight. Suddenly, the springy, overly polite voice spoke near the shrubbery. "Down here young ones!"

Brandon turned around in a circle, moving branches around and peering into the pink and red rose bushes. "I wasn't the only one who heard that right?"

"I did too. Um...hello? Anyone there?" Lily called out.

The voice squeaked. "A little further down if you please. Slightly more..."

Lily and Brandon slowly bent down towards an overgrown red rose bush, but still, they saw nothing.

"Oh right right! Course Course! How silly and presumptuous of me. Hold a moment if you please!" The voice replied in a consternated tone. Lily and Brandon waited a moment, then something wet hit them in their eyes. Lily grimaced, wiping the mysterious liquid off with a frown.

Brandon fell with a yelp. He rubbed his eyes, yelling out. "Wha- What was that for?!"

Lily's eyes were still hazy as the squeaky voice continued. "I do beg your pardon. Although the method isn't quite the most proper, based on the dreadful circumstances we've been placed in, the most expedited means for you to properly see is a necessity." It pipped primly. "Now, if you please, if you can direct your gaze towards the left side of the shrubbery. It may take a moment, but I assure you it will be that and nothing more."

Lily focused on the rose bush and slowly when the haze cleared, a small figure appeared. It was a homely little thing, roughly about a foot tall or thereabouts with brown overalls covering a crisp pressed white shirt. An equally boring brown cap covered brown hair that framed two very large eyes so black they swallowed up the light. A rather large nose jutted out from a clean-shaven face. The dark eyes were friendly and twinkled as lengthy thin arms with spindly long fingers grasped the weathered cap in a flamboyant show as the little fellow bent forward in a proper bow.

"It is a pleasure to meet the new master's children of the house." The fellow spoke with an extremely formal lilt. The tiny man raised himself with a straight back, the cap resting above where his heart should be, the other hand behind his back. "I trust that you both can see me quite clearly as you can hear me, correct?"

Lily looked curiously at the creature. "Yes, we see you."

He placed the cap upon his head again with a flourish and clapped his hands with satisfaction. "Excellent. Now, if you please, we must discuss this matter with urgency." Suddenly he slapped his hand on his head, the cap was seemingly forgotten as it smashed down with a squish. "Oh my stars, how could I be so rude? Oh, my goodness, how could I be so ostentatiously ignorant? I must confess this is my first time speaking with humans, but I can assure you both I was raised to the highest standards of proper etiquette."

Lily couldn't follow. "Umm...if I may ask mister-"

The little creature waved his hands offhandedly with a prim smile. "Of course of course – how improper that I did not even introduce myself. Where are my manners? You may call me Brom, Miss Lily."

"Ah - What are you?" asked Brandon, still wiping his wet face.

Brom turned to frown at Brandon, chin jutting up with an indignant air. "That was unnecessarily rude sir, but for the sake of time – that which we do not have regrettably – I shall tell you who I am. Who I am is what I am, and that is me. My mother, let the household keep her close to its heart, always said I was made of the finest propriety this side of the Atlantic." He gave a dramatic sigh as he stared toward the house, placing his hand over his heart.

"And that is?" pressed Brandon.

Brom tapped his foot impatiently. "My goodness, are all humans this impatient Miss Lily?" Brandon's eyes widened, annoyed.

Lily clasped her hands together nervously. "Umm, with

respect Brom, I know you said this was an urgent matter, but I'm sure you can agree that we may have some general questions."

"Oh quite right, quite right. Logical as always my lady, something us brownies do appreciate." He proudly beamed at Lily.

"Wait – brownie? What's that?" Brandon scratched his head.

"I believe it's a type of fairy," Lily pointed out. Pleased with her answer, Brom again clapped his hands.

"Brilliant Miss Lily! Quite clever of you I must say, for a human, if you don't mind my saying so. But again, I did just say so, didn't I? Please understand no disrespect intended."

Brandon's eyes got bigger. "You've got to be kiddin' me. Where's the joke? The camera crews? We got punked right?" He moved a few branches aside from the bushes, checking to see if there were any hidden microphones.

Brom huffed. "Household preserve me on the apparent nescience of humans."

"The who to the what now?" Brandon asked.

"The 'who' in question, Mr. Brandon is a brownie. A brownie that I am, therefore, a brownie is what the question is on." Brom brought a fist to his mouth, deliberately clearing his throat. "A brownie is-"

"An arrogant, prissy, stick in the mud – that's what a brownie is," said another loud voice. With a POP, another figure appeared out of thin air next to Brom.

Lily and Brandon blinked. Another one? This 'fairie' was around the same height as Brom, but with reddish windswept hair. He looked slightly disheveled with blue pants and a wrinkled brown shirt that was covered in soot. Smudges of ash graced his cheek, and his fingernails and hands were covered in dirt. The newcomer sported a stubble along his jaw with a slightly smaller nose.

The newcomer snorted. "Why are you bein' such a blether Brom? Yer chatterin' it up somethin' awful when we've got no time fer it."

Brom puffed his chest, clearly quite upset with the interruption. "I beg your pardon! I'll have you know, Alasdair Hob, that providing essential context to correctly absorb what is conspiring is polite and considerate towards our human caregivers. And no one is more adequately equipped to explain this than a brownie. I'll have you know we brownies are essential for the innermost workings of creating the most perfectly comfortable and acceptable home. Unlike Hobs...who are quite unrefined...and dirty." He sniffed the air around Alasdair with a grimace as if he smelled something foul, particularly glaring at the hob's dirty shirt.

Alasdair snorted. "Rather be a mink than a pretentious fandan any day, ya pansy. I mean who has a hissy fit when one wee glass is smashed? Hard ta believe yer from the old country."

Brom gave the Hob an affronted look. "I'll have you know I came from the Queen's country! And raised in the most refined and elegant manner. Why don't you take yourself back up to the North! And as for your accusation...those savages," he shuddered, "last night were utterly uncouth and would have done much worse to our dear home and haven. They needed to vacate the premises posthaste."

"Wait! What do you mean vacate?" Lily interrupted, trying to keep track of the conversation, which was proving difficult.

"He means throw out. Awa' an bile yer heid, get lost, bye bye." Alasdair shrugged.

Brom sniffed. "I wouldn't put it like that."

Alasdair rolled his eyes. "Then how would you put it?"

Brom glanced up at her with pleading eyes, ignoring the hob. "Oh Miss Lily, do forgive my impertinence. As the head brownie of this household, it is my solemn duty to protect the hearth and home." He placed his hand over his heart again, bowing his head. "Those ruffians last night were out of control if you don't mind my saying so. I merely provided a simple illusion to make them leave."

Brandon blinked, and his mouth dropped. "Dude! You mean the fire? You made it?"

"I'll have you know Mr. Brandon I created no fire." Brom spoke with indignance. "No no no. I simply 'crafted' an expertly designed illusion of a fire."

Brandon's eyes widened with excitement. "That's totally awesome! How did you do it? Pyrotechnics? Holograms?"

Brom sighed. "What is it with human boys being cave heathens obsessed with fire? I did nothing of the sort."

"Ack - all his eggs are double-yoaki." Alasdair glanced over at Lily and Brandon. "He's full of rubbish he is. He caused the fire," he said bluntly.

Brom huffed. "I most certainly did not 'cause' it!"

"Aye, you did!" Alasdair sported back.

"I'll have you know everything I did was protecting the hearth and home!"

Alasdair looked with disbelief at the brownie. "From teenagers?"

Brom threw up his hands. "They were savages! The house would have certainly been destroyed. And she wouldn't have liked that, not at all!"

Alasdair snorted. "I don't believe you! Yer always makin' a troll outta a fly." He looked up at Lily. "There was this one time he thought a tornado was coming to destroy the house. He got in such a tizzy that he boarded up all the windows and doors. He was shoutin' things like 'batten down the hatches' and 'don't worry I'll go down with the house Alasdair' and here it was just a human plane flying overhead -"

"Oh shut it you," hissed Brom.

Alasdair snickered. "Oye Brommie, and I'll have ya remember that I handle all the fires and heat in this household. What got your knickers in a twist was the lads and lassies were stompin' all over yer pretty floors."

Brom flushed crimson. He opened his mouth, but Lily stepped in.

"I'm sorry to interrupt, but you do realize how impossible this is to comprehend correct? I mean...well...you're...well..." She stammered. Everyone looked at her expectantly to finish. Lily was tongue-tied, the words drying up in her mouth.

Alasdair sighed, his gaze sympathetic. "Lass yer lookin' a bit peely wally. A little pale if you know what I mean. Are you tryin' to say we shouldna' be real?"

Lily nodded mutely. Of course, she wasn't feeling well. She was talking to fairies for goodness' sake! They were only supposed to be in stories. In all the places she had visited, the tales about these creatures were just that. Stories. There was never any scientific evidence that suggested anything else.

Brom shuffled his feet, his back straightening even more rigidly than before. "We are as real as you are. It was due to the Treaty circa Human Year 1889, 5th Age of the Rising Star, that we have kept in our existence secret on this side of the Veil. However, circumstances as they are, Alasdair and I felt the proclivity we needed to reveal ourselves to you. As you have gathered, we oversee, serve, and protect the Hemlock home and, subsequently, the denizens of the house who reside there. That includes you Miss Lily and you as well Mr. Brandon. Should anything portend that duty, we must act accordingly."

Alasdair rolled his eyes. "What this one's sayin' in gobbledie gook is that," he held up his fingers. "One, we're as real as you lot are. And two, there's a danger to you. So since we protect this house, and you are in it, we came ta warn ya."

"That's what I said." Brom huffed, crossing his arms over his chest.

Alasdair chuckled. "He didnae say that we've also grown fond of ya lass and would hate to see you hurt." He winked at her, giving a cheeky grin.

Brom snorted, his ears even pinker. "Personal feelings are irrelevant. We are doing our job."

"Yea yea," dismissed Alasdair.

"Threat? What threat?" asked Brandon.

Lily chewed her lip, asking quietly. "One of you tugged on my foot this morning, didn't you?"

Brom raised his hand slowly, looking slightly abashed. "It was me, my lady." He gazed at her with a serious expression. "I will say in my defense that it was necessary. I am relieved you heeded the warning. You would have been in a perilous predicament if you had entered that room with no knowledge of what you were facing."

A cold lump settled in the pit of her stomach. It spread out to the tips of her fingers, raising the hairs of her arms in little goosebumps.

Brandon put his face in his hands with a long groan. "I knew something was off with Ari."

Brom shook his head, looking at them with pity. "Oh Mr. Brandon, there is nothing 'off' about your sister."

Brandon looked at Brom in confusion. Brom continued. "The reason there is nothing 'off' about your sister is that the creature in there," he gestured towards the kitchen, "that is partaking of all the hard work I've put in creating the morning meal...is certainly NOT your sister."

Lily looked at Brom, her eyes widening in horror as the gears started clicking into place. Something dawned on her as she recalled all the tales she read about. She blurted out the first thing that came to mind. "A changeling?"

Brom nodded solemnly. "Indeed my lady, astute as always."

Brandon gave everyone the universal, *I don't know what you're talking about,* look. "Uh-huh, and that is?"

Lily, in shock, spoke numbly. "A changeling swaps places with a kidnapped human or baby. They take the human's place in the human world. Did I get that right?"

The brownie nodded. "That is fairly accurate. A few minor details are missing. But, of course, you would not be privy to such information, human as you are. Now changelings...well...where to begin? I guess at the beginning I suppose. Well, long ago the Fair Lady tried desperately to have a child. Children are quite rare with the High Fae as you know...oh my you wouldn't know, would you. Terribly sorry."

Alasdair stomped his feet with impatience. "Oye! Get on with it. Yer focus is jumpier than a squirrel in a den of foxes."

Brom coughed discreetly, his ears going a deeper shade of pink. "Apologies. Now, where was I?"

"The changeling! Ya daft brownie." Alasdair rolled his eyes.

Brom's head bobbed quickly. "Yes yes...of course...well when the Fair Lady finally had a child, it was quite sickly. Fae are rarely sick, since our physical constitutions are quite robust. And the High Fae, well, to put it kindly. They consider themselves quite extraordinary and their children must be the same as well. Having something...not as exceptional is utterly unacceptable amongst them. Since that was the case, the Lady couldn't keep the child so instead, the child was...given...yes that could be the correct word. She was 'given' off to the human side of the Veil. She had grown fond of another little child and took the human to her palace where the child was a servant for the rest of her days."

"You mean, she abandoned her baby and stole a human child?" Lily was flabbergasted. She couldn't imagine a mother being so heartless.

Brom looked at her pityingly. "High Fae are not human my lady. They are not like us lesser Fae either. Simply put, changelings are the cast-offs of the Homeland. Truly pitiful creatures they are, quite unfortunate. I do feel a bit sad for them, they must feel terribly inadequate with no meaningful purpose."

"Bloody disgusting wretches if ye ask me. They're crabbit as -" Alasdair spit on the ground.

"Be that as it may," interrupted Brom, glaring at Alasdair. "Back to the current matter at hand if you please. Changelings are particularly dangerous. And the one that happens to be posing as Miss Ari is quite a vicious one."

Brandon digested this, his eyes widening. "But, if that 'thing' inside is a changeling...then Ari is -" He stared off in horror when he came to the same realization as Lily. Brom looked sympathetically at them.

Lily closed her eyes. "It means she was taken. And from what we've seen, I'm positive she was taken by something that isn't human."

CHAPTER
NINE

Brandon and Lily spent the better part of the afternoon racking their brains trying to digest a few key facts. 1) Fairies existed. 2) One dangerous fairy was in their house looking like a homeless version of Ari. And 3) Ari was kidnapped.

Brom and Alasdair were insistent it was too dangerous to go back into the house until they had a plan. Alasdair assured them they were safe outdoors because changelings did not like the bright sun. That suited Lily just fine. She was not inclined to step one foot back in the house anytime soon.

Laying down on the soft grass, she turned her gaze up at the gauzy clouds. How were they going to fix this? Where was Ari now? Was she okay? Was she hurt? Scared? Lily groaned, rubbing the heels of her palms into her eyes until all she could see was the reddish tint inside her eyelids, blocking out everything but faint shadows.

"Ack lass, dinnae worry."

She opened her eyes. Alasdair stood over her, looking down with a curious tilt of his head.

Lily groaned. "Ugh! Where do we even begin."

"Well...takin' care of that changeling fer starters," said Alasdair giving her a 'duh' expression.

"And what about Ari?"

Alasdair shrugged. "To be honest lass, yer sister is not my concern. The changeling is a danger to the house." He saw her shocked expression. He explained very matter of fact. "I'm a Hob lass. The home comes first."

Brom interjected. "But what my uncouth compatriot failed to mention my lady is that once we deal with the present problem, we may be able to discern some valuable information about the whereabouts of your sister."

Lily sat up quickly. "Of course! We can find out who sent the changeling and find out who has Ari."

With renewed determination, she wracked her brain as she asked the group, "Okay, so how do we get rid of the changeling?"

Brom and Alasdair looked at each other for a minute. They spoke at the same time.

"Barlow."

Lily frowned, confused. "Who's Barlow?"

"He's my mother's uncle's cousin's son once removed," said Alasdair.

"He's the Lob that is in charge of the stable." Brom pointed towards said stable.

"What's a Lob?" asked Brandon.

"They are keepers of livestock and farming equipment. Barlow handles everything outdoors," replied Brom.

"Aye – Lobs are cousins to us Hobs. But Hobs handle the inside the house 'cause we're more reliable," Alasdair said proudly.

Brom furrowed his brows as he sniffed in disapproval. "Both of you are quite uncouth if you ask me."

"And I didnae seem to have asked ya, did I brownie?" quirked Alasdair.

Lily sighed inwardly. "Well then. Should we go get him?" She started to stand up but Alasdair and Brom stopped her. They waved their hands frantically.

"No no, Miss Lily. It is...well...going to the stable at this moment in time...well..." Brom stuttered. He looked over to Alasdair, his eyes wide.

Alasdair stepped in, talking low. "Best do it privately. Dinnae want certain ears to be listenin' in. I'll go get Barlow. You lot head down to the basement. Dinnae worry, that part of the house is safe. We'll meet you there." He pointed to the outside doors to the basement. "Be there in two shakes." And with a POP, he blinked out.

Lily was nervous about going back into the house. But she was taught that if she did not have all the answers, there was always someone who had an answer. That meant she had no choice but to trust this brownie as he would know about a changeling better than she ever could.

Brom sighed, breaking her from her thoughts. "I'm not looking forward to this. Not at all."

"What do you mean?" Lily asked

"Well, to put it politely. In regards to Barlow...well...don't tell that Hob this, but I always believed Alasdair to be the more refined of the two." Brom closed his eyes, taking a deep breath.

"Okay. But what about being in the house? The changeling?" asked Brandon.

Brom smiled awkwardly. "Well...ah. That is quite true Mr. Brandon. But do not worry. I temporarily sealed the basement door inside the house with a simple spell. The changeling won't be able to come downstairs. I also believe Master Tony sound-proofed the area to give his wife privacy am I right?"

Lily nodded. She continued to stare at the basement door with trepidation. The brownie smiled softly. "It is as safe as outside. I promise Miss Lily." He nudged Brandon on his shin. "Now come along this way if you please. This way this way."

Lily sighed and stepped into the darkness.

CHAPTER

TEN

L ily waited in the basement. The dark, quiet, cold, dank basement. Lily rubbed her arms. She really *really* didn't like the dark. Darkness outside with moonlight or starlight she could handle. But pitch darkness always made her uneasy.

She kept herself distracted by scolding Brandon to keep his hands off his mother's equipment. As the time ticked by, Lily was getting anxious as she kept pacing back and forth. Where was Alasdair? She had half a mind to go upstairs saying something like, 'get out of this house or you'll regret it' and the changeling would be so scared and tell her where Ari was and run away. She grimaced at how stupid that sounded. Ugh, what was she thinking!

"Well, what's this? What are ya doin'? Standin' around with your hands in yer pockets? You lazy wallopers! I have half a mind to kick yer bahookie's." A gravelly voice growled in the darkness.

Lily turned to the person she could only assume was Barlow. He seemed short of two feet tall and wore nothing but a tattered potato sack. He sported a grisly red beard with streaks of grey that reached to his waist. The same red/grey hair dusted the tops of his callused hands and very large bare feet. He had a rather large nose that was screwed up to accompany an equally big frown as he clutched a small hammer dwarfed in his massive hands.

Lily gulped softly. "Are you Barlow?"

The lob frowned as he continued to growl. "Of course I'm Barlow. See any other lob? Who else do ya think it'd be lass?" His eyes narrowed at them. "I'm guessin' Brom spit in yer eyes since you can see and talk to our kind."

Not waiting for an answer, Barlow walked up to the side wall where a frame was slightly out of place. He took up his hammer and started to pound. Lily stood, shocked as the lob began to mutter in a gruff tone. "Geez what was your father thinkin', he screwed up the framework! Glaikit dumb human," he groused.

Brom coughed politely. "Excuse me Barlow but I must say, that language is quite uncalled for. And as you are well aware, it is my job to take care of the household, which does include the basement. You need not trouble yourself with this small task."

The lob glared at Brom, his hammer pausing mid-strike. "Fine then mister prissy pants. Then why didn't YOU fix this already?"

Brom sputtered. "I beg your pardon! That is most rude."

"Awa' an bile yer heid. Get lost brownie!" Barlow turned away, his hammer resuming.

Lily stared incredulously as the two bickered, her mouth slightly open. Brom was right when he said that Alasdair was the pleasant one. Barlow seemed to be all vinegar and nails. Lily frowned as one thing the lob said earlier stuck out.

"Wait! Did you say spit?"

Barlow ignored her, the hammer falling loudly, drowning out her question. She closed her eyes ruefully, thankful the room was soundproof. She waited a moment, feeling awkward because she wasn't sure if the lob had heard her question, but Barlow turned his gaze towards her with a huff.

"Yeah, how ya think you could see us? Simply by wishin'? Och! Dafty humans!" grumbled Barlow.

Lily closed her eyes and prayed for patience. *Spit? Really? Okay, it's over and done. Don't think about it too much...* She groaned. She was thinking about it too much.

"Wait – that was spit in my eyes?!" Brandon's eyes widened as he gave her a goofy grin. "That's epically cool! Magic loogies."

Lily turned accusing eyes at Brom, who had the decency to look ashamed.

Brom shuffled his feet, embarrassed. "I do express regret for the delivery method. But it was necessary as it is the most expedited way."

She rubbed her temples, trying to focus on the problem at hand. "Barlow, did Alasdair talk to you about the changeling?"

Barlow threw down the hammer with a thunk. "I already knew!" He snarled, startling Lily. "How could I not? That stupid changeling stink is reeking all over the place. It's gotta go! You'd better hurry up on that!" He pointed a finger accusingly at her.

She stared at him dumbfounded. "Me? How am I supposed to do that? For your information, in less than four hours I found out my stepsister is missing and that fairies exist. Can you give me some slack here?" She put her hands on her hips and glared at the surly lob.

Barlow squinted his eyes then sighed, rubbing his hands over his face. "Listen girl don't get your knickers in a twist. I know this all feels like a skelp to the face. Sorry, I'm angry cause of that thing." He pointed upstairs. "And it didnae help that Brom and Alasdair can't do anything about it since your sister switched places with it and all."

"What do you mean? Can't you just 'POOF' it away?" Brandon waved his hands.

"None of us can 'POOF' anything away." Alasdair remarked, joining the group with a POP.

Barlow looked at Brandon with disdain. "Are all humans really this daft?"

Brom stepped in, his hands slicing down. "Pardon! But I do not believe Miss Lily deserves such deplorable treatment. Also, as unenlightened and impatient as Mr. Brandon may be, I am of an astute mind that name calling at present is not very conducive as we have an interloper invading our beloved abode." He raised his eyebrow at Barlow. "I do trust that we need a coordinated plan of action for our endeavors to provide a fruitful outcome where we are no longer plagued by this pestilence."

Alasdair let out a deep sigh. "Forgettin' the blether's prose, the brownie's got a point cousin. We need the changeling gone and quick. The lad and lass didnae ken nothin' of our world. You've dealt with changelings before. How do we make it leave?" He put his hand on the lob's shoulder with a squeeze.

Barlow picked up his hammer and twirled it in his hands, his brow furrowed in concentration. "If you can get the sodden thing to attack someone connected to the house, you lot can probably make it leave."

Lily frowned, puzzled. "Why's that?"

Brom's eyes lit up as he snapped his fingers. "Oh of course! Brilliant Barlow!" He looked at Lily's questioning gaze. "Because Miss Lily. The home has special protections. We cannot do something unless the home or its denizens are threatened within its walls. I mean I certainly could have prevented it from coming inside the house, but it was invited by one of the owners of the household." He pointedly looked over at Brandon.

Brandon's eyes widened. "So THAT'S why she asked me if she could come home."

Alasdair nodded. "So now Brom can't make it leave. Not unless it tries to hurt someone."

"Can't we uninvite it?" asked Brandon.

Barlow stared at him incredulously. "This isn't a vampire you roaster."

"If it was that simple my dear boy, I can assure you that we wouldn't be asking Barlow for assistance." Brom replied primly, giving the lob a look of disdain.

Barlow rumbled, twisting the hammer. "Watch it brownie!"

Alasdair slid next to Lily and tugged her sleeve as he whispered in her ear. "Better step in lass, brownies and lobs have been known to get into fights for months and we dinnae have that kinda time."

She gawked. *Months?* What is it with lobs and brownies? Shaking her head, she put her hands up placatingly. "Okay okay, so Brandon invited it in. We're past that now. I think we can all agree that the changeling needs to leave. And it sounds that the only way to kick it out is for it to attack one of us. Am I correct?" Both Brom and Barlow nodded mutely, still glaring at one another.

Lily closed her eyes. "Okay now that we have that settled that still leaves one thing. We need to find out where Ari is."

Barlow scratched his beard with a huff. "Lass, the changeling came to replace your sister. Ask the changeling. Geez, you humans are bloody dumb sometimes."

Lily let his grumbling slide as she continued patiently. "I understand that. My concern is that we need the changeling to talk BEFORE we kick it out of the house." She bit her lip, thinking hard.

Barlow tugged his beard harder. "That's gonna be tricky lass. Changelings are devious. Handling them requires trickery, which, quite frankly you dinnae seem to be mighty good at." He looked at her, slightly apologetic.

Lily looked at Brandon, a sly grin spreading across his face. "A trick huh? Leave that to me."

CHAPTER
ELEVEN

"**B**randon it's too dangerous."

Lily took a deep breath, grateful to be outside finally. The sun shined, but she still felt chilly. They ended up back at the stables, the horse eerily silent, watching them.

When Brandon told her his plan, she wanted to say, *Are you out of your mind!* However, she didn't think screaming would deter Brandon. Apparently, going in 'guns a' blazin' was the only genius deceptive plan he could come up with on the spot.

Brandon whined. "Ah come on! The beardy guy says we need this thing to attack us. I can annoy anything, it's simple. Just a smoke bomb to the face and it's a done deal." He snapped his fingers and clicked his hands together.

Lily stared at him in disbelief. *He's going to get us killed.*

Barlow groaned, clapping a hand over his face. "Oye, gonny no dae that." He shook his head as he took in Brandon's undeterred expression. "The youth today, so impatient. Don't do it ya moron! That thing would hang you by yer toenails faster than you can say, 'ouch'. Why when I was in Edinburgh there was a changeling that ripped off a man's- "

Alasdair slapped a hand over Barlow's mouth as he whispered urgently. "Haud yer wheesht. Be quiet everyone, I hear it coming." He glanced at Brom, who inclined his head in silent agreement. "We'll meet you kids later. Whatever you do, dinnae let on you know about us." And with that, the three fairies vanished.

No sooner than they disappeared the faux Ari skulked up the side of the house, staying in the shade and shadows. It sniffed the air, and curled its lip, looking for something. *Or someone*, thought Lily. It squinted its eyes around frantically before setting its sights on them. The eyes narrowed in recognition as it zeroed in and raced up to Lily and Brandon.

It cocked its head to the side, slowly blinking. "Sooo...what you doing out here? You've been gone a long while." The faux Ari asked suspiciously, its voice hushed.

Lily shuddered. The way the changeling stared at them reminded her of Jake's (her father's current intern) pet python. Once, she was waiting for her father to finish his lecture on Aztec Engineering Methods. Jake let her stay in his common room where the python was in a large glass terrarium, covered in bright green branches and a small pond of water. Before the lecture started, Jake put some mice in the terrarium in case the snake got hungry. Lily stared, horrified, as the python slowly slithered towards the mice, assessing them with an unblinking stare – then – BAM - no more mice. After that, she never went back to the common room. Lily had nightmares of that python's stare. The changeling was giving Lily that same stare.

Lily looked over at Brandon, who nodded. *Well, it's now or never I guess.* She hoped she could be convincing. "Oh, nothing much." She gave what she hoped was a nonchalant shrug. "Just checking on the horse." She gestured over towards the stable where said horse was eerily quiet.

The faux Ari peered as if searching for something. The horse gazed back, its eyes intense. Lily didn't realize she was holding her breath. Concerned the changeling would scare the horse, she put her hand out to stroke the horse's mane. The horse tensed under her palm, its eyes blazing. Lily continued to pet in slow, cautious strokes. She breathed a sigh of relief when the tension receded. The horse looked back at the changeling, giving a dismissive snort.

The faux Ari raised its eyebrow, undecided. After a pause, it gave a satisfied nod. It looked back at Lily and Brandon with a crooked smile.

"Good. Wouldn't want my siblings to get lost. The forest out there is wild and massive. Tons of bad things come in...and out of that forest, you know. Must be very careful." Its voice ended with a lilting raspy singsong note. It sneered, its gaze rested on Lily's hand which still rested on the horse's mane. It looked back up at her, and with a wink, it walked lazily back into the house.

Brandon let out a long breath. "Boy, I thought it wanted to rip us to pieces or something."

Her shoulders slumped in relief as she scratched behind the horse's ear. "I hope it didn't scare you too much pretty boy. I promise we won't let that changeling near you." She cupped the horse's muzzle with her palms, bringing her nose close for a nose kiss. The horse jerked back with a sharp neigh, seemingly surprised. Lily laughed. "Aww sorry boy, guess you weren't as scared as I thought." She smiled, even though she knew the horse couldn't understand her apology.

"Okay well, now we crossed that bridge, what do we do now? I still my plan is the best option," said Brandon.

Lily shook her head. "Oh no! I don't think so. Your mom would never forgive me if something happened to you."

Brandon crossed his arms, annoyed. "Okay then, so what's the plan?"

Lily rubbed her temples, uncertain of what to do. She gnawed her lip. "We don't have time to wait. Dad and Tabby will be back in five days. And who knows what's happening with Ari right now."

She looked back at the house, taking a deep breath, the wheels turning in her brain. *They only said they didn't want the changeling to not know about them...sooo...* Technically Barlow didn't specify she should wait for them. She closed her eyes a moment, her heart thumping loudly in her ears. *Please let me be right about this.* Before she could talk herself out of it, she started running towards the cottage.

Brandon yelled after her, his feet stumbling loudly as he sprinted after her. Lily pumped her legs to quicken her pace, knowing she had to stay ahead of him. All she had to do was get to the door before him.

Almost there....

Her fingertips touched the smooth metal of the handle as she pried it open. She slammed the back door for good measure to make sure she was heard and quickly locked it. She pressed her back against the cold wood as Brandon pounded behind her, screaming to let him in. She heard the horse neighing, but only faintly. Her palms began to sweat. *Come on Lil, you can do this.*

She yelled out. "Hey, Ari!" Silence. She took a deep breath and called out again. "Do you hear me you ugly stinky piece of manure! Where are you?!"

The cottage was eerily silent. Not even a breeze could be heard. "What you scared?! We haven't finished talking about last night," she taunted. Again, no response. *How can I make this thing mad enough to want to attack me?* She ran over to the kitchen counter to grab the sugar.

Here goes.

She yelled out, holding the sugar in the air. "Alright if that's how it's gonna be, I'm gonna pour all your honey and sugar down the drain." She began pouring the sugar down the sink, the slight whisper of the granules echoing within the silent kitchen. She stopped a moment to listen. At first, she heard nothing. Then she heard the faint pounding of feet above her, more animal than human. A hiss of scraping claws slid down the staircase accompanied by a low growling howl.

Before she could blink, something flew down the stairs, the walls shaking in the process. A loud THUD resounded through the cottage, and that was when she saw it. The changeling.

It was standing in the hallway, its ratty hair covering its face. The warped version of Ari's face twisted in anger, a growl coming deep within its throat. Lily's own throat slowly closed up. She silently gulped, the sugar still dangling in her hand. *Good going Lil,* she thought regretfully. She drew a deep breath, pulling together her remaining wisps of courage. *Well here goes nothing...*

Its lips peeled back in a silent snarl. Lily continued. "That's right. You heard me!" She tried to keep her voice steady. "I'm gonna throw all of this down the sink. Every...last...bit. What are you gonna do about it, huh?"

By the time Lily finished, the changeling seemed to double in size. Its face morphed and shaped until it revealed the true face of the changeling. And it was truly hideous. Lily's skin crawled. She started to second-guess her entire plan.

Perhaps this wasn't the best idea.

With an angry snarl, the changeling's claw-like hands reached out to her. Lily quickly backed up to the counter, her arm stretching behind, grasping for the nearest thing she could get her hands on. Her hands felt nothing but air as the changeling careened towards her. She tensed, bracing herself against the counter for impact. *Oh man, this is gonna hurt,* she thought grimly, her eyes closed instinctively.

Lily knew it was going to hurt. She underestimated how strong the changeling was. The changeling threw her against the cupboards with such force Lily lurched, the breath flying out of her body. She coughed, her chest burning. Lily cringed, desperately searching for something to throw. Thankfully, luck was on her side. Her hands grasped her dad's favorite tea kettle. With a frantic swing, the kettle gave off a nice clear *ding* when it made impact. The changeling staggered back, surprised by the sudden assault. Lily regained her balance as she held the kettle high, ready to throw it again.

Before the changeling could prepare for another attack, the cottage windows and doors started to slam open and shut repeatedly. The changeling darted its head around in confusion. Brom appeared with a CLAP, putting himself between Lily and the changeling.

Brom looked over at Lily, amazement dotting his features. "I must say. Very well done Miss Lily. Very well done indeed. Now if I may take it from here." He looked at the changeling in disgust and snapped his fingers. Silver ropes appeared in the air, writhing as if alive. With insane speed, they wrapped themselves around the changeling, caging it securely. The changeling struggled, howling like a caged animal, unable to break free.

Brom huffed. "Oh do keep it down, please." The howling continued. Brom glared. "That is *quite* enough thank you very much. I do not wish to silence you as that would be highly improper. But I will."

Silence.

With a nod, Brom walked up to Lily with a triumphant grin. "You may rest easy now Miss Lily. The threat has been contained."

Lily looked down warily, the adrenaline slowly receding. Her hands trembled, metal biting into her skin. She was still holding the kettle. Slowly, she lowered it, prying her fingers off the handle with some difficulty.

She blew out a wobbly breath, rubbing her aching shoulder. "I thought you said you could stop it when it attacked me?"

Brom looked abashed, his cheeks-tinged pink. "My sincere apologies Miss Lily. You see- "

"Sorry lass, we were arguing outside. Time got away from us." Alasdair popped in with Barlow in tow.

Lily's eyes narrowed. They were arguing? While she was getting pummeled? She was about to tell them what they could do with their 'time' when the door burst open.

Brandon rushed in, panting, his eyes frantically searching until they landed on her. "Lil are you alright?! The door wouldn't open and -" He stopped in his tracks, blinking, the changeling writhing on the floor. "Well then, I guess things are under control."

Brom lifted his nose in the air in a haughty fashion. "Well of course Mr. Brandon. I take my job as caretaker very seriously you must know. Why I've been the caretaker ever since-"

Brom took a breath, ready to continue with the lecture, when a loud pop echoed in the room. Lily turned to see Barlow sitting on the floor in front of an opened cupboard door, a large green bottle sitting between his legs. Brom scowled as the lob took a big swig of the contents with a loud gulp.

"I beg your pardon-" the brownie sputtered.

Barlow burped, wiping his mouth. "Didnae mind if I do. Nothin' like a good honey mead to cure what ails ya,"

Alasdair glanced over at the changeling, which, still tied up, was softly screeching and clawing at the floor. "Ah – cousin. Much as I enjoy a good drink as the next hob, we really should get rid of this thing."

Barlow burped again, wiping his mouth with his sleeve. "Eh, why are ye askin' me?"

"Because...it is YOUR bloody rope!" Brom gritted out. He glanced over at Lily and Brandon as he apologized. "Apologies. While I was able to use the rope to bind him, the magical workings of this item are beyond my knowledge."

"Oh, that." Barlow barely glanced at the changeling, taking another swig. "That's just some dwarf rope I keep laying around. Made with silver, silk, and a few spells intertwined makes for a good binding rope. Don't worry your little brownie head. I'll drag the fan-dangled thing outta here before you can say 'bloody' again."

"Okay, so one thing settled. Now what about Ari?" asked Lily. "We need to know who took her."

Barlow stared at her, sighing. "Oh fine. Go on, just ask him." He gestured towards the changeling. "Ye better be answerin' the lass's questions."

Lily knelt on the floor until she was at eye level with the changeling. It had morphed its face back to a misshapen version of Ari. When she got closer, it glared at her with a hiss. She flinched even though she knew it was bound. Involuntarily, her hand went to her bruised shoulder. The changeling saw where her hand drifted and gave a sly smile.

"Oh? Does it hurt?" It asked sweetly. Its eyes burned into her. "Come a little closer and I'll tell you something interesting..."

Brom stepped to Lily's side, putting himself between them. "Ask your questions Miss Lily, but carefully."

Lily tried to keep calm. "Do you know who took the human girl you were impersonating?"

It chuckled darkly. "Of course. I wouldn't have come otherwise."

Okay, I guess that was too vague.

"Who took Ari?"

Silence.

"Who...took...Ari?" She ground out.

The changeling spit at her feet, growling at them with beady eyes. It opened its mouth, but out came a series of clicks and growls that Lily couldn't understand. The floorboards began to shake as the cabinets banged open, dishes spilling out. With wide eyes, a shatter resonated as the bottle broke in Barlow's hand, liquid dripping down his fingers.

The lob's eyes, which were previously dull with apathy, had narrowed, burning with anger. He twisted his finger towards the changeling with a flourish, droplets splashing onto the floor. In answer, the ropes slowly tightened, the changeling struggling to break free. The cabinets silenced; the floorboards stopped. The house held its breath.

Barlow glared daggers at the changeling. He growled out into the silence. "I'll gie ye a skelpit lug if you do that again ye mink. Behave!" The ropes jerked; a muffled squeal emanated from the captive. Barlow continued. "And ye can get rid of the glamour now, it's so weak you dinnae even look like the girl anymore."

The changeling panted a few breaths, unable to move. It finally slumped its shoulders in defeat, giving a frustrated glare. "Fiiiiine,"

Lily and Brandon stood in disbelief as the changeling's body began to twist and bend. Its limbs elongated, the cracking of bones making Lily wince. Soon a humanoid, malformed creature with a spindly legs and arms along with a wrinkled, weathered face stood before them. It was skinny. Very skinny. Gray papery skin that looked like it was out in the sun too long hung-over visible ribs. Gone was the Ari double. In its place was something like looked like it was preserved for hundreds of years.

Barlow raised his eyebrow. "Now that yer done with yer hissy fit, tell the nice lass here who took the girl."

The changeling glared back at Barlow. "I'll tell you, but it'll do you no good. No good at all." Its voice was a deep grainy cadence like the crushing of autumn leaves.

"Well, where is she?" Brandon asked impatiently when the changeling paused. The changeling bared its fanged teeth in a grotesque smile.

"She's beyond the veil of human eyes. Past the boundaries of human imagination. She's -"

Exasperated, Brom stopped his foot. "Oh bloody hell just spit it out already!"

Brom, shaking, flamed bright red when he noticed the group staring at him.

"Apologies." He mumbled, his face shining a brighter red.

The changeling snorted with a sneer. "So emotional you all are. But if you must know little brownie, she was taken by the Prince of Prophecy."

Lily noticed all the fairies seemed shocked as the changeling's sinister laugh echoed throughout the kitchen. Barlow's mouth hung open, Alasdair's eyes had gotten so wide you couldn't see anything but black, and Brom started tugging his hair out.

The changeling turned its dark gaze back to Lily. "See? They know. They understand what's happening." Its voice danced in a singsong lilt. Its eyes sparkled with a wicked twinkle as it giggled. "You'll never find your sister now. Forget you ever knew her. And… if you did ever find her, you'll never be the same. If you make it out alive that is."

Brom clapped his hands together nervously. The rope curled around the changeling's mouth, gagging it from speaking. "Alright! That is quite enough out of you! I believe your presence is no longer required and you shall be vacated from this premise immediately."

Alasdair stood next to the brownie and glared down at the changeling. "Do not even think about coming back here. Next time it'll be worse than a dwarf rope." He pointed his finger at its face. The changeling shrugged nonchalantly, unable to talk of course.

Alasdair yelled out. "Barlow!"

And with that Barlow snapped his fingers. The changeling disappeared, the rope curled on the floor.

Lily and Brandon stared at the empty space. They looked at each other, still not quite understanding what had transpired in the last two minutes. It was a lot to take in. A changeling, magic rope, and fairy princes. Yeah, that was just a little bit to process.

Brandon spoke up first. "So, who is this prince that took my sister?"

The trio glanced nervously at each other. Barlow looked down into his empty smashed bottle. Brom magically produced a brush and pan as he proceeded to sweep up the broken glass.

"The Prince of Prophecy," whispered Alasdair. He sighed, not meeting the children's eyes. "Oye cousin, get another bottle will ye? I need a cup." With a pop, Barlow had produced another bottle, pouring the liquid into the cup.

"Yeah duh. We got that part. But who is he? Like we can go get her now right? You should know where she is." Brandon stared hopefully at them.

Barlow shook his head. "Aint that simple lad. This is one of the princes we're talkin' about here. This is NOT just some run of the mill fae."

Barlow sighed when they didn't budge. "Och, fine! Come on kids. If we're gonna talk about history might as well do it over a fire and something to eat." He grumbled to himself, waving them towards the living room.

Brom clapped his hands. A bunch of knives appeared, hovered in midair. The brownie moved his hands like a conductor and soon the cutlery began cutting vegetables with a flourish. The savory aroma of garlic, butter, and onions filled the air.

Barlow groaned. It sounded like a few bones popped when he plopped himself down on a stool next to the fireplace. Muttering to himself, Barlow rubbed his hands in agitation as he yelled over into the kitchen.

"Cousin, ye mind gettin' a fire going?" asked Barlow.

Alasdair came up with a pint of, what Lily thought, was her father's emergency beer. The hob sat on the floor in front of the fireplace and wriggled his nose. Immediately the fireplace lit up.

The reddish glow of the embers warmed the house, as if to burn away all traces of the cold changeling. The fire's heat started to ease the chill in Lily's body. Barlow, noticing Brandon and Lily were still standing, gestured them towards the couch.

"Alright have a seat. Brom should have everything ready in a minute." He took out a wooden pipe. No sooner did Barlow finish his sentence when out of nowhere Lily and Brandon's hands held a small bowl filled with a tantalizing soup. Brandon dug in immediately, his slurps resounding in the silence of the crackling fire. Brom popped into the room and stood quietly in the corner, watching them anxiously.

Barlow grunted. "Well go on. Eat lass."

Lily stared at the soup. It did look and smell delicious. It smelled of warm cozy winter nights as she could smell a perfect combination of root vegetables blended with butter, cream, and garlic. It reminded her of comfort and safety, but the pit in her stomach wouldn't go away. So much so that Brom could have put a slice of her favorite blueberry pie in front of her and she wouldn't have touched it.

With regret, she put her bowl aside gently without so much as a sip. "Okay. Let me understand this, Fae royalty kidnapped Ari, correct?" Barlow nodded. She continued. "Can you tell us who are the princes?"

Barlow put his hands on his bouncing knees, his pipe making a multitude of smoke rings. "They are the sons of High King Finvarra." He paused when he saw her blank face. He scratched his beard as he took another puff of his pipe. Large rings of a sweet smoke wafted up to the rafters, each one smaller than the one before, making a pretty pattern. "Let's start at the beginning, shall we?" He stared in thought a moment, a few more puffs before he began.

"Long ago, and I do say long ago cause it was ancient. Us fairies don't really measure time in the way you humans do-"

"So when he says a 'long time' I think you get the point." Alasdair interjected.

Barlow glared. "Anyways, as I was sayin', long ago the world as you know it was separated into facets,"

Brandon, soup running down his chin, tilted his head. "What's a facet?"

If looks could kill, Lily believed that daggers would have come out of the lob's eyes. After a heated glare, more incoherent grumblings, and a few more agitated puffs from his pipe, the lob continued. He blew out a large ring of smoke towards Brandon face, to which Brandon sneezed.

He growled. "Ack! Daft kids. Think of a diamond. When light shines on the stone, it gives off a lot of different lights right? A facet is one thing that holds several different pieces. Now, can I get back to the story?"

Brandon nodded, slurping another spoonful of soup.

Barlow settled back in his chair, looking up at the ceiling. "Now, where was I?" He gave a warning glare to his audience to not answer him. "Oh yes. When our reality was originally created, there was the Human world, the Underworld, the Upperworld, and the Otherworld."

Brandon interrupted, spoon halfway towards his mouth. "You mean like dead people?"

Barlow threw his pipe in the fire with a growl. "Are you gonna let me finish?"

"But you're taking too long. It's boooring," whined Brandon.

"Brandon-" scolded Lily.

Brandon's ears got red, and he quieted immediately.

Barlow produced another pipe. Rubbing his temples, he ground out. "As I was sayin'. The Otherworld is where we fae reside. These worlds were completely separate, each unable to cross to the other. It wasn't until the first of the High Fey, the Sidhe, used their magic to break the barriers between our world and yours." Barlow gaze saddened as he continued. "However, the Great Beings who had created the barriers between the worlds in the first place, they were angry with the Sidhe. They realized with that bloody stunt the Sidhe had power, much more than they originally thought. So, as punishment, they created the Veil. A limbo between the Otherworld and yours. They trapped the Sidhe in the Veil, barring any passage to the Otherworld. The Great Beings said that since the Sidhe wanted to visit the human realm so badly we can be a part of it, in a sense, but we will never quite fit in and never return home. It's been thousands of years since the Veil was formed."

Lily stared into the fire, the story playing out in her head. "All the stories, they're true?"

Barlow nodded. "Yup. Everything you thought was a myth really was some being from the Veil that came through to your world."

"Like aliens?" asked Brandon excitedly. "You mean you guys are from other planets?"

Barlow frowned. "No. We're not from the bloody moon! Are ye daft? Didnae hear a word I said?"

"These princes are from the Veil?" Lily asked, trying to keep the conversation on course.

Barlow coughed. "Well, their father, High King Finvarra, is a direct descendent of the Sidhe. His father, Dagda, was actually their original king. No one knows where the Sidhe are. No one has seen them in thousands of years."

"How big is it?" asked Brandon.

Barlow thought a moment. "The Veil touches your entire world. The High King needed assistance, as you can imagine, with overseeing it. Finvarra appointed his sons, the Seven Princes, to aid him. Now make no mistake. The High King knows with seven sons there is bound to be a lot of fighting. He didn't want too much bloodshed between them, so he decided to give each prince the right to rule over a piece. He broke the Veil into provinces. I believe you refer to these areas as continents. The High King reigns supreme, but the princes are next in authority." Barlow took a breath from the pipe, going silent.

Alasdair, who had been quietly staring into the fire, turned back to look at Lily with a pensive expression. "Your sister was taken by one of the seven princes. That isn't something to be taken lightly. To catch the attention of a prince is no small feat and once taken, he won't give her up easily."

"Why not?" Brandon tipped his bowl back, drinking the remaining soup.

Brom sighed from the corner, his lips curled in slight disgust as trails of soup dripped onto Brandon's shirt. "Because Mr. Brandon. If you were dealing with a common fae, they would either lose interest in your sister or you could barter with them... deplorable as that may be. High Fae are more refined but harder to negotiate with. To put it simply, it's an impossible task for a human."

Lily groaned. *Great,* she thought sarcastically, *of course Ari got the attention of a prince. She couldn't have gotten the attention of some unknown fairy. But noooo...it had to be the equivalent of a main character of some ridiculous novel for crying out loud! Just keeps getting better and better.*

She rubbed her forehead, her nose crinkled with annoyance. "Well, we can't just leave her there. What do I have to do?"

Barlow raised his eyebrow.

"Lass, not trying to stir the pot or anything but, from what I've seen, that stepsister of yours has given you nothing but grief and misery. She's got no sense of respect for anyone or anything. You sure you wanna go through the ringer to bring her back?" His brow furrowed.

Heat hit Lily's cheeks, embarrassment flooding her. How would he know how Ari had treated her? She glanced over at Brandon, who stared at her quietly with a solemn face.

Brom saw her expression and said gently. "Miss Lily...if I may. Your altercation with your stepsister was rather jarring to be delicate on the subject. And you seemed slightly perturbed last eve especially."

Alasdair scratched his ear with a puzzled look. "What are ya sayin' it like that for?"

Brom closed his eyes, gritting his teeth. "This requires some discretion Alasdair."

The hob cocked his head to the side, clueless. "Huh? Why? Everyone heard the racket the both of them made the other night. What's discreet about that?"

Brom stared openmouthed. "Because!" He stopped a moment and took a deep breath. "The lady is finding out that we have seen them in their vulnerable moments. It's quite shocking, I'm sure."

Alasdair huffed. "Ack, yer fine right Lily?" The hob asked Lily directly with a straight face. She blinked, trying to keep up with the conversation. Alasdair seemed to take her silence as agreement and looked over at Brom. "See? She's good."

Brom groaned, putting his face in his hands.

While the fairies started to argue again about manners and discretion, Lily mulled over what Alasdair asked. Why would she risk it for Ari? Brandon's warm hand fell on her shoulder, jarring her for a second.

"Lily. I know how Ari has treated you, but she's my sister." Brandon's eyes were pleading. "She's not all bad. You know that."

Lily fiddled with the satin hem of the teal and lavender bridesmaid dress. In five minutes, she was supposed to walk down the aisle to her father's marriage. She took careful steps back and forth in the room, making sure she wouldn't trip on the new heels Tabby had given her. What happened if she tripped? Or if the heels caught on the dress? People would be staring at her. She didn't want to embarrass everyone. Her heart pounded, her palms becoming sweaty. The door opened and Ari sauntered in. She looked stunning in her matching dress, the green accentuating her blonde hair. She frowned at Lily.

"Lily? You ready?"

Lily blinked. "Yes. Why?"

Ari stood a moment, her hands on her hips, as she looked at her. She motioned to a cushioned chair.

"Sit."

"Um..."

"Sit Lily."

With wobbly knees that Lily hoped didn't show from her long dress, she sat awkwardly on the pink cushioned chair. Silently, Ari grabbed a brush and carefully started working Lily's curls. The soft scrape of the bristles hit Lily's scalp, calming her. After a minute, Ari took a little hair oil from her purse and gently squeezed the curls.

"Take a look."

Lily looked and saw her normally frizzy curls were soft and shiny. She touched her soft hair in wonder, her anxiety forgotten. Ari came up behind her and gently put Lily's hand down. She took out a white laced embroidered ribbon from her purse.

"This is one of my favorites," said Ari softly. She gathered Lily's curls and tied the ribbon to make a half up hairdo where the curls cascaded down Lily's shoulders. Ari smiled through the mirror.

"There. All better." Ari patted her shoulders. She turned towards the door as she looked back to Lily with a small smile.

"Let's go!"

Lily absently fingered the same ribbon was holding her hair up. She looked at Brandon's pleading face and nodded, no doubt or hesitation in her mind. Ari may be selfish, but she was family. They looked at each other in silent agreement before she turned to the rambunctious trio.

"Regardless." Lily said loudly, interrupting them.

They stopped their bickering to stare at her, eyes wide.

"Ari's family," she said. "Regardless of how she acts, I won't give up on her. So, how do I get to this Veil?"

Brandon frowned. "Why do you keep saying, 'I', Lil? It's, 'How are WE going to get to the Veil'."

"I'm going to get Ari back, you're staying here," she said firmly.

She held up her hand as Brandon jumped up from his seat, beginning to protest. "Think about it Brandon, we can't have all of us leave. What if Tabby and Dad call? Or something else comes to the house or what if Ari comes back on her own?"

Lily was unsure on the last part, but it was a possibility. Truth was, she didn't want Brandon to put himself in danger. She couldn't handle it if something happened to Brandon too. She looked at Brandon sternly. "Someone needs to stay here."

She could see that Brandon wanted to protest, but Alasdair spoke up.

"She's got a point, lad. We can't intercede if your folks call or happen to come back early. Even though the changeling is gone, we do need an owner on the premises. Who knows what will come next."

Brandon looked around. He was outnumbered. He sighed, falling back down in his seat. "Fine. But Lil, I'm worried. You can't go on your own." He gazed at her, concerned.

Barlow grumbled. "Well first things first. You have to find out where the Prince of Prophecy and your sister are. And that in itself is tricky. They could be anywhere."

Brom tapped his finger to his chin, deep in thought. "Actually, there is a revel at the Forest Prince's palace. His province is the closest."

Alasdair sighed wistfully, taking another sip from his cup. "Ah a revel. How I miss those. The dancing, the singing, silly humans that would pass by and dance til their shoes burned off-" He paused when he saw Brom glaring at him. "What did I say?"

"Okay, so how do I get there?" asked Lily.

"You have to go through the Veil. But, you'd be stuck in the Wood," said Barlow.

Brandon snorted. "That's nothing. The whole back yard is a forest. How hard will it be to get to this guy's place?"

Barlow shook his head. "It's not that kind of wood lad. The cottage borders the Forest Prince's territory. We call it the Wood because it's a labyrinth of trees. Stretches for hundreds and hundreds of miles. You can get lost by just turnin' yer head if you're not careful. And that's IF the trees dinnae play any games with you."

Brandon blinked. "Who?"

Barlow groaned. "Dinnae you hear me lad? Prince! There are seven of them. You have to go through another's kingdom to find her."

Brandon threw up his hands. "Well why didn't you say that earlier?"

Lily put her head in her hands.

Brom added. "From what I have heard, the revel will be held in five days' time. After the revel has concluded, the Forest Prince and his entourage will leave for his winter palace."

"And where's that?" asked Lily

Barlow looked at her, expressionless. "Up in Canada some-place. You see his province is what you humans consider North America."

Lily's eyes widened. That was a lot of ground to cover. Ari really could be anywhere.

Barlow nodded as if he heard her thoughts. "Your best bet of finding yer sister is at the revel. That means you only have five human days to reach his summer palace before he's gone."

"Why the revel? Isn't there anyone else that would know where Ari is?" asked Lily.

Barlow coughed but it sounded more like a laugh. "Pfft! Doubt it lass. The Prophecy Prince's domain is where you call Antarctica. Dinnae see how there's anyone there that can help ye, but go ahead, try yer luck with the penguins."

Lily tried not to glare, but it was getting rather difficult.

Barlow noticed. He smirked with a good-natured chuckle.

"Calm down lass, only havin' a bit of fun. Look, he took the lass from here. That means he's in the Forest Prince's domain. The revel is the only current place they're all together. Got it?" He took another long puff, the large smoke ring splitting into three.

Lily sighed, resigned. "Yeah I got it." Sounds like there was no other alternative. "Alright so how do I get to the revel?"

Barlow tugged his beard, thinking. "Hmmm...Normally I wouldn't do this but you do need a guide. And the three of us here cannae leave the property." He looked over to Brom and Alasdair with a silent stare.

Alasdair huffed but nodded his head.

Brom's eyes widened in panic.

"Absolutely not Barlow Lob! You cannot seriously imply what I think you are!"

"You have any other ideas you fandan?" Barlow crossed his arms, his eyebrows raised.

Brom's face got red as a tomato. "It...it's...he is not decent company! The poor girl, you would be sending her out with the wolves!"

Lily tried really hard to ignore the part about wolves.

Alasdair pipped up. "Why don't we ask Parrin to help?"

Barlow grimaced. "Ock! That'll be a pair."

"But at least there would be a proper escort for Miss Lily and not...that...heathen brute!" Brom shuddered.

Alasdair sighed, running his hand through his hair. "Brom – that 'heathen' has to go too. You know it."

Brom's face crumpled, his eyes large. "...Fffi...fine...but let it be known that I am thoroughly against this." He crossed his arms with a humpf.

Lily jolted as she heard the thump of Alasdair's tankard hitting the fireplace. "Alright lass it's settled! Gie it laldy!"

Barlow smiled at her, eyes twinkling. "Aye. Give it your best lass. Whit's fur ye'll no go by ye! Whatever will be will be lads!" With a yell towards the ceiling another tankard appeared in his hand as he threw back the contents with a gulp. Somewhere, a few doors slammed open and shut.

Brom groaned as the two kept pouring cup after cup. Brandon watched the fairies bicker, fascinated. Brom even had to smack Brandon's hand away from one of the empty tankards.

Quietly, Lily got up and began walking up the steps towards her room. She paused halfway up the staircase as everything had gone quiet. She turned. Everyone was looking at her in silence. Brom scampered up to the bottom of the staircase and looked up at her.

"Miss Lily?" His eyes filled with concern.

Lily refused to look at him. "I'm okay. I just – I just need a moment."

Not waiting for a response, she turned around and ran up the rest of the steps. As she closed the door to her room and leaned against it, blood rushed in her ears. In less than a day her world had turned upside down. She tried not to feel bitter, but she couldn't help the slight kernel of anger lodged in her chest. Ari, always the victim. Lily, always cleaning up the mess. Lily gritted her teeth, stewing a moment.

As soon as the anger came, shame replaced it. She shook her head, forcing the icky feeling away. It was no good to be angry. What she needed was a clear head for the next step.

Lily bit her thumb and ran down the facts. Who was this 'Parrin' guy? And what about the other guy Brom was so upset about? Overall, this information wasn't exactly comforting. As she willed her racing heart to slow, she realized that all she had, other than a sporadic array of seemingly meaningless facts, was hope. Hope. A fickle thing hope is. But fickle though it may be, she hoped that it would be enough to find Ari.

CHAPTER
TWELVE

Brandon, Barlow, and Alasdair were waiting for her by the stable once she composed herself. Barlow held an unusual silver collar in his hand. It glinted in the setting sun, casting sparkling fragments. She kept staring at it, vaguely hearing Brandon as he laughed at Alasdair's rendition of a prank played on Brom that involved a sheep, mud, and feathers. She jerked when she felt a tug on her sleeve. Barlow motioned her to lean down towards him.

Barlow cupped his mouth to whisper in her ear. "Time to be gallus, you gotta be bold and brave for this to work. You see this?" He motioned at the silver collar. "Look at it closely lass."

Lily squinted at the collar again, trying to focus more clearly. There was a symbol etched in the middle, similar to a Celtic eternity knot. Barlow placed it in her hand. The metal was cool to the touch and smooth against her palm. He stared at her, his voice still a whisper but laced with urgency.

"Now when I say the word, take that collar and place it around the horse's neck." He gestured his thumb towards the stable.

Lily looked back at the collar, confused. "But the horse-"

Barlow jumped up, covering her mouth. "Shhhssssh! Haud yer wheesht lass! Stay quiet will ya? We dinnae want him to hear us. If he caught wind of what we're planning, the changeling is the least of our worries."

Lily kept silent, though she grimaced. The lob's hands were covered in grease and dirt. With a raised eyebrow, she silently motioned at Barlow's hand covering her mouth.

Slowly he peeled it away, mumbling an apology.

Lily stared at the collar, confused. *Maybe it's how I'm supposed to ride him. Yeah, that's it! This must be one of those fairy horses or something and for him to take a human I need this collar.*

Brandon appeared at her side as he whispered, loudly, to Barlow.

"So, what is it then?"

"What is what then?" Barlow looked at her stepbrother, baffled.

"You said, 'Now when I say the word', so what is the word?"

He glanced Lily's way with a playful grin. Her lip tilted up, giving a half smile. He was trying to lighten the mood for her sake. She was grateful for the moment of levity, even if it was brief.

Barlow pulled his beard, showing his exasperation. "Ack! Save me from these daft humans!"

Alasdair gave him a cheeky grin. "He's got a point cousin."

"I think we get it guys." Lily walked towards the stable door. She looked back at them. "Ready?"

She opened the door, face to face with the magnificent horse. It snorted as it began to walk through. It paused right before stepping outside with, what she thought, was a glare directed towards the lob. It didn't seem possible, but the horse seemed bigger while it stared down at them coldly. She frowned, not confident she could put on the collar. Especially when the subject in question would probably trample her at any moment. But personal safety didn't seem high on Barlow's priority as he marched right up to the angry horse.

The horse neighed loudly at the lob who looked up at him with a smirk. "Alright ya mangy creep, you promise to behave I'll let you out."

The horse went silent, staring at Barlow unblinking. Then, to Lily's amazement, it shook its' head side to side as if saying no.

Barlow shrugged his shoulders. "Suit yerself ya hairy coo. See how far ye get outta this stable without my help." The horse angrily neighed back at him, pawing the ground with its hoof. Barlow tilted his head, then nodded.

"Okay, but ye best be behavin' yourself. Dinnae even think about tricking the lad and lass here. We got our eye on you understand?" Barlow wagged his finger in emphasis. The horse bared its teeth at the lob before making a reluctant whinny.

"Alright, now dinnae say I dinnae warn ye." Barlow snapped his fingers. An iridescent wall appeared over the doorway for a moment before dissolving, fragments popping in the air with small sparks.

The horse warily looked out towards the group. Cautiously, it took one step forward, then another. As soon as it passed the gate, it let out a soft huff of relief. It dug its hooves into the dirt, bending over to sniff the ground. Lily watched the horse, fascinated. Before she knew what she was doing, she found herself beside the animal, her hand buried in its mane. The horse jerked up in surprise, eyes glued to Lily. Everyone else stared at her with equal parts shock, horror, and disbelief. As the horse continued to stare at her, Barlow quickly regained his composure. He shouted at Lily.

"Now lass!"

Lily stood frozen. All she saw were those deep eyes, swallowing her conscious. She winced at a biting cold that stung her hand. She had forgotten she was holding the cold metal collar which dangled by her side. Gathering her resolve, she quickly lifted the collar, reached around the horse's neck, and fastened it. Then...nothing happened. Lily thought maybe she had done something wrong, until she looked up and found herself staring at some very angry eyes. The horse's lips pulled back into a snarl, showing extremely large teeth.

Oh my, what big teeth you have, Lily thought uneasily. She slowly pulled her hand away, backing up. She jumped, startled when snorting laugh came behind her.

Barlow, quivering, held his stomach as he doubled over in laughter. "Ha! Will ye look at that! Looks like the trickster was tricked. By a bonnie human lass no less. Bet that gets your wet britches in a twist huh you bloody wetbag,"

The horse glared at the lob, snarling. Barlow wiped tears from his eyes, ignoring the horse. Eventually, his laughter died down. He pointedly looked at the horse. "Och time to put on yer formal-wear. You need to talk to the lass and ye cannea do it like that."

The horse shook its head with a snort.

Barlow raised his hand. "Get movin' prissy pants!"

Slowly, a silvery mist crept up from the stream towards the stable. It snaked around the horse in tendrils until it was nothing more than a vague shadow. The scent of sea salt and crisp rain washed over Lily in gentle waves. She felt refreshed and invigorated, as if she could run nonstop. The fog encompassed the group until she could barely see in front of her face. Where was it coming from?

Lily peered into the mist, eyes squinting, as the outline of a figure moved closer. As the mist began to fade, a man appeared where the horse stood. And a very handsome man at that. He stood almost a foot taller than her, her head barely reaching his shoulders. He had a lean build, like a swimmer. Thick wavy black hair streaked with dark red glinted in the sun as they brushed the man's chin. He looked of Asian heritage, sporting a porcelain complexion, which stood out amongst the black shirt and pants he wore. He had a chiseled jawline and full red lips, but it was his eyes that shocked Lily. Long dark lashes framed almond shaped eyes of such an intense blue green they glowed in the fading mist. He reminded Lily of one of her dad's archeology students she met in South Korea when her father was researching the Royal Tombs of the Joseon Dynasty. Not in looks, but their eyes. Lily thought that student had the most kind and expressive eyes. But there was no hint of kindness in the striking eyes of the man that stood in front of her. Nope, those beautiful eyes happened to be the icy glaring type. And they were glaring right at her.

Lily grimaced. *So, horses can be fairies and can turn into obnoxiously handsome guys with an attitude problem. For crying out loud how cliché is this?*

"Well human, how can I be of service to you?" His deep smooth voice flowed over Lily like water gliding over rock. She wasn't a fool to notice that deep voice was dripping with sarcasm with a sprinkling of hatred.

Lily gave a polite smile. "I need help to find my sister Ari. Could you help me bring her home?"

The horse/man looked at her in surprise, before narrowing in suspicion. He crossed his arms over his chest as he stared down at her.

His eyebrow lifted. "You mean the annoying blonde one?"

Lily nodded, ignoring his insult. "Yes, that would be Ari. She was taken and I need to speak with the Forest Prince at the revel so I can bring her home. Can you to take me there, please."

Barlow raised his eyebrow at her, motioning his head silently. She frowned. Was she missing something? Barlow huffed, making gestures with his hands. Lily's eyes widened as the light bulb clicked.

"Oh um...safely...please." She quickly added, casting a nervous glance at the guy. Barlow sighed with relief.

The horse/man blinked, silent a moment. Then, his full lips curved in a silky smile, a small dimple appearing in the corner. Lily couldn't help but notice how perfect his teeth were, and slightly pointed. *And of course, he's got a dimple...ugh!* She mentally smacked herself.

Even though his lazy smile gleamed, Lily could have sworn his eyes flashed with annoyance. But then, too quickly she must have imagined it, his eyes warmed to change the irises into a mesmerizing sea green. Her eyes narrowed slightly. She didn't imagine that, right?

However, her thoughts didn't go beyond that. Her legs began to wobble, her body warming. It was too warm really. It was like being wrapped in a fluffy blanket or having a cup a warm hot chocolate. Her mind was hazy and muddled. She wanted to sink into that warmth as she vaguely realized she was smiling back at him. Wait! Why was she suddenly smiling?

It doesn't matter, her fuzzy mind whispered.

His smile deepened seeing her expression. He held out his hand, speaking in a low, warm tone. "I could show you where the revel is. If," he pointed at the collar around his neck. "you take this little thing off me. I would be sooo grateful." He winked, his eyes sparkling playfully.

A tug jerked in her stomach. A pulling sensation that made her want to go to him. A voice, not hers, whispered in her ear. It slithered in her brain, tickling her senses in a faintly unpleasant way. The voice told her it was wrong to have the collar on him. It said he'll help her not because of the collar, but because he thought she was nice. Special. The whispering grew louder, telling her that he never met someone like her before, this pretty human girl.

*Wait wait wait wait...*her own voice mentally growled. *Hold on one minute.*

The unknown voice stopped a moment, as if confused. When it tried again, she interrupted it before she could hear another word.

Excuse me?! What in the world am I hearing? Is this some B-movie pick up line?

The voice seemed to struggle a bit. Lily could feel it trying to speak over her, but Lily imagined pushing it down. Waaaay down deep into a black hole. She imagined covering it up with a shovel and dirt. She mentally stomped on it a few times for good measure until she couldn't hear a peep anymore.

Now that her mind was quiet, a prickle of cold awareness glided down Lily's spine. She blinked her eyes, the haze clearing. She had moved, unbeknownst to her, less than a foot away from the horse/man. Her hand was on the collar, frozen. Her eyes widened, the blood draining from her face. What had she almost done? She snatched her hand back, her fear quickly being replaced by anger. How stupid did he think she was?! Did he really think she was foolish enough to take that collar off for a pair of pretty eyes and a heart stopping smile? Shaking her head, an icy prick seeped into her chest, dissipating the heavy warm languid feeling as she focused on the arrogant man before her. And the worst part? He was smirking. That jerk!

Lily's cheeks burned from embarrassment, but she tried to ignore it. She glared, her voice cold. "Does that line actually work?"

The horse/man's perfect smile faltered slightly. His eyebrows knit in confusion while Barlow's guffaws could be heard a mile away. Barlow smacked his knee, tears streaming down his face.

"HA! Take that ya bampot!" Barlow hollered with mirth. He fell to the ground, rolling with laughter.

Alasdair whistled in awe. "Whooee! Pure dead brilliant lass." He turned to the horse/man, waggling his fingers as he scolded. "Now best be forgetting that nonsense seaweed brain."

To add emphasis, the little hob kicked the horse/man in the shins. Since the horse/man was still in shock from Lily breaking his spell, he didn't notice the kick until it was too late. He yelped in surprise, holding his shin. When he tore his gaze away from her to grab his smarting shin, the last bit of fog in her brain completely lifted.

Lily knew her face was bright red cause she could feel the heat coming off her cheeks. She prayed no one noticed as she tried to ask calmly. "What happened to me right now? What did you do?!" She put a hand to her head, feeling the beginning of a headache creeping up the back of her skull.

Alasdair came up beside her, patting her knee in a fatherly fashion. He glared at the horse/man. "That Miss Lil, was glamour."

"Glamour?" asked Brandon, confused. His worried gaze rested on Lily.

Alasdair nodded. "Aye lad. Glamour can do many things for us fae. Conceal, entrance, reveal. For example, a brownie or hob's glamour is being invisible, so humans don't see us."

Barlow got up, wheezing, his cries of laughter beginning to subside. He went over to the horse/man, grunted, and started delivering kick after kick on the same poor offending shin. "And this wee bugger," KICK "uses glamour," KICK "to charm lassies allll the way home." KICK KICK "Well, his home to be precise about it,"

"Ow! Enough with the kicking!" The horse/man growled as he jumped out of the way as Barlow attempted yet another kick.

Barlow grumbled, ignoring him while looking for another opening. "And this fella is especially good at charming young ladies. Be careful around this one lass." His warning was accompanied with a stern expression. "His kind is known to lure humans-"

"Yeah yeah you already said. To their home," interrupted Brandon.

Barlow paused, giving a fake smile at Brandon. "Ya kinnae know where that is lad?"

Brandon blinked. "Umm...no."

"The sea lad. They lure you to the sea and you drown," said Barlow with a deadpan expression. He turned back to Lily's shocked face.

"Seriously?!" Lily didn't realize she had screamed until she noticed everyone had covered their ears.

Barlow anxiously scratched his beard, giving her an apologetic look. "I'm really sorry lass. Normally I wouldn't recommend him as a guide but there's no time and we're short on folks who know the way. You want to rescue your sister, right?"

Lily wasn't so sure about being paired with a lady killer. Literally a lady killer. But what other choice did she have? Resigned, she nodded.

Barlow took her hand, holding her gaze firmly.

"Then listen well lass. No matter what he says or does, do...

NOT...take that collar off. You follow that rule, and you should be safe. That collar is all that is protecting you from him, and you're the only one that can take it off. Remember that!"

Lily took his news to heart even more than before. She rubbed her temples. Great, another wrinkle to add to her growing list of complications. *So now I have to watch my back against a 'death by drowning' fae who happens use his model looks and some glamour mojo thing to have girls fall for him...literally...fall for him to their death. Oh goodie,* she thought sarcastically. She wished she could call it a day, but there was no other option. For all she knew, Ari was in danger. She was probably getting tortured right at this very moment.

Solemnly she focused on Barlow, hoping he could see she was serious. "I understand. Can you guys give me and 'my guide' a moment please?"

"Ah, you sure Lil?" Brandon cast a suspicious glare at the horse/man. "I mean I can stay with you. Someone should make sure he doesn't try that again."

The horse/man smirked, but it wasn't as alarming since he was still rubbing his aching shin. "Awww, are you worried for her welfare little boy?"

Brandon's eyes narrowed. He started towards the horse/man before Alasdair stepped in-between. The hob glanced over at Lily, concerned.

"You sure girl?"

Lily shrugged. She wasn't sure, but if she was stuck with this guide, she had to get on some type of common ground with him.

Alasdair looked between them, sighing. "Okay...ten minutes

then lass. We'll round up Brom and Parrin. Come on lad." He shooed Brandon towards the house. Brandon kept glaring, but reluctantly followed. Barlow mumbled something about 'daft humans' again as he blinked out.

Lily took a moment, making sure they were alone. She sat down on the fence, taking a moment to collect her thoughts. She gave a side-glance over at the horse/man and motioned him to sit beside her. He laughed as she jumped when he leaned against the fence, a little too close to her. She scooted over quickly, ignoring his chuckle.

"Okay." She breathed out, feeling her cheeks finally cooling. She attempted a pleasant smile. *One of us needs to be civil.* "So, what's your name?"

Again, the horse/man looked surprised, tilting his head to the side with a lazy smirk. "Why do you want to know?"

Lily shrugged. "It's a simple question. We'll be working together, and I don't want to call you horse/man the whole time."

"Horse/man?"

She continued. "Plus, I believe you know mine. You can call me Lil by the way."

He regarded her for a moment, staring. "You know it already."

"What?" Lily's brow furrowed, confused.

He sighed. "You already called me by a name remember?"

She pondered, her finger resting on the tip of her chin. His name...what was his name?

"Cabyll?"

He nodded, rolling his eyes with a dramatic sigh. "Yes, that is what you can call me. After that there's really nothing else you need to know." He dismissed her, his tone flippant as he crossed his arms loosely over his chest.

"Oh." She lapsed into an awkward silence. *Well didn't take him long to stop with the pleasantries.* This guy seemed to ping pong emotions faster than a bunny hopping around the yard. She bit her lip while the frosty silence stretched on, Cabyll continuing ignore her.

Come on Lil, no time to stay quiet. She discreetly coughed to clear her throat. "Um, so then you did say your name the first day I met you. When you were a horse I mean." Her face warmed.

Cabyll nodded, seemingly reluctant to answer.

Lily didn't give up. "Sooo...how did you speak to me in my head? That must have been by magic or something huh? Well, maybe not magic. There has to be a logical explanation for it. Are you able to use more than ten percent of your brain? Maybe some type of psychic connection through neural pathways-"

Cabyll shook his head, looking down at her. He rolled his eyes as he gave an aggravated huff. "I don't know about neural whatever, but it's basic mind projection. Even simple sprites could do it if they wanted, unlike weak humans," he said drily with a smirk.

Lily looked back at him, schooling her features to remain neutral. His arrogant tone really was grating on her ears. But, nevertheless, she was determined to remain undeterred by his rudeness.

Cabyll eyes narrowed when he realized he wasn't getting a reaction out of her. He ran his hand through his hair in agitation, his wavy hair falling in his eyes. His fingers grazed the silver collar around his neck, a flinch passing over his face.

Lily inwardly sighed. She really couldn't blame the guy for being a jerk right now.

She looked over at him in sympathy. "For what it's worth, I'm sorry that happened to you. But, from what I gathered you wouldn't have helped us out otherwise. Does it hurt?"

Cabyll's eyes narrowed at her, before quickly giving her a sly wink. "If I said it did, would you take it off?

Her eyes widened. *Boy he doesn't pull punches, does he?* Though she really didn't like the idea of anyone being in pain. Maybe there *was* something she could do to help. A more agreeable person is a more helpful person, right? And she could definitely use as much help as she could get.

"No, but how about I make an amendment to the deal."

Cabyll's ears perked up, paying closer attention.

She clasped her hands tightly in front of her. "Once you lead me to the revel safely, I promise I'll remove the collar." She chewed her lip, worrying she missed an important part of her agreement. *It is what it is, I need his help,* she mentally shrugged.

Cabyll looked at her, not saying a word.

Lily swung her feet awkwardly, keeping her head down. Her cheeks were warm as she could feel his gaze bore a hole into her head. *Why is he being so quiet! Just say something!* Her anxiety spiked and she swung her feet so hard she almost fell off the fence. Awkwardly she caught herself, her heart jumping.

Before she could break the silence, he laughed loudly.

Startled, she whipped her head up. He was close, so close she had to crane her neck up. Without warning, he bowed low, his hand over his heart. Stunned, she moved back. The man honest to goodness bowed at her. Lily didn't know whether she wanted to kick him or be flattered. *This is probably another trick*, she thought ruefully.

Cabyll's laughter died down to a flirty chuckle. "Well, this is an unexpected development. I do like the unexpected." He peered at her through his dark hair, giving a playful smirk. "As you wish...little master."

Her mouth gaped open in shock. *You've GOT to be kidding me. Now we're back to the flirting. Yup, I definitely want to kick him.* She took a deep breath in. *Keep it together Lil, you need him to take you to Ari. Breathe!*

Lily rolled her eyes to the heavens, calling on everything she knew to keep calm. She grimaced. "Please don't call me that."

Cabyll, ignoring her, smoothed his hair, kneeled, and grabbed her hand as if to kiss it. "Oh human master, why would I – your mere guide – presume to address you by any other means? I will gladly hear all your wishes."

Lily yanked her hand back, her cheeks stinging. "Seriously?! Stop clowning around! Enough is enough. It's Lil, just Lil alright? Will you please get up?"

Lily was so embarrassed she couldn't think straight. Completely unaware of what she was doing, she went forward and placed a hand on his arm. She tugged, trying to lift him up. Cabyll pulled back, shocked. He jumped to his feet, brushing the sleeve she touched absently.

Okay, note to self. Fairies are skittish when touched.

She tried to school her expression so he wouldn't know that she noticed. "This is a partnership. I'm counting on you."

Satisfied she got her point across, she turned to walk up to the house. Lily paused and turned around, seeing Cabyll still standing by the stable, unmoving.

"Are you coming?"

Cabyll gave her a confused look, but it swiftly melted away as he directed a handsome grin her way.

"Oh, by all means, lead the way my little human."

CHAPTER
THIRTEEN

L ily walked back to the smell of freshly baked bread and cheese. The table was strewn with a variety of dried meats, cheeses, bread, and dried fruit. Brom must have really gone out of his way. Where did he have the time? Lily shook her head, telling herself it wasn't the time to figure out brownie cooking habits.

She was grateful for the food. Every moment was crucial. Not only was it essential to get to the revel in time, but she also had the clock ticking down until their parents came home. Explaining what happened to Ari was definitely not a conversation Lily wanted to have. *Hey Dad, Tabby, have a good trip? Oh, where's Ari? Well long story – random info - did you know that fairies exist? Yeah, it's true and Ari flirted with one of their princes and decided to go traipsing around the fairy world. Surprise!* Lily had a headache just thinking about it.

"I hope this fare is satisfying Miss Lily." Brom appeared on the countertop with a hopeful look on his face.

She smiled. "You really took care of everything Brom. I really appreciate it."

Brom beamed at her compliment.

Cabyll yelled out, a pastry in both his hands. "Hey brownie! Do you have any more of these meat pies?"

Brom's smile slowly faded to a disgusted scowl as he watched Cabyll help himself to his sixth or seventh helping of the flaky savory pastry. Lily had lost count after he ate his fifth pie.

Alasdair snorted. "Why dinnae you be helping instead of eating and go pack up some of the food for the journey. Goodness knows you'll be needing a full cart just for yourself with how much you eat!"

Cabyll winked over at Lily. "Aw, don't be like that. These are so delicious I can't help but want another. But being the gentleman that I am, I will assist. Show me what you want packed."

Lily shook her head. *Please let there be enough food for everyone else.*

She turned her attention to Brom. "We should leave soon. Can you tell me about Parrin?"

Brom nodded. "Yes Miss Lily. He actually should be here any minute now." Brom cupped his hands, calling out. "Parrin?"

Silence.

Brom frowned. "Parrin VonBrown! Tardiness never looks good on a brownie. Pop out if you please!"

Lily realized she was starting to become used to random

appearances now as another POP hit the air and a neatly dressed smaller brownie appeared on the counter.

He was much younger than Brom sporting curly tawny hair and big almond eyes. He had a much rounder face, which gave him a pleasant air. His eyes and lips crinkled with several laugh lines. Though the little brownie wasn't smiling currently. He glanced furtively between her and Brom. He twisted his blue cap in his hands nervously.

"Ah yes...good afternoon, Miss Lil," said Parrin, his voice soft.

Brom sighed, exasperated. "Parrin! You must address the lady as Miss Lily. As one who will be serving a fine house such as this, you must be precise with your honorifics." He waved his finger in a scolding fashion.

Parrin pulled on the cap, fidgeting anxiously. "Oh...Uh...Sorry." He looked at Lily, his eyes reminding her of a sad cat. "I apologize Miss Lily. I heard the others addressing you differently."

Lily sat on the barstool which put her on eyelevel with the brownie. His scared face shot through her chest. "You can call me Lil. All my friends do, and I do hope we can be friends." She smiled, putting her hand out.

Brom placed his hand on his chest, his eyes glazing with unshed tears. "Oh, what a kind and generous lady you are Miss Lily. To bestow such an honor on such an inexperienced caretaker, you indeed have a huge heart."

Lily didn't understand the big deal. It was only a nickname. But the young brownie looked positively crestfallen when he was scolded, she really wanted him to feel better. He looked like such a kind little guy.

Parrin's eyes widened in awe at her. He slowly reached out to grasp her hand, shaking it vigorously. "Then...if you please...you can call me Parr."

Lily's smile widened, immediately liking the little brownie. Curious, she looked over at Brom. "But I thought brownies couldn't leave the house. Why can Parr come?"

Parr coughed discreetly, looking at Brom. "Umm, if I may." The head brownie nodded in encouragement. "Brownies that have made a pledge to the home's hearth can't leave. And for brownies to pledge themselves to a home...well...they must be very good at what they do. Their magic needs to be able to protect it. And I'm...well..." He gestured lamely to himself. "I'm just me you see. Well, what I mean to say is that I am only an apprentice. I haven't taken the pledge yet. So, I can accompany you. Well, that is, if you're okay with it, Miss Lil."

The poor brownie looked so anxious Lily wouldn't have had the heart to say no, even if she wanted to. She tried to reassure him. "Oh of course I'm okay with that." His smile returned, positively beaming with delight.

Brom clapped his hands with approval. "Well, now that we are all sorted, I suggest Miss Lily that you procure your things while Parrin and I finish the preparations." When he noticed that she hadn't moved quickly enough for his liking, Brom gave her a shooing motion towards her room.

Lily ran upstairs to take one last look at her small pack, taking stock on what she had. A weight fell heavy on her chest. She wasn't prepared. Not really. She held up a can of bug spray with a frown. What good was bug spray in an enchanted forest? Were there even bugs? She sighed, throwing the can back into the pack and zipped it up.

She unlocked Rox's cage and waited for the little sugar glider to jump onto her shoulder. He chirped happily while she rubbed his neck. "Well Rox, you think I can do this?" She chuckled softly to herself, her nerves bubbling to the surface. "I'm way out of my league. But, Dad *would* say this is a story worth telling."

She felt a little better thinking about her father. Apart from the whole 'Ari being kidnapped by fairies' scenario; her father would have jumped up and down at the chance to see the Veil. Lily could picture her dad walking around with his notepad taking in every little detail. She put her cheek against Rox's soft fur, closing her eyes. "You be good for Brandon, okay? Don't manipulate him into giving you more treats."

Rox nuzzled into her neck, eliciting a giggle from her.

Feeling more relaxed, Lily began placing Rox back when she heard a creak by the door.

"You really like talking to animals, don't you?"

Cabyll leaned against the doorframe lazily, his arms and legs crossed with a graceful air. He looked at her with unreadable eyes, a smirk in place giving her that hint of a dimple. Instead of making her blush, it reminded Lily of a predator staring at its prey.

Maybe this bug spray will be useful after all.

Before Lily could open her mouth, Cabyll continued. "Tell me human, why tell an animal your secrets?" He whispered as he slowly approached her.

Lily ducked her head down, hoping her hair covered her

heated face. Abruptly, she recalled all the times she came down to feed the horse (technically Cabyll). She had rambled about anything and everything. Mostly it was stories about the antics she and her father got into, or how Ari treated her, or whether people would find her weird when she started college. She thought she was speaking to an animal who didn't understand her. But in reality she was talking to a person. Wait, correction... fae. And he had understood every embarrassingly awkward word.

Lily envisioned a big giant hole swallowing her up. *Nope, no luck. Still here,* she thought ruefully. Wishing her red face would cool down, she gave Rox a kiss on the head and put him in the cage, slowly, buying herself time.

"I know it seems silly, but it's comforting to have someone simply listen," she said softly. "And I think it comforts him too, because he knows he's not alone." When she felt for certain her face wasn't flaming, she turned back to look at him trying to change the subject. "Are you ready to go?"

Cabyll gave a puzzled look. "Ready to go? Why do we have to leave just yet." He placed his hand on the cage as he lazily looked down at her. He leaned closer, never looking away. "Let me scout ahead. I will provide us with a direct route. You can stay here, stay safe. What's another day?"

Lily stared down at the floor, watching him in her peripheral vision. *He's doing that eye thing again!* Her hands clenched at her sides. She gritted her teeth, feeling a twitch coming on.

She shook her head, replying firmly. "No. Delaying another day could mean Ari disappearing forever. I can't let that happen."

Cabyll narrowed his gaze, the lazy aura dissipating. He quickly straightened, his smile melting away in annoyance.

Ah – there we go, bye bye teen drama star, she thought with a small sense of relief.

"As you wish human." He briskly adjusted his shirt, refusing to look at her. "I will meet you downstairs. We leave as soon as you eat." With a dismissive nod, he sauntered out.

Lily let out the breath she didn't realize she had been holding. Seriously? *This* was the guy she had to rely on to find Ari. She was wound up, her stomach twisting in knots. She tried to take a steady breath.

Remember, it's just words. You control your response, no one else. Let them say whatever they want.

With renewed determination Lily roughly grabbed her backpack, taking one last look at her room. She paused when her gaze fell towards Rox. He stared back at her with, what she thought, a sad understanding.

"See you soon Rox," she reassured the little animal. "Miss you already."

CHAPTER
FOURTEEN

You know the saying reality is overrated? Yeah, it's very much rated. They hadn't even been in the Veil for ten minutes and already Lily felt the beginning of a throbbing headache. She kept reminding herself Ari was in trouble or else she was tempted to run back to the cottage.

She rubbed her temples to disperse the pounding. She figured arguments between hobs and brownies was something to get used to, but that was nothing compared to an argument between a cabyll and a brownie. Apparently, the other arguments were only the minor leagues. It began when she met Cabyll at the edge of the bridge. It didn't help matters Parr had a panic attack when he caught sight of Cabyll's towering frame He had stuttered so hard Lily thought he was going to pass out. She closed her eyes as she relieved the awful memory:

"Umm...no. No no no no thank you. Not today!" Parr kept pointing to Cabyll and babbling.

Cabyll, meanwhile, was casually leaning against a tree. "Aww. Little brownie has his hat tied in knots?" His eyes were wide in a seemingly innocent expression. Lily tried not to overthink it, but the wicked scimitars strapped behind his back and several potentially dangerous objects fastened to his leather pants definitely didn't give off an 'innocent' vibe.

Parr opened his mouth to argue, but nothing came out. He glanced over at Brom with disbelief.

"You cannot seriously be thinking of him accompanying us, right?"

He was waiting for Brom to do something, say something. Anything! Brom dejectedly shook his head. Parr sputtered, throwing his arms in a wild gesture towards Cabyll, all gentility gone.

"Oh come on! Brom...this is a cabyll! A CABYLL! For goodness sakes, having him be our guide is basically inviting a wolf to lead a lamb to dinner. *His* dinner!"

Brom sighed, closing his eyes. "Yes, but he's the only one that knows the way to the revel."

Cabyll gave a cocky smile to the group, slowly rubbing his hands together. "Right then. Since we've recognized you can't do anything without me..." He walked over the bridge and paused at the edge of the forest.

He tilted his head back, motioning towards the densely packed trees behind him. "Shall we go?"

Parr wildly shook his head. "Nope. No thank you! Not going to happen,"

Lily looked at the little brownie with sympathy. "It's okay Parr, if you're not comfortable you don't have to go. But, I have to find my sister." She walked towards Cabyll, trying to ignore his triumphant grin.

Parr stared, fidgeting side to side. He looked around and, seeing as no one was jumping in to intervene, he gave a reluctant sigh and joined them.

Lily was towards the edge of the bridge when Brandon reached out and gently held her arm.

His hand trembled. "Lil..." He looked at her with a very serious expression. "Be careful."

She nodded, covering his hand with her own. She tried her best to reassure him. "You too."

She turned towards the motley fairy bunch. She wagged her fingers at the head brownie, hob, and lob. "I'm counting on you guys to make sure Brandon is okay." They bobbed their heads in agreement.

"Dinnae worry Lily, things will right as rain here," assured Alasdair.

"Aye – ye take care of yourself lass," agreed Barlow.

Lily smiled in gratitude, quickly turning around to give Brandon a hug, surprising him into silence. Before she lost her courage, she turned back and stepped over the bridge towards the Veil.

Stepping through the Veil was the equivalent to having a hefty dose of vertigo. Barlow had warned her the sensation would be perfectly normal. It had felt like she stepped through a mirror and wound up upside-down. *This is what suffocating must feel like.* Her entire body was compressed and tight. She wobbled slightly. As soon as she thought she couldn't take anymore, the tightness had fallen away. Thankfully, Parr held her hand as the dizziness finally subsided.

Lily didn't even realize she had closed her eyes until she cracked them open slowly. At first, she couldn't see anything. Nothing but blurry shapes and foggy outlines. She rubbed her eyes. Blinking a few times, she tried to get her eyes to focus. When everything came clearly, she looked around and saw.... nothing. Well, nothing too out of the ordinary. *Well, what did you expect,* she thought, disappointed. *The trees to be purple or something? Get a grip.*

But a keener eye noticed there were slight differences. For one thing, the trees were immense. Similar to the redwoods in California, these trees were so tall Lily couldn't see the sky, only filtered light playing upon the branches as it sprinkled down onto the forest floor. The trunks were so wide that the naked eye couldn't see the entire width, let alone put one's arms around their massive girth. Large tufts of emerald moss and tendrils of blooming vines littered the ground to create a soft pathway amongst the tall sentries. It really was quite a spectacular sight in Lily's opinion. Songbirds gave soft lilts of a soothing melody that gently echoed in the air. Semitransparent butterflies flittered around, dancing around the vines. If Ari wasn't kidnapped, Lily was tempted to sit for hours, if only to listen to the gentle melody of the forest. And the smells. She took a deep cleansing breath. Oh, it was unlike anything she had ever smelled. It was fresh and crisp, a combination of every flower she could think of and more. It was indescribable.

"It's beautiful." She breathed softly, her gaze taking in the vast forest. She realized she must have spoken out loud when Cabyll looked at her with a puzzled frown.

"I guess you can consider this place beautiful," he said. "But it is not nearly as beautiful as other places in the Veil."

"Like what?" she asked.

He paused, his eyes debating. After a minute he replied. "The ocean."

Lily noted a hint of sadness in his eyes. He shook his head, refusing to look at her as he turned back to continue walking along the mossy path.

Parr came up beside her. "Don't mind him, his kind are from the sea you understand. You could say he's probably homesick, being landlocked by trees and all."

Cabyll turned back to glare at them. "I suggest you mind your business brownie."

Parr gulped. "Sorry!" He paused, biting his lip. Then it rushed out as if he couldn't help himself. "But I'm sure it must be terribly inconvenient for you...being far from the sea and all. I mean do you have a mum? A sister? Family? Does your skin feel incredibly dry in such high altitudes?"

"Does your mouth feel tired from talking nonstop?" asked Cabyll, eyebrow raised.

Parr flushed. "I was checking to make sure that everyone was feeling alright."

Cabyll smirked. "Nothing a glass of wine and a dryad wouldn't cure."

Parr's eyes widened as he sputtered. "That...that I must say. That is quite crass!"

Cabyll's grin widened and...

.... Here they were. Lily, rubbing her temples in agitation as Parr and Cabyll continued their...well she didn't know what to call it. Cabyll's snide risqué remarks got Parr more insulted and flustered. The brownie's response seemed to delight Cabyll who, in turn, kept turning up the comments. And where was Lily in all of this? Stuck between two bickering fae who squabbled like Hatfields and McCoys all the while she was desperately trying not to throw up as her head pounded. Yup, what a day.

Finally, Cabyll must have noticed her discomfort. He glanced her way, but thankfully didn't say anything. Instead, he clapped his hands together with a loud bang, making her wince.

You little- She thought angrily. He smirked as she glared at him and continued.

"Alright! First things first. You!" He pointed at Lily. "If you want to reach the revel on time you have to be faster. At this rate, a snail will make it before you. Are all humans this slow? Perhaps your little legs are too weak. Or your brain is taking too long to process the concept that one foot goes in front of the other." He looked down his nose at her, a sneer gracing his handsomely smug face.

Lily's eyes narrowed. *Well, count your blessings Lil. At least he's not flirting anymore.* This was a side of Cabyll she could handle. She rearranged her pack and looked at him, schooling her expression.

"I would be faster if my headache went away." She quipped, pretending the stabbing pain between her eyes didn't exist.

Parr looked at her, concern etching his face. "Miss Lil, you were unwell?" He came over as he gently scolded. "You *must* tell us these things sooner. Humans are so frail after all."

Lily, eyes wide, bit her lip to hold her tongue. First, she gets insults from the one fae saying she was basically as dumb as an amoeba and the other one is afraid she'd keel over from a sneeze.

She rubbed her forehead, dispelling the image of throwing both of them off a bridge. She forced out, calmly. "I would have mentioned something sooner, but I would have hated to interrupt your verbal sparring." She looked at them pointedly, her eyebrows raised.

Parr looked positively ashamed. He stared down at his feet, his face reddening. Cabyll, on the other hand, didn't seem the least bit concerned as stared back at her unblinking. He even had the gall to wink at her.

Disgusted, Lily hefted her pack to a more comfortable position, trying to ignore the pulsing of her veins. Winking?! *He has some nerve!* She stared straight ahead towards the path.

"So...this way?" she asked.

Not even waiting for an answer, or looking to see if her companions followed her, Lily started walking down the mossy path.

Lily could hear the both of them behind her as they scrambled to catch up. Though, if she would make a bet, it was probably only Parr she heard. From what she could tell, Cabyll was quick and silent on his feet. She couldn't figure out how a guy so tall could be so quiet. *Not a guy Lil, a fairy. A girl drowning fairy.*

Cabyll's deep voice sounded beside her.

"We go this way."

She jumped, placing her hand over her pounding heart. Never glancing her way, he gestured towards a darker part of the forest. He motioned toward the portion of trees where the branches twisted and gnarled together. Lily looked between the two completely opposite paths with trepidation, which reminded her of a poem. *Two roads diverged in wood...*

Parr took one look at the dark path and shook his head emphatically. He gestured towards the other path, which was very brightly lit. "Excuse me! But, I do believe this way may be a better course of pursuit. Wouldn't you agree?"

Cabyll blew out a breath, grabbing the brownie by the collar. Parr squeaked.

Cabyll rolled his eyes, clearly exasperated. "Not that way you brainless brownie. We have to go this way," he said sternly, his finger pointing back towards the other path.

Parr shuffled his feet, tugging his hat off. "I'm sure you are a wonderful guide and all can provide us with a suitable route...a route that takes us through a well-lit area that in no way spells doom for us."

Cabyll opened his mouth for, what Lily speculated, was

another scathing remark, but he stopped. He stood a moment, thinking.

She groaned when he glanced over at her and gave one of his slow smiles. She was starting to dread those smiles.

"Brownie?" Cabyll called, never tearing his gaze away from hers. "The human seems awfully hungry. I don't think the snacks we packed will be enough. Why don't you find us something to eat, and I'll get us on the right track?"

Lily's stomach bottomed out. She wasn't hungry. Wasn't the point of Parr coming was to make sure that their guide behaved himself? Cabyll's smile widened at her panicked expression, his teeth seemingly glowing in the soft light.

Parr furrowed his brows a moment, then beamed, not noticing Lily's growing panic. "That actually sounds like good idea. There are some delicious flowers and roots I could gather for a quick meal."

Lily's eyes widened and she had the immediate urge to smack him on the back of the head. If she had a hundred bucks, she bet Parr didn't give two hoots about dinner. She saw him glancing warily at the Ichabod Crane path. She was fairly certain Parr wanted to be as far away from that path as his little brownie legs could take him.

Well not on her watch. She was not going to be alone with a drowning fae. Lily tried to dissuade the little brownie. "We shouldn't separate. What if you become lost? How will you be able to find us?"

Parr gave her a large grin that spread from ear to ear, either completely oblivious to her dilemma or completely apathetic to it.

She inwardly growled. *Oh no you don't! He is NOT leaving me here with this outlandish flirt.*

"Oh, not to worry Miss Lil, not to worry at all really. You see you're still a member of the household. Because of that, I can POP in whenever you need me."

Lily's eye twitched. *Just POP in whenever huh?* But, of course, it was easier to say in her head as real words failed her. She could feel them, stuck to her tongue, refusing to come out. Instead, she could only stand silently, staring at the brownie, quietly pleading him not to leave.

Parr put up his hands at her shocked face, misunderstanding her pleading eyes. "Oh no need to be concerned Miss Lil, I shall only be a moment. I know you must be starving so I'll make sure to gather only the finest. Simply the most scrumptious. I refuse, simply refuse to let you eat something horrid. I shall be but a second, I teensy tiny moment. Call out if you need assistance."

And before she could finally open her mouth to protest, he disappeared.

CHAPTER
FIFTEEN

S
ilence. That's what Lily was left with now. Absolute
silence. Now Lily enjoyed peace and quiet like anyone else,
but this long stretch of quiet was borderline ridiculous.
Cabyll and Lily had been hiking through the woods for, what
seemed like to her, hours in complete silence. Even the sounds of
the forest became muted to her. Parr had still not returned yet,
which made the walk even more awkward. Not to mention creepy
as they took the less traveled trail. Lily scoffed to herself thinking
back on how she felt it was unnerving when Cabyll smiled. Turns
out it was even more unsettling when he didn't speak at all. He
kept walking ahead of her with a confident gait that didn't seem
to show any signs of fatigue or slowing down. Lily, on the other
hand, was fairly certain the blisters on her feet were going to have
blisters.

Lost in thought, she tripped on a large root that twisted

around the path. Fumbling around, she sidestepped around a patch of mushrooms. A sweet aroma entered her nostrils, almost like a butterscotch scent, which caused her stomach to grumble.

No girl! You are not hungry!

The mushrooms were a large, shaped like an oyster shell. Framed by an outer white ring, the inner portion of the cap had a lustrous brown, purple blue gradient. Her survival guide 101 told her bright colors meant dangerous – but then again, she really had next to zero survival skills in an enchanted forest. She bent down to take a closer look at them. Before she could pick one up to examine it, a black boot appeared and smashed the toadstools to smithereens. The noise seemed to echo louder than normal as it broke the heady silence.

Lily looked up, not surprised to see Cabyll's face looming over her. "Psilo mushrooms. You can call them sleeping mushrooms." He answered her unspoken question. If possible, his voice took an even deeper, velvet tone. "They're known for their delicious smell, but they are not for eating. A thorn emerges from the cap and pierces your tongue, which puts you to sleep. It is a common ingredient in a lot of potions fae use."

Lily wiped her hands, relieved she didn't pick one of them up. Regardless of how much of a jerk Cabyll was, she owed him. "Thank you." She sighed. She looked up to see Cabyll give her a grin, dimple on full display.

"What will you give me?"

"Huh?"

He gestured to the destroyed mushroom pile. "The mushrooms. Although they do not harm you, per say, you could have been in a deep sleep for a long time. I've seen some fae sleep for years after taking a bite and when they wake up..." he trailed off with a chuckle.

Lily raised her eyebrow at him. "So, you're saying you saved me from becoming Rip Van Winkle?"

Cabyll shrugged. "I do not know of this Van Winkle, but if he suffered from the Psilo sleep, well then yes my dear human." He gave her a nod, lips tilting up in such a handsomely arrogant grin she didn't know whether she wanted to kick him or laugh. To her astonishment, it looked like he actually was waiting for her to praise him. He continued when he saw her blank look.

"I am being VERY generous you know." He raised his eyebrow at her innocently.

She waited a minute before a realization hit her hard like a semi-truck, her throat closing. In his roundabout way, he was letting her know he could have let her eat those mushrooms. She could have been asleep for years. Since she wouldn't have been poisoned, technically it wasn't a violation of their agreement. While the rational part of her knew she should be wary and afraid, annoyance passed over like a storm cloud. She couldn't believe his nerve. Did all fae think that humans were brainless amoebas or something? *And this arrogant jerk expects me to be so grateful that I'd simply fall at his feet!*

Still crouched down on the ground, she gathered her thoughts and rested her chin on her palms. "So, what are you expecting?"

He leaned down over her until he was half bent over. He curled his finger around a stray hair that came loose from her ponytail. She batted it away.

He tilted his head, keeping his gaze downward as he said coyly. "Nothing much. Only something of equal value."

Lily's eye started to twitch. *This guy*, she growled. Counting to ten, she thought hard. He said something of equal value. He must be implying that since he believes he saved her life, that she should do the same for him. *What a trickster! He wants me to take the collar off.*

Brom had warned her on equivalent exchanges between the fae. Right before she left, Brom gave her a boot camp session in fae society. One thing he repeated over and over was that most fae enjoyed word play since they never could tell a lie. The next basic rule of thumb was they could never resist a bargain. With the look in Cabyll's eye, she knew without a doubt he was trying to force her into a bargain. *Wait.* An idea formed in her mind. *He has no clue I wasn't going to eat the mushrooms. Maybe...*

She slowly got up, noticing Cabyll's eyes glowing as he show-cased a savagely eager expression. *Yup, it's a bargain.* She winced inwardly. Why did it have to be a bargain? It wasn't like an IOU a few bucks. The fae bargains were like giving away first born children and losing limbs kinda crazy. Schooling her anxiety, she stood very still and folded her hands together. Taking a deep breath, she forced a smile.

"I appreciate the lesson. As you probably know, human survival skills make us wary of eating anything brightly colored so I'm sure you're *so* relieved that I had no intention of eating that mushroom. But, since you gave me knowledge about it, I'll give you some knowledge about my world as well." She paused, reaching into her backpack. She fished out two granola bars and tossed one over to him. He deftly caught it, confusion etching his brow, the gloating look beginning to fade from his eyes.

"We have a saying where I'm from – don't look a gift horse in the mouth."

He frowned as she blinked her eyes at him, trying to look innocent. She bit into the salty sweet goodness of her granola bar and resumed walking. Lily hoped he wouldn't notice her tense shoulders as she mentally prayed her word play worked. *Keep walking. Keep walking. Fake confidence, be brave Lil.*

She looked back over her shoulder at him, copying his smirk. "Shall we?"

Out of the corner of her eye, Cabyll assessed her with a calculated gleam in his eye. He shook his head with a reluctant chuckle.

"Well played human...well played."

As she turned to continue walking, she thought she heard him mutter.

"Next time..."

The sun was starting to fade into the hazy violet sky, darkening the wood in a twilight glow. Lily closed her eyes, the fatigue of the day kicking in. The forest was indeed a labyrinth, each twist and turn the same as the last. At first, she tried to figure out which direction they were going, but even the placement of the sun kept switching on her. She couldn't even tell what time of the day it was. She knew it must have been hours since they started, as she was still quite hungry after her granola bar.

Man, if I tried to do this on my own, I never would make it to the revel, she thought dismally.

Cabyll abruptly stopped, jolting Lily from her musings. He

looked upwards towards the sun a moment and paused. He quickly bounded over towards the nearest oak tree, a particularly large one with hefty branches that leaned down towards them, and placed his hand on the weathered trunk. He closed his eyes, his head tilted to the side. She was about to ask what he was doing when he spoke over his shoulder.

"It's getting dark, we need to camp for the night." He opened his eyes and pointed through a thicket of oaks slightly off the path. "There's an open meadow a few yards ahead. We'll rest there."

Lily raised her hand over her eyes and squinted towards the trees but couldn't see anything other than more and more trees. "Are you sure? I don't see anything."

"Yes – ." He moved so fast Lily had to scramble to catch up.

"Hey Cabyll? How did you know there was a meadow out there?" She was nervous leaving the path, but tried her best to remain calm.

Several minutes passed by and he didn't answer. He didn't look her way, making Lily wonder if he heard her. *Or maybe he just doesn't care to answer me,* she thought annoyed. She opened her mouth to ask again, but he spoke softly.

"The trees."

"What? You can talk to trees?" Slowly, Lily went up to the nearest oak and placed her hand on the trunk. The rough bark scraped against her hand. She could hear the rustling of the wind, but, nothing else. Frustrated, she scrunched her eyes tight, pushing against the tree. Still nothing. Then, a cool hand covered hers. Cabyll stood behind, giving an exasperated huff.

"For crying out loud. Relax! You look like your head is going to pop."

He sighed softly as his hand squeezed hers. "Let me help as you're clearly so *ordinarily* human."

Lily tried not to take offense, but it took a lot of willpower now to elbow him in the gut. *He's offering to help you talk to a tree girl, lighten up for a moment.*

"You don't think I'm weird?" She hoped she didn't sound as uncertain as she felt.

Cabyll looked down at her, frowning. "What do you mean?"

She gestured towards the oak. "You don't find it weird that I want to hear the tree?"

Cabyll shook his head. "Why would I? Honestly, I find it weird that humans wouldn't want to learn what's around them. They're too busy being blinded by shiny toys."

Lily hid her smile as she laid her hand on the bark again, but suddenly got swept with guilt. Cabyll must have noticed, his tilted his head to the side curiously.

"What's with that look?" he asked.

"Um...just thinking."

"About what?"

She looked at him, her hand still curled over the bark. "I shouldn't be..."

"What? Curious? Happy? Excited?" He seemed genuinely curious.

She nodded. "Ari is out there somewhere. I shouldn't be getting distracted. I should be focusing on getting her back."

"Why?" He asked, nonplussed. "She wasn't the nicest human from what I could tell. Especially towards you for that matter."

Lily stared up at him, taken aback by how blunt he was. "Well, she's family. And she's alone. No one should feel alone." She ended with a mumble, rubbing her hair ribbon.

Cabyll's face turned up in a quirky grin. "Human, she's with a fae prince. She's not alone."

She groaned. "She has no idea what she's gotten herself into. Family looks out for one another. And she's family."

"Not by blood."

Lily's eyes narrowed at him, hoping he saw how serious she was. "Family is family. Blood doesn't mean anything."

Cabyll stared at her for a moment, face blank. Lily wished she knew what he was thinking.

Her hand twitched under his as the bark itched her palm. Lily shifted awkwardly. She should remove her hand from his. Before she could slip underneath his palm, he leaned over. A cool sensation washed over her, like rain. Time slowed down; the world was walking at a snail's pace. She could hear every leaf rustle in the wind. Then she heard it. A whisper. Actually, it was more like a sigh that traveled through her veins.

"It's happy." She closed her eyes with a smile. She opened them to find Cabyll's surprised expression.

Lily was so happy, she beamed. "Thanks Cabyll, that was amazing!"

He stared at her, quiet. He pulled back his hand back as he rolled his eyes, taking a step away from her.

"Amazing? That's normal. You humans never relax. You're too

jumbled inside. And don't get me started on how you 'think' you all are so smart. I mean if it wasn't for me, you wouldn't have heard anything." He nonchalantly inspected his nail, his arrogant smirk in place.

Lily's mouth hung open. *This arrogant, two-bit horse needs a muzzle!*

"Excuse me?" She glared. "Look I understand you're not a fan of humans, but I'd like some common courtesy at least. Just who do you think you are anyways."

Cabyll gave her a devilish smirk as he quipped. "Me my dear? Why I'm your humble guide. I am Cabyll, a simple cabyll." He winked.

It amazed her how he could insult her one minute and charm her the next. *That takes real talent.* She rolled her eyes skyward. "Let's get to that meadow alright?"

"Right this way." Cabyll gave an overly dramatic bow, his hand outstretched for hers.

He's mocking me! With a huff, she ignored his hand, stomping past him. She heard his chuckle faintly as she stepped into the clearing

She stepped into a painting. An array of brilliantly colored flowers danced everywhere. And everywhere was not an exaggeration. Flowers were strewn all over the ground as well as from above. Hanging upside down in ropes of vines between trees dangled a variety of blooms, emanating sweet fragrances that were indescribable. The dying light of the setting sun cast a glorious ruby haze over the long grass which was speckled with golden wheat. What really caught Lily's eyes was scattered throughout the meadow were giant cherry trees, their pink blossoms illuminated like gemstones. She was amazed that they were still in full bloom, as they were in the middle of summer.

Of course they are, magic world Lil remember, she scolded herself.

Cabyll was obviously not as impressed by the sight as she was. "I'll be right back. I need to scout ahead for a moment." He looked down at her with a serious gaze. "Stay here and do...not...move." Without waiting for her reply, he took off, disappearing amongst the tall grass.

Lily stood, alone, unsure what to do. She looked towards the edge of the meadow and saw a group of deer. She frowned. But normal deer weren't the size of a bull. And they weren't grey in color either that shimmered in the sun. These 'deer' had antlers so large they arched upwards towards the vines in various twists and turns. Some of them had flowers and vines draping from their ivory antlers. They were stunning. She gently kneeled down on the soft grass, trying to keep her movements slow and quiet so she wouldn't scare them.

"Wow," she whispered in awe. She sat silently, watching them, when a familiar quiet POP appeared by her side. She didn't even look over check it was Parr. She could feel the brownie's presence. It was comforting, so she wasn't as annoyed that he showed up now and not when she needed him on the creepy trail.

Parr sat quietly with her, not breathing a word. They both gazed calmly at the iridescent creatures reflecting the gilded crimson rays. It was peaceful.

One of the 'deer' creatures lifted its head when the brownie appeared. It stared at them with uninterested eyes, then leaned its head down to nibble on the tender grass. To Lily's surprise, its coat started to change. One minute the stag was grey-brown, and then it was golden like the wheat. The others in the herd followed suit, some turning green while others turned gold, others blue.

"Amazing," she gasped.

Parr coughed discreetly. "Eh em...quite Miss Lil." He rocked back and forth on the balls of his feet, his curious gaze following her.

"What are they?"

Parr explained. "They are Busse. Similar to deer in your world but – as you can clearly see – with some alterations. Just um, don't get too close. If they see you as a threat...well...they have very sharp horns as you can clearly tell. You don't want to be skewered like swiss cheese. Not saying swiss cheese isn't good mind you, it's very good over some nice brioche. Just um, not so good if you looked like cheese. Which you don't look like cheese, oh what am I saying? I mean you do not want to be skewed. But, you know, I guess they really are like a deer." He laughed awkwardly; his face flushed in embarrassment.

Lily hid her smile, not wanting to embarrass him further. "I'll keep that in mind." Though, she never had to worry about deer skewering her. Now that she looked closer, those antlers appeared really *really* sharp. With that slightly chilling observation, Lily was perfectly fine gazing at them from a distance.

Gazing across the meadow, Lily realized Cabyll still hadn't returned. *Guess he still scouting.* But how long did it take to scout around a meadow?

She nudged Parr with her elbow lightly. "Did you find anything when you were gone?"

The brownie perked up, eyes brightening. "Oh quite indeed Miss Lil! I found so many ingredients. Good, solid, quality ingredients! Some I'm certain I haven't seen in almost a century." He chuckled. "It was quite a find I must say. Quite indeed. I already have in mind to make some lovely tarts over the fire tonight. I do so hope you'll enjoy it." He waved his hands around eagerly, a hopeful grin on his face.

He continued talking, very animatedly, about what he was going to cook up. Lily remained silent, listening, but anxious. Maybe she was being too impatient. It was only the first day, she scolded herself. Unbidden, a cloak of exhaustion settled over her and she started to yawn. She discreetly covered her mouth, not wanting to be rude to Parr who was still chatting away. After a minute he fell silent. He must have finally noticed how tired she was.

He reached over and gently shook her shoulder. "Oh, dear Miss Lil you look positively exhausted. Has that," he lowered his voice to a conspiratorial whisper, "uncouth behemoth been running you ragged? Say the word Miss Lil and I promise you I'll... well...ummm...I can't do much. But I can certainly make sure he has a good tummy ache."

Lily giggled. "It's okay Parr. The walk tired me out. But the more we walk, the closer we are to the revel. I think I just need to rest my eyes a moment."

Parr nodded in agreement as he lightly patted her leg, reminding her of her father. "Of course, of course. You rest a moment and I'll start supper." He bounded off to the edge of the clearing, far away from the Busse. She got up, staggering as her legs had fallen asleep. She managed to lean against one of the other cherry trees. *Just fifteen minutes.* She rested against the tree, her legs sprawled out. *I just need a few minutes to catch my breath.*

She looked up at the light pink blossoms falling on her face, the petals so delicate. A light, perfumed fragrance tickled her senses. The petals glided over her face, smooth as silk. Lily never felt so light, almost weightless. Her eyes started to close. Soon, a deep heat began to seep into her body, particularly centered around her legs. Slowly her tired achy legs began to feel better, as if she had taken a relaxing dip in a warm Epsom salt bath. Lily gave a drowsy contented sigh, wondering if maybe cherry trees here had healing properties. *I mean, they do have sleeping mush-rooms,* she thought with a chuckle. *Five more minutes, then I'll help Parr.*

The pleasant warmth in her legs continued to rise. Slowly, it traveled up to her stomach, then her chest, then her throat. The warmth coiled and tightened, getting warmer and warmer, as if she was in a sauna. Sweat started to bead on her forehead. She frowned. What was going on? She tried to open her eyes, but was unable to, her eyes sealed shut.

A prickle of fear lodged in her chest. She could hear Parr give a frightened yelp, but it sounded so far away. She tried to move her legs, but they wouldn't budge. It was like an invisible rope tied her down, preventing her from getting up. Soon, her body was on fire. Her legs grew tight as they began to swell. Her throat and nose began to close up. Involuntarily, she reached to grasp her throat, but realized her arms were paralyzed as well. While she was still processing that nugget of information, Lily rationalized she was suffocating, black spots flickering above her eyelids.

She struggled, desperate to take a much-needed breath through her nose, her mouth, anywhere! *Parr! Cabyll?! Can anyone see what's happening? Someone please help me?!* Oh...the heat, it was too much. She was drowning and burning at the same time. The darkness was engulfing her, pressing her down. Her father's voice penetrated the fog. *Lily Ambrosino, don't you dare give up now! Combattere! Fight!* Lily tried moving her head side to side in desperation as she heard someone calling her name before the darkness took her.

CHAPTER
SIXTEEN

"Ouch!"

Brandon jerked his hand from the stove, waving his index finger up and down. Grimacing, he stuck the burning finger in his mouth. Bad idea! With a yelp he ran to the sink, holding it under the cold running facet. As the burning sting began to fade, he frowned, frustrated. It was his fifth attempt to make himself noodles and the third finger he burned. So far.

"At least the pot didn't catch fire this time right Brom," snickered Alasdair.

Brom sighed dramatically. "Really Mr. Brandon, must you strain yourself so? I can quickly whip up a quaintly delish five course meal. It shall only take but a few minutes."

Brandon shook his head. The cold water quickly soothed the

blister beginning to form on his hand. It may seem ridiculous, but his mother always made him noodles when he had a bad day. He just wanted noodles. And noodles that HE made. Was that so hard? Groaning, he looked over at the stack of dirty dishes from his failed attempts. Brom would probably nag him about that, too. The brownie was a stickler for cleanliness. Specifically dirty dishes in the sink.

He waved his aching fingers with a smile. "See? It's fine guys. No problem! Besides, I need to learn how to do this myself ya know."

Brom jumped on the counter, frowning at the dishes – as Brandon had predicted. The little brownie sat down on the side of the sink with a huff, beginning to wash a large pot. Brom looked up at Brandon as he grumbled.

"I do not understand why you are so greatly determined to cook." He glanced at the noodles again with a raised brow. "What was it again?"

"Ramen. It's called ramen."

"Oh, yes. Ramen..." Brom shuddered, wiping vigorously at an imaginary grease stain.

Alasdair snorted. "Oye – it's only noodles. Have ya never had it brownie? Or are ya too prissy?"

Brom sniffed, his nose in the air. "That stuff is practically sodium on steroids. Quite unappealing, unappetizing, and um... well...um..."

"Well? Go on ya dafty twit! Can't find another 'un' word to keep it alliterate can ya?" Alasdair grinned from ear to ear.

"It is just not proper supper! The young mister needs a

balanced nutritional meal. As you well know, proper diet is essential for-"

"Oye – we get it." Alasdair rolled his eyes.

"I was not finished Alasdair Hob." Brom coughed dramatically. "As I was saying, a proper meal is essential. Mr. Brandon! I can make you a very nice roasted lemon chicken with a lovely roasted cauliflower and leek soup and-"

"Holy Moly! The ramen!"

Brandon ran to the stove. The water boiled over, covering the stove top with a white froth. Brandon hastily tried to mop up the mess, putting the towel on the hot burner. The kitchen began to smell of smoke.

Brandon knew he could have let Brom cook. But he didn't want to admit it to the 'guys' as he started calling them, that it wasn't about ramen. What he really wanted was to show Lily he could handle this. The house, his meals, everything. He imagined when she got back, she would be smiling at him with admiration. She would say how responsible he was. How mature. She wouldn't look at him like a kid anymore. However, the first part of his plan wasn't going as well as he hoped.

The brownie and hob watched, dumbfounded, as Brandon waved the towel, flames spreading around the terry cloth. The two fairies looked at each other.

"Hmmm..." Alasdair mused, watching Brandon jump around, desperately trying to put out the flames.

Brom gazed over, concerned. "Do you think Mr. Brandon has this under control?"

"Dinnae be stupid. You really think he's got this under control?"

Brom sighed. "You have a point..."

Brandon twirled around, the fire spreading over the towel. His dance took on a more dervish twirl.

Brom palmed his face. "Well, one of us should step in."

"Aye – one of us should." Alasdair nodded nonchalantly.

"Yes...quite right."

There was a pause as they looked at each other. Alasdair shrugged.

"After you brownie."

"Oh no my dear Alasdair Hob. After you."

"Oh! I wouldna dream of oversteppin' your authority as 'head' brownie."

"It's quite alright."

"Nay! I cannae possibly."

"Oh, but I do insist."

"Ummm...naw."

"Bloody-" Brom cleared his throat. "I do believe that it should be age before refinement as the saying goes and all."

Alasdair scoffed. "I'm only fifty years older than you ya hairy coo! You should take care of this." He swept his hands toward a scrambling Brandon, who had begun stomping on the towel, the flames creeping higher, almost catching his ankle.

Brom raised his eyebrow. "I distinctly heard you say earlier that *you* take care of fires sir."

"Oye – well...let's see what our little human friend can do

huh?" Alasdair crossed his arms over his chest and sat down on the counter with a thump.

Brom looked between Brandon frantically smacking the towel against the countertop and Alasdair calmly watching the scene unfold. Alasdair looked over with a smirk, shrugging one shoulder, daring the brownie to make a move.

"I cannae wait to see what he does next. Ye got this lad!" Alasdair yelled in encouragement at the frantic Brandon.

Brom growled. "Fine...fine! I'll take care of this mess. Like always." With a snap of his fingers, a bucket of water appeared above Brandon's head.

Brandon, oblivious, turned, eyes wide.

"Hey guys, a little help here-"

SPLASH

Brandon stood frozen, the water dripping down his hair. At least the towel was no longer on fire. He looked over at the pot, realizing his noodles were still on the stove top.

Brandon shrugged. "Eh...still good." He scooped up the soggy noodles into the bowl and began eating, water dribbling down his shirt onto the floor.

"Great assist guys!" He yelled over his shoulder, a noodle dangling from his mouth.

Alasdair laughed. "Brandon me lad, you will never make this place boring."

Brom groaned, rubbing his face. "The Veil preserve me. I now have two ragamuffins."

Brandon slurped some more noodles. His gaze turned outside towards the forest, his face pensive.

"You think Lil's okay?" He turned to his new friends with an uncharacteristically serious expression.

The fairies looked at each other again in silence before they slowly nodded.

"Here's hoping lad. Based on what I've seen, I believe she has a chance," said Alasdair.

"Miss Lily is an exceptionally bright young lady. And with Parr at her side I do believe she will be at least well versed. Though that cabyll-" muttered Brom.

Brandon's ears perked up.

"Yeah, what's the deal with that guy." Brandon had a bad feeling about that dude from the first moment he popped out of the smoke.

Alasdair grimaced. "That 'guy', well...We dinnea want to say anything in front of Lily you understand. To be honest lad. He's definitely a dangerous fae, there's no doubt about it."

Brandon frowned. "Then why send him with her?"

Brom put the last of the dishes away wearily. "Because Mr. Brandon, cabylls are one of the best trackers in the Veil. Even though they are deceptive that use subterfuge to obtain what they require – dastardly business if you ask me. But, that being said. If anyone can get Miss Lily to the revel in time, it's that cabyll."

Brandon wasn't convinced. "I still don't like how he tried to manipulate Lil." He grew angry remembering that moment. He saw how that guy tried to use his looks to sway Lily. Thankfully she didn't buy into that. Brandon was so afraid she was going to fall for those cheesy lines. It was something his sister would have done. One of the many differences between her and Lily. Brandon broke out of his musings when Alasdair barked out.

"Ock – dinnae worry lad. That sister of yours could see right through it. Threw him for a loop she did. Ha! Such a sight to see." Alasdair chuckled at the memory.

Brom smiled, trying to reassure Brandon. "It was indeed. I do believe Miss Lily is immune to such blatant displays of deception. You need not worry Mr. Brandon."

Brandon twirled his fork around his noodles aimlessly. He certainly hoped so. Suddenly losing his appetite, he put his bowl down and ran his hand through his slightly damp hair.

"Well, what should we do here?"

"Protect the hearth and home." Brom answered, his fist over his heart.

"And how do we do that?" Brandon was getting kinda tired of Brom repeating the same creed over and over. Hearth and home, hearth and home. Frankly, that hearth and home creed was giving him a hefty headache.

Brom placed his hands on his hips, mumbling quietly. "The impertinence and impatience of youth." He spoke up louder. "I do believe you require some basic manners Mr. Brandon. Shall we start with some simple etiquette lessons? First thing you must do is learn how to address someone properly. Lesson one-"

"Ah...Brommie..." Alasdair tugged on his sleeve.

Brom shrugged him off dismissively. "Not now Alasdair. I need to import some real-life lessons on this youth today."

Alasdair tugged harder. "Broooom...."

"Not now," gritted Brom.

"Oye! Fandan! Look!" Alasdair took Brom's head in his hands, squished his cheeks together, and turned the brownie's head towards the window. Brandon followed where the hob pointed. Something moved across the bridge. A shadow had come out of the forest and was scurrying around their backyard. Brom's mouth dropped open.

"Oh....no no no! No!! Absolutely not!" The brownie sputtered.

"Ack – ya see now don't ya? You prissy pot with your *'oye let me talk to the human about etiquette lessons'*. Ya missed that sly weasel and he slipped right through!" Alasdair removed his hands and glared at Brom.

Brom moaned, clutching his head. "That...heathen...is back?! The nerve! The gall! The audacity of that mongrel! He is going to cause an enormous amount of mischief. I just know it! Oh no! This is dreadful. Positively, absolutely, dreadful! I swear on this house if he so much as takes one more paw closer-"

Brandon stared outside, confused, as Brom continued to rant. The shadow darted around his makeshift ramp, pausing by the trees. Brandon squinted until the outline of the shape came into focus.

Brandon eyes squinted, then he laughed. He pointed out the window. "Guys? That's a raccoon. Is that what has your pants in a twist?"

Brom sputtered. "Just...a...raccoon?"

Alasdair smacked his hand over his face. "Now ye done it."

"Just.... just...a...raccoon?!"

Alasdair patted Brandon's arm. He motioned to sit down, away from the brownie. "Best stay back lad. He's gonna blow."

Brom's chest started heaving as he gasped for breath. "A BLOODY RACCOON?!" The brownie grown a bit in size, his pressed shirt stretched a little too thin, the thin arms getting a tad bigger with muscle. Wait...were those teeth getting a tad pointy?

Alasdair put his hands up in a placating gesture, slowly approaching the brownie. "Hey...Brommie? Let's take a minute and breathe alright? The lad didn't know. Did ye Brandon?" Alasdair motioned with his head over to the brownie, his eyes wide.

Brandon nodded emphatically. "Oh yes! I had NO idea." Honestly, he had no idea, but Brom did not seem to be in any mood for follow up questions.

Alasdair nodded in approval. He turned back to the heaving brownie that was beginning to remind Brandon of a version of what "Hulking Out" might have looked like brownie style.

"See Brommie? It was a mistake. We'll fix it yea? We'll make sure the trickster is gone won't we lad?"

"Sure Alasdair. It'll be gone before you know it." Brandon gave a thumbs up.

Brom began to breathe normally. Brandon stared, dumbstruck. The Hulk brownie was slowly returning to normal size. With no pointy teeth, thank goodness for that. Brom took a deep breath. When he began to resemble himself, he staggered towards the countertop, his shirt in ruins. Blinking, he looked down in shock.

"Oh...my..." Brom straightened up, trying his best to look dignified, as much as possible in a tattered shirt and pants. Face turning red, he sputtered out. "Apologies Alasdair, Mr. Brandon. It seems my emotions got the better of me. It shan't happen again I can assure you." He looked over at Alasdair, contrite. "I am afraid due to my...vulnerable emotional state as it were...I will be unable to sufficiently remove the threat. Can I leave this for you two to handle?"

Alasdair nodded, patting Brom's shoulder. "Aye Bromie we got this."

Brom inclined his head slightly, eyes still wary. "Then I take my leave at once so I can...rebalance myself. Goodnight." And with a slight bow he winked out of sight.

Alasdair waited a moment to make sure the brownie was gone. He scratched his head, wearily sitting next to Brandon.

"Oye – that dafty brownie will be the death of me."

"So, what was that about?" asked Brandon.

Alasdair glanced over, pointing his finger up in the air. "One thing to learn about brownies lad. One! They are quick to anger and can turn into, well, you saw what he almost turned into."

"But you tease Brom all the time and make him angry."

"Aye – but that's because that fandan has a stick so far up his keister that he doesn't get genuinely angry too often. Much too disciplined for that." Alasdair sighed and pointed his thumb at the window. "But that rocket out there, that guy is one of the very few things that truly gets Brom riled up."

"But a raccoon?" Brandon asked in disbelief.

Alasdair scoffed. "Lad, after everything you've seen in the last twenty-four hours. You really believe that is a normal, everyday raccoon?"

Brandon had to admit that did make sense. There was no use

believing anything here was 'normal'. "Okay good point, so what is he?"

"That, laddie, is Azeban. A trickster of the tricksters if ever there was one. Last time he came for a visit half the cottage was destroyed and Brom went-"

"Brownie-Hulk?" Brandon interjected.

Alasdair stared at him, confused. Then his face split into a grin as he laughed loudly. "Ha! Never thought of that one. Needless to say, Brom said he'd tear the fur off his tail if he ever showed up again. Trouble is Azeban is a favored fae among the Forest Prince's court. So we cannae have Brom and him going at it you understand?"

Brandon let that sink in a minute. These guys had so many rules. Way too many for Brandon's liking. What did it matter if this raccoon guy was a favorite of the prince? What did that have to do with Brom? Then a light bulb clicked in Brandon's head.

"Wait! If he's part of the court..." Brandon trailed off, putting the pieces together.

Alasdair nodded. "Aye lad, now yer thinkin' big picture! If we can catch the bugger, we may be able to acquire some information on your sister."

Brandon leaned down, his eyes eager. "Alright! What's the plan?"

SEVENTEEN

L ily woke up with a pounding headache. Her eyes were crusty as she struggled to peel them open. Squinting, her headache pounded harder, she tried to ascertain her blurry surroundings. She could make out faint purples and reds before she closed her eyes again. A fresh wave of pain thumped at her temple. *Is it dusk?*

She tried to move but whimpered, a fiery jolt of pain shot through her legs. The burning pain made it nearly impossible. Even the slightest twitch of her muscles brought about a fresh wave of agony.

Tears sprung to her eyes. This reminded her of the time when she had the worst sunburn ever when she was twelve years old where they spent the summer with her Aunt Ravenna. Instead of swimming in Capri's beautiful waters, she had to lay in bed for three days covered in aloe.

The pain brought her back to the present, the pounding heat radiating from her body. Cracking her eyes open again, she noticed she was lying flat down on the grass. All she could see was the purplish sky above her. Lily gritted her teeth through the discomfort, pulling her upper body to a sitting position so she could look around. Nothing seemed out of the ordinary. Then she looked down. Her eyes widened in shock. Her legs were covered with cherry blossom petals. But it was not the petals that startled Lily. It was the condition of her legs underneath the blooms that worried her. They were twice their normal size, burned bright red, shiny, and swollen like big, steamed crab legs. If someone put a stick of butter on them, it would melt. Panicked, she looked at her hands, afraid they had fallen to the same fate. Thankfully her upper arms were unblemished, but her palms had met with the same fate as her legs. She cringed. They looked worse than third degree burns. Did fairies have hospitals?

"You're awake."

She jumped at the deep voice behind her. Lily struggled to turn around, but a firm hand lightly touched her on the shoulder, holding her still. "Don't try to move, it'll only make the swelling worse."

She tilted her head up to see Cabyll looking down at her with a frown.

Lily wet her dry lips as she croaked out. "Wha – what happened?"

Cabyll sat down beside her, holding a container with, what she assumed, was water.

"Drink some water first. Then we'll talk."

He held the bowl to her lips, helping her drink since she couldn't move her hands. Lily gulped the cool water down, wishing the cool feeling in her throat could be moved to her legs and hands.

"Slowly human. You'll get sick." Cabyll scolded softly.

Once she had enough, Cabyll sat the bowl down and took a few herbs and leaves from a pouch on his waist. He put the herbs in the bowl, grinding them into a fine powder. He mixed it with some water, creating a purple greenish paste. Carefully, he picked up her lobster leg, examining her injuries. Lily winced, sucking in a breath. The pain flared up her body in a wave, which nearly made her pass out again.

Cabyll whispered, in a surprisingly kind tone. "It will be only a moment."

He scooped up the paste and gently applied a heavy layer to her legs and hands. As soon as the paste touched her inflamed skin, Lily felt better. Forget aloe vera. Lily determined this paste was a miracle. She almost wept as the blistering heat started to fade, a relieved sigh escaping. Cabyll glanced over as he spread another layer on her right hand. He frowned.

"You're lucky I got back when I did or this could have been worse," he reprimanded, shaking his head. Lily gave him a confused look.

He sighed as he spread more cooling paste on her other hand. "I should have told you not to go near the cherry trees, but I thought you wouldn't even notice them. Way to prove me wrong Lil."

"That's the first time," she murmured.

Cabyll looked at her, head tilting to the side, waiting for her to continue.

"That's the first time you said my name and not 'hey human'." She gave a small smile.

Cabyll's face was struck dumb, that is if she believed he had emotions like that. Was he flustered? Before she could tell, he ducked his head, concentrating on wrapping her legs with large leaves.

"Anyways, thanks for helping me," she said sincerely.

Cabyll, still keeping his head down, muttered. "You know, you say that a lot."

"What?"

"Saying thank you. It's annoying," he grumbled.

Lily's lip quirked. She lightly patted Cabyll's hand, briefly stopping him from finishing up the bandage. "Well, I mean it. And from what I can tell, I had a close call right?"

His hand stilled under hers, refusing to look at her as he whispered. "You have no idea."

Lily gave him a grateful smile. "Truly, thanks for saving me Cabyll."

Lily still was not able to see his expression under the dark hair that covered his face. She tried not to think too hard about how close she may have come to...well...yeah, she tried to put those thoughts aside. He muttered something unintelligible as he finished tying up the bandages before he quickly pulled away. He sat back on his heels a moment, deep in thought. She wanted to say something else, but he stood up staring down at her. Then, as if by magic, his signature handsome smirk returned. And with it his arrogant tone, much to her annoyance.

He stared down at her, sneering. "Only doing my job human. You need to reach the revel 'safe' remember? Isn't that in the agreement? Humans are so fragile. It looks like you can't do anything without me huh?"

She inwardly rolled her eyes. It wasn't lost on her that he didn't answer her question, but she decided to change the subject.

"How long have I been out?" She tried to turn her head. "Where's Parr?"

Cabyll rubbed his forehead as he muttered. "So many questions. Always the questions with you."

Lily waited for Cabyll to answer, but of course he didn't. She closed her eyes and groaned. *He probably thinks those questions are unnecessary.*

"Cabyll! Can't you just answer one question?"

He rolled his eyes, letting out a long-drawn-out sigh.

"Fine."

His eyes softened. He coughed loudly, breaking eye contact. "You've been out the whole day." He gestured towards a clump of trees. "Parr left to gather more medicine to take with us the rest of the way. Your frail human body is taking longer to heal, and we have a time limit."

Cabyll crossed his arms as he glared. "There, I answered your ridiculously long list of questions. Are you happy?"

Lily wet her dry lips again, wincing at the sting. Though she couldn't tell if it was from her ripped up lip or from her guilt. They lost a day, an entire day, all because of her. *Way to go Lil*, she thought ruefully. But something niggled in the back of her mind. She tried to place her finger on it. Wait! Didn't he say he should have warned her about the trees? What did he mean by that?

Her brow furrowed. "I don't understand about the tree. Isn't it a cherry tree?"

"Just a cherry tree huh?" He quipped, raising his eyebrow.

Cabyll turned suddenly and walked to the offending cherry tree. Before Lily could process what was happening, a flash of lightning streaked down across the sky, splitting a branch into splinters. To her surprise, the bark did not burst into flames and burn. Instead, something was thrown out of the tree. It hit the ground with a resounding thud, petals dancing in the air frantically.

The figure laying on the petal-strewn ground was gnarled and twisted, its skin dark and rough similar to bark. It straightened itself up, as much as it could in its twisted way, and looked over at Lily. She felt a chill when she stared at its eyes, or what she thought were eyes. Because where the eyes should have been, there was nothing but empty blackness. Even though she was itchy and hot all over, staring at this creature brought a burning cold at the same time.

The creature rubbed its bark hewed arms, grimacing. "Now why did you do that for?" It grumbled, its voice like crackling leaves under someone's footsteps. It made her shiver. Well, she would have shivered if she could move.

Cabyll crossed his arms over his chest as he stared hard at the twisted thing in disgust. His eyes were ice green which made Lily nervous. Gone was the carefree, insufferable flirt. This was the

Cabyll the others warned her about. Cabyll may appear to be harmless, but he was still dangerous.

Cabyll raised his eyebrow as he spoke in a non-nonsense tone. "Enough of your games Aer. You have information. Talk."

Aer sighed, which sounded more like an autumn breeze ruffling leaves. "Should have known. Can't get anything past you Cabyll. Word is you want information about the revel."

Cabyll didn't answer.

Aer rubbed its hands together, examining its claws flippantly. "Gossip through the trees says that Prince Jacy is indeed having the revel in three days." The tree fae trailed off with a faint hiss.

Cabyll glared. "And..." He prompted.

Aer blinked. Or it seemed like it blinked. Lily wasn't sure since the creature didn't have any eyelids.

"And what?" asked Aer innocently.

Cabyll raised his eyebrow. He held up his hand. Blue-white light ignited from the tips of his fingers. Startled, Aer's gnarled arms shot up to shield its face. It scrambled backwards to the tree trunk.

Aer hissed, its eyes peaking between its arms. Cabyll didn't move, nor did he quell the light in his hand. He merely stared at Aer. Unafraid and unfazed. Aer turned away first with a snarl.

Aer grumbled reluctantly. "Fine! They say the revel will be held at the Fern Palace off to the East."

Cabyll snapped his fingers, the light disappearing. He spoke to himself, tapping his fingers lightly on his chin. "So, we have to go by the gorge."

Aer's mouth curled. "Yeaaaah. Not only that, but you must

also go through the marsh. And," Aer put its twisted fingers over its mouth and whispered playfully. "SHE is waiting...waiting. Word says she is eager to see you Cabyll."

Lily wondered who the 'she' was. Aer appeared anxious when it mentioned the mysterious woman as its gaze darted around cautiously. She inwardly scoffed. It didn't take a genius to figure that out. Cabyll was a flirt. Pretty easy to deduce honestly. *He probably doesn't even care or remember who she is.*

Cabyll shrugged as he waved his hand dismissively. "She doesn't matter. You know as well as I do we don't have to go through the marsh. We can take the Ohneganohs path by the river."

Lily mentally sighed. *Yup...doesn't give two hoots...poor girl.*

Aer giggled darkly. It shook its head. "So you say Cabyll. Well either way you go, be on the lookout if you near the gorge. The Bloody Caps are having some stirrings in their ranks. They're all over the place. Destroying everything. Even the trees." Aer spat on the ground in anger.

He glanced over at Lily, a sly smirk creeping across its weathered face that gave her the creeps.

"A 'friendly' piece of info. I'm not the only one who knows you brought a human here. The human could be a burden to you. You could leave it here with me." Aer gave her a twisted smirk, revealing very long and very *very* sharp teeth.

Lily shuddered. She really did not like the way Aer was looking over at her as if she was dinner. She replied in, what she hoped, was a confident annoyed tone. "Hello? Said human here. I think I have a say where I go."

They ignored her. Cabyll looked at the tree fairy, paused in thought. Lily's eyes widened. He was actually *thinking* about it. *Seriously?!* With what seemed like forever, Cabyll shrugged, shaking his head. "Thanks for the offer Aer, maybe next time."

Lily blinked. *Wait what? Next time?! You slimy no good* – She must have spoken out loud as Cabyll turned around, looking shocked.

Aer laughed loudly, the sound scraping against her ears. She winced. "Well that human has got some spirit. She seems to be made of strong stuff Cabyll, she really gave me a struggle she did." It said it with an almost appreciative tone.

Lily's brow furrowed. *Struggle?*

Cabyll turned back to Aer, growling low. Aer's head ducked in a submissive pose. "Not trying to steal your thunder," it mumbled.

"Ignore her," commanded Cabyll. He turned his back to Lily, but she heard him whisper. "Tell me the rest."

The creature nodded as it lowered its voice, probably thinking Lily wouldn't hear them. However, unbeknownst to them, Lily had remarkably good hearing. She even taught herself how to read lips a few years back because her father's digs were so incredibly loud. Reading lips made the digs a lot easier. Though she admitted this was situation was harder since Aer didn't have lips per say. She thought Aer said. "The glamour...not worked Cabyll? You're losing your touch." She noticed it smirked, its' bright pointy teeth gleaming.

Cabyll's back was tense, but she couldn't see or hear his response, but she definitely took note when Aer responded with,

"Well time you don't have 'friend'," it emphasized. "you're losing days." It pointed a gnarled finger toward the setting sun.

Cabyll must have said something else since Aer nodded. But Lily couldn't hear anything else. Cabyll turned back to remark loudly. "Later Aer."

"Oh and Aer?" The tree fae paused mid hobble towards the trunk. "You're losing your touch. You didn't kill her."

Lily held her breath at Cabyll's casual tone. It was as if he was commenting on someone forgetting to tie their shoe. The casual way these folks spoke of violence was really unsettling.

Aer scoffed as it waved its hands in a shooing motion. "Ah she was fine geez. How about next time you don't be so flashy to summon me hmm? Be gone by dawn will you?"

Lily watched the creepy tree fairy fade back into the cherry tree. She would never look at a cherry tree the same way ever again. Cabyll, deep in thought, sat down slowly. He looked at her curiously. As if debating with himself, he seemed to make up his mind about something.

"I suppose you have questions, right?" His head tilted to the side.

Dude, I have them spades, she groused inwardly. She held her tongue though, afraid to say it out loud.

Cabyll scoffed. "None? Did the petals get your tongue?" He chuckled at his joke, his hair falling over his eyes.

Lily narrowed her eyes at him. Did he really find that joke funny? The salty prick of tears began to form on her eyelashes, but she couldn't rub them because her hands were still wrapped.

His smile faded, realizing his error. "Here," he mumbled,

reaching into his pouch to hand her some berries. They were bright pink in color and gleamed in the twilight. They reminded her of candy gumballs from those old candy machines. They were too pretty in Lily's opinion.

"What am I three years old? I don't need candy."

"They're medicine. It'll help with the rest of the pain." He gruffly insisted, gently pushing the berries into her hand.

Bewildered, she kept the berries in the palm of her hand, still uncertain. Cabyll must have noticed as he ran his hand through his hair, not looking at her. "Parr found them."

Lily's shoulders sagged, relieved since she knew he couldn't lie. After looking at them one last time, she popped one in her mouth. Flavor burst on her tongue, a syrupy sweet mint. Not awful per se, but definitely not what she was expecting. The medicine was quick acting since she started to feel the remaining ache from her burns fade away.

Cabyll cleared his throat before he barked out. "Now relax!"

He gently pushed Lily against the mossy bed, tucking the blanket from her backpack around her in a clumsy fashion. If Lily still wasn't in so much pain, she would have laughed at the handsome fae attempting the normally boring art of tucking a blanket. She winced as a broken chuckle escaped her when he tried to arrange, and fail, a makeshift pillow for her out of soft moss with a sprinkling of fragrant white flowers.

She put her hand over her smile. "You've never done this before have you?"

His hands stilled. He jerked back, giving an annoyed huff. "Now," deliberately ignoring her as he changed the subject, "about your question on what happened to you. You, human, happened to sleep next to the wrong cherry tree."

She rolled her eyes. "I gathered that Sherlock." She paused a second, her voice dropping. "The blossoms did this to my legs right?"

Cabyll nodded. He gestured towards the tree. "That cherry tree happens to be inhabited by a demon. An Aerico demon to be precise."

"A demon? I thought he was a tree fairy."

He sighed, exasperated. "The Veil has more creatures than the fae you know. Aerico demons live in trees, particularly cherry trees because they like the blossoms. They love pretty things because... well, Aer is not the prettiest thing to look at. In exchange for protecting the tree to a long life, the demon can live within it." He paused, looking up at the tree with a half-smile. "On the bright side, the tree's blooms forever. However, the blossoms become poisonous. Anything they touch will swell and burn."

There was a stretch of silence.

Cabyll stared at her, his serious expression radiating chills down her spine.

He spoke gravely. "Remember this well human. Beauty means death. And Aerico demons do not like anyone messing with their trees." Cabyll concluded with a flippant shrug. "I would think even a human could grasp that simple concept."

Maybe he didn't mean to be cruel, but the patronizing gesture struck her as strongly as a punch to the gut. He had the nerve to act like a resigned schoolteacher scolding a forgetful toddler. If Lily's legs weren't swollen, she swore she would have kicked him.

Then she remembered the lightning from his hands. *Yup, keep telling yourself that girl...*

She frowned. "Simple?! Cabyll, in case you forgot, I know next to nothing about your world, your culture. Basically anything!"

Cabyll pursed his lips, nodding. "Yes, you appear to be quite uneducated."

Keep calm Lil....

Lily ground her teeth together. "Do you really think based on that assessment that I would have heard of an Aerico demon? Are they even from North America?"

Cabyll mirrored her frown, tapping his chin absently. "Well... no. Aer's people are originally around Albania or Greece I believe you humans call it."

Lily puffed out an annoyed sigh, rolling her eyes. "Well, oh genius one. Riddle me this. If I clearly do not know about fairy culture, how am I supposed to recognize a demon infested cherry blossom tree? I'm not Zatanna!"

She shook her head at his blank look, clearly not understanding her comic book reference. And it was a pretty good reference if she did say so herself. Zatanna was a master of mystic arts. This would be a walk in the park for a superheroine like that. But Lily wasn't a superhero.

"I mean do YOU know anything about the human world?" Again, she was met with a blank look. *Or rather*, she thought dryly, *you don't care enough to know about it.*

Lily closed her eyes, calling upon her innermost responsible adult to take the high road. "Look, I'll admit. I made a mistake. No more sitting near demon trees. But consider I've recently learned about your existence, dealing with Ari being kidnapped, being attacked not once but *twice* mind you, and putting up with your attitude. Can you give me a break?!"

Cabyll's eyes widened, dumbfounded. Probably because even though she reminded herself to stay calm, she ended up yelling. For the record, she really tried to remain calm.

Lily stopped to take a breath. She bit her lip, feeling guilty. It did not help anyone for her to be mad. They needed to move forward with a mutual understanding so they could reach Ari. Her eyes began to close, the berries doing their work. It was hard to keep her mind straight, but she pushed through as a small tear trickled down her face. "I'm sorry. It's just been a lot to process. I understand I should be more aware of my surroundings." She struggled to keep her eyelids open.

Cabyll looked at her in silence, frowning, as still as a statue. With a frustrated growl he ground out. "And I should have understood that you needed some guidance in a world you don't know anything about." He conceded with a resigned sigh. "Here you are, with no knowledge of what you are facing and yet you march through it with a determination that even had an Aerico demon praise you."

Lily chuckled, her eyes half-mast as exhaustion crept in. "I guess I can put that on my resume. Demon praises."

Cabyll's lip quirked slightly. "I wouldn't dismiss it lightly. Demons don't praise fae often, let alone humans."

"Well, I guess that's really lucky of me huh?" she asked, not keeping the sarcasm out of her voice.

"Yes. It is indeed lucky." He answered seriously, either not noticing or ignoring her sarcastic tone. "Especially *that* scourge of a demon."

Another wave of exhaustion settled in her bones. Any minute now she wouldn't be able to keep her eyes pried open. Sleep seemed like such a wonderful idea at the moment. But she didn't want the conversation to end. It was the first time they were not arguing. Although the calmness was only temporary, it was still a welcome reprieve.

"Sounds like perfect dinner company." She rolled her eyes.

He tilted his head, confused. "Of course not, they are a plague. Literally, an actual plague."

Lily softly giggled. It was obvious he had no idea she was joking, but it was funny to see the bewildered look on his face. She tried to smooth down her grin so he wouldn't be offended.

"Speaking of company. What brought you to the cottage? I never did ask."

Cabyll remained silent. She could see the wheels turning in his head. He sat down next to her, focusing on her bandages. He waited a moment before lifting his gaze towards hers.

"I saw your sister."

Lily gave him a surprised look. "Ari?"

He nodded, clasping his hands together, his fingers steepled. He stared at her intently.

Lily narrowed her eyes. "When?"

"When I came the first time. I was at the edge of the forest and saw her by the bridge." He paused a moment, searching for her reaction. She intentionally kept her face blank. He waited a beat, eyes intense, before shrugging. "She was pretty. And I'm the kind of fae that-"

"Likes to drown pretty girls," supplied Lily with a deadpan face.

He raised his eyebrow. "Cabylls have been known to drown people yes."

"But, you didn't drown Ari. You came over to me and Brandon instead."

Cabyll scratched his temple, not looking at her.

Lily's eyes were drifting shut. It took a lot of effort to keep them open. It was so hard to focus on what he was saying. But she had to ask. She groused out.

"Cabyll? Why didn't you go to Ari?"

"I'm the patient sort. It wasn't the right time," he said quickly. Maybe a little too quickly.

He rested his hand on top her head and gave her a somewhat brotherly pat. He sighed softly. "Enough of that. Get some rest human, we have a long hike tomorrow."

"It's Lil," she grumbled sleepily, not bothering to mention he didn't answer her question. Her eyes drifted shut and her breathing slowed. Was it her imagination or was his hand still in her hair? Nope, had to be her imagination. As she drifted off to a dreamless sleep, she thought he whispered something.

"Sleep Lily. I will watch out for demons tonight."

THE SUN FILTERED through the trees, creeping towards a cloudless sky when Lily woke up. It was close to mid-day and her legs were much better. Obviously, Aer did not make good on his promise for them to be gone by sunrise since the demon remained silent in the tree all morning. Maybe it had something to do with Cabyll making a show of sharpening his scimitar in front of the rustling branches.

Parr, having returned, had been fussing over her all morning. As soon as she woke up, he had shooed Cabyll away - who apparently had stayed by her side all evening - all the while muttering about propriety, manners, etiquette and the like. Before he left to scout, Cabyll fluffed up the brownie even more by telling a tale of past exploits that made Lily wish for more of the pain numbing, sleep berries.

Lily noticed the 'serious' Cabyll from the day before had vanished, replaced by the flirting nonchalant trickster she was used to. In a way, she wondered if she had dreamed it all the other day. But the clean bandages that were meticulously wrapped around her legs told her otherwise.

Trying to keep herself busy, she attempted to get up and walk around. She failed thanks to Parr. She insisted she was well enough, but he was in full mother hen mode. Parr fretted over her injuries, redressing her bandages. He made sure she ate plenty, and he preened when she complimented the strawberry tarts he had made.

They sat in the meadow, the bright blossoms surrounding them – which made Lily a tad nervous based on her last encounter. As soon as she finished her tart, Cabyll returned.

Silently, he pulled out a walking stick. He handed it to Lily, promptly leaving to wait at the edge of the meadow. Lily held the walking stick in her hands, the wood sturdy and polished to a glossy sheen. Parr peered over her shoulder.

Parr whistled appreciatively. "Oh my! How considerate. Considerate indeed. Why it's even your exact size Miss Lil."

Indeed, it was. The walking stick was whittled down to her height so she could walk comfortably. She clutched it, glancing over at Cabyll who stood with his back to her. He seemed to be keeping watch, quietly, unmoving. Lily inwardly smiled. Maybe this was his way of calling a truce.

On cue, Cabyll yelled over his shoulder. "Hey human! Brownie! Get a move on will you? We need to get to that revel in-" he looked up at the sky, "less than four days. You're frolicking is eating up time."

She groaned, tapping her head softly against the wood. *Never mind. Spoke too soon.*

They quickly gathered up their supplies and rushed to meet Cabyll at the edge of the clearing. Lily snuck one last glance at a group of young Busse. They jumped around the meadow, pink cherry blossom petals dancing in the air. It was extremely beautiful, if you got past the fact the petals were acid and the deer could skewer you. Shivering, she quickly followed Cabyll back into the dark woods. Beauty is death indeed.

CHAPTER
EIGHTEEN

Brandon wondered what he got himself into as he followed Alasdair, hunched over, sneaking around the bushes like a thief. Alasdair explained they needed to catch Azeban unawares. Hence why they were acting like amateur stealth operatives. Brandon's feet crunched and smashed over every single leaf and gravel stone. He grimaced. Definitely not stealth material. His mind swirled. How does a fae become a raccoon? Or does a raccoon become a fae? Does he eat trash? Does he talk? Does he speak English? Would this fae have even seen his sister? As these questions raced through his head, a hand smacked into his chest, abruptly stopping him in his tracks.

"Quiet!" Alasdair whispered. He stared straight ahead, not looking back at Brandon. "He's right ahead of us."

Brandon peeked above Alasdair's head. The raccoon was indeed close, about ten feet in front of them. It seemed to be sitting down and assessing his vert ramp. Brandon was pretty proud of the plywood half pipe; all 12ft width and 14ft height of it. The curvature and schematics always gave Brandon a thrill for his next trick.

Alasdair spoke, not turning around. "You ready?"

Silence.

Alasdair turned back, frowning.

"I asked if yer ready lad?"

Brandon, perplexed, whispered back. "You told me to be quiet. Which is it? I stay quiet or answer you?"

Alasdair opened his mouth, but stopped. He crinkled his nose before he nodded. "Alright fair point, lad. Let's go."

They slinked up to the side of the halfpipe. Azeban was laying down on the other side, back to them. Brandon could see up close this was no ordinary raccoon. It was much too large, the tail too thick, the body too long. Why it was almost the size of Brandon. Alasdair motioned with his hand, holding up three fingers. Brandon rolled his eyes as the fingers counted down. Three... two....one. They jumped across the ramp –

SMACK!

They both fell into something, an invisible wall slamming into Brandon's face. He rubbed his nose, wincing. A high-pitched laugh rained down around them.

"Ha! Ha ha ha ha!! Fooled you!" Azeban came around the corner, laughing so hard his paws clutched his shaking furred belly.

"I mean...honestly! Who do you think you were fooling? I

could see you coming from a mile away." The raccoon giggled, whiskers twitching.

Alasdair dusted himself off, groaning. "It worked on ya the last time rodent."

Azeban snorted. "Pfft. Maybe you Alasdair Hob, but that-" He pointed at Brandon. "That hulking mass was like a big 'HERE I AM' sign. In bright neon letters. Ha ha ha!"

Brandon didn't have anything to say to that. He was pretty horrible at being quiet. "Hey what's with the mime routine with that wall?" He rubbed his still smarting nose. His hand reached out slowly, thinking he'd touch the wall, but it wasn't there anymore.

"Bah! Just another one of that mink's tricks," grumbled Alasdair.

"I am a raccoon, thank you very much." Azeban looked over at Brandon. "You know, after two hundred years you'd think he'd have better manners. I mean there was the one time we-"

Alasdair jumped in front of Brandon, interrupting the fae. "Az, what are ye doing here?"

Azeban laid back on the halfpipe, his tail swinging side to side in merriment. He looked at them with mischievous eyes.

"Oh me? I was only wanting to see how my good old pals are doing. How's that stickler Brom?"

"Ye know Brom, the last time you came here-"

"Yeah yeah, he went on a rampage that lasted for a year. I mean it was hardly my fault. It was just a little eensy weensy mistake."

"You covered the house in tar! And feathered it with the chickens!"

"Bah! Those chickens were always spoiled sports. I was simply helping them out by reliving that burden." His paws crossed behind his head.

Brandon covered his mouth with his hand, preventing his chuckle from bursting forth. Alasdair took note, however, and gave Brandon a warning look.

"Dinnae encourage him lad."

Brandon nodded, a small snort popping out.

Alasdair retorted. "Well, we dinnae want whatever you're planning today, Az. Tis time you go home alright?"

Azeban tilted his head to the side, thinking. "Nah...besides," he jumped up and peered at them with a grin. "I know you Alasdair. You don't want me to go. You wanna know something."

"Dinnae know what yer talking about." Alasdair scoffed, briefly glancing at Brandon.

"Come on! I normally like this game, but it's a little old," whined Azeban.

Alasdair sighed. "Ye got me. What do you know about the girl?"

Azeban clapped his paws together. "There we go, way to be a sport Alasdair! And yes, I do know about the girl. That human has the forest in an uproar. It's been practically all anyone can talk about from here to the Evergreen Estate." He looked at Brandon with a conspiratorial wink. "That's way up north you know."

Brandon stood waiting to hear more, but the raccoon looked at him with a big grin. Alasdair waved his hands impatiently.

"Well? Go on!"

Azeban blinked innocently. "With what?"

"Ack! Tell us something we can use Az! The girl needs to come home. She has family."

The trickster scratched his fur, a grin spreading. "Oh, well... maybe there is something. I'll tell you. For a price of course."

"Figures," mumbled Alasdair.

"What do you want?" asked Brandon.

Azeban's eyes twinkled. "A game! I do so love games you know. Play a game with me. If I win, I have some fun with your cottage again. But if you win, I'll tell you what you want to know about the girl and the prince. Maybe I'll even tell you about what happened to that human trying to find her." He winked.

Brandon's heart stopped. Did something happen to Lily? He looked at Alasdair, panicked. The hob shook his head. He put his arms out in a placating gesture as he turned back to the trickster.

"IF we agree, we pick the game." Alasdair insisted.

Azeban sighed dramatically. "Okaaaaaaaay...fine. I'll give you two minutes to discuss." He flopped back down on the halfpipe, looking up at the sky whistling.

Brandon tried to calm his racing heart. A game? He was really good at games. He smiled but paused. Alasdair wasn't smiling. The hob frowned; his eyes narrowed. He gripped Brandon's shirt, pulling Brandon close as he whispered frantically.

"Lad I have no idea what yer smilin' about but knock that grin off your face."

Brandon rolled his eyes. "Oh come on Alasdair. It's a game! I can do this with my eyes closed."

Alasdair groaned, smacking his forehead. "You dinnae even know what game you'll be playing. Even so, Azeban has lived lifetimes. Lifetimes boy! He has played every game you can think of."

"Well, what do you suggest?"Alasdair put his hands on his knees and sighed. "I guess it can't be helped. We want information. Az wants a bit of fun."

He looked squarely at Brandon. "But we need to pick a game we have a chance at winning lad. We have no chance otherwise."

Brandon thought about all the games he played. Then he thought harder. He could hear Alasdair muttering to himself names of games he never heard of.

"Is there any game he hasn't played?" asked Brandon.

"I've played every game ever invented human!" Azeban called from where he sat. Brandon saw the trickster sporting a smug grin. He pointed to his large, tufted ears when he saw Brandon give him a questioning look. "Good hearing." He chuckled with a shrug.

"Stop eavesdropping ya blether," yelled Alasdair.

Azeban, unbothered, kept whistling as he reclined back, staring up at the night sky. He sang out.

"You got one more minute hobbie."

Brandon's eyes widened, a plan beginning to form. He tugged Alasdair's arm.

"I got it!"

Alasdair gave him a skeptical look. "You sure lad?"

Brandon nodded. "Trust me."

He could see the gears turning in Alasdair's mind. There was doubt, definitely a huge dose of doubt in his face. However, the hob's shoulders slumped, giving him a resigned nod. Alasdair's breath went out in a low hiss as he clapped Brandon's shoulder

"Alright lad. Let's see what ye got."

Brandon and Alasdair walked over. Azeban jumped up with a flourish, his tail waving.

"You gonna play?" Azeban's eyes were wide with anticipation.

Brandon nodded. "Yes, I'll play."

Azeban bounced around, giggling in merriment. "Wonderful, wonderful! So as agreed, you pick the game. What game do you want to play human?"

Brandon smiled back and pointed up at the halfpipe. "I want to vert skateboard."

Azeban cocked his head to the side. "Vert?"

"What?!" Alasdair yelled in disbelief.

Brandon crossed his arms and nodded. "Yes. This," he motioned to the ramp, "is a vert ramp. Here's the game. Whoever does the best trick on the ramp and stays on his board wins."

Azeban giggled. "Oh! I do like tricks."

Brandon smiled back with a secret grin. "So do I."

CHAPTER

NINETEEN

"Pardon, but I must ask...again...how far is the river?" Parr asked breathlessly as they trudged along.

"Close," said Cabyll, not turning around and not stopping.

Lily followed along, leaning against her walking stick. They had been going for hours nonstop. But at least her legs were recovering from the burns where only a slight ache remained in her shins. Parr's medicine worked wonders, far better than medicine at home. She absently patted her pant pocket; the psilo mushrooms from earlier were tucked away. Parr had said there was a way to smoke the mushrooms to use them in an incense to get rid of bad dreams.

Lily squinted as the trees opened up, bright light momentarily blinding her.

"Excellent, we've made good time," said Cabyll.

Lily blinked. Yet again, the scenery changed. The path opened up to reveal a large apple orchard. Rows and rows of apple trees stretched for miles around. The trees were in various stages of growth. Some had beautiful white blossoms, others were bright orange, and some sported bright candy red apples dangling from their branches. It was as if they were all in various points of the season. It was utterly beautiful and logically impossible. The apples were proof, glistening in the sunlight, looking as if they were freshly washed. Lily was tempted to grab one of ruby gems and take a juicy bite. But, if she had learned anything in the last few days, it was anything that was beautiful and too good to be true...pretty much was.

Parr sighed loudly. He was not in awe of the magical field. Just another Tuesday in his eyes. The brownie yelped when he tripped over a downed apple. Grumbling, he kicked the offending fruit off the path as he called out to Cabyll.

"Close?! Good time?! Last time you said that we almost ended up in quicksand. Oh, and when we were almost set upon by those carnivorous vines that were hiding in the maidenhead ferns. Oh oh oh! And my personal favorite. You said we were sooooo close, 'go down towards that cave Parr, scout for the river around it. It'll be *fine*' and I almost got caught by that family of Kee-wakw!"

Cabyll shrugged his shoulders. "We needed a diversion. The Kee-wakw would have smelled her. If they did, they would have tried to eat us. There's no way she would have made it past them."

"I'm NOT some ball you throw at a dog!" Parr threw out his arms.

Cabyll waved his hand, dismissing Parr's protest. "Oh stop

barking brownie. There were only three of them. And look at you, you're perfectly fine."

"Fine? Fine?! They are cannibals Cabyll! Cannibals!!"

Cabyll scoffed, not bothered. "You weren't in any danger." He paused, his finger tapping his chin in thought. "Well...maybe they would have eaten a few fingers. Only a few though I suspect."

Parr's mouth dropped open.

"A few fingers?! Why you insufferable-"

Dropping the walking stick, Lily jumped in between them. Ignoring the ache in her legs, she held out her hands to break them up. Parr grew larger, his eyes pitch black. She noticed a few times when Cabyll would get such a rise out of the brownie, Parr would begin to transform into something frightening. While he never fully transformed, she really did not want to find out what the mild-mannered brownie could become.

She took a deep breath, trying to keep her voice calm. She focused on Parr. "Relax guys. It's been a long day."

Parr, still annoyed and panting in anger, began to shrink down. He took a deep breath and held it a moment. When he calmed, he focused on Lily, his lips turned downward in a remorseful frown.

"Forgive me Miss Lil. It's that...that." He gestured towards Cabyll.

Cabyll smirked over her head. He gave Parr a 'what are you gonna do' look. Parr sputtered, outraged.

Lily turned, but Cabyll quickly turned his gaze away, rocking back and forth on his heels. She put her hands on Parr's small shoulders, smiling gently at the flustered brownie.

"I get it Parr. You don't have to say anything. Here." She reached up and grabbed an apple, handing it to him.

The apple was so large the brownie had to use both his hands to hold onto it without dropping.

She whispered playfully. "They say an apple a day will keep Cabyll away."

Parr snickered.

"I heard that." Cabyll smoothly called out over his shoulder.

Lily rolled her eyes, ignoring the smirk on his face. Instead, she mulled over what Parr had said. They had gotten into a strangely high number of mishaps that day. One or two setbacks is unlucky, but more than five was shady. Especially with how *great* a guide Cabyll claimed to be.

She bit her lip, a terrible thought creeping into her conscious. She glanced over at Cabyll, frowning. *He wouldn't.*

She narrowed her eyes at him. "Cabyll?"

"Hmmm?" He tilted his head, waiting.

No facial response? She raised her eyebrow, her suspicions growing even higher. "Are you leading us in circles?"

There was a beat of silence. Lily focused on his body language. If there was one thing she noticed about Cabyll was not to listen to him, but to observe. His jaw tightened slightly, his foot tapping to an irregular rhythm.

She clenched her hands at her sides, furious. *Yup...he would.* He saw her glare and put his hands up in a placating gesture.

"Now now human."

She glared as she spit out. "CABYLL?!"

He groaned, running his hand through his hair before responding, his tone matter of fact. "It was necessary."

"WHAT was necessary?"

Cabyll rolled his eyes. "You know what or else you wouldn't have asked."

"Um, excuse me." Parr interrupted as he walked up next to Lily, displaying an equally annoyed frown. "But how is leading us on a wild goose chase necessary!"

Cabyll softly growled, refusing to look at her. "It just was."

Lily threw her hands up in the air. "That's not an answer."

Cabyll crossed his arms, refusing to respond.

Parr and Lily both glared at him. When the silence became unbearable, finally, Cabyll's let his breath out in a whoosh.

He spread his arms, annoyed he broke the stalemate.

"Okay you got me! I was having us avoid the marsh alright? And every time, every bloody time, I got away from it, the wood would switch course to take us back there again." He raked his hand through his hair again, frustration evident. His eyes peered through the wavy mess, piercing. "So, I had us take a few detours."

Lily bit her lip, her concern obvious. He lowered his voice, trying to ease her fear. "Don't worry, we'll make it to the revel in time."

Lily remembered Cabyll and Aer's side conversation. "Is the marsh the fastest way to the revel, isn't it?"

Cabyll exhaled. "Yes, unfortunately."

Parr gripped the apple tightly. "So why didn't we go that way in the first place?"

Lily looked at Cabyll, concerned. While he appeared calm, his mouth had tightened, his lips slightly pinched. She remembered Aer mentioning the mysterious 'she', Lily took a risk. "Is there something or, someone you don't want to meet?"

If Lily hadn't been watching him closely, she would have missed the flicker of shock dance across his eyes. Quickly, his expression morphed into a suave grin.

"I am a popular guy. Too many admirers and we don't have time for that." He winked.

Lily rubbed her temples. *Yup, my concern for you went out the window.* Though she couldn't help the strange feeling after seeing the genuine shock and panic in his eyes. She was certain she didn't make that up, and it didn't escape her that he didn't answer the question.

She pressed. "Why aren't we going through the marsh Cabyll?"

He looked down, eyes growing cold. "The marsh is not the place a weak human like you would be able to handle. Going this way is safer, even if it is longer." His tone gave no further arguments. Lily continued to glare at him.

Parr rocked back on his heels. He coughed awkwardly.

"Okay...right then. How far away it is from this orchard?"

A lazy drawl echoed from the trees.

"I'd reckon it's about two clicks if you keep heading the way you were goin'."

Parr jumped and screamed like a little girl. Lily's eyes darted around the green branches but couldn't see anything.

Cabyll, unfazed, called out with a slight grin on his face.

"Hey old man! Show yourself."

Lily looked over at Cabyll, eyes wide. She blinked twice to make sure she wasn't imagining things. Cabyll was smiling. Like a genuine, honest to goodness, real grin. It was blinding.

"Who ya callin' old, pretty boy?" The voice joked good naturedly, a shadow darting through the branches.

A figure of a man appeared in the branches of the apple tree, lounging. The man laid on the sturdy branch, his leg propped up as he rested his head behind his hands. He looked a bit older, not too old, but not too young. A piece of grass was caught in between his teeth which he chewed noisily. He had a pleasant face, clean shaven, rugged. He sported a nose that looked like it was broken a time or two. He tapped his fingers on his bald head, grinning from ear to ear. He twirled a weathered tarp hat around his hands, his boot tapping the branch in a steady rhythm. What really caught Lily's eye was this fae was wearing jeans and a plaid shirt. This was the first time she was seeing familiar clothing. It was, quite frankly, very weird.

The man laughed, a full belly laugh, when a scowl darkened Cabyll's face at being called a 'pretty boy'. He unfurled his arms and lithely dropped onto the ground deftly twisting the cowboy hat onto his head with a flourish. He went up to Cabyll and gave him a big bear hug, slapping his back loudly with a thump. What surprised Lily the most was Cabyll wasn't shoving off the stranger like she expected. Instead, he returned the hug! Actually, Cabyll lightly tapped the guy on the shoulder, his body stiff as a board. But Cabyll was still allowing to be hugged.

The guy spoke loudly in a jovial tone, giving Cabyll one more hard thump on the back. "Cab, my man! Whatca doin around these parts?"

Cabyll let out an involuntary cough, the force of the blow forcing him to bend over. "We're headed to the river," he wheezed out, rubbing his chest.

The guy snorted. "Well I dang dong there guessed that. But whatca *doin'* here Cab?"

Parr coughed discreetly, gathering the attention of the rest of the group. "If I may...sir...we are-"

The man focused on Parr, chewing his blade of grass noisily. He spit it out at Parr's feet with an audible splat. Ignoring the brownie's gasp, he addressed Cabyll. "What's with the kid?" The guy jerked his thumb over at Parr.

Parr glared, red blotches on his cheeks. "Of all the - I am not a kid! Are you blind? I am a brownie, sir!" Parr blinked, appalled. "Uh...what I mean is...."

The guy shrugged, hooking his thumbs in his jean pockets. "Eh – brownie, kid, whatever. Speaking of brownies you know," he dismissed Parr again, smiling at Cabyll. "Did you know that humans make the most wonderful brownies. Their baked goods are pretty spectacular. They have cupcakes, cakes, and-"

"Sir!" Parr interjected. "I am NOT to be compared to a food group, thank you very much!" He took a deep breath, "I believe the question you had asked prior was that you wanted to know why we are here correct? Well, we are here to attend the Forest Prince's revel"

The newcomer finally centered his gaze at the fidgeting

brownie, everyone growing silent. The man whistled low while he scratched his chin. "Waaa? Prince Jacy? Y'all sure you wanna do that?"

Cabyll gave him a resigned look as he pointed to his neck. "No choice."

The man peered at the collar encasing Cabyll's neck and, after a moment, a huge grin slowly spread across his face.

Cabyll rolled his eyes. "Don't say it," he warned.

The newcomer laughed hard, slapping his knee in amusement. "Hooo weee doggies. You gone got yerself bamboozled! The great tracker and lightening fae himself. HA! Was it this here fella?" He pointed to Parr.

Cabyll face flushed in embarrassment.

Lily stepped forward, raising her hand hesitantly. "Um, it was me."

The man looked at her, eyes wide in astonishment. He pointed back and forth between her and Cabyll, his gaping mouth opening and closing. He remined Lily of a fish struggling to take a breath.

"You...you?!"

He had sputtered out the words, choking back laughter as his entire body started to shake. His lips split in a wide Cheshire catlike grin, watching Lily with eager eyes.

Lily nodded, unsure if he was asking rhetorically or not. The guy kept looking at her like he spotted a unicorn. Well, maybe that was a bad analogy. Maybe there were unicorns here. Lily had no idea. But the guy was starting to get on her nerves. She breathed a sigh of relief when he turned back at Cabyll who, Lily noticed, was grinding his teeth. The newcomer continued laughing.

"The great Cab...fooled...by a little human lady! Oh man! This is a GREAT story. I had this feelin' when I saw y'all walk by and heard your yappin. I said to myself, self, these folks have a story."

The man was laughing so hard he had thrown himself forward, clutching his knees as his whole body shook violently. Cabyll glowered, his eyes stormy. A small bolt of lightning zapped the man on his foot. The fae man jumped up and down, still laughing as tears began pouring down his face.

The man threw up his hands in surrender. He sucked in a breath, his chest heaving. "Now now Cab. Whew! Just give me a minute here. There's no need to throw a meaner tantrum than a two-dollar rattlesnake. I'm only messin' with you." The man wiped a tear from his eye, his body still quivering. Whether he was shaking from laughter or lightening Lily wasn't able to tell.

"Excuse me, but are you a friend of Cabyll's?" asked Lily.

"Oh where are my manners Miss."

The man bent forward and took her hand in a courtly gesture.

"The name's Randy darlin'. And I've known this grumpy fella over here for longer than a tortoise takes to finish a race. Ya might say I'm one of the few friends this rouge's got."

Lily chuckled, a grin tugging at her lips. "Nice to meet you Randy. I'm Lil."

Cabyll stomped over to them and smacked Randy's hand away from hers. "Enough of that – we have a river to get to."

Randy pouted. "Aww Cab, don't be like that. You might have a collar on ya, but at least you got it from this pretty little lady." He winked over at Lily. She shook her head, grinning. It was hard for her not to. Randy practically screamed the phrase, 'puppy dog look'.

"You said earlier the river isn't too far?" Lily wanted to make sure she heard correctly.

Randy nodded. "Yup! Just go forward two clicks and you should be good to go."

Cabyll lightly touched Lily's shoulder, steering her away from Randy. "Okay Randy. Then we'll be on our way."

Cabyll ushered with a shooing motion, urging them to move it along.

"Good luck!" Randy called out to them, sporting a lazy grin. He must have found a new blade of grass since a tall stalk magically appeared between his teeth again.

"Thank you!" Lily waved back to him.

Lily found herself grinning. It was refreshing to finally meet someone nice and helpful. *Soon,* she thought with relief. Soon they'd be at the river. Then, the revel. And after that? Her heart squeezed a little, trying not to be bogged down with speculations. Like, what was happening to Ari right now? Was she hurt? Was she scared? She saw the shadow of the river ahead when...

She blinked. She was standing back in the middle of the orchard.

Lily and Parr shared a glance, confused. It wasn't just they were back in the orchard. They were in the EXACT same spot they had left. Parr pointed ahead and behind him, his head bobbing back and forth.

Randy was still lazing in the tree, exactly where they left him, chewing his new blade of grass, his feet crossed over one another. He peered one eye at them, eyes flashing with mirth.

Cabyll watched Randy, a frown forming. He groaned in frustration.

Randy ignored him. "Y'all are back already?" he asked innocently. "How was the river?"

Cabyll growled as he gritted out. "Alright Randy. Enough games."

Randy waved his finger at them with a tsk. "Aww come on Cab. You can't blame me. Y'all are the most interesting story I've seen in decades. I couldn't let you walk away like that. I mean just you and the lady over here are a hoot and a holler. The little fella over there is simply a cherry on top."

"Cherry?" Parr asked astonished. He looked over at Lily concerned. "Is that a good thing? Or..."

Lily said nothing. She was trying to piece together what was going on. "What happened?"

Cabyll rumbled. "This old timer put us in a time loop."

Randy gave a delighted smile as he pinched his fingers together. "Tweaked it a *little* bit. Not a time loop per say, but it'll keep sending you back to this orchard no matter where you go. 'Fraid you won't be leaving anytime soon. Y'all are just too interesting."

He picked an apple, tossing it in the air.

Lily's eyes followed the bright red apple, her panic flaring. "But, I need to find my sister." Her voice wavered slightly.

Randy eyes narrowed at her, the apple landing deftly in his palm, a gleam flashing. His grin widened, his tone perking up.

"A sister huh? Why do you need to find your sister darlin'? She lost?"

Lily paused, uncertain. She glanced over at Cabyll and Parr. Cabyll shook his head silently in warning. Randy took note of their silent communication. He tossed the apple up again even higher.

Randy tsked, his hand over his heart. "Bless your heart darlin'. Look at you trying to be cautious and all. As you should be, of course. But," his eyes started to glow a bright yellow, swallowing up his irises, "that makes your story all the more exciting."

Lily heard a rumbling growl. Cabyll's eyes begin to glow as well, a brilliant green, as he gritted his teeth. Cabyll's voice deepened to a rumble, as if echoing from within his chest. "Spider... break this magic or-"

Randy's eyebrow shot up, unphased. "Or what Cab? You know when someone's stuck in my weave they can't get out unless I say so. And you're not asking politely."

Cabyll's hands curled inward, sparks flickering on his fingertips. He took a few steps forward, his aura menacing. "Keep talking nonsense. I can still turn you into a crispy bug."

Randy blinked. "Arachnids aren't bugs Cab," he deadpanned.

"Doesn't matter. They all fry the same." Cabyll taunted with a roguish smirk, the sparks making frightening shadows across his face.

As they continued their glowing eyed staring contest, Lily knew this could go sideways real fast. The tension was suffocating. Before she knew what she was doing, she found herself grabbing onto Cabyll's arm. He tensed, looking down, giving her an incredulous look. Lily couldn't blame him. She shook her head silently. Cabyll took a deep breath and slowly, his eyes started to fade to normal, the blue sparks extinguishing from his hand. When he calmed down, he pointedly looked down at her, motioning to his arm.

Lily jerked her hand back, focusing her attention to the other troublemaker. Said languid fae was leisurely passing the apple back and forth between his hands. His eyes weren't yellow anymore, but that didn't stop his schoolboy grin as he watched their exchange.

Lily walked up to Randy. "You say you're the only one that can break this." He nodded. "Then what do we have to do?" She quickly added, "Please?"

Randy grinned widely at her, the apple stopping in midair. "Woo! Darling, I do like you! See Cab why can't you be as polite as this wonderful lady here? She could teach you a thing or two about manners."

Cabyll's eyes burned a hole in her back, but she refused to look at him. She kept her focus on Randy.

Randy scratched his temple, deep in thought.

Suddenly, he snapped his fingers, eyes lighting up. "How about we play a little game?"

Parr jumped in excitedly, "Oh I do so love games. Cribbage, cricket, polo and the like. Oh, what a marvelous gentleman sport!"

"The who to the what now?" Randy scratched his head.

Parr's shoulder's slumped and Lily could hear him muttering the word 'savages'. Randy shrugged. "Well, it doesn't matter. Cause I'll be playing with the lady here."

"Wait me?" asked Lily.

Randy winked. "Of course! Gotta make it fair right?"

Lily frowned. *How is it fair when you are a magical being and I'm me?*

Cabyll groaned. "We'll never leave." He glared over at her. "She can't possibly win against you Randy! She's a weak human."

Okay that sounds more insulting when spoken out loud.

Randy patted Cabyll's shoulder. "Don't underestimate humans Cab." He gave Lily a side wink. "In my years, there ain't nothing weak about humans."

Cabyll scoffed. "You're getting soft old man."

Randy leaned over to pinch Cabyll's cheek. "Old man? The ladies and men still think this 'old man' is handsome ya know."

Cabyll smacked the hand away, glaring.

Lily cleared her throat, ignoring Cabyll's earlier jab. "What game would you like to play?"

Randy smirked as he sat back against the tree. He closed his eyes and hummed a minute. Lily paused, confused. Was that a showtune? After a few minutes, the humming slowed down, eventually stopping. He peaked at her, his eyes twinkling.

"I want a game of riddles," he said playfully.

"What?" she asked dumbfounded.

Cabyll scoffed. "You don't even know what a riddle is? We'll be stuck here forever!"

His arrogant tone made her bristle. "Of course I do! But riddles? Isn't that a bit cliché?"

Randy put a hand over his heart. "Ah! You wound me little

rabbit. It's a classic. Don't the fancy young folk like the old-fashioned games anymore?"

Lily rubbed her forehead, a headache beginning to form. *Little rabbit?*

"What are the stakes?" asked Cabyll with a raised brow.

"Well, since we have a human lady present, I'll make it simple. If you win little rabbit, you and your 'friends' will be able to leave the orchard. But, if I win." He paused.

Lily waited, anxious. He simply stared at her.

"If you win?" she asked.

He leered, showing off some slightly pointed teeth. Lily gulped nervously. Why hadn't she noticed those sharp teeth before?

He chuckled softly. "If I win, I can eat you."

Her mouth gaped open. "Seriously?"

Randy raised his hands, giving her an innocent look. "Can't be much simpler than that right? Plus, now I know you'll play with your whole heart, right? Cause no one wants to lose theirs." He snapped his teeth.

A cold shiver ran down her spine.

Parr chuckled nervously. "Oh, I'm sorry. I must be going mad. But I thought you said you would eat Miss Lil." He gave an awkward giggle. "But, that would be utterly absurd of course."

Cabyll sighed, exasperated. He shook his head at the clueless brownie.

Randy gave Parr a 'duh' look. "Um...yeah...that's what I said brownie. Eat, as in, 'Randy winner human dinner'." He looked over at Lily with a thoughtful expression. "I think you'd go good with a nice hard cider, not chianti. I'm not a fan of wine."

Cabyll rubbed the back of his neck. "Randy..." he warned. "That's a bit-"

Parr sputtered. "Now see here you neanderthal! You cannot eat Miss Lil!"

"Only if she loses. But she still has to agree to the game." Randy dismissed the brownie, his focus on Lily. "Whatca say darlin? You were smart enough to collar the best assassin in the Veil. I think you can handle a simple game of riddles."

Lily tried to process it all. Especially that little, teeny tiny detail about Cabyll's occupation settled in. *Assassin?*

Cabyll looked at her with an unwavering stare, hand still rested on the back of his neck. His face was blank, betraying no emotion. But it seemed like he was waiting for her to say something.

"So...an assassin huh?" she asked, her eyebrow raised.

Cabyll shrugged nonchalantly. "Yes."

"And you didn't mention that because..."

Cabyll crossed his arms over his chest, lifting his lip with slight smirk. "Why would I?"

She threw her hands up in the air. "I dunno! That may have been helpful information to know that my guide is an assassin." *Though why am I not surprised.*

He laughed coldly. "And that would make a difference how? My my, I didn't know you were interested in dangerous guys."

Lily glared, not amused. "Cabyll!"

He sighed, running his hand through his hair, suddenly serious. "Human you do not have to fear death from me." He pointed at the collar.

"It's Lil and you know it!" She gritted out.

Randy laughed, clapping his hands. "See! Now this is what I'm talking about! The drama, the anger, the quid pro quo." He got up and took both of her hands and gave them a slight squeeze. "So how about it darlin', wanna play?"

Parr pleaded with Cabyll. "You cannot seriously be okay with this! You promised she would be safe!"

Parr chewed his cheek while Cabyll remained impassive. The tension swallowed up the air. Cabyll met her eyes, but she still couldn't get a read on him. He stood there; his head tilted to the side with his hair hanging over his face.

Well, he wouldn't let something bad happen to me...right? He just said so.

Cabyll's deep voice interrupted her thoughts. "It's her choice to make. I cannot make it for her."

Normally, Lily would have considered that considerate. However, based on Cabyll's tense shoulders and Parr biting his nails, obviously this wasn't going to be as 'easy' as Randy was making it out to be.

She sighed, thinking of Ari. *Well, what choice do I have?*

Her gaze rested on Randy's thousand-watt smile. That smile which was so warm earlier was now chilling. Probably because he was nonchalantly talking about eating her. *And he seems not bothered at all about it,* she grimaced.

Resigned, she nodded. "Okay, it's a deal."

Randy lifted both their hands up over his head, giving a loud whoop. Dropping her hands, he grabbed the apple that was still hovering in the air and tossed it to Lily. She clumsily threw up her hands, barely catching the apple. Cabyll deftly plucked the apple from her hands, taking a large bite.

Randy spun around, snapping his fingers, looking at her eagerly.

"If there are four sheep, two dogs and one herds-men, how many feet are there?"

Oh...right to it then huh?

Lily put her fingers to her chin and thought. *Sheep, dog...*

"Two."

Randy gave her an approving smile. He motioned at her with his hands enthusiastically.

"Okay now darlin, your turn."

She pondered a moment. "What has many keys, but can't open a door?"

"Piano." Randy rolled his eyes. "Too easy, give me something harder next time alright? Hmmm...let's see. I am not alive, but I grow; I don't have lungs, but I need air; I don't have a mouth, but water kills me. What am I?"

Lily tapped her foot, thinking back. This one was familiar. She was certain she had heard it before. Tap, Tap, Tap.

"Fire."

"Good! Good golly I was right. I knew this game was for you." He smacked Cabyll's arm playfully. "She's good right?"

Cabyll didn't answer but rolled his eyes as he took another leisurely bite of apple.

Randy shrugged.

"Well?" He pressed when he saw her hesitate. "Don't stop now. Ask away!"

Think Lil, think. It was her turn, but she wasn't sure what to ask. She chewed her lip, concentrating.

"The more you take, the more you leave behind. What am I?"

Randy whistled a tune, putting his hands behind his head. "Hmmm...now lemme think about that one."

Lily felt a prickle of anticipation. Was he stumped? It was taking longer than the last time.

"Aha!" He wagged his finger at her laughing. "Footsteps. Am I right?"

Her breath whooshed out in disappointment. "Yes."

Randy clapped his hands together in glee. "Yee haw! That was a good one. Maaaan was that good. You almost got me there, like a rattlesnake with a roadrunner. Okay...now! You can see it every day but cannot touch it at will. What is it?"

See it every day but can't touch it. She bit her lip, her mind racing. *What is it, what is it?!*

"Um..." Her mind blanked. She tried not to panic, but she could see Parr's eyes widening. Even Cabyll seemed tense. He paused mid bite, watching her silently, which made her even more nervous. What could you see every day but can't touch? Her brain sped up, her thoughts starting to jumble together. Time was ticking by. Was there a timer on this? Randy eyes took an anticipated gleam watching her struggle.

"You stumped?" He started to whistle slowly, a dangerous glint in his eyes.

The melody was low and discordant. It reminded Lily of a tune played in a horror movie. Precisely at the point where the main character gets jumped by the killer. It was definitely not giving her any warm and fuzzy feelings that was for sure. She imagined whether he was dreaming of different ways to cook her. Roasted with a demi glaze? Perhaps baked with truffle shavings. She shuddered.

She adamantly shook her head, trying to focus. "Ah, no. I just need a moment."

"Not too much longer now little lark. You look greener than frog. And I do so looooove frog's legs." He ran his tongue over his lips, making an exaggerated smacking sound.

Lily felt her throat close up, bile burning down her esophagus. *Okay, stop thinking of Lil burgers. Think of this riddle. What can't you touch? Focus!* Of course, it didn't help seeing Randy licking his lips and rubbing his hands like he was about to go to the best buffet this side of the Hudson River. Her heart thumped faster, so hard it pulsed down to her fingertips. All her senses heightened; the sun was brighter, bird calls pierced her ears, even the sky was falling down on her.

Wait...

"Sky?" She whispered, afraid.

Randy's smile faltered, which made her confident. She repeated louder.

"Sky!"

Randy huffed, clearly unhappy. "Well aint that lucky of you darlin'. I can't wait to hear your next one."

Lily gave an audible sigh of relief. *That was close.*

Cabyll's shoulders relaxed. Parr's legs had given out as he sat sprawled on the dirt.

Her relief was short lived. Randy was patiently waiting for her next riddle, and she was running out of things to ask. Taking a deep breath, she tried to think of another riddle. Her father loved puzzles. He had told her hundreds over the years. *Think Lil. How hard is it to try to remember another little riddle?* She bit her lip. Apparently, it was very hard.

Come on! Dad wrote all these down and showed you...hold up...

"I am white when I'm dirty, and black when I am clean. What am I?"

Randy tiled his head to the side. He drummed his fingers on his legs.

"Well let's see." He paused. "A black swan? Wait no! Let me think here. A road with bird poop? Yeah, that's it! Am I right?"

There was a pause.

Lily grinned. "Nope."

Parr jumped up and clapped. "Well done Miss Lil. Well done indeed!" He marched up to Randy and wagged his finger at the tall fae. "And let that be a lesson to you sir that eating people is rude. Not appropriate behavior. Not...at...all."

Randy grinned, holding up his hands in surrender. "I yield darlin'. You can call off your brownie."

Much to Lily's surprise, Randy leaned over and clapped his hand on her back, laughing loudly. "I must say, that was quite thrilling. Yer sharp as a tack little lady."

Lily was shaking but managed to nod weakly. Whether it was from the back pounding or the nerves she didn't know. Her heart pounded as she wiped her forehead, her hand shaking and clammy. *Yup, definitely nerves.* She couldn't believe it. She won.

She barely heard Parr's exuberant cheering over her pounding ears. But she noticed Cabyll watching her with an approving grin. She rubbed her chest. What was this feeling? It may have been fleeting, but for a moment she felt she could do anything. She smacked her face lightly. *Wake up Lil!* What was she thinking?! This wasn't a time for a celebration or a pat on the back. They had to keep moving. She smoothed her clammy hands over her pants, hoping she could grasp some composure.

Cabyll must have noticed her shaking hands. Without a word, he walked in between her and Randy, blocking her view until all she saw was his back. He crossed his arms over his chest as he pressed. "Okay old man, you had your fun. Now, the river?"

Randy rolled his eyes. "Y'all are so impatient. I'm a being of my word after all."

Closing his eyes, Randy put his fingers together. With a snap, the wind picked up, the apple branches swaying in all directions. Something moved in the distance. The air itself shimmered and danced, particles darting back and forth. It grew and the particles began to resemble floating waves. They rippled and swelled until it pulled apart the air itself. Suddenly, the air ripped open and slightly beyond the orchard Lily could see a river. She blinked and rubbed her eyes, looking again. Yup, there was a river that wasn't there before. She glanced back at Randy who sported a haughty smirk.

"Told y'all it was two clicks." He moved towards the river.

"Hold it!" Cabyll held his hand out, smacking Randy's chest.

Randy stopped mid step. "Yes?"

Cabyll glared. "You're not coming."

Randy returned Cabyll's glare with a big grin, his pearly teeth blinding. "Of course I am Cab! I wouldn't miss this for the world."

Cabyll rubbed his hand over his face as he gritted his teeth. "There's no way to convince you not to come is there?"

Randy shook his head, his toothy grin wide.

Lily wasn't so keen on having Randy join them. Maybe it was because he wagered to eat her. She tried a different tactic. "We don't want to impose. I'm sure you have other things you'd prefer to do." Honestly, she couldn't imagine why he wanted to join them.

Randy looked at her as if she was an adorable puppy. To her surprise, he patted the top of her head, his fingers tangling through her curls softly.

"Bless yer heart darlin' you're so polite. But, being by your side...Well, this is exactly where I need to be."

His hand lifted off her head abruptly as he nimbly jumped away, narrowly avoiding Cabyll's fist. Randy's peal of laughter echoed in the trees. "Now now Cab, yer lookin' quite flustered my friend. Let's go everyone!"

Randy took off towards the river, the rest of the party following behind. Cabyll grumbled his displeasure the entire way. They reached their destination rather quickly, almost in no time at all. They had wasted so much time and for what? A game? Lily buried her frustration, trying not to dwell on the past. She needed to think about Ari. This was not the time or the place to indulge in her emotions.

The party reached the edge of the river as the sun began to set, the warm rays dipping down through the trees. Cabyll quickly scouted the area and said they needed to settle down for the night. The Bloody Caps had hunted that area recently, from the faint reddish hues that dotted the river rocks. Cabyll mentioned if they continued ahead, there was a high chance they would run into the deadly creatures, and he wanted to keep their distance. Lily paced as her anxiety scratched the surface.

Another day gone. How many are left? Three?

She walked away to have a minute alone. The river glistened in the sun's dying embers, its frothy current sweeping silently in the distance, dark as molasses. The bowed willow and swaying reeds danced around the gurgling brook. Translucent butterflies drifted over the patches of clover that blanketed the slippery rocks and cool earth surrounding the riverbank. Lily could smell the fresh, clean scent of green clover and wildflowers in the breeze. She leaned against her walking stick, taking a deep breath, letting the rumbling of the steady flow of the river calm her anxiety. A clear voice interrupted her fleeting solitude.

"The Ohneganohs river."

Randy stood next to her, staring down the river as it met the setting sun. They remained silent for a beat, both of them looking out towards the winding and twisting current. He wasn't looking at her, which made her a tad more comfortable and a little less nervous. Not by much, considering what happened the last few hours. Still facing the river, he spoke as if she asked a question.

"If you follow the river down that way," he pointed towards the sun, "you'll end up at the Susquehanna Bridge. Or as I call it the Oyster Bridge. Those darn fellas cling to the sides something fierce. Takes a lot to pry those morsels off. But, once you cross it, you'll be 'bout half a day walk from the revel."

"Really?"

Her hopeful gaze followed the winding river. Were they really that close? It seemed so far away, yet he made it sound so easy. It reminded her of every car ride she took to a new place. It seemed like it took forever to get there. It was even worse when you needed to get there quickly.

Randy nodded. "Yup, I reckon knowing how much a slave driver Cab is, you'd get there even faster."

He patted her shoulder lightly, giving her a kind smile. Lily tried not to flinch, but muscles tensed under his hand. Slowly backing up, she discreetly tried to put some distance between them.

He tilted his head to the side, gazing at her, concerned. He moved his hand away. "Hey, what's up with you? You're sweating like a whore in church."

Lily blinked a few times, warring between being flummoxed and insulted. "Um, that's...wait. Excuse me?"

Randy chuckled. "I mean to say you look nervous. More nervous than a dog that wouldn't bite a biscuit. What's goin' on in that pretty head of yours darlin?"

Lily furrowed her brows. *He's got to be kidding.*

But he wasn't. He stared with an openly curious gaze, not a hint of malice or mischief. He really was wondering why she'd be nervous. Resigned, she decided to tell him.

Hello, Captain Obvious!

"Well, you wanted to eat me."

Did or did she not have a game of riddles with him where the outcome was possible filet a' Lil?

Lily flinched, waiting for his reply.

He snorted, dismissing her with a wave of his hand. "Oh, that's why you're pitching such a hissy fit huh? Don't worry darlin' that was all hat, no cattle."

Lily took that in for a second. "What do you mean?"

Randy's nose crinkled. "I wasn't planning on eating you, you silly girl. No offense but humans are not something I prefer. Much too tough for my liking." He grimaced.

She chose to ignore the 'humans being too tough' comment.

"But you said in the bet that if you won, you'd eat me! Did you lie?"

"I didn't lie! Fae and the like of me can't." He put up his hands when he saw she didn't believe him. "I mean we physically cannot tell a lie. It hurts like the dickens. But that doesn't mean we can't twist and play with it. Just can't lie outright."

Lily frowned, not understanding. "But, if you weren't going to eat me and if you won..." She stopped when she saw his eyes twinkle.

"You said the magic word girl. You said...IF."

Lily stared at him, astonished. "You weren't planning on winning, were you?"

Randy winked. "I knew you were a smart one."

Lily pinched the bridge of her nose. "You lost on purpose!"

She was conflicted, but she couldn't understand why. She should have been happy Randy didn't want to eat her. And she was happy about that. But he let her win on purpose. Was she really not as smart as she thought?

Randy scratched the top of his head, wincing. "Darlin' you're hurtin' my heart when I see your face scrunched up like that. I wouldn't say I completely lost on purpose. You did almost have me there for a moment. Truth, scout's honor!" He held up his hand over his heart.

He noticed her glum expression and sighed. "Listen, I hate to admit it in front of Cab, but I am an old lark. Like, really old. So old that you'd be making 'my grandmas grandmas grandmas grandmas' jokes and not get to my grandma yet. Still handsome as the day is long, but-"

Lily grumbled. "Yeah you're old I get it."

Randy snorted. "Okay fair enough. But what I'm trying to say is well... I've been around the block. And not tryin' to toot my own horn or nuttin', but most folks, human *and* fae alike, aren't able to beat me at riddles. But you little lark. You did have me hesitating for a minute there. So be proud of yerself. You did well, and that's the honest truth." He reached out to ruffle her hair again.

Her lip quirked up in a grin.

Randy looked up at the sky, staring at the purplish wisps of stratus winding through the willows. "Can I let you in a secret?" She nodded as he continued. "There's only been one being who has ever really thrown me for a loop."

Lily followed his gaze to see what he was staring at, but only saw the purplish ink blots dotting the darkening canvas. "Who was that?"

Randy remained silent, as if in a trance, his hand still nestled in her curls. He shook himself, pulling his hand back. His goofy smile disappearing to reflect a somber expression. His eyes began to glow before he turned his back to her.

Not facing her, he muttered. "No one you ever want to meet."

He turned around, a small scowl in place as he said bitterly. "They would crush you like a bug beneath their feet just for the simple reason was because they could." His somber, angry tone shocked her.

Lily warily bit her lip. He was abnormally tense. "Sounds like someone pretty evil."

"Family...evil...in this immortal life is there a really a difference?" Randy replied cynically.

Lily kept her gaze on the blazing sky. "I think so. I don't believe it's as cut and dry like you made it sound."

Randy snorted. "Darlin' no offense but sounds like if you're here for your sister that y'all care about each other. Not so much with my family."

Lily paused and then said quietly. "I wouldn't say my step-sister and I are close."

The intensity of his stare burned a hole through the back of her head.

Lily gulped but continued. "Family may hurt you-" The words got stuck in her throat. "But, holding onto that hurt. Holding onto hate. It doesn't help anyone, least of all yourself."

Now practice what you preach, her inner voice scolded.

She sighed, rubbing her hair ribbon absently.

"My stepsister may not be my family by blood. But family is

more than that. I choose my family. We may not get along, but that doesn't mean we can't work things out."

Silence followed. Lily's face flamed. Did she sound foolish? A few minutes passed and Randy still didn't say a word. It wasn't long before her stomach growled, breaking the stillness. He cleared his throat, glancing at her awkwardly.

"Well darlin', sounds like your insides are gonna hurt if you don't eat. Speaking of eating, I wanna see for myself what that brownie's cooking." He gave her a playful nudge, his dandyish air returned.

He cupped his mouth near her ear as he whispered loudly. "Oh, and don't tell Cab that I lost on purpose. He was prickled like a cactus when he thought you were gonna be dinner. Let me tell you that was a hoot and a holler. Seeing his face all ruffled. Ha! But, if he knew the truth, he'd probably zap me six ways to Sunday for scaring you."

With a parting wink, he walked back towards a cluster of willows where Parr started a fire, whistling as he went. Lily was alone again, the river keeping her company. The sun started to turn crimson and indigo, the twilight burning out slowly. Lily squinted, trying to make out a faint outline over the river.

That must be the bridge.

If they rested tonight, by her calculations they could make the bridge, cross over, and make it to the revel with time to spare. Maybe? Even though it seemed far away, maybe it was quicker to return home once she found Ari. Right? She'd be home with Ari before their parents would be back. They just had to be.

Ari. Lily closed her eyes, her chest hurting. Was she okay?

What was Ari going through in the Veil? Was it anything like her experience? She winced. She had to find Ari as soon as possible. Lily had no doubt why Ari went with him willingly. The prince was probably gorgeous, judging by the fae she encountered already. Most of the fae were otherworldly beautiful, but it hid how dangerous they were. Speak of the fae, one of those handsome devils was heading her way now, much to her chagrin.

"Come on human, stop staring into the clouds. Time to eat!" Cabyll shouted over the rushing water. With an impatient wave he strode back to their small campfire. Lily suspected he was still cross with Randy, if the boisterous laughter and angry barking drifting on the wind was any indication.

Reluctantly she came back and was greeted by a crackling fire. Lily sat down on the cold, soggy earth, reaching out to warm her hands by the flames. She tried to ignore the dampness that seeped into her jeans, but it was difficult. Parr handed her a bowl of stew, which she took gratefully. She was starving! He beamed as she devoured the entire bowl of roasted vegetable stew. Cabyll and Randy were already digging into their meals.

They all ate in comfortable silence, dusk settling in. Parr fussed here and there, making sure everyone had a full plate and equally full bellies. Randy slurping noisily, broth running down his chin. Even Cabyll, ever keeping a watchful over the camp, gave off an air of contentment as he sipped his stew. Smiling to herself at their rag tag band, Lily allowed herself to enjoy the camaraderie for the moment.

And a fleeting moment it was. And it was gone in a flash when Cabyll moved to sit down beside her. He deliberately coughed, trying to gain her attention. She bristled, forcing herself to ignore him as she continued to eat. Honestly, it was hard not to notice him. One, his presence alone was overwhelming. Two, he still smelled of sea and rain, which was distinctly different from the damp mossy musk surrounding them. Lily kept her head down, wondering if he would leave her alone if she kept ignoring him. But, in typical Cabyll fashion, he leaned over as he whispered condescendingly.

"You look like you're having a fine time."

She jerked her head up, glaring. Her spoon clanked against the bowl. "Excuse me? A quiet moment doesn't equate to a 'fine time'."

Cabyll clucked his tongue, his arm draped casually over his knee. "True...but I wonder what that sister of yours is doing right now? Think she's having a grand time? Do you think she's eating good food and dancing the night away?"

The remaining soup turned to ash in her mouth. It stuck in a lump in her throat, making her unable to swallow. Her throat burned; her face flushed in shame. She bit her lip, staring into her half empty bowl. Suddenly she didn't feel hungry anymore, putting the bowl aside.

Cabyll noticed her silence. He cleared his throat. "Well...um... so the riddle game. Never thought a human could be so reckless."

Lily refused to answer, wrapping her arms around herself.

Cabyll frowned slightly. "What's with the silence? You were confident enough you'd win that riddle game and suddenly you can't answer a simple question?"

She glanced up, eyes widening. "Confident? I was terrified!

What if I had lost?!" Granted Randy told her that wouldn't happen earlier, but she didn't know it at the time.

He raised his eyebrow, leaning back against the tree, his legs sprawled out lazily. Ever the picture of cool flippancy. "I would have figured something out."

"Like what?"

"I said..." He said slowly, pursing his lips. "I had it under control."

"Uh huh..."

He bent his leg, his elbow resting casually over it, his arm draped towards the earth. His fingers toyed aimlessly in the dirt while he stared at her. His green eyes glowed lightly in the fire-light. Lily knew those glowing eyes for what they were. Not human.

"You would have been alive human. I am to protect you. Remember?" He gave her a roguish grin.

She stopped herself from rolling her eyes towards the heavens. *He really must think I'm an idiot. What a great choice of words, 'Would have'.* It would be fine and dandy if she was missing an arm or a leg as long as she was alive. *Gosh how grateful I should be because I am alive. What's a missing limb or two? But no worries Lil, the big bad water horse would protect you from certain death,* she thought sarcastically. *You'd just be a paraplegic...a minor setback. Nothing to worry at all, cause he had it 'handled'.* She repressed her disgusted groan, trying to focus.

"Regardless of what you would or would not have done. The facts are that I'm alive because I won. And the only reason why you would have done anything would be because of that." She gestured towards the collar. "Am I right?"

Cabyll blinked, rubbing his neck, his fingers toying with the smooth metal. His other hand trailed figures in the dirt. He peered at her through dark lashes, his eyes reflecting the firelight. He tilted his head as his dark hair fell over his face.

"It's true. The collar does make sure I protect you. But," He paused a heartbeat, his lips quirking upward in a boyish smirk. "Maybe I would have stepped in for another reason. After all, you are...unexpected."

This time Lily couldn't hide her embarrassment. She smacked her palm flatly on her face. The loud crack reverberated in the dark, probably startling everyone, but at this point she didn't care. She ignored the sting on her face as she kept her palm over her eyes, blocking out what she assumed was another annoying smug expression on his face. But curiosity got the better of her and she peeked between her fingers. Sure enough, Cabyll was sporting a self-satisfied grin that was dripping with one hundred percent male ego. He looked positively thrilled.

That smug faced, pretty boy, she inwardly growled.

Her chest burned hotter than her flaming face. She was tired. Emotionally, physically, mentally, you name it. Just plain tired. And annoyed. She couldn't ignore the rising irritation which tangled inside her chest. And right in the center of this frustration was smirking right in front of her.

"Okay! That's enough! I need a minute!" She jumped to her feet, knocking her stew on the ground. Vaguely she told herself she should apologize to Parr for wasting food, but that inner voice was nothing but a faint whisper as the blood rushed in her ears.

Parr and Randy looked up, shocked, as she stomped towards the river. She thought she faintly heard Randy say something akin to 'oh this is getting gooood', but she was beyond the point of caring. Her heartbeat thumped in her ears, drowning everything out. Was she really an amusement to these people/fae/whatever? She didn't know why it angered her so much, but it did. She was someone, darn it! Someone to be treated seriously, with respect.

When her mind cleared, she found herself standing back on the bank of the river, blankly staring at the dark current. She struggled to listen to the soothing melody of the river, but the roaring in her temples drowned it out. Taking a few breaths, she heard it, over the pounding in her head. The voice that was the source of elevating her blood pressure. The deep voice scratched her ears with its droll amusement.

"Little human...you okay?"

She whipped around, tense. Cabyll looked at her, worried. Which definitely had to be fake because of that awfully arrogant tone. Oh, sure at first glance one would think the furrow in his brows displayed genuine concern, but she knew better. Nothing but smoke screen and mirrors. A very good acting gig if she ever saw one.

Lily simply stared at him, unmoving. Inside, she was struggling desperately to grasp the last bit of decorum she had left. She wanted nothing more than to throw him in the river. *Keep calm Lil, just remain calm.*

Oblivious, he had the nerve to wink at her. "You're embarrassed." He snapped his fingers, his eyes twinkling as his full lips stretched in a grin. "That's it! I know a handsome fae like me can be overwhelming."

Lily's mouth gaped open. She shook her head as she stuttered out. "It's...it's not that. Cabyll you really need to-"

Cabyll chuckled softly, cutting her off. His shoulders shook with laughter as he looked at her with mock pity. "It's okay human. There's no need to be nervous." He ran his hand through his hair. "Attracting females is what I do. You can't help but fall for me eventually. Look, I'll do you a favor since we're bonding over this little adventure. I'll be your perfect guy. Anything you want, name it and it's yours! But, for one day only. I just want a little itty-bitty favor in exchange."

Her eye twitched. *Don't say it jerk...*

Before she could respond, he leaned forward slowly until he towered over her, the smug expression still plastered on his face. "The collar. You know you want to take this off of me."

She blinked. Seriously? Was there something she could hit him with? With regret she realized she left the walking stick back at the fire. Her hands clenched the air. Did he really think she was stupid? "Cabyll, I really think you are misunderstanding..."

Ignoring her, Cabyll bent down until his breath fanned her face.

Lily stopped herself from knocking him back with a roundhouse kick. *Patience Lil. Keep calm. Your sanity is a precious thing.* She ground her teeth, trying to find the words to reply when...

She froze, even her heart seemed to stop momentarily. Somehow, he had learned down far enough that his cheek brushed next to hers. He whispered in her ear, his breath tickling her hair.

"Besides, your sister left willingly, right? I bet she's having the time of her life at this moment. She probably doesn't even want you coming for her. We both know she doesn't even like you. So why don't you take this time and have a little fun? Just say you couldn't find her and let it go."

Her jaw dropped with a snap. Her stomach clenched as she tried to ignore the pain in her chest. Instead, she focused on the kernel of anger rising to the surface. She couldn't deal with the other emotion that churned her gut. But anger? Anger she could work with.

Of all the insufferable, arrogant...

Brain loading...ERROR... ERROR...REBOOTING

"...Pigheaded, pompous, actions this is the worst! Seriously, how many times are you going to play that stupid card?! You may think you're a Don Juan or whatever, but KNOCK...IT...OFF!"

Yup, goodbye sanity...Arrivederci...I wish you well.

Cabyll stepped back, putting his hands out to her in a placating gesture, his suave smile still in place. "Oh, come now. Don't be like that little water lily."

Did he seriously try to play a feeble cutesy word game with her name? This guy couldn't take a hint. Did he deliberately play stupid or did he clearly not understand?

"You...are...*pazzo*! Absolutely insane!"

He waggled his brows, his pearly whites gleaming. "You say crazy, but I've been told some women like a little crazy."

Lily groaned, putting her face in her hands. "Ugh! No, no, no, no, no! I do not want to know! Please for goodness sakes can't you go bother one of them!"

He laughed and pretended to wipe a tear from his eye. "Aww, you don't mean that. You'd miss me too much human."

She kept her face covered, refusing to look at that him a moment longer. She groused out, her voice muffled. "Your arrogance is overwhelming. Why are you wasting so much time when you know I won't... Wait!" She paused, peering at him suspiciously through her fingers. "You're doing it again. Why are you pushing this?"

Cabyll's smirk slowly evaporated, his laughter dying. He stared at her, all hint of his earlier playfulness gone. His eyes were dark, swallowing up her gaze, a familiar fog creeping in.

"I don't know what you mean. I don't think you do either," he said slowly.

She glared at him, wishing again she had the walking stick to smack him on the noggin. Too bad she left it where she sat by the fire. "Knock off the glamour!"

Cabyll's eyes widened as he took a small step back. Lily breathed, her mind clearing.

She pointed her finger at him accusingly. "That's it! When you were talking to Aer about losing time! This has to be about why your sweet talking me with all this nonsense am I right?!"

His eyes narrowed at her. "Hold on. You heard me talking to Aer? What did you hear?" He asked suspiciously, a dangerous glint in his eye.

Lily threw up her hands, ignoring his tone. "Of course I heard you! And now it's clear what he meant. You really are a bumblefoot! You were talking about doing everything possible to get that stupid collar off!"

"Bumblefoot?!" Surprise etched on his face.

Lily glared. Did he really think she was a moron? "Honestly, did you really think those lines would work? I mean, seriously, it's so much worse than any ridiculously cheesy teenage romance movie."

He shook his head, frowning. "You believe the collar..." He paused a moment, his brows creased. "Wait a minute. I have you know I do *not* give cheesy lines."

Lily rolled her eyes. "Are you kidding?! You memorized every cheesy line known in existence! You might as well be called Cheesy Cabyll!"

"Watch it Lily," he growled.

She refused to acknowledge the slightly happy feeling of hearing her name. "I don't know whether you would be considered swiss cause your lines are full of holes or limburger cause you just reek!" She could have sworn she heard herself growl right back. "Do us both a favor and admit it already."

He narrowed his eyes, his arms crossed over his chest. "Admit what?"

"This..." She gestured between them. "The whole smirking, flirty thing you're doing. Can you please just admit it's all fake so we can move on already. Frankly, it's exhausting. I have more important issues to focus on. Like getting Ari back."

"Why would you think it's an act? Fae have been taking humans to our realm for centuries. And you are intriguing." He ruffled his hair. "In your own mortal way. Humans are colorful wisps of smoke. Poof!" He snapped his fingers with a lethal grin. "And you're gone."

She gritted her teeth. "There! Right there! All those thinly veiled insults wrapped in pretty words." She was elated by his shocked expression. Finally, that infuriatingly pompous expression disappeared.

"You can't stand humans. Don't think I can't notice every time you give that grin that you're putting on a show." She jabbed her finger at him, glaring. "You are a pretentious, dramatic, showy-"

"Oh fine." He rolled his eyes, his voice dripping with disdain. "Is that what you want to hear Lily? It was an act? That you were right? I wouldn't insult a beautiful fae with the dribble I have been forced to spew." He glared down at her, his glacial eyes spearing daggers in her chest.

Lily threw her arms up in the air. "Then why in the world did you bother?!"

He glanced at her, the roguish grin he was sporting earlier transformed into a cruel smirk, devoid of any compassion.

He sneered. "You know why I say those 'cheesy' lines as you call them Lily? Cause humans are so foolish they would believe anything as long as it's coming from a pretty face showering them with attention."

Lily gasped. "Excuse me?!"

"It worked for your sister didn't it?" He raised his eyebrow. "Like I said, humans are foolish."

She gritted out. "Don't talk about her like that!"

"Why not? She's off having fun. She probably wouldn't care

about everything you've gone through. You almost died and she probably hasn't even thought about you once."

Lily bit her lip, hugging herself. "How dare you! Barlow was right about you! You're nothing but a prancing pony! Pretty face my boot!"

She stomped her foot down, barely missing his toes. He jumped with an astonished yelp.

Quickly, he got right in her face, his voice gritty as he growled softly. "Say that again. I dare you..."

By this point, Lily began to feel the teensiest bit of a warning tickle the back of her mind. But she swatted it away. Her anger was boiling over and wouldn't be stopped. She stood up on her tip toes to be as close to eye level as she could. Which was quite diffi-cult as even standing on her tippy toes her head barely reached his shoulder. But that didn't stop her from leaning in and jabbing her finger hard into his chest.

"Little...prancing...pony." She clenched her teeth as her finger poked his chest with each word.

Cabyll's eyes widened, shocked. His shoulders tensed a beat before he let out a deafening roar that echoed across the river. Lily felt the electrified current spark in the air as blue electricity crackled around his clenched hands. Her body tingled and she could have sworn her hair was rising from the static, but she refused to break eye contact to check.

Now at this particular moment, the rational, mature part of Lily's brain knew she should duck and cover. Maybe try to smooth things over. Apologize perhaps? After all who wants to be BBQ human. Certainly not her. But rational, responsible Lily had gone out the window. More like bungee jumped out and was free falling. What replaced calm and collected Lily was her 'I don't give a flying toot' doppelganger who happened to stand – toe to toe – as Cabyll held back his fury.

"Lily…" He ground out slowly, his chest vibrating against her finger. "You are the most-"

"Oh, I can't WAIT to hear this one." She interrupted, finger still stabbing into his sternum.

If Cabyll's eyes could widen any further, they did, his eyes almost completely green as they got brighter. His body shook harder. "Why you *little-*"

A sharp whistle cut into the argument. Lily and Cabyll both turned their heads to see Randy sitting high in the weeping willow.

Randy removed his fingers from his mouth, cutting off the whistle with an audible snap. "Well now kids. Normally I'd *hate* to break up this shin dig. Especially cause it was getting to the really good part-"

Cabyll scowled. "Stay out of this spider! I'm warning you."

Randy huffed. "Well yeah that was the plan. Didn't you hear me just now that I didn't wanna interrupt? But darn it Cab you don't listen do ya. Because…" He paused and pointed towards the river. "I think we got company."

Lily, her finger still pushing hard against Cabyll's chest, slowly followed where Randy was pointing. Cabyll's gaze followed hers. The dark current swirled and frothed in a manic fashion. It twisted and rumbled, reminding Lily of a winding snake as it seemed to curl in on itself. Her mouth opened, gaping like a fish, as the water level rose, the twisting and frothing motion continuing, until she found herself face to face with a silo of water. It towered over them, blocking out the moon, droplets cascading down onto the embankment. To her surprise, the water drops hissed and simmered as they hit the ground.

Wait...there is a hole in the ground. Why did the water make a hole?!

And that was when she noticed it. The previously fresh, crisp air surrounding the waves soured. A brackish, fetid stench emanated from the growing cyclone. *Oh my god...it's acid...*she thought in a panic. She turned to Cabyll, who happened to look at her with the same open-mouthed expression.

"Don't tell me-" he whispered.

A rock sank to the bottom of her stomach. Up until this point, she had never seen Cabyll look afraid. The fact his porcelain complexion was ashen, his pupils swallowed up his eyes, decimated any feelings of reassurance Lily tried to give herself.

Randy called out sarcastically. "Yuuuup. Y'all woke Iya. Good job there slick. Taunt the lady some more. Yell at her more for all the good it did ya."

"Yeah yeah I get it Randy," muttered Cabyll.

Parr squeaked behind them, arms laden with their supplies. "Um...pardon. But considering how loud the two of you were, well, I suggest that you two kindly put your differences aside for the time being, so we move away from the disease demon. Very far away if you please."

Lily kept staring at the writhing water. *Disease demon?* The wall of putrid liquid was growing larger by the minute, but try as she might, she couldn't see anything past the rushing waves. She was frozen, her limbs heavy.

"Lily-"

Her blood pounded in her ears. She turned when Cabyll called out for her, the sound dulled through the rushing in her head. He stared at the water like it was a snake ready to strike. Their fight forgotten, he gingerly reached out his hand to her as he slowly backed up.

"Lily." He repeated her name quietly. "Take my hand. Slowly, we need to get out of here."

She turned to hear the droplets falling faster, the hissing and sulfur smell getting more poignant in the air. She peered into the raging currents, a shadowy outline lurking behind the wet curtain.

"Don't look at him!" Cabyll whispered frantically, trying to catch her attention.

Lily limbs were unable to move. If blood could freeze, her veins would have iced up. She tried to shut her eyes but realized she couldn't. She stood still, transfixed, at the Iya. Some type of invisible weight held her in place. It was utterly terrifying. Words couldn't even describe it, but Lily knew she'd have nightmares for years about what she saw behind the glistening depths.

"Don't breathe it in!" Cabyll snapped, breaking her trance as he forced her to look back at him. "It's poison. We have to leave. Now!"

"Miss Lil. Please! There is no time, he's moving over the bank," cried Parr.

Sure enough, the water tornado started moving out of the

river, towards them. It started to pick up speed, swirling faster and faster. The ground became bare where the water had splashed down. Lily realized, in horror, that it was indeed poison.

"Please Lily!" Cabyll begged.

It was the desperate tone that snapped her out of it. She looked into his eyes as he gazed at her, frantically pleading with her to follow him. His outstretched arm shook, his fingers grasping towards hers.

Lily heard the howling of the funnel behind her, her hair whipping around her face. Adrenaline and determination thawed her frozen state as she put her hand out, clasping his cold fingers. As soon as their hands touched, a thunderous roar made the ground tremble.

Cabyll cursed. "*Aigo...*"

He yanked her towards him the same moment the water tendrils reached out towards Lily. Cabyll, clutching her, took off like a rocket. The ground shook as the Iya chased after them, the rotten sulfur rank in the air. Lily felt, rather than saw, the rest of the group running with her. Randy was jumping tree branches in a blur. Cabyll pushed them onward in a sprint, holding tightly to her hand. Parr kept popping in and out as fast as he could go.

Parr yelled out. "Cabyll! You're supposed to be this awesome fighter! Can't you do something?"

Cabyll grunted. "Like what?"

"Oh, I don't know! You have a sword for pity's sake!"

"A sword against acid? Why didn't I think of that?" Cabyll quipped, rolling his eyes.

Still gripping tightly to Lily, Cabyll spun around. In one

smooth motion, he pulled out a dagger and threw it at the Iya. His aim was perfect. The dagger spun in the air, hitting the water. However, when the dagger passed through the wall of water, a hiss echoed in the trees, and the dagger disappeared. Cabyll glared up at the brownie.

"That's why oh smart one!"

Parr, face paling, nodded mutely. They picked up the pace, the Iya closing in.

Lily struggled to keep up. She ran and ran until her chest burned and her arm hurt from Cabyll's vice like grip. He refused to let her go. She flinched as the wind whipped her hair around. Strands smacked her face, the small stings hitting her eyes, temporarily blinding her. Her legs pumped so hard they went numb, but she kept running. She ran so fast that she couldn't avoid the wayward branches above her head. She winced as a few caught her cheek, a burning bite that began to throb. She willed her legs to go faster as the frightening roar of the Iya against the cold damp air churned around her. It wasn't until she her legs became jelly that they gave out. She tripped over a branch, her hand wrenched out of Cabyll's grasp. Cabyll spun around, his eyes wide.

"Come on, you gotta get up." He reached towards her. He frantically looked back, his face paling. "Hurry Lily!"

Lily panted; her breath strained. "I'm trying...my legs-" Her voice died when she saw the Iya was almost upon them.

She trembled. "Cabyll...."

Cabyll gritted his teeth. "Hold on!"

Next thing Lily knew, an electric charge crackled in the air. A large bolt of lightning hit the Iya. It screamed in anger, vines of water splashing out against the trees. Lily's eyes widened in fear at the hissing of acid, blackened dying pieces of branches fell to the ground near her foot. She scrambled back on the ground, staying far away from the water. Thankfully, the acid didn't move further. The Iya paused momentarily, shaking itself from the attack.

A loud neigh echoed in the trees. Cabyll had transformed into his horse form. He whinnied frantically and nudged her to get on his back. Problem was, he was too big. She couldn't find a way up. As she tried to gain purchase, hands effortlessly lifted her and, with no ceremony, promptly plopped her on the horse's back. Randy grabbed her fingers and guided them to the mane, making sure she had a steady grip.

"Hold on tight darlin'. Time to get a move on, and this ride's not gonna be smooth. That zap won't stop him for long,"

Randy jerked his thumb toward the whirling vortex behind them. He put his fingers up in a salute and promptly jumped back to the trees in a blink of an eye as he hollered back at them. "Cab – time to lit outta here as fast as you can!"

Cabyll nodded, needing no more encouragement. When a shake of his mane and a loud neigh, he took off with a jolt. It was so abrupt Lily almost fell off. She scrambled to grab hold and clasped on for dear life as he galloped down the path. The trees whizzed past her eyes. She could vaguely make out her companions keeping up with them, surprisingly. The icy breath of the Iya tickled the back of her neck. The disease demon yowled, tearing through the forest having regained momentum. And the demon was angry.

"Don't look back!" Randy yelled from above the treetops.

Of course, Lily did the opposite. She glanced back, clinging to Cabyll's silky mane desperately, unbalanced from vague twinges of vertigo. The Iya tore through the forest, the water mass smashing trees, uprooting rocks and roots. Nothing escaped the Iya's wrath as it devoured everything in its path. The demon moved with a single-minded focus, showing no signs of slowing down.

Dread creeped up her spine. It was catching up! Even though Cabyll was going unnaturally fast. Her gaze darted back in front of her. She reared back, panicked. They were heading towards the edge of a cliff. Cabyll kept moving, hooves digging into the earth. What was he thinking?! She couldn't see how far the drop was, but she could tell that it was definitely not a short fall.

Her heart dropped into her stomach when she realized Cabyll was not slowing down. The edge of the cliff grew closer and closer as he gained speed. She saw Randy jump off the ledge with ease. Parr blinked out.

"Cabyll-" She squeaked; her tongue stuck in her throat. Trembling, she buried her face in his neck, squeezing her eyes shut, her knuckles tightening around his mane. Her heart pounded loudly in her ears. She could feel Cabyll's muscles tense, preparing to jump. She yelled out.

"If I die, I'm going to haunt you!"

Her eyes opened the moment Cabyll lifted them into the air. Lily ducked as a water tendril lashed out, barely missing her head.

Cabyll soared through the air and...for a moment...Lily felt the weightless thrill of flying. Until gravity took control, pushing them downwards toward the awaiting ground. The wind, cleared from the astringent acid, bit her face. She couldn't even scream because of the pressure bearing down on her, freezing her cry. All Lily could do was desperately hang on to Cabyll and pray she didn't lose her grip. She tensed, waiting for the inevitable agony of smashing into the ground. But, it never came. Miraculously, the wind ceased, and the falling sensation in her belly subsided.

Lily waited, her heartbeat pounding in her ears. When it calmed down, the only thing she could hear was silence. Hesitant, she cracked one eyelid open. Cabyll, still a horse, was standing firmly on the ground, unhurt. She tried to lift herself off him, but it proved difficult when her limbs shook and wobbled. Shock hit her, causing her body shake uncontrollably. She tightened her arms around his neck to remain upright. She heard him shift, giving her a soft whinny. In the back of her mind, she thought he sounded concerned, that is if she wasn't focused on not passing out from shock.

Deep breaths girl...keep breathing.

After a few deep, purging breaths, she slowly lifted her head. Feeling steadier, she slid off the horse's back, looking up the cliff they had jumped from. She almost passed out again. It was high. And by high, it was ridiculously high. Lily couldn't believe it. How did they get down here and not become flat as a pancake? She wrinkled her nose. *Remember Lil, magic horse...duh.*

Cabyll sighed behind her, his horse form disappearing into the mist. He raked his hand through his already tousled hair, following her gaze. She could hear the faint roaring of the Iya above. Letting out a relieved breath, Cabyll turned his gaze away, dismissing the demon as it bellowed in anger at them. Lily couldn't stop the shudder that ran through her body. She jumped, startled, when a voice called out.

"It's alright girl. Ol' Iya hates this place, he won't follow." Randy dusted off his shirt with his hat. His brow furrowed, concerned. "You okay girl?"

Lily panted. "I'm fine...just...getting back my legs." She hoped her trembling hands weren't noticeable. Randy looked down at her and patted her shoulder gently, his eyes kind. If felt strangely comforting and her tremors subsided.

Randy gave a half grin. "Girl, I've known full grown fae tremble when Iya would get even slightly annoyed. Y'all managed to get him madder than a wet hen. There's no shame in being a little rattled."

"That's right!" Parr patted himself off, clouds of reddish dust and leaves swirled around him. He looked at her with admiring eyes. "It took great courage to trust that ruffian over there to carry you over the cliff. Quite the bang up to the elephant I must say Miss Lil. Perfect indeed. I am in awe of your bricky fortitude. It is only natural you'd be in some state of shock. Not to worry, we're here!" Parr beamed at her.

Cabyll scoffed, rolling his eyes at the brownie. He turned to her with an inscrutable look. "I must admit, not many fae, let alone a human, could have stared at Iya without dying on the spot in terror." He tugged his lip between his teeth before glancing away. His focus remained on the landscape before them, but not before she heard him mutter reluctantly. "Pretty impressive indeed..."

Lily smiled, her teeth still chattering from the left-over adrenaline kicking through her system. She had to admit, save for the whole "almost dying part" ...again.... she actually was relieved. For a second, just a second, she didn't have to worry about taking care of someone else. She didn't have to make sure everyone else was okay. She didn't have to be the strong one, the responsible one. Instead, these people she had only known a few days were making sure she was okay. And not only that, but they were telling her it was okay to not be okay. When was the last time she felt that? Yes, almost dying from a disease monster with acid water was going to give her nightmares for a long time to come. But, for that moment, she was truly grateful for this motley crazy crew.

She took a deep breath, pulling in a new sense of confidence as she surveyed their surroundings. Her feet sunk into the soft earth. Mossy pathways wound through patches of brackish shallow water. They had entered the marshland. The grassy desolate wasteland was extensive, brownish grey tendrils of mist emanated from the sulfuric water surrounding them. Reedy marshes swayed in the light breeze as stagnant green water plopped and gurgled underneath their feet. Lily got a whiff of the swampy salt air, the humid breeze causing her curls to stick to her neck. She looked over at Cabyll, who was sporting a resigned expression.

She already knew the answer but asked anyway. "We're in the marsh, aren't we?"

"What was your first clue?" Cabyll's sarcasm was hard to miss.

And there's my answer. Lily sighed.

"Since we're here, care to share now?"

Silence.

She frowned, noticing since the danger was gone, he was back to being prickly. *Well, I said I didn't want the fake flirty Cabyll.*

Lily opened her mouth when Randy's hand patted her shoulder. He shifted to her side. His playful eyes, directed at Cabyll, were cold, even as his warm hand seemed gentle.

Randy wagged his finger at Cabyll, reminding Lily of a parent scolding a child. "Look Cab, I know your madder than a bee in a hornet's nest, but right now we're caught in two different buckets of possums." He pointed upward. The Iya was still looking down at them, acid droplets sizzling off the cliff. She imagined if walls of acid water could glare, that's what it was currently doing at them.

Parr wrung his hands together. "So...what shall we do now?"

Lily peered at Cabyll, crossing her arms over her chest. "Seems like there's no other way. You said this is the quickest way to the revel."

Cabyll rubbed the back of his neck and sighed, resigned. "Yes. The marsh is the quickest way."

Randy raised his eyebrow. "You sure Cab? Like really sure?"

Lily watched the two of them exchange a glance.

Cabyll was quiet, furtively glancing over at Lily. He finally gave Randy a nod. They shared another look that made Lily furrow her brows. What was it about the marsh that Cabyll didn't want to venture in? She was about to ask when Randy tucked her walking stick in her numb hand and steered her around, turning her away from the cliff.

"Alright folks, let's get a move on. The revel won't be waiting for us to arrive now, will it?" Randy called out in a sing-song voice.

"Can we get some sleep at least? I am terribly exhausted." Parr complained, lugging the provisions over his little shoulder.

Randy whistled. "We will little brownie. Once we put some distance from the old coot up there." The Iya roared again in answer.

Randy pushed her forward with Parr in tow. Lily glanced back over her shoulder to find Cabyll not moving, unfocused, sporting a dark somber expression on his face. A trickle of unease ran down her spine. Even when he was angry or annoyed, there was always an undercurrent of flippancy. Well maybe apathy was the word she was searching for. She never saw him take anything on this journey, quest, whatever this was, seriously. He never looked this solemn and somber. Just what was in the marsh that would even make Cabyll this nervous? Lily took once last glance upward at the roaring Iya. She hoped they wouldn't find out.

INTERLUDE

Ari stood, staring out the window of the Evergreen Estate. Nothing but miles and miles of ponderosa pines stretched the landscape. She looked down, the fading mists of twilight blanketing the dark forest. She was miles above the ground with no way to get down. Ever since she came through the Veil, nothing was as it seemed. Everything was not what she envisioned. How long had she been gone? What were Brandon and Lily doing? Did they know she had left? A dark voice spoke from behind, startling her.

"It's time human."

TWENTY

"Um, lad? Are you sure about this?"

Brandon strapped on his helmet. The hob was scratching his beard, staring down the ramp with uncertainty.

"I mean...yer supposed to what? Ride that piece of plank wood down and back?"

Brandon rolled his eyes as he adjusted his wrist guards, his knee and elbows pads secured. "It's more than that, but yeah, you can say that's what you do in a nutshell."

Alasdair tugged his beard a little harder. "Brandon, you do understand if you lose-"

"I get it Alasdair. But not to worry man." He glanced over to catch Alasdair's distrustful frown. "Seriously, I've been boarding for years. I got this."

Alasdair opened his mouth to retort when Azeban called out.

"Brandon! Oh human Brandon! Do you think this will do?"

Brandon and Alasdair turned. Azeban climbed up the ramp, a makeshift skateboard in his paws. Honestly, Brandon was amazed Azeban was able to make a skateboard. Granted it looked rough since it was made from bark and stone. Brandon wasn't sure it would make it down the ramp. That was no skin off his back though and he hid a snicker when Azeban jaunted up next to them. The racoon spirit eagerly raised his board with a triumphant smile. A twinge of guilt crept up in Brandon's chest. Azeban looked so excited, he didn't have the heart to not be fair about this.

"It may. Let's do a test run and see. It won't count as the game," Brandon said.

Azeban nodded enthusiastically. "This will be ever so much fun! So, you go back and forth on this ramp am I correct?"

"Yeah – there are tricks you can do with the board and that will count as points. I gave a list to Alasdair on the ranking of tricks. We'll each take a turn and do a trick. The object of the game is we must outdo the other's trick. Whoever falls off their board or fails to do a better trick will lose. Sound good?"

"Splendid! I agree to your terms. Now you said a 'test' run?" Azeban put his board down on the edge of the ramp.

Brandon nodded. "Just do what I do, and we'll see if your board will work."

He looked at Azeban and Alasdair who both nodded. He stood on the edge of the ramp and let himself go. The wind hit his face, his stomach experiencing the familiar free fall. Brandon did a simple axle stall and came back to the other side of the ramp easily. Alasdair's raised his eyebrow while Azeban clapped his paws together excitedly.

"Oh my! That looks like so much fun! Is it like this?"

Before Brandon could reply, the racoon shot off like a rocket. Brandon's eyes widened, surprised. Azeban was fine, better than fine. He glided effortlessly on the ramp. Sure enough, the racoon had no trouble going to the other side and copied the exact same move as Brandon. Azeban came back up the ramp with a jump and a squeal.

"Yes yes yes! That was thrilling! Alasdair you *have* to try this," cried Azeban with a wave of his board.

"Oye, I'm fine with both of my feet planted firmly on the ground. Thank you very much." Alasdair shook his head. "Well now lads, are we ready?"

"Ready!" Both Azeban and Brandon shouted.

"Alright ya mangy mongrel, you're first. Get to it." Alasdair grumbled.

"Yay!" And off went Azeban down the ramp. He took off, so excited his legs kicked out in opposite direction while he grabbed the board. He came back with a flourish, a wide smile on his face.

"Well?! How did I do? That felt like I was running on air!"

Brandon scratched his ear, nervous. "Well, you kinda did an airwalk..."

"Airwalk? How appropriate! Show me what else you can do with this!"

Brandon put his board towards the edge of the ramp, held his breath, and went. He decided to go with a simple Rock and Roll – his board rocking back and forth on the other side. A simple enough trick, but he was sure that it was only beginners' luck for Azeban. He came back to the racoon furiously clapping.

"Marvelous! Simply marvelous! Now let me see..."

Azeban took off so fast Brandon could barely follow the raccoon. A deep pit formed in his stomach when Azeban shot up in the air, spinning one and half times. Brandon's mouth gaped.

How in the world did he do an FS 540?

Azeban's tail twirled under the night sky, his shadow reflecting down on the ground as the board spun perfectly. Brandon groaned silently when the trickster came back to their side.

Azeban jumped up and down. "Oh my! What fun! How was that?"

Alasdair slowly raised his eyebrows to Brandon. "Umm...lad?"

Brandon took a breath, reluctant to answer. "That was a pretty good trick." He winced when Azeban screeched in glee.

"Good enough to win?" Azeban's eyes were wide. He clutched the board in his paws, hopping from one foot to the other.

"Hey! I didn't get my turn yet remember?" reminded Brandon.

The trickster waved his paw side to side dismissively. "Oh quite right, quite right. Well then, let's not delay." An eager glint appeared in his eyes that made Brandon feel an uneasy prickling across his skin. Brandon steadied himself, trying to remind himself this was the first time Azeban was on a skateboard. It was a fluke, totally a fluke. Right?

Time to turn things up.

He shot off the board and the wind hit his face. He knew he needed a little more momentum up the ramp. Brandon felt a thrill when his hand hit the edge, his board flying, nailing his Eggplant trick. He finished his handplant, staring down at the bottom of the ramp with his board above him in a perfect handstand. His lip curled. *See if that little fluff ball can beat that.*

Brandon got back to the other side with a grin. His chest puffed out.

Alasdair seemed impressed. "Wonderfully done lad."

Brandon grinned. "Well I have been practicing since..."

CLAP CLAP!

Alasdair and Brandon looked over to see Azeban still clapping his paws loudly. He was still sporting that weird gleam in his eyes. Brandon wondered why the trickster didn't look the least bit worried.

Azeban held his paws together, his board tucked to his side, his tail curling around. "Well, this has been thrilling. But," his eyes took a dangerous glint, "now it's my turn."

Before Brandon could blink, Azeban took off in a sprint. He was even more confident than before, the energy changing. Instead of the appearance he was figuring it out, the fae shot up to the sky and did two perfect rotations. Azeban smirked in triumph, landing back on the ramp.

He leaned on his board, his tail twitching, a triumphant smirk spreading between his whiskers. "Beat THAT fellas! I believe that is what you humans call a FS 720 right?"

Alasdair and Brandon's jaws dropped. Brandon blinked, trying to clear his head. That uneasy feeling grew to a stone sinking inside his stomach. Shaking his head, he stammered.

"Wa...wait...so you're saying..."

Alasdair jumped up in front of Azeban, his face reddened and shiny, the sweat beaded on his brow. Spittle flew out of his mouth as he yelled. "Ya cad! You blighter! Ya *knew* and played him fer a fool!"

Azeban cackled. Alasdair's eye twitched in response. "This has been a delight let me tell you. But did you really think the Master of Games hasn't heard of skateboarding? What nonsense." His laugh rang throughout the dark still air. He looked pityingly at Brandon, who refused to meet his gaze.

Azeban waved his board in front of their faces mockingly. "You can try to beat me human, but I doubt it looking at your skills. I must admit, it was fun, and you are pretty decent. But, no one beats me."

Alasdair smacked the board out of his paws, glaring. He called over to Brandon. "Lad! Dinnae believe one word that comes out of that lavvy heid's gub."

Brandon gulped, the spit stuck in his throat. His eyes fixed on his feet, his thoughts swirling. How would he pull off a better trick than a 720?

"Human! Since you did so well, I can give you a hint about your sister." The trickster hummed. "In the Emerald Estate she awaits. Only a willing human can change her fate."

Brandon's stomach clenched. That made no sense. He wanted nothing more than to walk away. He always hated when things got too serious. He shuffled his feet, inching backwards, then stopped. The image of Lily's disappointed face floated in his mind. Guilt hit him square in the chest. Lily was out there, alone, doing everything she could to get his sister back. Was she scared too?

Lily wouldn't give up. He clenched his hands, his fingers clasping his pants. He didn't want to see that look of disappointment again.

Brandon wiped his sweaty palms against his pants and rolled his shoulders, picking up his board. He stared hard into Azeban's beady little eyes.

"I believe it's my turn."

Alasdair jerked, surprised. The hob saw Brandon's determined face and smiled. "So it is lad. So it is." Giving one last glare at Azeban, the hob went back to Brandon's side. "Ye got this lad. Kick that blighter's furry little behind."

Brandon stared down the ramp and took a deep breath. His mind zipped through a dozen tricks. Each scenario came back to the same one. There was only one trick he could try, but it was super hard. He grimaced. He hadn't gotten the trick right yet, each time resulting in a massive fall. But what choice did he have? *Go broke or go home,* he thought wryly.

As he kicked off the ramp, he felt the familiar weightlessness as gravity did its job. He made an inward plea for this to work.

Faster...

Suddenly his eyes met the vast expanse of the sky, his breath caught in his throat. The stars twirled in a dance around him. He swirled, once, twice...

Just a little more...

His breath whooshed out, his stomach dropping, his body descending. Brandon braced himself as his board landed with a thump down the ramp. His balance teetered, a flicker of panic causing a cold sweat to break out on his back. Sure enough, by some luck he didn't know how, he stayed on the board. Dazed, he realized he was back on the other side of the ramp, staring into the shocked faces of Azeban and Alasdair.

"You couldn't have done that." Azeban murmured. His tail whipped in a frenzied motion.

Alasdair looked back and forth between them. Blinking excitedly, the hob deliberately coughed into his hand, breaking the tense silence.

"Well lad. Care to tell us what that was?"

Azeban ignored the hob. The trickster pointed his claw out towards Brandon angrily. "You COULDN'T have done that! There's no way you pulled a FS 900."

"A 900 whatzit now?" Alasdair pressed, fighting a grin at the happy trickster losing his composure.

Brandon's hands, still trembling with adrenaline, slowly smiled. "Yeah, I did. So beat that!"

"AHHHH!!!!!"

Azeban threw his board down, splintering across the platform. He growled and pulled at his ears, tufts of fur flying about, all the while stomping with a flourish.

"NO NO NO! I DO...NOT.... LOSE!"

Brandon stared, dumbfounded. The happy go lucky fae suddenly morphed into a caricature of Mr. Hyde. Brandon could only stand there, stunned, as the screaming and hollering wounded creature rolled around on the ground. He ducked when the board flew over his head.

The hob wiped a tear from his eye, chuckling. "The trickster finally got tricked! Didnae think I'd see the day." He bobbed, a rock flying over his head, his laughter booming even louder.

Alasdair chuckled harder. "Ack! Don't get yer knickers in a twist. Yer actin' like someone's shoved a hot poke up yer buttocks. Calm down Az, how old are ya anyways? Yer actin' like a baby kit."

Azeban's wailing keened over the warm air. He snorted loudly, his chest heaving, saliva frothing from the corner of his mouth.

Brandon looked at the trickster, concerned. He bent over the side of the ramp where a little door hid some essentials he kept on hand: an emergency kit, sunscreen, some repair items in case his board broke, and bottled water. He pulled out two sealed bottles of purified water.

"Here." He tossed one over to Azeban, who narrowly caught it in his shaking paws. Brandon calmly twisted the cap off his and took a long swallow. The water, though lukewarm, coated his dry mouth. He watched the racoon out of the corner of his eye. Azeban paused, staring at the bottle, before biting into the side of the plastic, taking mouthfuls of liquid with loud slurps.

After a pregnant pause, the tension slowly dissipated into the air. Azeban finished the bottle with a loud sigh.

"Thanks. I needed that"

Alasdair snorted. "Always did follow yer stomach."

The trickster giggled.

"You're too right, too right. Sorry 'bout that. Never lost my cool before cause...well...never lost I suppose." He scratched his ear a few times, his whiskers twitching.

Brandon smiled. "Hey man, no harm no foul. Honestly, I didn't even think I'd make that trick."

Azeban smiled back ruefully. "But you did make that trick kid. Pretty well I might add." Brandon's eyes twinkled, his excitement pouring out. "I know right! I've been practicing for forever on that! Never thought I'd make it."

For a brief moment, his sister's disappearance and Lily navigating an unknown world, it all disappeared. Brandon was thrilled he accomplished something he had been practicing on for forever! He could not contain his delight.

Azeban and Alasdair both chuckled as Brandon hopped up and down. The hob ran his hand through his beard, glancing at Azeban.

"Well Az...."

"I know I know. A deal is a deal after all." He clapped his paw on the back of the hob. He looked over at Brandon, his smile fading away to a serious expression. Brandon's elation slowly receded when he stared into the fae's troubled eyes.

"First thing's first kid." Az took a deep breath. "I'm sorry to say this but, the girl is in trouble..."

TWENTY-ONE

Sulfured clay and silt stuck to Lily's boots as she waded through the brackish muck. Her thighs strained but she pushed herself through the thick shallow water. A foggy haze descended around the group, leaving the sun peeping through a misty veil. Lily could hear only the sloshing of their feet as they trudged among the cattails. And the smell...she grimaced... the smell was awful. She barely could sleep the previous night, the only solace she had was to cover her face with her jacket. Now, all she could do is breathe through her mouth as much as possible, but she could not rid her tongue of the acidic bitter residue it left behind.

She desperately wished for a bath. Actually, she suspected two baths would be necessary. The stench and muck were so intense it would require several scrubbings to make her feel somewhat clean. As Lily gazed amongst the group, she was convinced everyone needed a good wash. Save for Parr. Lily shook her head. The little brownie kept popping among the bulrushes, not getting wet in the slightest. She stopped a moment to catch her breath.

"Please...tell me...we're almost there." She panted, her thighs burning as she rubbed feeling back into them.

Randy paused next to her, laying his hand on her back, giving her a fatherly pat. "You alright girl?" His voiced was laced with concern.

Cabyll, in the lead, yelled behind him – not stopping. "She's fine! Get moving!"

"Cab? Maybe we can wait a moment. Gather our bearings ya know?" Randy protested.

Cabyll glanced back at Lily. He frowned at her. "I said...Get a move on human! Or do you not want to rescue that sister of yours?" He turned his back on them and kept walking.

"Guess that means no," Lily mumbled to herself. "I'm coming!" She straightened herself up, shrugging off Randy's helping hand politely. She couldn't hold back the grimace when she began moving again.

Lily could feel Randy's gaze on her back. As much as she hated to admit it, Cabyll was right. There wasn't much time left to find Ari. She had no right to take a break. Even now she felt the time slipping away, ticking faster and faster.

Randy, refusing to leave her to her musings, appeared beside her. "Don't let him get to ya. He's all hat no cattle that one."

Lily sighed. "He's right you know. I need to find Ari and I can't get distracted."

Randy tilted his head to the side, giving her a puzzled stare. "You really are something girl you know that right?"

Lily laughed, bitterness tinging the edges. "Yeah, are you about to say I should know better?"

Randy whistled low. "You know what I find so fascinating about humans?" He continued as Lily stared at him in confusion. "Your will. Ya see, fae are tricky tricksters but basically there's a code we follow. And I mean strictly follow. To – a – Tee. Pretty easy to figure us out, ya know? But you-" He chuckled. "Humans grow and change. The fortitude and loyalty they display when they love something...well...that's something to be admired. Even if it's kinda foolish." He winked at her as his strode off ahead, his whistling a tinkling sound in the air.

Lily stood still a moment, letting Randy's words seep in. Was she being foolish? Perhaps. Then she thought of Brandon, Tabby, and her dad. Being foolish didn't always mean being wrong. With renewed energy, she pushed her tired legs and kept moving.

Time passed slowly. They trudged through the mist, the hazy sun silent in the sky. Lily believed it was close to noon, but she couldn't be sure. Honestly, she wasn't trying to figure it out anymore. Time was different in the Veil, so they kept telling her. That didn't matter to Lily as long as they made it in time for the revel. Cabyll said they had until tomorrow night. Lily's lips pressed downward. Not much time left.

The group reached a cluster of barren trees, the bark peeled back, hanging in clumps. The branches resembled claws, curling out towards the pondweeds and bulrushes. Cabyll abruptly stopped which, to Lily's chagrin since she wasn't paying attention, caused her to slam into his back. She wondered if you even call it a back as it felt more like a brick wall.

Lily rubbed her nose, smarting from the impact. "What are you-"

Cabyll raised his finger to his lips, prompting her to clamp her lips shut mid-sentence. He jerked his head towards the bulrushes. There...within a clump of cattails and pondweeds, nestled a bushel of white branches. They were smooth and clean. A handful of them scattered amongst the silver waterlilies.

"See those?" Cabyll whispered.

Parr tilted his head to the side. He clapped his hands together excitedly, yelping. "Oh how lovely! These birch branches are wonderful for burning. I could make a proper fire out of these, and we can something scrumptious to eat." He bent forward, gathering them up in his arms.

Cabyll put his fingers to his lips. "Shush!!" He peered around them, gesturing to keep quiet. "They aren't branches they're -" He stopped, his gaze darting towards the horizon. His shoulders tensed, his stance alert.

While he was preoccupied, Lily peered down closely at the 'not' branches. They were indeed smooth, but too smooth to be from a birch tree. She frowned. They looked like they were picked clean...like they were... Lily gulped. A dreaded, unbidden thought crossed her mind.

Oh please no...let it just be my overactive imagination.

Parr looked blankly around the group, confused. "Pardon. But I must ask what are you all staring at? I mean if they aren't branches what else could they..." He trailed off, his mouth gaping open.

Randy raised his eyebrow as he asked quietly.

"Think about it fella. Not much to eat 'round here huh?"

Parr's eyes widened in horror, his arms still laden with the remnants of something's last meal. Lily closed her eyes. She held back her stomach from bringing up the granola bar she had nibbled on earlier.

The bones dropped out of Parr's hands faster than if they were hot coals. They sloshed into the muck with a splash. Parr hastily wiped his hands over his trousers as he moaned.

"Oh my oh my! Get it off, get it off!"

His tone hit a fevered pitch. He began dancing up and down frantically. His cries echoed across the swamp.

Cabyll glared as he furiously whispered, "*Hajima!*" He cut Parr a cold look, effectively freezing the brownie's squeal.

Cabyll looked around, scouting the area, lowering his voice even further. His tone a deep rumble as he instructed firmly. "Stop doing that. We don't want to attract them."

Randy sucked in a deep breath, his eyes wide. "Cab, ya thinkin' the Hecesiiteihii?"

Cabyll nodded, never taking his eyes off the landscape.

Randy groaned.

Parr's hands froze mid wipe. "Hecesitte- what?" He flinched, glancing over at Cabyll, afraid of another rebuke. Cabyll kept scouting so Randy answered.

"The little people." His face was pained.

"Ummm…" Lily finally found her tongue. "You mean leprechauns?"

Randy shook his head. "Naw not those greedy fellas. These are the little people, enemies of the Arapahos tribe."

Lily stared at him, blinking, cause of course that meant nothing to her.

Cabyll breathed out, exasperated. "He means dwarves."

Parr sighed with relief, fanning himself with a chuckle. "Oh dwarves. Why didn't you say so? Oh my goodness, all this fuss about dwarves. You know my uncle's mother's cousin's sister's son twice removed dated a dwarf. He was quite charming, even with all that hair -"

Cabyll palmed his face, annoyed. Lily swore she heard him mutter under his breath, "*Jinjja*? Really?"

Randy shook his head as he said solemnly. "Not that kind of dwarf Parr. These were dwarves in direct service to Prince Jacy. They are strong, a lot stronger than your average dwarf. And if you thought a dwarf had a bad temper then you never met a Hecesiiteihii. They make a regular dwarf look like your sweet grandma covered in sugar baking cupcakes with coconut frosting."

"I don't particularly like coconut." Parr mumbled.

"The point," interjected Randy, "is these folks are not your average run of the mill dwarf. They were Prince Jacy's personal shadow force. Until well…"

"Until they ate his favorite deer." Cabyll scoffed, his arms crossed.

"Huh? Can you repeat that please?" asked Lily. All this was because of a deer?

Cabyll sighed, his eyes still searching, not looking at her. "Look! The prince cursed them. Said they let their hunger drive them, so now they are exiled. Until the prince forgives them, they're cursed to live with an inescapable hunger."

"For brownies?" Parr interrupted, his face going white.

Randy shrugged. "You might could say that."

"I think he means they are hungry for anything. Am I right?" asked Lily.

Cabyll didn't answer her, which Lily took as a sign that she was right. She snorted softly. *These fae are really petty aren't they...*

Cabyll looked on ahead, his lips pursing in concentration. "Now that you have had your history lesson of the day, can you all please be quiet now? These bones don't look fresh, but we shouldn't take any chances. We keep moving, for now. Need I remind everyone we only have until tomorrow."

They all nodded and continued to press forward. Reshouldering her backpack, Lily moved quickly, far *far* away from the clump of cleanly picked bones as fast as her legs could carry her. She hoped the further she went, the further the image would leave her. But she suspected that it would take a long time before those bones would leave her.

The group continued onward for a few more hours until Lily heard a faint tinkling in the distance. She stopped briefly, leaning against her walking stick to take a breath, her ears perking. The sound reminded Lily of wind chimes singing through the air. It was soothing, calming. Cabyll and Randy stopped a head of her. She wanted to ask Cabyll what was making that noise and gasped when he turned towards her. His normal porcelain skin was bone white, unnaturally pale, his eyes glazed over. Concerned, she reached out to touch his arm. He flinched, jerking away, his eyes frantic.

Lily began to get worried. "Cabyll, what's wrong? It is those dwarves?"

Cabyll stayed silent, his gaze wide and unfocused. The bells echoed around them.

He looked at her, regret passing over his face. He reached out to her. "Lily, I'm so-"

Cabyll stopped midsentence, his arm frozen.

Randy, alarmed, ran over. His chest heaved as he tried to catch his breath. "Ah Cab? This is bad. Real bad!"

Cabyll didn't respond.

Lily's body went cold. Cabyll's gaze was unfocused, his mouth slightly open. Her concern grew when he didn't move. Not an inch. She tugged on Cabyll's arm, but he was stiff as a board. No insult, no scoffing, not one reaction. It was like he was a statue. Lily tried to keep down her growing fear. She pleaded anxiously.

"Cabyll? Cab!"

Lily tried shaking him, but nothing. Cabyll stayed frozen as the bell-like tinkling grew louder. Soon it became a song – a beautiful song that rivaled the joyous songbird. It grew uncomfortable to Lily's ears. Like an itch she couldn't scratch. She put her hands on her head, dropping the walking stick. She wanted to drown out the sound. It hurt so bad.

Clutching her ears, Lily looked around. Parr sported a similar glazed look. She ran to the brownie but, same as with Cabyll, he was frozen. Lily's panic grew as she turned to Randy. He was still moving, barely, slightly swaying.

Lily cried out, desperate. "What's wrong with them?! Randy? Help them!"

Randy regretfully shook his head. He slowly backed up, his eyes widening. He lifted his hands, palms up. His eyes scanned around them, afraid of what was coming, then gazed back at her full of sadness.

"I'm sorry darlin'. This is where I have to leave you for now. If she gets a hold of me it's all over. I have to leave before she ensnares me too."

"Her who?!" asked Lily.

The song grew louder, but instead of a pounding sensation, it slithered and snaked along her ear drums. Trying to slide into her subconscious. She gritted her teeth, focusing on Randy's retreating form. She barely could make out when Randy whispered.

"Sirin."

Randy appeared in front of her, clutching her shoulders in a tight grip. She winced, whether from his grasp or her pounding head she wasn't sure. His eyes bore into hers with laser intensity. "You need to focus Lil girl. It's up to you to keep your wits. The fellas are lost right now, but you have a chance."

He glanced above her head, looking off to something...or someone. Closing his eyes, he took a deep breath, wincing as the song grew closer. He opened his eyes, they were glowing. The yellow irises met hers, pleading.

"Little lark. You need to save them. Save Cab. He needs you darlin'. I'll be back as soon as I can."

Randy disappeared in a flash of light. Lily shook her head, goosebumps breaking out across her arms. A trickle of cold sweat dripped down the back of her neck. She shivered. The melody pressed down on her, a weight holding her in place. Lily held her breath and tugged feebly again at Cabyll's arm. Of course, nothing happened. She placed her hands back on her head, spinning around in a panic, moving a little away from the group, trying to gather her thoughts. The eerie melody wafted along the mist, right on top of her. She was trapped.

Lily saw a figure emerge from the wispy grey vapor. Her heart froze. In front of her was one of the most beautiful women she had ever seen. Pale, unblemished skin gleamed under the misty light. Glossy red tresses tipped with gold streamed down her shoulders, framing large doll-like black eyes sporting a sharp, pointed nose and bright red lips.

A long cloak covered the woman from the neck down, completely covering everything, even down to her feet. The cloak was an assortment of feathers, tightly fastened together. An array of colors accentuated the cloak, from coppery reds, to burnished golds, warm ambers, and browns, and even a smattering of deep black and rich white speckled throughout. It looked like she was floating on the marsh, not even a ripple appeared where she moved.

The mystery woman, Sirin, Lily assumed, glided past her. Ignoring her and Parr, the woman made her way directly to Cabyll. Lily watched as he stood there, still as stone, while the beautiful fae approached him. The fae tilted her head, birdlike, and blinked up at Cabyll, studying him. A wide smile displaying brilliantly white sparkling teeth split her red lips.

"Cabyll..." Sirin whispered. Her voice was delicate and flowery. This did not surprise Lily in the least. The woman was like a walking supermodel, only way more fragile.

"Cabyll." The fae woman repeated, as if he could hear her. She continued in a slightly scolding tone. "It's been too long. Did you miss me? I missed you, you wicked Cabyll."

Lily mentally rolled her eyes, trying not to gag. She wanted to make a snarky comment of leaving the two lovebirds alone, but she noticed Cabyll's face. He may have been frozen, but his eyes were alert and focused. They gleamed in the mist. They were angry but anxious at the same time.

Okaaaay...it doesn't seem like he's happy to see her.

The fae woman paid no attention to Cabyll's glare. She pouted, her red lips pursing. She continued her one-sided conversation. "How could you leave like that Cabyll? I thought you'd stay with me." The woman's hand, still under her cloak, reached up to gently rub feathers over his cheek. "Don't you know by now..." She paused, her eyes brighter as her tone became possessive. "No one leaves me..."

Lily stayed quiet, trying to school her expression watching the manic glint grace the fae woman's eyes. She grimaced. *I guess we can add a fatal attraction to the list of Cabyll's past girlfriends.*

Facetiousness aside, Lily became increasingly worried at the obsessive stare the fae woman gave Cabyll. The woman opened her mouth again, and that beautiful song echoed around them. Lily winced, a sting stabbing into her ears. Were her ears bleeding? She wasn't sure, but didn't want to check, keeping her eyes on Sirin.

Though she really didn't want to attract any attention, she knew she had no choice. She couldn't leave her friends there. She bit back a groan as she grudgingly trudged toward the woman and Cabyll. She opened her mouth but couldn't speak. It was like a vice was pressing against her throat.

Lily coughed, her voice sounding paper thin to her aching ears. "Um, excuse me. Can you tell me what's wrong with my friends?"

Sirin turned her head slowly towards Lily, which was a feat since Lily was almost directly behind the fae woman. The woman turned her head in a one hundred ninety degree turn. Her eyes were wide, unblinking, as they stared down at her. Unnerved, Lily took a small step back. Her body knew instinctively she was dealing with a predator, and she wanted as much distance as possible. Not that it mattered. Lily had a feeling this woman was faster than she looked. Then, unexpectedly, the woman blinked, her lips curving into a syrupy smile.

"Oh? Hello," she cooed.

Lily held up her hand in an awkward greeting. "Um...hi."

Silence.

"Are you Sirin?" asked Lily.

"Yes," replied the woman.

Silence again.

Lily shuffled her feet, nervous. She tried again. "Okay. Um about my friends?"

"Oh? You'd like to know what's happened to them?"

Lily nodded.

Sirin cooed again. "Nothing is wrong with them dear. They're simply in a trance." She tutted, glancing back to Cabyll, giving him a soft smile. He wasn't looking at Sirin though. Cabyll's eyes were staring at Lily, wide and urgent. If Lily didn't know any better, she would have sworn he was concerned. Or maybe that was her own subconscious thoughts. Because she was concerned. Very concerned.

"A trance?" asked Lily. She mentally kicked herself. *Stupid question Lily.*

"Would you like to take a closer look?" Sirin asked innocently. She trailed her cloak down Cabyll's shoulder. Cabyll eyes began to glow.

Sirin jumped, surprised. She pulled her hand back as small sparks shot around him, creating a soft blue aura. She giggled.

"Naughty *naughty* Cabyll."

Lily pinched her nose. Even the woman's giggle sounded like bells.

Sirin caressed the feathered cloak against Cabyll's cheek once more. She spoke over her shoulder offhandedly to Lily. "He's really trying so hard to free himself. But I'm not surprised, he is so strong after all. That's why he is so dear to me."

She gave Lily a dismissive look up and down. "Honestly, I'm quite surprised you're not under the spell. Being a lowly human and all. Maybe it's because I never bothered with women. But not to worry, my song has never failed before. Well, save once with my dear Cabyll here. But...he is..." She tittered. "Well, let's just say he's not your normal fae."

Lily kept her face blank. She already knew he was a big-time assassin. What else could he be? *Not the time for that Lil!* Lily slowly backed up a few steps as the fae woman began to glide closer to her.

Sirin stared unblinking at her. "Not that you'd be special enough to know anything about him."

Lily silently gulped. *Yup, not just cuckoo. Definitely certifiable. Geez louise Cabyll you sure know how to pick them.*

Lily raised her palms, trying to show she wasn't a threat.

She internally scoffed at herself. *A threat? Human = no threat according to these guys.*

With her palms still raised, she discreetly looked for any kind of weapon on the edges of her vision. While the woman didn't appear hostile, Lily wasn't taking any chances. What did she have on hand? Her foot hit something. Glancing down she saw her walking stick.

Great...how can I be sneaky about this?

She spoke slowly, bending down, her hand cautiously reaching for the walking stick. "Yup, you're right. He's definitely not normal and it's none of my business. But, he kinda has to take me somewhere first. How about we take care of that first and you guys can talk about whatever you want. Sound good?" Her hands grasped the cool wood firmly and gradually hid it behind her back.

Sirin tilted her head more to the side until it was almost down to her shoulder, her crimson hair spilling over her face. A cheshire grin spread over her lips, her blinding teeth peeking behind her dazzling tresses.

"Aww, little human, you're so naïve it's cute. I already know all about what bargain my Cabyll has with you." She kept moving forward. "I'm going to relieve him of that burden. Now that he's with me, I'll never let him leave. He won't be attached to a *thing* like you." Her syrupy tone laced with venom, causing Lily to flinch.

Lily protested. "Look. I'm not trying to get between," she waved her hand, "whatever this is. He needs to help me with my issue and then you two go about your business." Lily swore if statues could glare at her, Cabyll was shooting daggers her way. She inwardly yelled at him.

Dude! I'm saying whatever I can so this crazy obsessive lady does not go stan fan on me.

Sirin appeared in front of her in a flash, jostling her out of her thoughts. Lily brought her walking stick to her chest, feeble as it was. Seeing Sirin's large eyes up close made Lily cringe. No pupils. Just inky blackness held her gaze, like a snake.

Sirin purred. "What issue? You won't need to worry about anything anymore."

"What are you talking about?" Lily demanded, trying to hide how unnerved she was.

Sirin smirked. "You'll see."

"See what?" asked Lily. Her heart hammered in her throat. She didn't want to 'see' what this crazy fae woman was talking about.

Sirin chuckled darkly, her teeth becoming sharper in Lily's eyes. "Oh foolish little human. Your perfect life of course." She tsked, which made Lily think of a parent scolding a child. "Don't worry dear, just let sister Sirin take care of everything."

Sirin extended her hand out to Lily. Except, it wasn't a hand. No...it was a claw. Wait! No, not a claw, a talon. An owl talon to be precise. Lily gaped at Sirin, fear settling in her belly. Sirin paused, then looked down to where Lily was staring. She giggled.

"Oh dearie, you really are a treat. I wonder if Cabyll thought about eating you. You seem too gullibly sweet."

Lily forcefully ignored that statement. Why was everyone intent on eating her? On further analysis, she realized the fae woman's cloak was actually feathers. The only thing 'human' about her was her face. Everything else from the neck down was the body of a large horned owl.

Why do the crazy ones have to have the fangs and claws and...

Sirin brushed her feathers over Lily's face, immediately stopping Lily's inner tirade. Sirin whispered.

"Time to dream little human."

Sirin began to sing. Lily tried to move the walking stick to give a good whack, but she found herself paralyzed as well.

The haunting melody flooded Lily's ears. It wrapped around her, squeezing her like she was a tube of toothpaste ready to pop. Black spots crowded her vision. Distantly, someone called her name.

Lily!

Lily....

Lil....

"Hey! Lil? Lil!"

Lily's eyes snapped open. She glanced around anxiously, her heart pounding. The cream and yellowed walls of the cottage greeted her. Lily frowned. Wasn't she at the marsh? Wait...what marsh? She rubbed her ears, trying to lessen the lingering ache in her ear drums. When the pain subsided, she was able to focus more clearly. She was sitting at the dining room table. Brandon, Tabby, and her dad were all staring at her, concern etched on their faces.

Brandon looked at her worried. "Hey Lil? Are you okay? You seemed pretty out of it for a minute."

"Sorry! I'm supposed to be somewhere. Um, what am I doing here?" she asked, confused.

The clink of a dishes rang in the sink. Lily was immediately engulfed in a warm hug. The scent of lemon and dish soap tickled her nose.

"Oh honey, the studying has been way too hard on you hasn't it?" asked Tabby, her arms tightly wrapped around her.

Lily blinked, surprised. She slowly reached up and tentatively held onto Tabby's sleeve, her heart tugging. When was the last time she had a hug like this other than her dad? Hold on. Tabby always gave her hugs, right? Yes, always. Tabby would shower her daughter with hugs and kisses until Lily grew sick of it.

Wait, daughter? She fingered her curls, her hands tangling in her hair ribbon. What was that she was thinking about just now? Didn't Tabby already have a —

"That's my *Fiore*! She's gonna be at the top of her class you watch!" Her dad exclaimed, while he forked down his dinner.

Tabby looked over at him, her eyebrow raised. "I don't want her over-extending herself Tony."

Brandon interrupted. "Hey Lil, wanna go to the movies tonight? They have the latest horror film playing. It's gonna be awesome!"

"Wait, you want to go with me?" asked Lily.

Brandon laughed. "Duh! You're not missing out on our bimonthly movie night, right? We always go rain or shine. I want to eat bottomless popcorn and grab ice cream afterwards."

He reached out and grabbed her hand to give it a reassuring squeeze. "You sure you okay sis?"

Lily blushed, feeling foolish. "Oh yeah – I'm fine. Maybe I am tired." She looked around, everyone was staring at her with smiles and caring eyes. Her heart expanded as Tabby leaned in and kissed her on the top of her head.

Tabby gave her a warm smile. "Well worry not! This will be a stress-free night. Want to help me clear the table for dessert?"

Lily jumped up, an eager smile spreading over her face. "Of course! So, what's for dessert?"

Her dad laughed loudly. "That's my girl! Never too full or sad for dessert!"

Tabby chuckled, her shoulders shaking. "You're so like your father. We're having your favorite sweetie, lemon panna cotta with wild berries."

Lily's eyes lit up. "I can't wait! But doesn't Ari hate that dessert. Is it okay?"

Brandon tilted his head to the side. "Who's Ari?"

Lily put her hand on her head, a pounding beginning in her ears.

"Um..."

Her thoughts shut off when Tabby placed a plate in front of her, displaying a large helping of the sugary treat.

"Go ahead sweetie, it's your favorite."

Lily shook her head, unable to touch the dessert. The migraine began to spread down her body like a tidal wave.

"Sis! Let's go spend some time together!" Brandon tugged on her arm.

Lily panted, finding it hard to breathe. "Hold on...something isn't right..."

"Sweetie?"

"*Fiore!*"

"Sis!

"STOP! STOP IT!!" yelled Lily, clasping her hands over her ears, desperately trying to drown everyone out and stop the pain.

Silence...

A voice drawled out.

"Tsk tsk tsk. You are a stubborn little human, aren't you?"

Lily slowly opened her eyes. Brandon, her dad, Tabby, they were all frozen. Lily, hesitant, reached out to touch Tabby's outstretched hand. It was cold and hard as stone. She pulled back quickly, frantic. She called out.

"Who's there?"

The voice snarked back. "Only someone who is trying to give you what you want!"

Lily's nose wrinkled, thinking. The voice sounded so familiar, but from where? Wracking her aching brain, she pushed through the pounding pain. In an instant, a fog seemed to lift from her as she blurted out. "Sirin? Is that you?"

The voice – Sirin – scoffed. "Way to ruin the fun. Why do you hurt yourself like this? I'm only trying to give you what your heart desires little human."

Lily glared into the darkness, trying to find where Sirin was hiding. "And what do I want oh knowing, whatever you are?"

A tinkling chuckle rang throughout the house. "Oh, aren't you just cute."

Lily frowned. *She makes me sound like a fluffy pet.*

Sirin continued. "Silly human, I'm offering you a happy life of course. A family who loves you, cares about your feelings and ideas. You'd have a father, a brother..." A pause. "A mother..."

Lily tried not to react, but she couldn't stop herself from glancing over at the frozen Tabby, a hollow ache spreading in her chest.

Sirin drawled out, noticing where Lily's gaze fell. "Ah yes, a mother. You always wanted a loving mother, haven't you? Well, now you can have that all for yourself. You can have it all human. All you have to do...is go home."

"Go home?" repeated Lily.

"Yes yes! Go home. Leave everything behind here and go back. Simple, yes?"

"But what about Ari?" protested Lily.

Sirin scoffed. "What has that girl ever done for you? Hmmm? Shall we have a little look."

The house blurred in front of Lily's eyes. As it came back into focus, she found herself in the same dining room, but it was different. Sitting at the dinner table were the same people, but with Ari and someone else. Lily's eyes widened. There was another Lily sitting, frozen as the rest. Unnerved, Lily tried to reach out but jerked as a shock ran through her fingers. Sirin clucked in the darkness,

"Nu uh human. No touching."

Then, as if a start button was pressed, the phantoms, figures, whatever they were, began to speak. Lily took a deep breath, watching the scene play out.

Ari clanked her fork against the table, her face curled in disgust. "Umm, what is this?"

"It's puttanesca." Tabby replied.

"Tastes good," said Brandon, stuffing his face with a forkful of pasta.

Professor Ambrosino twirled the pasta around his fork in methodical movements. "It's one of our favorite dishes. Lil wanted to make something special for you guys before Tabby and I left."

Oh...this happened few days ago. Lily remembered, the memories coming back.

Ari frowned. "Are there sardines in this?"

Lily saw her double wring her hands nervously. The double replied. "They're anchovies with capers."

Ari's eyes widened. "Eww gross!" She threw down her fork, pushing the plate away in disgust.

"But, it's actually good. If you'd only try it," insisted Lily.

Dr. Ambrosino halted her, raising his hand. "It's fine Lil, if Ari doesn't like it, we don't need to eat it."

The double stared at her dad, opened mouthed.

"Are you sure Tony?" asked Tabby, glancing at the Lily double.

"I refuse to eat this. It's disgusting!" Ari crossed her arms, her nose up in the air.

Dr. Ambrosino waved his hands dismissively. "It's okay, right Lily? We'll order a pizza."

Lily protested. "But Dad..."

"Yeah pizza!" yelled Brandon, still stuffing his face.

"Mom, order at La Sol, they have gluten free options and salads." Ari ordered, her nose lifting in the air.

"Okay if we're sure guys. Are you okay sweetie?" Tabby asked as she came over to the Lily double and Ari.

The double opened her mouth to reply but Tabby went over and gave Ari a hug.

"Oh I'm fine Mom, thanks," said Ari.

The scene froze again with Tabby's arms around Ari. Lily's double was standing there, alone, looking down at the ground.

"Aww...how sad. They didn't even give you two seconds of their time," clucked Sirin, unsympathetic. "And they had no idea how hard you worked on that meal did they?"

Lily clenched her hands, her heart aching. She did work hard. She drove an extra hour and back to the Italian market. She hand-picked the tomatoes, the anchovies, the fresh pasta. She remembered the stinging tears running down her face when she cut the onions for the cucumber onion salad she made specifically for Ari. It didn't escape her notice that Ari didn't take one bite of the salad because she claimed she 'hated vinegar'. Though on more than one occasion Ari ate pickled vinegar-based vegetables.

But it was more than just the cooking. Every time Lily was sad, her dad would make puttanesca for her. She remembered the days when they had no money, the days where they didn't know whether the dig would be called off, living paycheck to paycheck. Those particularly bad days she could always count on the comfort of this warm meal for her. As if to say things would be okay as long as they were together. She wanted to share that with Ari and Brandon because she knew they weren't really happy moving to the new house. But instead...instead, she was ignored, again.

Lily focused on her frozen dad. She bit her lip, the anger growing. *Dad knew. He KNEW how important that was to me. And he still dismissed it because of her. All because of her...*

Her nails cut into her palms.

"Hurts doesn't it dear?" Sirin tsked in her ear. Lily looked up trying to find where her voice was coming from, but only saw darkness. Sirin's siren call blanketed her, echoing throughout the room.

"But it doesn't have to hurt anymore. That girl made her choice. Now you can make yours. Let her go. She doesn't care about you. Just go home. If you go home, they will forget about her. You will be their only sister, their only daughter. You'd like that wouldn't you?"

That alluring suggestion spread deep down into Lily's bones. Oh, it was tempting, so tempting. Sirin was right. Ari did make her choice. She didn't want to be around them. She chose a stranger over her family. She walked away from her mom over someone she barely knew! For what? A guy?! And Lily, who dreamed of having a mother, a sibling. Ari had it all and she didn't care! Instead of treasuring that, Ari threw it away for a handsome face and pretty words. Lily gritted her teeth, anger seeping through the ache. Dark thoughts crept in. She would not have thrown away her family. She would be a better sister. A better daughter.

"Yes!" Sirin's excited voice called out. "You have a right to be angry. Be angry! Just look at how they treated you. You have to sit there and be such a good girl all the time. Isn't that exhausting? While this one..." Sirin's voice gestured to Ari, her infuriating smirk frozen in place. "This one they jump all over themselves to please her and she doesn't have to lift a finger. And she takes it all for granted. You would treasure this family."

"Yes, I treasure them." Lily murmured.

Sirin's excited voice grew more encouraging. "Of *course* you do dear. You deserve to be selfish for once."

Lily's eyes glazed over. "I do deserve it..."

Sirin continued, her alluring tone slithering in Lily's ears. "Go home little human. Go home and be with your family. I'll take care of the rest. Don't worry about the others. You can forget your time in the Veil. Think of this as if it was a passing dream. Go be happy."

Lily nodded. Yes, she should go home. What had this trip gotten her? She almost died, multiple times, trying to find Ari. And for what? Ari probably wouldn't care.

"All you have to do," called Sirin, "is to tell me to take you home. Make a deal. That's it...just say three...little...words."

Lily bit her lip. "Take..."

"Yes! Go on."

She took a deep breath. "Take...me..."

Lily paused.

Sirin called out, impatient. "Go on go on! Go be with your perfect family!"

Lily stopped. Something wasn't right.

She whispered. "Family isn't perfect."

Silence.

"What did you say?" Sirin hissed.

Lily opened her eyes. The dark anger was dispersing. Her mind became clearer, her body less heavy. She said louder. "I said, family is not perfect."

Abruptly, as if a plug was pulled, the red-hot anger drained out of her. Why was she so angry? Yes, she was hurt, but she would never leave Ari behind. Brandon was counting on her. And how could she leave Cabyll and Parr to this crazy woman? She'd never forgive herself if she left them like that.

"I need to get back to my friends. I have to get to Ari. Let me out!" Lily yelled.

The scene darkened, the house, everyone disappeared before her eyes. She was encased in total blackness. A frustrated growl echoed around her.

"Why you foolish little human! Why didn't you take the deal? Just leave this place and leave Cabyll with me!" Sirin's syrupy voice was gone, becoming more animalistic.

"Sirin?" Lily reached her hands out in the darkness as she said firmly. "Sirin! Let me out right now!"

Sirin ignored her. "I would have let you have a happy life. I really am too generous and nice for my own good." She sighed dramatically.

Nice?! This is her being nice?!

Lily looked around, trying to find a spot where she could walk. Everywhere she turned, it was pitch black. She stepped forward and could not even hear an echo of her footsteps in the gloom. She glared into the darkness, wishing she could kick something.

"Where am I Sirin?" asked Lily.

"You're in your mind silly. Does, 'in a trance' mean something different in your human language? My goodness are all humans this slow?" scoffed Sirin.

I'm in my mind. Okay, at least she confirmed what I suspected.

Lily tried to concentrate on the darkness, willing it to lighten. For a brief moment, she thought she saw the shadows flicker. A sharp pang rang in her head. Something wet trailed down her lip. She wiped her face, and her fingers came away smeared with blood.

A tinkling sigh rang around her. "Well, I guess I have no choice since you seem to be breaking free of my trance. You really are quite a nuisance." Sirin commented, as if disappointed. Her voice trailed off, an eerie silence stretching into the darkness.

Dread creeped in. Lily asked cautiously. "What are you talking about?"

Silence.

"Sirin?"

Sirin's tinkling voice rang out. "Sorry dear, had to make a quick call. I'm afraid if you won't take my gracious offering of a happy life, then I'll simply hand you off. I really have no need of you after all, I was only doing what I was asked to do. My cousins may find use out of you though. Just remember, I tried to give you a chance."

Lily's brows furrowed. Someone asked Sirin to do this. But who? She had a feeling placating Sirin may get her some answers. It seemed better to stall her than the alternative. Lily figured meeting these 'cousins' was not a good option.

Lily changed tactics. She asked politely. "Who asked you to do this? What I mean to say is, why would a beautiful fae like you even bother with a silly little human like me?"

Sirin scoffed but seemed to take the bait as she replied. "Normally I wouldn't. You're so beneath me. But..." She paused and sighed longingly. "He said I could have Cabyll. And now I have him. I did *my* part of the bargain. No one guessed you wouldn't leave. Now, I don't care what happens to you. Besides, if my cousins are fed, they can stop bothering me for a while." With a flippant tone of finality, Sirin's presence started to fade.

"Wait! Wait!" Lily called out, trying to hide her growing panic.

A pause – "Yes? I'll answer one last question before I go human."

"I'd like to know about your cousins. Are they like you?" Lily asked, hoping to stall for more time.

Sirin giggled darkly. "Oh child, they are nothing like me. They are the Tah-tah-kle-ah. I sing and give you what you desire, but my cousins prefer to give you your darkest nightmares. They are especially fond of children for dinner..."

Lily gulped. So, they were 'that' kind of fae. *Of course they are...*

she thought ruefully. *Everything here either wants to eat me or mess with my sanity.*

Sirin kept giggling, then gave a startled yelp. A slight vibration shook the ground. Lily's legs wobbled, then it calmed down. A moment later, Sirin's voice returned.

"That was unexpected." Sirin said in a slightly surprised tone.

"What was?" asked Lily.

"It looks like my dear Cabyll was angry. It is quite puzzling. That bargain you made must be strong for him to try so hard. No matter though. That bargain will disappear when you're gone."

Lily blinked, unable to respond.

Sirin gave a dainty snort. "Well, I guess you can take some comfort in that he did try to help you. I hope you remember how courageous my Cabyll is while you 'live' through your nightmares. Ta ta darling!"

Sirin's laughter faded away, the tinkling bells disappearing in the darkness.

Maybe I can snap out of this before those crazy sisters show up.

Lily closed her eyes to concentrate again when something slithery slide up her leg. Instinctively she kicked out, dislodging whatever it was. She winced as a feathering sting raced down her calf muscle. Something skittered across the floor.

"Oh...sisssster..." A dry and papery voice hissed in the darkness. It was so scratchy Lily could swear it glided over her like sandpaper.

"Yessss...sister..." Another voice hissed back.

"Look! Our cousin gave us a little young human to play with. Wasn't that niiiice of her?"

"Yessss...sssso nice of her sister."

The air grew colder, Lily's breath coming in puffs. She rubbed her arms, the slippery chill climbed up around her, tightening.

"Um, I don't suppose you'll let me go if I ask nicely huh?" Lily joked.

The sister's voices hissed in delight.

The first voice laughed, or at least Lily thought she laughed. The laugh sounded more like nails raking down a chalkboard. "Oh! This little human is funny! Normally they are so terrified, like little rabbits. It's an interesting change."

"Yes indeed sisssster. It's too bad that she'll break in the end," remarked the second. If Lily didn't know any better, she could have sworn the voice seemed a little remorseful.

"Maybe I won't break. How about we play a game to find out?" Lily asked.

"Oh! I like games!" exclaimed the first voice.

"Dear ssssister...do you think that's a good idea?" questioned the second.

"One game!" Lily encouraged. "If I win, you let me out of this, whatever this is. If you win well...you get to do what you're doing right?"

The first voice whined. "Hmmm...well what's the fun in that?"

Lily tapped her chin with her finger, hoping to appear flippant. "Hope. You mentioned breaking me, right? Isn't hope the best way to do that? If you let me play one game that gives me hope and if I lose, well that's an even a better win for you." Lily held her breath, her fingers quivering slightly. She silently pleaded.

Please work please work please work.

A ringing clap resounded in the darkness. The second voice remarked gleefully. "Ah! That sounds wonderful! Devastation does make it ever the sweeter."

"Okay little human. We'll play a game with you. But here are our terms. We'll give you fifteen minutes. If you do not speak or scream in that specified time, you win. If you make a sound – you are ours," said the first voice.

Lily bit her lip, steeling herself. *Okay...I can do this.*

"I agree." She replied, hoping she sounded calmer than what she was feeling.

The sisters snickered. Lily peered through the darkness, still not seeing them. They were only voices in the darkness. The darkness slightly lifted, Lily's eyes squinting to adjust. Two figures were walking towards her. The sisters were tall, very tall, and bone thin. While Sirin sported beautiful bold feathers, these two looked like emaciated owls with their tattered and frayed black and grey plumage. Their talons were long and razor thin. Their noses were sharp and pointed, their mouths stretched wide to reveal black lips and rows of needle fangs. Lily contained her gasp. She tried to remain still while their black beady eyes held hers. They mirrored each other's movements, cocking their heads to the side and continued to stare at her. The first's smile grew wider, showing something stuck between the sharp fangs. Lily tried to hide her disgust. She didn't want to think about what was caught between those fangs.

The Tah-tah-kle-ah pointed their long talons at her, their

high-pitched laugh rang hollow, and they trilled in unison. "Your time starts now."

Lily grimaced. *As if they weren't creepy before...*

The sisters paused and dipped their heads down, reminding Lily of lions ready to pounce. She started to back away slowly as they stalked towards her.

The second grinned evilly. "Run little rabbit."

CHAPTER

TWENTY-TWO

Brandon paced back and forth, chewing his thumbnail down. The kitchen floorboards could have shown the worn treads of his sneakers with how often he was dragging his feet from one end of the room to another. Alasdair and Brom looked over at him with worried glances.

"Lad..." Alasdair began.

Brandon spun around, his eyes frantically searching until they landed on Azeban.

"What's going to happen to my sister? You still won't tell me."

Az, perched on top of the countertop, ran his claws through his fur and scratched his neck awkwardly. He closed his eyes and sighed. "Look kid, I really don't know. It's like...it's like I catch a glimpse. Fragments, pieces, ya know? Not much to go on."

Brandon blinked. "A glimpse? A glimpse?!"

Az's ears dropped, flinching at Brandon's tone. Brandon didn't care. It was as if he could see himself from the outside. And this Brandon sure looked mad. He dimly heard his voice getting louder, his anger rising.

Brandon glared. "Well, what 'glimpse' did your all seeing yet not seeing wonky powers tell you?"

Azeban paused, indecision written over his furry face. Brom groaned, putting his face in his hands.

Brom coughed deliberately, waving his hand in a flourish. "While we're still young if you please."

"Well, if you insist. Must you all be so impatient?" Az sighed dramatically as he lounged back on the granite top, his tail wafting back and forth.

Brom's eyes bugged out as red spots appeared on his cheeks. "I beg your pardon? This is only about the young misses' life. And you are one to talk about patience. I swear on the Veil Azeban if you so much as-"

Alasdair snorted and spat out, interrupting Brom midsentence. "Come on ya old rat. Out with it!"

Brandon clenched his fists, feeling desperate. "Az, it's my sister." He couldn't breathe, wondering what was happening with Ari.

"Fiiiiiiine. Well, it's not much anyways." Az drawled while examining his claws. He ducked his head, turning away from them, but not before a glint of guilt reflected in his eyes.

"Sorry kid. I tend to forget emotional attachments come with human sociology. There's not much to tell. Just the usual story with fae and humans. Your sister is in a dark place right now and may not see the light of day again. Savvy?"

"Savvy?! Dark place?!" Brandon was freaking out. Was Ari okay? Didn't Lily make it in time? No, he shook his head silently. Lily wouldn't have failed, he just knew it.

"Manners Azeban! You are scaring the poor child!" admonished Brom.

"Sheesh sorry Brom, but you guys can't see what I see up in here." Az tapped his head, his ears flapping.

"Well why dinnea we?" asked Alasdair.

Brom gasped, looking at Alasdair with horror. "You can't be serious."

Az laid back on the counter again, putting his paws behind his head, his tail flicking lazily.

"Someone want to clue me in guys?" asked Brandon.

Brom and Alasdair ignored him as they continued to argue with each other.

Alasdair nodded. "Serious as a banshee calling a family member home."

"But it's dangerous!" protested Brom.

"Ye think the lad hasn't been in danger? A changeling isn't something to sneeze at brownie." Brandon jumped on the counter, startling Azeban who fell off with a thump. Brom and Alasdair jerked in surprise.

Brandon stomped his foot loudly. "Hey! I'm RIGHT here!"

Brom threw up his hands in exasperation. "Well fine. But I'll have the lot of you know that the potential damage to home and hearth must be kept to a reasonable minimum. Are we clear?"

"Yeah yeah prissy McPrissy Pants!" A voice growled behind Brandon. He turned to find Barlow scratching his beard, looking positively gruntled. Barlow's calloused fingers grabbed onto his arm and pulled him down roughly off the table, dragging him up the staircase.

Barlow, not looking back at Brandon, groused. "Alright lad, let's go. Dinnae have time to waste."

He led Brandon up the steps towards Lily's room. They barged into the room, the door slamming on its hinges. Rox squealed in protest over the loud disruption, rattling the cage. Brandon tried to keep up with Barlow as he marched towards Lily's vanity. Barlow motioned for Brandon to sit. Confused, he fell with a thump on top of the cushioned chair. He stared at his equally confused reflection within the silver mirror. Barlow was behind him, his thick hairy arms crossed over his chest with a look of impatience on his face.

"There ya go Chancer. Try yer luck."

Brandon shook his head. "I still don't understand." He was trying to make sense why he was in Lily's room. He struggled not to blush because he was in her room without permission. Before he could gain his wits, Brom, Alasdair, and Azeban ran in. Well, it was more like Alasdair and Brom ran in with Azeban trailing behind. Rox chirped in protest, not liking all this commotion.

Brom panted, bent over with his hands on his knees. "Listen well Master Brandon before you follow any advice from this-"

"Watch it ye clarty little-" growled Barlow.

"Guys guys! My sister!" Brandon reminded the group. They fell silent, the fae looking slightly ashamed.

Alasdair came forward, putting his hand on Brandon's shoulder as he said gently.

"Lad – Brom's just looking out for ya. There is a way to see what Az is seein' but...there is a price."

He pointed towards Lily's mirror as he continued.

"That is a scrying mirror. Miss Lily discovered it upstairs."

"Which is really quite remarkable. Much to show how brilliant and extraordinary Miss Lily truly is." Brom interrupted with a prideful tone.

Brandon stared at the mirror. "Will it help me find out what is going on with my sister?"

Barlow nodded. "It'll show ya what ye need to see lad."

Brandon gazed at his refection against the glossy surface and took a breath. "Okay. Let's do this."

Brom scurred forward. "A minute please Master Brandon. You must know with magic that there is always a price."

"And that is?" Brandon glanced down at the brownie.

Alasdair squeezed Brandon's shoulder again; his gaze filled with pity. "If the mirror wants ya ta see, then some sight must be taken away."

Brandon gulped. "Um, you mean permanently?"

Barlow snorted. "Nah lad – only fer as long as ye see. The longer you search and further back you go, the more sight is taken away."

Brandon rubbed his face. "So, I'll be temporarily blind."

They nodded. Brandon continued to stare at the mirror, unsure what to do.

Az's ears twitched. "Well well well. This just got interesting. Sight for sight. How curious! What are you going to do?"

Brom glared back at Az. "Will you please be quiet you insuffer-able mongrel! Give the boy a moment to think."

Az rolled his eyes. "I hate to break up this dramatic party, but if you decide to do this you must do it soon." Brandon held his breath, noticing Az's eyes beginning to glow. "What I saw about your sister is happening. Right now."

Brandon's heart dropped to his stomach. He scanned the faces of his new friends, all their gazes reflecting his concern and fear.

Brandon decided. "Okay, let's do this. How do I make this work?" He knocked on the mirror, running his hands over it's cool, smooth, surface. Alasdair slapped his hand away before Brandon could damage it.

Brom tapped his finger to his chin. "Hmm, it depends on its makeup. You see the different composition can change the wording of the spell. So, if it's ancient dwarf, seelie, ogre that can-"

Barlow growled. "Enough of listening to this namby pamby! Look here-" He pointed to the carvings around the frame. He looked over the symbols for a second. Then he grunted, confident on what he found. He gestured towards the mirror's surface.

"Alright lad. Touch the surface and think about reaching out to the person who needs you right now. No need for any of that harkey malarkey stuff that ole brownie said."

Brom's face heated as he crossed his arms with a huff. Brandon ignored them, keeping focused. Gingerly, he reached out to touch the cold silver inlay carvings. The cold metal warmed under his hand, and he held his breath.

"How will I know it's working?" He whispered.

Barlow shrugged. "You'll know lad. Now get moving."

Brandon turned back to the mirror, thinking hard about his sister. He pictured her in his mind, mentally reaching out his hand and –

Nothing.

Nothing happened.

Brandon blinked, thinking he missed something. But no, indeed the mirror looked the same. He frowned. What did he do wrong? He did exactly what Barlow told him to do. Right? He glanced over at the group with a confused look.

"Did I do something wrong?"

Barlow scratched his beard. Alasdair and Brom looked at each other nervously.

"Did you picture your sister?" asked Barlow.

"Yes! I pictured her and nothing!"

Az rolled his eyes, one busy eyebrow raised.

"Which sister did you pick little human?"

Brandon shook his head, confused. "What do you mean which sister. My only sister, Ari." Az shook his head. "Are you sure?"

Brandon paused, the whole group unnaturally silent. That pit grew to a cold weight that pushed inside his stomach, smothering him. Brom, pale in shock, stuttered.

"You...you...don't mean..."

Brandon whispered. "Lily..."

The trickster put his finger to his nose with a nod.

Brandon whirled back to the mirror, picturing Lily in his mind's eye. He thought he heard Az ask faintly over the roaring of his ears.

"Isn't she your sister too?"

Ignoring Az, Brandon focused on the cold silver warming in his grasp. He kept thinking of Lily and eventually the unblemished surface began to ripple and swirl. Waves of silver danced around the surface until Brandon saw a shape vaguely in the distance. He squinted his eyes, peering closer in the mirror. There! There was Lily, but she was lying on the ground. She seemed so still. Unnaturally so. Her normal golden complexion was so pale it stood out in the darkness surrounding her. Her eyes were shut, her arms and legs outstretched like a starfish. But, there was something else.

A dark figure sat on Lily's chest, curled over her looking downward. It was perched on top of her chest, reminding Brandon of a large bird. But it wasn't. Brandon watched in growing horror as the thing turned towards him. Wait! Things, as in plural! It was two beings set side by side, moving in perfect unison. Their beaklike noses and sharp teeth smiled eerily at him. Their black bottomless eyes stared, unblinking.

Az gagged. "Ugh! Those two get uglier every time I see them."

Brom gasped. "Oh my stars! Oh no! It's..."

"Dinnae say their name!" barked Barlow. Brandon felt Barlow's hand on his as the lob whispered to him.

"I know they're scary lad but don't look away or we lose our shot to save Miss Lily."

"What are they doing to her?" Brandon frantically whispered back, his fear making his voice shaky.

"They are trying to steal her soul." Barlow hissed.

Alasdair growled. "You mean they want to eat it."

Brandon gasped. "But...but why can't she move?!"

Barlow squeezed his shoulder. "Those two put their prey in a trancelike sleep. We need to get her out of their spell lad."

"How?!" Brandon was panicking. He couldn't lose Lily. How could he be so stupid. He just assumed Lily would be fine. She was always fine! How could he be so stupid, so forgetful, that she was the one risking her life.

The windows in the cottage blew open and slammed closed. The fae jumped to attention.

Barlow stood a moment, listening. He barked at Brom and Alasdair.

"It's time! Get it fellas!"

Alasdair nodded along with Brom as they popped out. Barlow turned back to Brandon. He spoke softly but urgently; afraid the creatures would hear him.

"Alright, listen to me. You need to go inside Lily's mind. It'll require to go a little deeper in the mirror. You may lose your sight a little longer. You willing?"

Brandon nodded, determined. "Whatever it takes to save Lily."

Barlow squeezed his shoulder again in approval.

"That's the spirit lad."

Brandon heard the familiar 'POP' indicating Brom and Alasdair were back

"We got it Barlow!" yelled Alasdair.

Brandon, unable to turn around, wondered what "it" was. Barlow placed something small in his palm. It was smooth to the touch, but he was afraid to glance down even for a moment. It warmed in his palm, spreading a comforting warmth through him. He gripped it tighter.

"Alright lad – you need to give this to her. She *needs* to take it," said Barlow.

"How? She's asleep!" cried Brandon.

Barlow growled. "I just said, you got to get in deeper. Go into her mind lad. It's the only way."

Brandon stared harder at Lily. Deeper in her mind? Taking a deep breath, he pictured getting inside her mind. He imagined a door between him and Lily with a large lock. The mirror transformed before his eyes. A door emerged, sporting a large lock like he imagined. With a 'click', the door creaked opened slowly. Nothing but darkness greeted him. Brandon hesitated for a moment as Barlow's voice echoed in his ear.

"Now lad!"

Pulling his shoulders back, he called out.

"Lily!"

He scanned around him, afraid it didn't work, when he saw her. She wasn't laying down on the ground anymore. Instead, she was running. Towards him! He could see her face, a mixture of fear and determination. She was almost to the mirror when he saw her gasp silently and stare right at him. She opened her mouth and he almost cried when she tried to call out to him, but she snapped her mouth shut.

Her mouth moved, forming the word, "Brandon?", but no sound came out. He stared at her, motioning to his ear.

"I can't hear you Lil! Talk to me!" He called out louder, unsure if she would hear him.

She shook her head. She must have heard him but refused to speak. She stared at him for a few more seconds then glanced behind her quickly. She turned back at him, regret in her eyes, as she started to move away.

Brand stood frozen while Lily started to walk away from him. Barlow pinched his arm, jostling him back to the task at hand.

"Ow! Lil! Don't go! It's not a dream."

She turned back to him, her mouth open in shock. She waved her arms trying to tell him something

Brandon frowned. "Sorry Lil, I can't understand you."

Lily shook her head at him again. She pointed behind her into the darkness and pointed to her throat. Brandon looked in confusion until he heard Barlow whisper.

"She's not allowed to speak lad."

Brandon nodded, though not quite understanding. "Look Lil, I need to give you something."

He reached out to her when he heard it. The distinct clinking of nails dragging on the floor. A high-pitched giggle echoed in the darkness. It reminded him of every scary movie he ever watched, but way worse. Brandon saw Lily back away her eyes wide with panic.

"Little rabbit..." cooed a voice in the darkness. Brandon and Lily turned towards the pitch-black emptiness at the voice. It called out in a singsong lilt. "Where are you?"

Barlow nudged Brandon harder.

"Lil! You need to take this!" Brandon reached out with his hand. It went through the swirling mirror with ease. His hand passed through the silver, appearing on the other side. It felt weird – like water and air mixed together.

Lily whipped her head back and forth between the

encroaching darkness and Brandon. He could tell she was debating whether to run for it.

"Please Lil!! I can't lose you!" cried Brandon.

She gazed at him, a small tear falling down the side of her cheek. She nodded, reaching out slowly. He felt her fingers gently brush against his when she pulled the object from his hand. He finally was able to see it. It was a pendant. It dangled off a dark black chain of unknown metal. But what caught Brandon's eye was the pendant held the most brilliant colored stone he ever saw. It swirled with a fiery red and yellow gleam, as if a ruby and citrine fused together. Surrounding the stone was a bird, its large wings protecting the stone.

"Put it on lass! Hurry!" Barlow exclaimed urgently.

Lily hastily put the necklace over her head the same moment Brandon saw a white clawed hand reach out of the darkness towards her back.

He screamed, his heart stopping. "LIL!"

Lily turned around and ducked, rolling to the side effortlessly. He saw her turn wordlessly to him, mouthing a thank you, and bolted back into the darkness. The last thing Brandon saw was the sharp smiling teeth following after her into the blackness. He shook his head in frustration as the mirror's surface smoothed until all he saw was his own reflection staring back.

"Wait...wait!! Did she get away? Is she okay?!" Brandon hit the mirror, shaking it. He barely felt Barlow and the others grabbing to pull him back. Brandon kicked, images of the creatures chasing Lily replaying in his head.

Alasdair called out into his ear, trying to reassure him. "Calm Brandon lad, it'll be okay."

Barlow sighed, watching Brandon slowly start to breathe normal again. "You got her the pendant lad. That is her best shot at beating those things." Brandon felt Barlow's hand pat his head softly. "Ye did yer best lad. Have faith in the lass now."

Brom clasped his shaking hands together, biting his lip. "We must have faith in Miss Lily. That is all we can do for now."

Brandon's tears welled up, spilling down his cheeks. The last time he could remember was his dad patting him on the head; it was the day he never came home. He drew in a shuddering breath, rubbing his arms, his own reflection staring back at him sadly.

"Please...please be okay." He whispered brokenly.

TWENTY-THREE

L ily raced through the darkness, her lungs burning. She could feel them behind her. Goosebumps spread on the back of her neck, which made her run faster. Who'd have thought near death experiences could make someone who refused to run in gym class become a professional sprinter.

Yeah...only every horror movie ever, she thought sarcastically.

She didn't have time to process seeing Brandon in this dark abyss. Questions danced the surface of her mind like, "how did he get there, was he okay, how much time had passed, what was with the pendant?" She touched the pendant over her neck and absently rubbed it. She couldn't dwell on it. Not with fae straight out of the Shining coming after her.

Lily assumed they were close, but she wasn't completely sure. How much time had passed? The darkness was beyond pitch-black. She heard whispers surround her, coming from every angle.

And she swore those scary talons were scraping faintly on the floor all around her. Her heart, and her feet, stopped when the muffled giggling came closer.

"Little mouse! Little mouse! Where are you?"

She groaned internally, biting her lip in frustration. *Dannazione! What am I going to do?*

More giggling echoed in the darkness. Lily crouched, scanning the dim empty never-ending void surrounding her.

"Look sister! There she is!!"

Lily took a deep breath, keeping quiet, as the outline of the sisters glided forward. They clapped their talons together, tinkling and scraping together is a dissonant note. Their thin lips pulled back, their cruel smiles an eerie beacon in the darkness. Lily shuddered when they sang out.

"Now come on little one. We won! It was a wonderful chase wasn't it sister?"

The other giggled. "Yes! Quite exhilarating. I don't remember the last time we had such fun!"

They focused on Lily, their heads tilting. Lily remained in a half crouch, ready to jump. One sister reached towards her, clucking.

"Alright little rabbit. Since you gave us such a good run, we'll be generous. Plead for your life. Tell us why we should spare you?"

Lily's eyes widened. They wanted her to *explain* why she should be spared? She shook her head.

The sisters frowned, but quickly smiled again. Lily figured they were trying to appear kind, but the gleaming fangs didn't give her any reassuring vibes. She knew they had no intention of listening to her.

The first one scoffed. "Oh come on little mouse! We are going to *eat* you! As in dinner. You should at least say why we shouldn't. I mean don't humans usually want to live and all that?"

Her sister nodded eagerly in agreement. "Come on, speak up little mouse."

Lily clamped her lips tighter, refusing to speak. She warily watched the sisters. Resolute, she shook her head again harder, slowly backing up.

The sisters began to growl, their feathers fluffing their annoyance on full display. Lily shut her eyes, her hair whipping against her face as the sisters' wings flapped around her angrily. She tried to keep still while the faint brush of their ragged feathers stung her arms. Lily kept slowly breathing in and out through her nose, grimacing as she smelled the musty decay of their breath.

"That's enough games rabbit. Sounds like we'll eat you since you're not going to say anything." They growled as one. In perfect sync, the sisters reached out with one hand towards Lily's throat. She squeezed her eyes tightly, her heart thumping, a burning warmth building in her chest. She winced, a burning sensation spreading from her chest.

This is it...

A moment passed.

Lily flinched, confused. She didn't feel the sharpness of talons slicing her throat. Or anywhere for that matter. Actually, she couldn't even hear anything. Only when her chest cooled down and her heart slowed did she crack her eyelids open. She held in her shocked gasp.

The sisters were still in front of her, so close that she could see individual spidery lashes framing their black eyes. Their hands were still stretched out towards her throat, but they were statues. Right before her eyes, they had turned to stone. Their faces sported a silent scream, fangs glinting in the darkness by a red faint flickering light.

Lily scanned the area, trying to find where the light was coming from. She refused to turn her backs on the statues. She was afraid they would break free at any moment, but she couldn't find the source of the light. The warmth in her chest flashed hot, forcing her to look down. The pendant was glowing in the darkness, a comforting burnished gold copper glow blanketing her body. The light covered the sisters, their grayed stone skin soaking up the pendant's rays. She clutched the stone in her trembling hands. Cautiously, she poked one of the sister's stone eyes, confirming they were indeed solid stone. She sighed, her muscles relaxing slightly.

Okay, one problem down. Now, how can I get back to...

Before she could finish her thought, the pendant's light increased. Her palm was hot, but she couldn't peel her fingers from the stone. Holding in the pain, she tensed as the light grew, forcing her eyes shut.

E adesso?! Lily grumbled to herself. *What's happening now?*

It was the soft breeze Lily noticed first. She greedily breathed in the fresh clean scent, not knowing how she much she missed it. Lily opened her eyes. She was back in the marsh. She squeaked, a bubble of hysterical laughter escaping her before she clapped her hand over her mouth. She was back! She never thought she'd be so happy to see that murky, dank landscape but she was so relieved she could kiss the moss at her feet. Imagined only, she still had some rational thought left. She cupped her hands, yelling out.

"Cab?! Randy!! Parr, you there?"

She looked over her shoulder, letting out a breath. Cabyll stood where she left him, still frozen. Sirin hovered over him, cooing, a greedy smile gracing her red lips. Sirin hadn't noticed her yet. Lily's eye twitched, frowning. She wanted nothing more than to wipe that grin off that owl lady's face. Her anger bubbled up, the pendant heating up against her chest in response.

"Sirin!"

Startled, Sirin finally noticed Lily marching towards her. She cocked her head in confusion, her feathers fluffing.

"Little human? How?"

"How am I here?" Lily threw her arms out and spun around. She stopped a few feet from Sirin, glaring at her. "I think the question should be, where are your cousins Sirin?"

Sirin's eyes widened in panic. There, in a patch of reeds, rested the stone statues of the sisters.

Sirin sputtered. "You couldn't! How could a mere human do that?" Afraid, she wrapped her wings around Cabyll.

Lily couldn't tell if Sirin was trying to protect Cabyll or simply refusing to let him go. Was Sirin seriously thinking she was protecting him? How deluded was this bird? If she had to bet what Sirin was thinking, she suspected it was the latter.

Lily glared and demanded. "Get away from him Sirin."

"NO!" Sirin shouted, desperately clutching Cabyll in her talons.

Lily crossed her arms. "Sirin...let him go. Let them all go."

Sirin looked at her with pleading eyes. "You don't understand. I finally have him! I've waited so long." She gazed at Cabyll's frozen face, her eyes softly taking him in as one talon gently grazed his cheek. She turned her gaze back to Lily, eyes half crazed. "You have NO idea what it's like to want someone so much and they ignore you."

Lily sighed, disgusted. "How is this any better?" She gestured to his still form. "He can't talk to you, hold you, or even smile at you."

Sirin's red lips trembled. "But he'll never leave again..."

"That is *not* how someone stays with you. He's not a thing!" Lily felt the pendant getting warmer. She gently clasped the warm metal, her anger draining away. She pitied the owl fae. To desperately cling to someone who does not want you. Lily reiterated gently. "Sirin, you need to let him go."

Sirin glanced at Lily's necklace, her face lighting up in fear as the pendant's glow began to move towards her.

"That necklace! It can't be! How do you have that?!" Her voice shook, her eyes getting impossibly wider.

Lily could practically feel the cold fear radiating from Sirin. The light grew, covering Lily and spreading outwards, reaching Cabyll. Sirin jumped away from Cabyll as if burned. Desperate, she spread her wings, trying to escape, but the light quickly encompassed her, cocooning the owl fae in a blazing ball. Lily heard her cry out in desperation.

"No! Please no – I just had him!"

Lily shielded her eyes, but she couldn't see anything but a copper haze. When the light dimmed, the pendant cooling against her chest, Sirin had disappeared. All that was left were a few burnished downy feathers falling around them in the dimming light. Ignoring them, Lily ran up to Cabyll, grasping him by the shoulders. She searched his face, but he was still frozen.

She shook him, or as tried to as much as she could for a guy twice her size and frozen solid. "Cab! Cab...please say something. Anything!"

He didn't move, still as a marbled statue. Lily kept shaking him until her hands ached, but still nothing. Defeated, Lily dropped her head to his chest, biting back tears.

Lily sniffed, hot wet tears running down her cheeks, sinking into the scratchy fabric of Cabyll's shirt. "Come on! I'm sorry for our fight. I'd even take one of your arrogant, smart-allic, comments if only that meant you were okay."

A faint purring rumbled against her cheek before his deep voice growled softly.

"Well...I do aim to please."

Lily's head shot up. Cabyll stared down at her with an unread-able expression. She stood still, blinking up at him. Cabyll's eyes smiled, his lip quirking upward.

"Lily?"

Lily continued to stare, forgetting to speak. She barely regis-tered his arm had moved up to cradle her shoulders. She knew she should smack him, but she was just so happy to see him back to his normal 'pain in the butt' self.

Cabyll coughed nervously, looking down at her, their noses practically touching. "Lily," he said gruffly. "You're standing on my foot."

She jumped back immediately. "Oh my gosh I'm so sorry! Does anything hurt? How's your foot. Oh man! Not just your foot, I mean you were practically a statue for how long?"

Cabyll chuckled, dusting his sleeves off, feathers fluttering around him. He opened his mouth when Lily clapped her hands, turning away.

"That's right! Parr, Randy – where are they?"

A moan rang behind them. Parr crawled from behind the brush, covered in muck. Lily rushed over to help him up.

"Parr are you okay?" she asked anxiously.

Parr moaned again as he slowly stood up. Lily gently held onto his arm.

"That..." he panted, "was...the most...horrific experience of my life!"

Cabyll raised his eyebrow. "You mean being paralyzed by a siren for eternity while being plagued by your either your best dreams or worst nightmares?"

Parr shook his head. "No! Being stuck in this disgusting muck and smelling that putrid smell. Look at me!" He stomped his foot with a resounding squish. "I'm positively rancid!"

"Wait. So, you could smell?" Lily asked.

Parr and Cabyll nodded.

"And see and hear as well. Sirin wanted us conscious first." Cabyll added.

"So...you saw?" Lily couldn't continue as her face reddened. He couldn't have heard her crying on his chest, right?

She ducked her head. *Oh, where's a hole to swallow me up now?*

"What Sirin did to you, yes," said Cabyll seriously.

Lily looked up at him confused. "Wait what? Oh, which part?"

Cabyll's eyes widened, his mouth opened in disbelief. "Which part? Which part?!"

He began pacing back and forth, raking his hand through his hair. He stopped, glaring. "What were you thinking Lil?! Going toe to toe with the sisters?"

Lily was confused. Why he was so mad? "Well, that wasn't part of the plan believe me. She brought them when she got a little upset."

"And why was she mad?" He demanded, eyes shining.

Lily paused. *Oh...he didn't hear that part I guess.*

"It doesn't matter," she mumbled.

Cabyll glared at her. "Doesn't matter? Lily you were almost eaten by owl fae! Did you know that I could see them hovering over you, ready to slice you and I couldn't-" Cabyll stopped, shaking his head. He looked at her coolly with a frosty tone. "What was so important that you had to take that huge risk?"

Lily looked down, tucking her hair behind her ear. "Because I wouldn't go home and leave you guys behind."

"Budeureoun maeum," whispered Cabyll, his gaze unreadable.

Parr clasped his hands over his chest. "Oh Miss Lil. You are truly an angel."

Cabyll scoffed. "More like stupid."

Lily felt her anger rising. "Stupid?! You would still be paralyzed being her stone boyfriend if I didn't do anything!"

Cabyll refused to look at her, crossing his arms over his chest as he muttered. "Maybe you should have left me to her."

"I wouldn't have," said Lily. "I don't leave friends behind. Even when they're a pain. Even if we had a fight." She stared pointedly at Cabyll

He still wouldn't look at her, but the back of his ears went red. Parr snickered. Cabyll glared at the brownie.

"You have to admit Cabyll, Miss Lil did a bloody well brilliant job." Parr beamed at her with pride.

Cabyll scratched his neck, glancing over at her. His face smoothed to his typical smirk.

"Well, I guess you could consider it pretty impressive." He coughed to cover his smile. "For a human."

"For a human?! I believe you mean for anyone!" Parr exclaimed. "She took on the sisters and survived! If that was *me* I would be chuffed to bits! What Miss Lil pulled off was quite an extraordinary feat if I do say so myself."

Lily blushed at the unexpected praise, especially coming from Cabyll. This was probably his apology for his part in the fight as well.

She smiled. "I'm just glad to have my friends back."

There was a slight pause, ending when Cabyll roughly groused out. "Okay that's enough." He turned to Lily with a nod of his head as he began to walk. "Let's get moving. We've lost enough time."

Lily stopped as she suddenly remembered they were missing someone. "Wait!" she called out. "What about Randy?"

Parr nodded vigorously. "Yes! We must not leave a party member behind! Am I right good fellow?" He struck up his fist, looking up at Cabyll, waiting for him to join in solidarity.

Cabyll stared blankly at Parr's fist. "He'll be fine. Don't worry, that spider will find us without anyone's help."

He turned away, leaving Parr behind as the brownie awkwardly put his hand back down.

Lily patted Parr's shoulder reassuringly. "Randy left before Sirin got there. He was okay then, and I'm sure he's okay now." She sounded more confident than she felt, but she didn't tell Parr that.

"Thank you, Miss Lily. You really are too kind." Parr glared at Cabyll as he called out. "Unlike some other chaps I know."

Cabyll groaned loudly, refusing to look at them. Lily giggled at Cabyll when he glanced gave her a halfhearted glare. She didn't want to ruin the moment by pointing out she could see the faint curl of a smile beginning to form on his lips. Then, as soon as the smile appeared, it disappeared, Cabyll's gaze stone cold. His gaze was focused behind her.

"Lily!" he cried out.

What now?!

Lily faced the tall grass. At first, she saw the swaying of the yellowed green fronds in the breeze. Something passed her vision. She peered closer into the foliage. Between the wispy strands a pair of burning yellow eyes stared back, camouflaged amongst the undergrowth. Parr gasped behind her. She held her breath, the figure and her staring each other down. Someone called out, but she couldn't make out who it was. She raised her walking stick.

I'd like to hit one of these guys just once!

"It's the Hecesiiteihii! Run Lily run!"

Soon as the silence was broken, the eyes jumped towards her. She tried to jump back, swinging the stick, but her foot sucked deep in the mud. Her arms flailed, dropping the stick, the sky tilting backwards. Her back hit the ground with a squelching thud. She let out a whoosh, the air leaving her lungs. Pain radiated up her back to her shoulders, the cold-water seeping into her clothes. She groaned, trying to catch her breath as seven small bulky shadows surrounded her. Her hand covered her eyes, the light too bright. The outline of the figures hovered over her, their yellow eyes staring down unblinking. She tried to kick out at them, but several strong hands held down her ankles, then banded around her arms. She squirmed, trying to break free. They lifted her into the air effortless. She sulked, remembering what Randy said about the Hecesiiteihii being unnaturally strong. She tried to calm down her racing heart and think. If she couldn't get out of this by force, she needed to keep a cool head.

"Make her go sleep sleep," grunted a low voice.

A sharp pang reverberated against the back of her neck. One last thought rang before her eyes closed.

Gosh dang it, can't I catch a break?

TWENTY-FOUR

L ily groaned. The first thing her mind registered was her heartbeat thumping against her chest, then her breath coming back to her. Finally, she started to hear voices beneath her. They were rough and gravely, like stone grinding over concrete. Calloused hands held her upright, like she was a plank of wood. She cracked her eyes open. Nothing but sky greeted her, the treetops outlining the edge of her vision. She must have been knocked out for a few hours as stars streaked across the sky. The voices continued to their conversation below her. She tried to listen closely, but it was hard to make out over her throbbing head.

"This her?"

"Neihoowóé'in!"

"What you mean don't know?! How many humans you see?" A lower voice growled.

The others continued their argument. Lily strained to hear more but she couldn't make it out entirely until she heard the same growly voice speak up again.

"We stop to rest. Then we take them to see him. Understand?!"

"Hee!" called one.

"Hee'ínowoo!" Others called out in a gravely chorus.

The growly one, Lily assumed was the leader, yelled out. "For His Highness!"

"His Highness!"

Lily bit her lip, trying to stretch to clear the ache in her neck.

You know, I would really REALLY like it if I could have about five minutes without having a life-or-death situation thrown at me. That would be fan-freaking-tas-tic!

The world tilted right side up again. It took her a moment to realize she was being lowered. She was placed against one of the tall trees. One of the dwarves tied her hands behind her back, the rough rope scratching her wrists. Cabyll and Parr were on the other side of the clearing. Parr was passed out. Cabyll was alert, but she noticed his hands were bound in front of him with some kind of metal gloves with runes etched into the surface. He caught her looking at him. She gestured towards the gloves. He gave her a nod, lifting them mouthing, *enchanted*. She leaned her head back against the bark with a soft thud.

Great, so no magic lightening help.

She looked back at him, wondering what they could do next. Before she could mouth something to him, two of the largest dwarves picked him up and dragged him out of the clearing.

Cabyll kicked his feet, but the dwarves easily pulled him like a kid pulling a sled.

"Cab!" Lily tried to yell, but her voice was scratchy.

He looked back at her and mouthed, *It's okay*, before he was pulled from sight.

Lily gritted her teeth in frustration. How could it be okay? This was so far from okay. She tugged at the ropes again, feeling helpless. It sounded like the dwarves were going to take her to see Prince Jacy. There wasn't much time left. Not to mention she wasn't sure what kind of condition they'd meet the prince as she smelled the beginnings of a stew. She refused to look at what they were using for meat. Or if there was no meat at all...yet.

"Gah! Think Lil, think. It's only a rope, you can do this," she muttered to herself.

"Really? Can you?" Lily flinched, startled as a bright chipper voice called from above. The voice continued.

"Wow I'd LOVE to see this!"

Lily twisted to find where the voice was coming from.

"Up here girlie! Up...up...there ya go!"

Lily stretched her neck so far up she felt she was bending backward, but she could finally see where the voice was coming from. Up on the lowest branches of the thick oak was a small cage. Lily wouldn't think about what it was made from, but the bleached white sticks were eerily similar to what she saw in the marsh.

Inside the cage was a young woman. She looked to be about Lily's age with alabaster skin and long platinum silver hair tied in a tight braid down her back. Her white teeth gleamed in the twilight, her eyes a brilliant violet. Those eyes were twinkling at Lily as the woman jumped up and down giggling, her voice clear as a stream trickling down onto Lily like dew drops.

"Wonderful! Now girlie if you could do me a teensy weensy favor please?"

Lily was confused. "Um, I'd love to help, but I'm a little tied up at the moment." She twisted her hands for emphasis. The young woman giggled again.

"Pffft! That's nothing! Tell you what, I help you and you help me. Savvy?"

"And how can you help me?"

The woman gestured behind her back and that's when Lily noticed a bow.

"Here – let me show you!"

With a flick of her wrist, the woman effortlessly pulled the bowstring taunt. Lily frowned. There were no arrows. What was the woman thinking? No sooner than she thought it, a beam of light formed on the string. The woman left go and the light beam quickly flew down to cut through Lily's ropes like butter.

Amazed, Lily rubbed her sore wrists, trying to get the blood circulating. Familiar pinpricks of feeling started to come back in her fingers. She kept her hands behind her, just in case, because she wasn't sure if the dwarves would come back. Quickly, she looked around the clearing to make sure they were alone. Unafraid, the woman called out lazily.

"Eh don't worry about them, they're busy eating. When they're eating there's nothing that can distract them. One of the downsides to the curse. Though they are strong – so very strong, but that reminds me of the time when I fought those mountain trolls and then I tore-"

"Peri..." rumbled a deep voice.

Lily turned to find another cage on the other side of the tree. The cage was huge and held the biggest fae Lily had ever seen. He was massive, probably about eight feet tall and just as wide. His tawny red hair was shaved on one side and braided on the other. He had a large scar that ran down from his left eye down to his chin. It made him look fearsome and dangerous. The large fae looked up at the woman, Peri, with a sigh.

"Don't scare the poor girl Peri," growled the large fae.

Wait...he's worried SHE might scare me?

Lily noticed there was a manic glint in the female, Peri's, eyes. She shuddered. Somehow, that glint was scarier than the large fae next to her. Unfazed, Peri rolled her eyes.

"Don't scare the poor girl Peri." Peri mocked in a low voice, putting her hands on her hips in an exaggerated fashion. "Come on Spyke I think she can handle a little story time."

The large fae groaned, the sound like thunder rumbling across the plains. "Peri, stay focused will ya?"

"Yes! Focused! I'm the epitome of focus Spykie poo!" Peri saluted with a flourish.

Again, the large fae, Spyke, groaned louder. He mumbled something like, "We're gonna die."

Lily looked at the two fae and asked. "Thank you for helping me. How can I get you out of there?"

"You're still going to help?" Spyke asked with an incredulous look.

Lily nodded.

Spyke snorted. "Foolish human."

Lily ground her teeth. What was it with fae thinking being kind was foolish? "You helped me. It's fair." She didn't care if they were dangerous, or it was foolish of her to help them. She didn't want anyone to be on the menu for those scary dwarves.

Spyke looked at her for a moment, then slapped his meaty hands together. "Alright, well for starters we need you to get Peri out of that cage." He pointed upwards.

"What about you?" asked Lily. Surely the big fae could take care of it himself.

Spyke shook his head. "You aren't strong enough to break me out. She can."

Lily didn't comment that Peri was smaller than her. She checked to make sure they were still alone. Assured, she slowly got up. She took a deep breath, staring up at the cage. Why was it so high? Peri called out excitedly.

"Don't worry girlie! We'll be a look out for you. Just focus on climbing up kay?"

Lily got her footing and started climbing up the massive oak. She tried to remember the last time she climbed a tree. She was maybe thirteen. And she fell halfway up, breaking her wrist in the process. She shook her head, dispelling the unpleasant thoughts, focusing on not looking down. One step, two step. She kept her gaze on the rough bark in front of her.

"Almost there! That's it! Just a little more! Liiiiitle more. Ha!" Peri triumphantly called out above her.

Lily glanced warily over her shoulder, hoping she wouldn't

look down. Thankfully, she was parallel to the cage, Peri eye level with her, the fae's eyes gleaming. Peri clapped her hands, jumping up and down again excitedly.

"You did it! What a champ! You know this reminds me of the time in the Maldives-"

"Peri, focus!" Spyke chided.

Peri rolled her eyes, giving an exaggerated groan. She looked back at Lily and grinned. She whispered loudly. "He's such a spoil sport you know. I guess there's no time like the present. Get me outta here!"

Lily looked around the cage. She saw no latches or mechanisms of any kind.

"How?"

Peri shrugged. "Eh just push it, it'll fall apart."

Lily was confused. "But, why can't you get out then if it's so easy?"

"Because I can't touch 'the bars'." She gave air quotes. "It drains me." She gestured towards her feet. Lily noticed Peri was hovering above the frame, not touching the white bars.

"That's why they put her in the tree. I can't free her from that." Spyke replied from down below.

Peri gave Lily a little pushing motion. "So do a little pushy push kay?"

"Why can't you touch them?" asked Lily.

Peri smiled. "I like you! You ask questions! They're enchanted...well I stand corrected. They're blessed. Holy things ya know?"

Lily didn't know. "But what are they?"

Peri took a deep breath.

Spyke interrupted. "Don't ask..."

Okay, here goes. Lily gulped. Digging her feet into the bark and holding on tightly, she shakily reached out to give the cage a slight push. She didn't have to push hard thankfully. Sure enough, like a domino effect, the walls collapsed on one another until it broke apart.

Peri stood in the middle as the cage fell around her. She twirled around in the air with a triumphant smirk, giving an eerie cackle.

"See?! Easy peasy!" She giggled again. She flew over to Lily to grab a lock of her hair, rubbing it gently. "Where *did* you get your hair done it looks so nice! Such a beautiful shade of black. Or is it brown? And these curls! Do you use product?"

"Peri! Focus! A little help here!" Spyke barked.

"Yes yes coming!" She called down flippantly. She started to zip down when it caught her attention Lily was still holding onto the tree trunk for dear life. Peri flew back up beside her.

"Need a hand down?" Peri asked innocently.

Lily nodded mutely. While the two fae bickered, Lily made the mistake of looking down. Now she was too afraid to say much else. Getting up was one thing. Getting down, well that was another matter. Peri pulled her into a hug and, to Lily's surprise, hoisted her up effortlessly from the trunk. The fae gently flew down to the ground, setting Lily softly to her feet.

Peri winked at her as she rolled up her gossamer sleeves. "Now to break the big guy out. You wait one second sweetie girl!"

Lily, wide-eyed, watched as Peri, little, small, diminutive

Peri, casually walked up to the cage. She cracked her knuckles, grabbing both bars. With barely any effort, the bars bent like they were made of play dough. Next thing the side of the cage was thrown overhead as it landed in the brush with a loud crash.

Lily blinked. *Note to self...don't mess with Peri.*

"Ugh, Peri. You're supposed to be quiet." Spyke rubbed his face.

Peri shrugged nonchalantly. "Pffft, it's fine. They're eating right? They're off in food baby la la land."

A horn blared in the distance. Gravely voices approached from the other side of the bushes. Peri and Spyke looked at each other. Quickly, Spyke ruffled through the brush, looking for something. He stood up, carrying the largest war club Lily had ever seen. Strapping it behind his back, Spyke glared down at the little fae. Peri sheepishly waved.

"Um...I guess they're done?" Peri rocked back and forth on her heels with an apologetic grin.

"Yup. Definitely will get me killed one day," mumbled Spyke.

"Okay time to go girlie!" Peri quickly ran over and grabbed Lily's hand. As she was being tugged forward, Lily pulled back.

"Wait! My friends!" Lily gestured over to where Parr was knocked out. She still had no idea where Cabyll was taken. She didn't want to leave them behind. What were they doing to Cabyll right now? And Parr, what would he think if he woke up and he was alone?

"Don't worry. We'll help your friends. But we gotta get outta here first. Savvy?" Peri tugged again at Lily's hand, harder.

Lily looked back, full of indecision. A heavy hand engulfed her shoulder. Spyke stared down at her, his face compassionate.

"They'll be okay."

She didn't know how, but she trusted him. Lily let out a huge breath and nodded. She turned and followed the two fae into the brushes away from the dwarves as fast as she could run.

THEY RAN for what seemed like hours. They finally slowed down once they reached a good spot that Spyke deemed was far enough away from the Hecesiiteihii. They sat down to catch their breath, Lily's lungs burning. Peri started laughing. Lily was beginning to think that Peri was a little insane.

Peri cried out with excitement. "That...was...awesome! So dangerous and thrilling! Let's do it again!"

Spyke groaned. "No Peri." He looked over at Lily, seeming to read her thoughts. "Yes, she is insane."

Peri snorted, delicately. Lily shook her head. Who could make a snort graceful? Well apparently, Peri could.

Peri pouted. "I'm insulted Spykie poo. I'm never talking to you again."

Spyke grunted with a roll of his eyes towards Lily. Looks like this wasn't a new threat from the female fae. He looked up at the sky and counted his fingers down from three, two, one. Right when he hit one, Peri turned around to let out a large sigh.

"Wow that was the longest time I've ever not spoken with you Spyke. Don't upset me again. You must be sooooo sad."

Spyke chuckled softly. He turned towards Lily with a warm smile.

"We promised to help your friends. But first, I think we need to hear your story human."

"Lily, my name is Lily."

Spyke nodded and gestured towards Peri. "You know Peri. My name is Shappa, but Peri likes to call me-"

Peri interrupted loudly.

"Spyke, Spykie Poo, Spkyster-"

Spyke put his hand over Peri's mouth, his palm so large it covered her whole head. He chuckled as Peri's arms kept moving, her voice not stopping even though it was muffled under his palm. Lily covered her mouth to hide her own smile.

"Peri calls me Spyke. You can call me that too if you like." He smiled down at Lily. She noticed his large face sported small tusks that jutted out from his lower jaw. Even though he seemed so fearsome, Lily couldn't help but smile back into his kind eyes.

"Thank you both for helping me out back there," said Lily, very grateful.

Spyke shrugged off the thanks, his massive shoulder rolling. "No need. You helped us as well. But I think you need to tell us why the Hecesiiteihii were holding you captive so we can help your friends."

Lily thought that was a very reasonable request. Soon the story came spilling out of her mouth. Her sister, the kidnapping, meeting Parr/Cabyll, and before she realized it, she had told them everything. In the back of her mind, she knew she shouldn't have confided in these strangers. But if she was honest with herself, it somehow made it seem more real and the weight lessen just a bit. Peri and Spyke listened silently, well mostly silent since Spyke had to shush Peri a few times.

Finally, when Lily finished her story, Peri was wiping a tear from her eye, turning to Spyke.

"Spyke, we HAVE to help Lily!"

Spyke nodded with a grunt. Peri came over and wrapped Lily in a warm hug. Lily swore she could smell sugared berries and peppermint.

Peri squeezed her tight. "You poor, beautiful little human. Don't you worry your precious head. Peri is here to make everything better you'll see! Can we keep her Spyke please?!"

Lily smiled, awkwardly patting Peri's hand. It was hard to move as the fae hugged her a teensy bit too tight. "Thanks Peri," she wheezed.

Spyke laughed when Peri immediately let Lily go to catch her breath. Inwardly she smiled. Somehow in a short time, these two ragtag fae became dear friends.

"Well first thing is first!" Peri announced, pacing back and forth. "We need to go to the revel. When is it?"

Lily couldn't answer. She didn't know how much time passed. Spyke answered for her.

"Tonight."

Lily gasped. She had lost a whole day. Even now the sun was setting at an alarming rate.

Peri, unnaturally serious, glanced over at Spyke with a raised eyebrow. He nodded.

"Is it far?" Lily questioned. She was really hoping they weren't too far away. There wasn't much time left.

Peri laughed, flippant again. "Pfft oh no! It's only a mile away. But I wanted to make sure this guy," she gestured with her thumb behind her at Spyke, "was okay going."

"Is everything okay Spyke?" asked Lily concerned.

Spyke tugged his braid, his face flushing red. Peri laughed so hard she snorted.

"Awww she's just the sweetest isn't she?" Peri came over to hug her again. "You're so cute! Spyke over here left Prince Jacy's service a while ago. The prince has wanted him to come back for so long. I just didn't want to put him in any hard positions. I could do this by myself if need be."

"Yeah, sure Peri," rumbled Spyke. "You'd be distracted by the first song or the first dryad."

Peri snorted. She stuck her tongue out at him.

"You were a soldier?" asked Lily.

Peri giggled. "Soldier? Lily sweetie. Spyke over here was one of Prince Jacy's Thunder Boys. Only the elite of the elite. You know his name, right? Shappa? It means Red Thunder. Spyke is one of the best." She folded her arms, a look of pride gracing her face.

"That's enough Per." His ears turned red to match his hair.

Peri ignored Spyke and continued. "So cause of Spyke, that means we have an open ticket to the revel. We just need to sneak in there without the Hecesiiteihii seeing us. Sounds like they're trying to get back in good graces with the prince."

Spyke growled. "They are dishonorable vermin. Even more so for bringing a helpless human to try to win back his Highness's favor. That is not honorable. Prince Jacy would never agree to remove their curse for that."

Peri clucked her tongue. "You're so noble. But why the prince wants Lily is what baffles me. I mean you're beautiful, cute, sweet, and innocent, but why would the prince send the Hecesiiteihii after you I'm not sure."

Lily blinked, trying to keep up with Peri's train of thought. Spyke noticed and chuckled.

"Don't try human. Peri is a moving stream. Best go with her flow than go against her."

Lily thought a moment before she tested a theory. "Unless he's trying to stop me from seeing my sister."

Peri tapped her chin. "Hmmm...good point. But that means that Prince Jacy is on good terms with Prince Dain. We may be rogues but we certainly would have heard about that development right Spykie?"

Spyke grunted in agreement. "They were never close in the past."

Peri shrugged. "Eh it doesn't matter. Point is we need to get there and fast to save your friends and sister." Peri clasped her hand firmly and gave Lily a warm smile. "You ready for a ball Lily pie?"

Lily nodded. "Let's go."

TWENTY-FIVE

*L*et's go to a ball she says...

Lily's inner sarcasm was in full swing. She frowned, tugging uncomfortably at the dress she was forced to wear. Peri was right. With Spyke they were able to walk right into the revel. Spyke explained the revel was always held in a glen outside the Fern Palace. Thankfully they made it right in time to blend with the crowd.

The music swelled, a cacophony of strings that blended harmoniously with crickets and cicadas, the steady drumbeats outlining the revel's main circle. Tall red oaks towered above her, reaching towards the stars, a perfect circle overhead allowing the moon and stars to shine down softly amongst the torches. Fireflies sparkled in a joyous dance around the oaks. They paid particular attention to a large one located in the back of the circle. In front of the largest tree there was a throne made of red cedar. Carved within the lustrous wood was a buffalo on one leg, a coyote on the other, the seat consisted of the turtle, the arms were the wings of a raven, and the crowning head was a massive eagle. Patches of sage, sweetgrass, and tobacco framed the base of the throne. Fae of all shapes and sizes filled the ferned glen. All the guests wore masks of various metals and images. They danced merrily with the creatures of the forest, laughing and drinking merrily. It was beautiful. Beautiful, but dangerous, as most things are.

Lily stared down at her dress, frowning. Peri insisted she wear this outfit made of spider silk and violets Peri put together. Spyke and Lily had to yell at the spritely fae twice to fix it so the material wasn't see through. Peri, confused why Lily refused to wear sheer spider silk, grumbled but complied finally. Lily shuffled from one foot to another, feeling ridiculous as she adjusted her mask, a delicate silver butterfly.

At least I got to keep wearing my pants, she thought with a sense of relief. She didn't find it very practical being in a dress when at any moment she knew she would probably have to run. And she didn't think she was being overly cautious. She was doing nothing but running away from something since she got to this place.

She looked around, trying to see if she could spot Ari or her friends anywhere. She jerked as a hand clasped her arm.

"Relax Lily pie, it's me," whispered Peri.

Peri looked otherworldly in her spider silk dress made with blue cornflowers. Her hair practically glowed in the moonlight as it framed her otter mask.

"You scared me Peri."

"Aww Lily didn't mean to. You seemed like you were about to

shake all those violets off, so I thought I'd come to give you some extra courage."

Lily smiled. It was nice to have a friendly face and she did need a little boost of courage. Peri continued to whisper urgently.

"You didn't forget the plan, right?"

Lily shook her head. "Yes, keep to the sides of the revel. I'll keep an eye out for Ari. Spyke is going to look for Parr and Cabyll and you will be up in the trees keeping watch above."

Peri smiled, squeezing her arm reassuringly.

"You are soooo smart for a human Lily girl! Okay, if you're good I'm going to go up oky doky?"

Lily nodded. Before she could blink, Peri disappeared into the crowd.

Okay...you got this. Just stick to the sidelines. How hard can that be?

Lily gulped, readjusting the hem again. She scanned the crowd, hoping to find Ari somewhere in the dancing circle.

"Well, howdy there, what's the plan butterfly girl?" A familiar voice asked behind her.

Lily jumped. Randy stared at her behind a bronze spider mask. He was definitely not trying to blend in. The outrageous fae was wearing a shocking outfit of what looked to be fur, gems, and... was that denim jeans? His smiling eyes looked down at her as he tossed an apple lazily in the air. She gaped a minute, happy to see he was okay. She couldn't even get mad at him for scaring her.

Lily grinned. "What's with you and apples?"

Randy barked a laugh. "Hoowee. Ain't that a hoot? Girl, you always do surprise me."

"I'm glad to see you Randy. I could just hug you!"

Randy smiled warmly, giving her a playful wink. "I'll take that hug later girl. And don't you worry yer pretty head. I'd not leave this story abandoned. But seems like we're missin' a few folks. Wanna bring me up to speed?"

Lily quickly told him what happened after he left them to Sirin. A few nods, frowns, and a knee slapping later, Randy tapped the bottom of his metal chin.

"Okay I see where this is going. I'll check over yonder to help that Spyke guy find Cab and Parr. You just sit tighter than a lid on a jam jar. If you need me, I'll be two hoots and a holler away got it?"

She nodded, reassured Randy was going to look for Cab and Parr as well. "Got it Randy."

As he headed into the throng he turned back, his eyes staring at her hard. He wagged his finger.

"I mean it Lily girl. Don't go diggin' up more snakes than you can handle. Just sit tight."

Lily rolled her eyes.

What is it with everyone thinking I'd cause trouble? They're the ones that are slightly insane.

But she listened, shimming backwards to hide behind one of the large oaks. She got to the edge of the massive tree trunk, off from the main crowd who were swirling in a hypnotizing dance. Several tables were strewn about, laden with all types of delectable foods and drinks.

One way to stay incognito. She picked up a flute of sparkling pink liquid that fizzed and popped. Her nose wrinkled as the bubbly mixture tickled her senses. She caught faint whiffs of wild strawberry and blackberries. It smelled so good. Lily was really tempted to take a sip. Then she remembered the stories of not drinking or eating fae foods, especially at revels.

Ug! Is that even real? She didn't want to test out that theory though.

Grimacing, she realized it would look more awkward if she didn't drink. She should have stayed hidden at the tree. Hoping she was being stealthy enough, she headed back towards the tree, praying not to attract any attention. Because she wasn't paying attention, she gasped when she plowed into something hard.

She fell backwards, her drink falling from her hands. Her hip caught on the table, catching her from making an even bigger spectacle. Wincing, she clutched her mask, hoping it was still in place. A deep voice asked, concerned.

"Oh my! Are you alright?"

Dang it! So much for being inconspicuous!

Lily looked up to find herself face to face with an extremely handsome fae. Clad in leather, painted with bright colors, he towered above her. His long straight dark hair fell down his back. Colorful feathers and beads were interwoven in his locks. His arms were bare, painted with unrecognizable green symbols. A gold puma mask covered the upper part of his face, his full lips smiling brightly as his moss green eyes glowed.

She managed to get out an, "I'm fine, thank you", hoping he would walk away. But he didn't. Confused, Lily looked down. To her horror, her pink drink was, much to her chagrin, all over the man's leather boots.

Mortified, she yelped. "Oh! I'm so sorry!"

Lily looked quickly for something to clean them. She grabbed a few large leaves from the table. On autopilot, she bent down to fix the mess. A deep warm chuckle tickled her ears. Lily paused, closing her eyes, embarrassed. Gosh she was stupid. A hand appeared in her vision, the fae reaching down to help her up.

He smiled warmly. "It is fine. Boots will mend, leather will dry. Do not bend for something that will come to pass."

"Still, I'm sorry for being so clumsy." Lily looked down, tucking her hair behind her ear.

"I must say it's quite refreshing to see someone so lively. Usually everyone here is-" He paused, searching for the right word.

"Perfect?" muttered Lily. Her eyes widened. *Oh, sugar biscuits! I said that out loud, didn't I?*

The man snapped his fingers, laughing. "That may be one word for it. I may find the term predictable more appropriate. You seem raw. More real."

Lily didn't respond, unsure what to say. She hoped maybe if she didn't say anything long enough the fae would get bored and move on. Certainly, there was something better he could do than talk to her. The center circle was swirling, the music growing louder. Maybe he could find a pretty fae to dance with and leave her alone. But that didn't happen as the man remained at her side. The silence between them grew. He kept staring at her with an unreadable expression.

"Please don't mind me," he murmured.

Umm...yeah exit stage left. Cautious, she turned to leave but stopped when the man whispered something to himself. He tilted his head, watching her intently.

"Butterfly..."

"Excuse me?"

He pointed to her mask. "The butterfly. Interesting choice for a mask. What made you choose it?"

"Well, not really sure. I just felt it was the right one. I've always liked butterflies." Honestly, she wasn't given many options. Peri gave her the choice between the butterfly and a large peacock. Lily was certain the latter was the opposite of blending in with the crowd.

He looked at her curiously. "Looks like you're on a journey that will change your life little butterfly."

He must have seen her confusion as he continued to explain. "The butterfly symbolizes change. I sense you're on a path that will change you in many ways. Mystery surrounds you little one. Like she's wrapped you in her inexplicable blanket."

If he was an ordinary human guy back home, she would have dismissed him without a second thought. However, Dorothy wasn't in Kansas anymore...well New Jersey. And this guy's words were way too sage/prophetic-like for her liking. Lily forced a bright smile while she backed away slowly. She realized she had to say something as she blurted out the first thing.

"Well, next time I'll bring the gang with my Mystery Machine. Um, if you'll excuse me."

He bowed low; his arm outstretched in a courtly gesture.

"By all means my Lady of Mystery."

Lily quickly stepped around him but stopped when she saw

the familiar faces of the Hecesiiteihii rustling through the crowd. Trapped, she tried to avert her gaze, turning back to puma guy to find another exit. To her chagrin, that idea failed as another tall fae walked up to her current talking partner, which she decided to dub as Puma.

This newcomer wasn't as tall as Puma, but he wasn't short either. He looked younger, dressed in all white and silver, with burnished red gold hair that curled around his crystal coyote mask which covered his entire face. Only his scarlet eyes were visible, which stood out against the clear crystal. Those eyes were cold and calculating, focused between Lily and Puma. Lily tried to think of another exit plan when Puma called warmly.

"Brother! Happy Solstice!"

The coyote stood unmoving for a beat, then finally gave a graceful bow.

"Good Litha brother," he said formally. His eyes stretched in a shrewd gaze.

The taller fae laughed and clapped his brother on the shoulder.

"No need to be so formal brother. While we don't see things eye to eye most times, you are family. And family is welcome at my court, especially during the Summer Solstice."

"I do appreciate that," the coyote said flippantly. He grabbed a flute of sparkling liquid. He lifted the mask briefly to quietly sip the drink, one arm behind his back in a courtly manner. Puma continued.

"Speaking of. How is your companion? Has she been enjoying her stay?"

Coyote nodded, the crystal mask glittering in the torchlight. "She has. Your hospitality knows no bounds as always brother Jacy."

The Puma, Jacy, smiled with a soft snort. "Oh Dain, you still are as cold as ever. I hoped your human would have thawed you."

The Coyote shrugged languidly. "I am who I am."

Jacy nodded. "As we all are brother."

Lily thanked her lucky stars she had a mask on to cover her expressions as she let those little information bombs sink in. How she wished she could drink that sparkling drink in her hand. Or disappear in the air, far away from these two.

Well, cavolo...

She not only found Prince Jacy, but also the prince who took Ari. Looking at the kidnapper again, she had an overwhelming urge to punch that crystal mask off his face. She wanted to yell at him, kick his shins, rip that pretty hair off his pretty head. Clenching her hands, she held her breath for a moment, willing her emotions to calm. She counted to thirty before she let it out with a soft puff. Logically, she realized it was no good to be upset in front of one prince, let alone two. But that didn't stop her from imagining throwing the drink in his face and hoping he'd melt like the witch of the west. She glanced around discreetly, looking for Ari. Was she locked up? She froze, heavy gazes centered at her.

"And who is this brother?" Dain asked curiously, his intense gaze burning her. That gaze made Lily cringe. She held back the urge to wipe her arms. In that moment, she wished for nothing more than one of those Looney Tune black holes to appear under her feet.

So much for a low profile, Lily grumbled to herself.

Jacy placed one hand over his heart and extended the other towards Lily in a gallant gesture, his warm smile full blast on her. "Oh! This is the mysterious Miss Butterfly." He bowed his head in apology. "I'm sorry my lady, my brother and I haven't seen each other in years. I forgot for a moment of present company. Please forgive me."

Lily smiled. Her mind inwardly screamed. *Don't mind me! Just forget I'm here and go back to your conversation. Please!* She felt like her face was going to fall off with the fake smile she forced.

Dain tilted his head, scanning Lily's outfit. He asked with slight curiosity. "A mystery brother? Hmmm..."

After a noticeable pause, Lily realized he was expecting her to speak. Reluctantly, she peeled her fake smile back to grit out a reply.

"A pleasure your Highnesses," said Lily softly with a slight curtsy.

She hoped her shaking legs wouldn't fail her. Last thing she needed was to fall, again. But at this point, she surmised, she already had embarrassed herself enough for the night. What was one more right? By some miracle she kept herself upright, her moderate curtsy successful. The icy calculating gleam in Dain's eyes had her on edge. Wasn't she supposed to curtsy? She assumed, but Brom never informed her about fae etiquette.

Jacy put up his hands, trying to reassure her. "Please my lady. It's the solstice. Enjoy yourself, no need for formalities on this night of revel."

Dain coughed discreetly, pulling Jacy's attention away.

"Brother Jacy. If I may remind you, the opening ceremony."

Jacy waved him off. "Yes yes brother of course. My lady Butterfly." He bent down to air kiss her hand. "Good travels on your journey. I will be seeing you soon."

"And to you with yours," responded Lily, hoping it was an appropriate response. It was hard to imagine this warm guy was part of Ari's abduction. But if these last few days taught Lily anything, nothing was as it seemed in this world.

Jacy smiled warmly at her. He motioned to Dain to follow him as he headed towards the throne. Dain waited a heartbeat longer, staring at her with narrowed eyes, before he turned to follow. Lily let out a long breath, willing her heartbeat to calm. After taking a few more deep breaths, she began to follow them slowly, trying to keep hidden within the crowd.

Lily couldn't see Peri, Spyke, or Randy anywhere. But she couldn't let this opportunity slip away. This was the guy who kidnapped her sister! It was times like these that she wished for a comm link, a walkie-talkie, even a brief mind reading would be great right about now.

She got to the edge of the circle where she had a clear view of the throne. Both princes stood up on the platform, engaging in a deep discussion. Lily rose on her tiptoes, hoping to catch a word, but the music and laughter were too loud. She couldn't hear a thing.

As she strained her neck upwards, she stumbled when someone roughly pushed passed her. She paled. It was the Hecesi-iteihii. Thankfully they didn't notice her as they rudely shoved their way towards the platform. Guests grumbled at them, but the dwarves ignored them. Their focus centered on the princes. They didn't bother wearing masks like the rest of the guests. And their stench...Lily tried not to gag. It was overwhelming. The Hecesi-iteihii stopped at the edge of the platform, making a semi ring. The largest stepped forward, kneeled, his voice growling loudly in the glade.

"Héébee your Highness."

The music slowed down until it quieted to a soft whisper. The guests stopped their dancing, looking up with curious eyes. Prince Jacy stepped forward, Prince Dain at his side. Jacy inclined his head towards the Hecesiiteihii, taking in their rough appearance. His voice solemn as he called out.

"Hecesiiteihii. It pains my heart to see you like this. Tell me, what brings the exiled to this revel. You do not need me to tell you that you are charged with pain of death if you would return. What would bring you here?"

The lead Hecesiiteihii looked up at the princes, his hand in a fist over his chest.

"We brought who you asked for Highness, but the other...she escaped."

Jacy frowned, but before he could open his mouth to speak another voice called out.

"Escaped? I wouldn't worry about that," droned a familiar arrogant tone.

Lily eyes widened. Cabyll walked up to the platform. He was dressed in a deep blue silk shirt and pants, his swords strapped to his back.

She frowned.

He was too clean and too finely dressed for a prisoner. He was also wearing a mask like the other guests. His was a fox made from black obsidian. He was too handsome, too otherworldly that Lily was tempted to believe that wasn't Cabyll. But Lily could see the bright green of his eyes. She could also spot that confident gait from a mile away.

Why was he walking up so casually towards the platform? Last time she saw him, he was being dragged away. Lily slipped through the throng of fae, who had gone quiet watching the spectacle unfold. Cabyll stood at the foot of the throne, his finger tapping unconcerned on the spear of the one guard. He looked between the dwarves and the princes, giving a smirk.

"That was a little oversight. I'm sure she's miles away by now. Just like you wanted. Nothing to worry about. She won't be here to stop any of your plans."

Jacy remained silent. Lily trembled slightly, watching the exchange. Her heart clenched as a pricking cold seeped into her bones. It slowly dawned on her. The delays, the flirting, the running in circles. The constant secrecy around Cabyll. Here he was...with the prince!

Lily's throat closed up, a stone dropping in her gut. She pushed the heel of her palm to her eyes, willing them to remain dry. She thought he was her friend. Granted he was an arrogant jerk, but she felt after everything that she could call him a friend. Lily tried to slow down her panicked breathing while her trembling fingers clenched and unclenched. She stared down at her hands, too pained to see the scene before her, when another hand covered hers, giving it a slight squeeze. Lily raised her watering eyes to find Randy staring down at her. He gave an apologetic smile.

"I know it seems bad, but don't worry yer little head darlin'."

"But-" she protested.

Lily looked up to find Jacy still staring down at the group, his eyes narrowed at the Hecesiiteihii. He sliced his hand down in a chopping motion and gave an order.

"I have no idea what you are all referring to. But enough is enough. Guards! Remove them!"

Before the guards could move in, the Hecesiiteihii jumped into action. They overtook the guards in a whirl of punches and flips. The subdued guards laid in an unconscious pile at the base of the platform, groaning. Cabyll stepped lightly over them as he walked up towards the princes. Jacy glared. He raised his hands, sparks and vines jumping from his fingertips, aiming at Cabyll.

"How dare you all interrupt this sacred time! You-"

Lily gasped. Jacy stumbled forward, his magic disappearing in a soft flicker. He fell to his knees with a thud, wheezing. Blue icicles encased his shoulder down to his hands. The golden Puma mask fell with a metallic thump. It echoed in the bower as it spun and rolled down the steps. Jacy looked up towards his attacker, his face pained with a mix of betrayal and anger.

He growled. "Brother! You?!"

Dain stepped forward next to Cabyll, slowly removing his mask with a calculating gleam in his eye. He casually flipped the mask in the air before throwing it at Jacy's feet.

"Betrayer!" yelled Jacy.

Dain shrugged. "You say betrayer, I say visionary."

Jacy shook his head, his arms trembling within the ice casing. "But the Hecesiiteihii...why?"

The lead Hecesiiteihii stepped forward and spat on the earth where Jacy lay.

"If his highness Prince Dain takes your territory, then he becomes new Prince of Forest. Curse will be removed. No need for pain any longer. No need for you."

Jacy's face darkened, a thunderous scowl transforming his face to a terrifying visage. Gone was the kind prince Lily had seen earlier. Even his voice deepened as it boomed throughout the glade, rolling like a mountain.

"I will remember this betrayer...once I am free, you will all wish the curse is the only thing I left you with. You will be begging for that instead of what I have planned for you!"

Dain clapped his hands, interrupting his brother.

"That's enough with the dramatics Jacy," he sighed disdainfully. He addressed the crowd, scarlet sparks dancing around him. "Either dance or leave!" The fae quickly set about their business, fear permeating the air. Lily focused on the throne.

Dain turned towards the dwarves and Cabyll, his eyes cold.

"You cut it too close Cabyll. You were supposed to lose the girl much sooner."

Cabyll shrugged, removing his mask, his hand smoothing his hair. "I had it under control. Granted there were...complications. But nothing I couldn't handle. Besides, it's done, isn't it? She's gone."

Dain chuckled darkly. "True. But it seemed you needed some help for a moment."

Cabyll narrowed his eyes. He crossed his arms, insulted. "Considering the bargain was first to bring you the sister, I should charge you more."

Dain shrugged. "I grew impatient. But as things stood, it was good you remained. I did not anticipate her family would come for her." He motioned to the collar around Cabyll's neck, giving a cruel smirk. "And you didn't anticipate that did you?"

Cabyll sighed. "As I said. Things got slightly complicated. Regardless, you knew I would have taken care of it."

Dain waved his hand. "Yes yes, I received your message when you crossed into the Veil. And you received my reply from that Aerico demon. But Cabyll, you were taking too long and that girl was not being deterred."

Cabyll raised his eyebrow. "Still, there wasn't a need to send Sirin and the Hecesiiteihii. I had it covered."

"Clearly..." Dain rolled his eyes.

"Dain-" warned Cabyll. "You knew my history with Sirin."

Dain waved him off. "Eh, you had it under control. You would have broken free of her spell, being the best assassin in the Veil. Besides, I knew about your bargain with the human. If Sirin took care of the girl you'd be free. I'd thought you'd be grateful."

Cabyll gritted his teeth. "Dain..."

"Yes yes. You said you wanted to keep that human alive. And she is alive right? No big deal. Besides, what's one more mortal in our immortal life?" He pressed at Cabyll, staring at him hard. "Am I right?"

Cabyll's face smoothed to a cold smirk. "True, mortals are mortals after all."

Dain glanced at the collar, amused. "I did find it rather enter-taining when I heard about the infamous Cabyll getting leashed."

"I'd like to think of it as a way to stay close to the target. But, a little assistance would be appreciated since she can no longer remove this." Cabyll drawled, pointing to the collar.

Dain laughed loudly, his handsome face glowing as he clapped a hand on Cabyll's shoulder. "Of course, I'll grant this favor for you. After all you've done for me."

Dain rested his fingertips lightly on the collar, tapping gently a few times. His eyes began to glow bright crimson. The collar vibrated, shaking wildly, until it shattered. Cabyll rubbed his neck, cracking it side to side.

Dain gave a triumphant grin. "Feel better?"

Cabyll smirked, his eyes dancing, "Very much. It was exhausting having that dead weight. It feels very thrilling to be free again."

Lily's face burned as she heard the exchange. How she wanted to wipe that arrogant smirk of that handsome face. In her angry haze, a strong arm held her in place.

"Woah there darlin'. Best stay put," warned Randy.

Lily hissed angrily. "Why? He's clearly on Dain's side."

Randy whispered in her ear. "Just watch the scene play out girl. Trust in that sly fox."

"But Randy!" she protested.

Randy looked at her with neither pity nor sadness. He was looking at her, willing her to understand. "I've known Cab a long time. Trust him Lily."

Lily jerked, insulted. *Trust him?! That two faced jerk —*

Lily was tempted to ignore Randy. Really tempted. She wanted to throw something heavy and sharp at Cabyll's head. She paused, conflicted. Randy seemed so sure. Well, she reasoned she could wait a moment. She couldn't see Ari yet, and she needed to keep the element of surprise. Last time Cabyll saw her she was still with the dwarves. And so, she waited, barely.

While she was having this internal debate, Cabyll was inspecting his nails causally. He gave a blinding smile to Dain as he asked curiously. "But why did you need to get rid of the other sister? I thought the more the merrier right?"

Dain grinned back, but the smile did not quite reach his eyes. "Oh Cabyll...I only need – Oh my dear you're here!"

Lily's mouth opened, ready to make a move. Randy held her back when Ari, clad in a shimmering pink dress strewn with rose petals walked across the throne. Flowers were woven in her cascading golden hair. She was so beautiful. Lily couldn't tell her apart from the fae.

Ari paused, searching until her gaze rested on the prince. She ran towards Dain, throwing her arms around the prince to kiss him on the cheek. Lily's eyes got huge, her mouth dropping. She couldn't believe it. Wasn't Ari supposed to be scared? Or sad? Instead, Ari was giggling at Dain, who smiled down at her. The prince asked smoothly.

"My special one, have you been enjoying the revel?"

Ari gushed. "Oh, it has been the best ever Dain! The music, the lights, oh everything is perfect." She looked down, finally noticing Jacy. Her nose turned up in disgust. "I thought you said you were going to talk to your brother. Why is he on the ground?"

Dain kept his charming smile in place, smoothing her hair as he shrugged. "Things escalated. Nothing to concern yourself with."

Ari, seemingly satisfied with the answer, clutched Dain's arm giving him a besotted smile.

Lily was flabbergasted. She was clinging to his arm? While a person was trapped on the floor in pain. Her shock soon gave way to the prickling of anger.

You have GOT to be kidding me-

Randy looked down, noticing her face. He whispered in her ear urgently. "Lily dear, I know what you're probably thinking, but this may be the time to keep your head down on this one."

Lily shook her head and looked up at Randy, determination in her gaze. She was tired of being told to stay put.

"I stayed put once Randy. Not again."

Randy shook his head. "Lily girl we really should-" He flinched when she glared at him.

She growled low. "Ohhhh no...not today."

Before she could think about it, she picked up her dress in both hands and marched through the crowd, up the platform. Out of the corner of her eye she could see Cabyll's eyes widen when he recognized her. He stepped forward but she gave him such a glare he stopped stone cold, his mouth dropping.

Taking a deep breath, Lily steadied herself. Hoping she appeared confident and strong, she called out loudly. "Arianna Greene! Can I have a word please?"

CHAPTER

TWENTY-SIX

Ari's grin fell, turning panicked eyes towards Lily. Lily managed to get on the platform, without falling thankfully. She placed her hands on her hips, her dress swaying in the slight breeze.

"Lil?" asked Ari dumbfounded.

Lily sighed. Of course, Ari must be confused. Lily guessed she looked completely out of place in a fae gown, a mask, and noticeably calling Ari out in front of a crowd.

Lily removed her mask slowly, raising her eyebrow as she asked. "So...wanna tell me a story? I'm all ears." She gestured to Ari's hand which was still clutching onto the prince's arm.

Ari opened her mouth and closed it a few times, which reminded Lily of a fish gasping for breath. She would have found Ari's face hilarious if it wasn't for their current situation.

Impatient, Lily prompted. "Anytime Ari."

Ari stomped her foot on the ground, reminding Lily of a petulant child. "What are you doing here?!" She screeched, her face mottled red.

Lily sighed, suddenly very tired. The anger fizzled out of her like a popped balloon. "I came to find you of course. We are worried about you."

Ari paused, startled at that response. She clearly expected Lily to berate her or yell at her. To be honest, Lily was too exhausted to yell. All she wanted was to bring Ari home.

"You...were worried?" Ari asked her, confused. She seemed wary, like a skittish colt.

Lily nodded, trying to keep her voice calm and soothing. "Of course we were. Brandon is worried sick about you. We imagined the worst. That you were dealing with goodness knows what over here."

Lily put her hands down to her sides. "We want you to come home Ari."

Ari stared at her in confusion, biting her lip. Her eyes were wide and bright. She opened her mouth to speak but stopped when the prince patted her arm. He interrupted politely, his voice silky and sly.

"Who is this nasty human my dear?"

Lily glared at him. She coldly replied. "I'm her sister. And who are you mister kidnapper?"

Dain tapped Ari's hand softly as he said flippantly. "Kidnapper? How dramatic! And not to mention simply rude."

Lily raised her eyebrow. "And 'nasty' human isn't rude?" She ignored the warning looks she was getting from Cabyll. She crossed her arms. "What else would you call it when you took Ari away from her home?"

Dain brought his arm around Ari's shoulders, giving a brilliant smile. He replied but kept his gaze on Ari. "I simply brought my special one to my home as she desired." His calculating eyes turned, boring into hers. "I only did what she requested of me. Hardly seems fair to say it's kidnapping when the supposed victim made the request."

Lily focused on Ari. Made the request? He's saying Ari wanted this. Lily frowned. Ari was staring at the prince with besotted expression, which worried her.

Please don't fall for those lines Ari.

Feeling she was losing a critical moment, Lily pleaded. "Please Ari, come home."

Lily watched, waiting.

Ari stared quietly at her. She looked back and forth between Lily and Dain with an unreadable expression. Slowly, Ari's eyes hardened until they were chips of blue ice. Ari turned away from Lily, her nose high in the air. In that moment, Lily's heart dropped, her face crestfallen.

Ari glared. "I'm not going!" She looked at Dain, her lip beginning to tremble as she whined. "She's no one. Please! Please make her go away Dain!" And with that, Ari buried her face in Dain's chest with a dramatic sob.

Lily palmed her face, too shocked to reply. *Seriously?*

The prince held Ari lightly. He glanced over at Lily, a satisfied grin spreading across his face. Lily's eyes narrowed. Something was really off about him. The prince raised his arm to call out loudly.

"You heard the lady. Looks like you need to go away Lily Ambrosino."

Lily scowled. So, he did know her name, that jerk. If he thought he'd get rid of her that easily, he didn't know her at all. "I'm not going anywhere without my sister."

Ari whirled around and scowled at her. "Sister? I can't stand you Lily don't you get that! You ruin everything! Just let me be happy."

Lily bit her lip, ignoring the sting. "And what should I tell Brandon huh? Your mom? That you don't want to be with them? That you can't stand them either?"

Ari flinched. Lily knew it was a low blow, but this wasn't the time to play nice. Actions had consequences. Ari just refused to acknowledge that. Ari clutched onto Dain's hand as she looked at Lily, her voice wavering.

"They'll be just fine without me. All of you will. None of you understand. When I'm here, the emptiness is gone. I'm special here." Ari rubbed her arms up and down uneasily, refusing to look at her.

Lily frowned at the raw hurt reflected in Ari's face. Lily took a deep breath. She knew she needed to open herself up for any chance of Ari listening, but she wasn't ready. But then again, who really is ready to bare their feelings. Bad enough to do it in front of one person, let alone a crowd. She hated crowds.

She said slowly. "Ari, I know things haven't been easy. Especially between us." Lily swallowed the lump in her throat. "I never knew my mother. I don't have one memory of her. I can't remember the feeling of her hug, her smile, or her laugh. I don't even have a memory of what she smelled like."

Lily couldn't hear anyone else over the blood rushing in her ears. She refused to look over at Cabyll or Randy as her own tears dampened her cheeks. She focused on Ari, who looked back at her in shock, tears streaming down her face. "I understand that anger. The anger of why someone you loved is gone."

Ari sniffed, her voice trembling. "I miss my dad so much."

Lily nodded. "Ari, you still have a mom who loves you so so very much. A brother who, even though he drives you crazy, and he doesn't know the first thing about giving you space. Regardless of all that. He would do anything for you!"

Ari shook her head in denial. "If they care so much, why aren't they here? Why did it have to be you?!"

Lily pulled in a trembling breath. "Because I care too!"

Ari blinked, stunned. "We're not sisters."

Lily breathed in, touching her hair ribbon, remembering that day. The words poured out, like a river flowing into the bay. "Maybe not by blood, but I care Ari. I care about your mom, and Brandon, and I even care about you. Even though you yell at me, make fun of me, I still care. Because at the end of the day, I choose to have you as my family. And family may have their differences. They may fight and sometimes we may not like each other. But you're still family Ari. You're my family."

Lily rubbed her eyes on the back of her hand, wiping the tears. She pleaded again. "Please Ari, please come home."

Ari waivered, uncertain. She stepped towards Lily but

stopped, looking back at Dain. He gave her an unreadable look. Ari paused to take a breath. She finally gave Lily an apologetic smile, her eyes sad.

Ari shook her head as she said ruefully. "I'm sorry Lil, but I'm staying with Dain."

Lily suppressed a shudder. It wasn't his confident smirk that caused her to shake, but the glint in his feral eyes as they bore into her. Lily's heart bottomed out when Ari returned to his side, clutching his hand again. She failed. She sniffed, holding in a small sob as she rubbed her cheek with a trembling hand. So, this was how it was going to be. Did Ari really hate her so much she'd leave her own mother behind? She bit her lip, hard. She couldn't let it end this way. She walked towards Ari when a rough hand twisted her arm, painfully.

Lily grunted, the pain forcing her to her knees, her arm twisted upward. Prince Dain appeared in front of her, jerking her arm upwards in his grasp. *Gosh dang it, these guys are too fast.* Lily cried out when a searing icy burn traveled down her arm. The prince looked at her with a raised eyebrow, his cold smile bearing down on her.

"I believe you heard her human...for a second time. I know you're not that smart, but I believe you heard her this time, correct?"

"Dain!" Cabyll shouted, his voice slightly panicked. "Let her go! You said she was to leave. It's not worth hurting her."

Dain, not looking at Cabyll, twisted his hand slightly. Lily cried out louder as her arm twisted even further, her elbow bending in a way she knew wasn't natural.

"Oh." Smirked the prince. "But this is just too fun. I was just being magnanimous. I gave her a chance to leave on her own. It's not my fault she didn't take my gracious offer when she had the chance."

Lily whimpered as the fiery cold seeped into her bones. Cabyll's terrified gaze held onto hers.

Dain clucked disapprovingly. "Cabyll, don't tell me you actually care about this one?"

Cabyll opened his mouth, but Dain interrupted him.

"Oh, it doesn't matter whether you care or not. Either way means nothing to me. I'm going to finish having my fun here. Oh!" He turned towards Ari. "You don't mind do you my special one?" he asked innocently.

Ari refused to look at Lily and shook her head, her blonde hair sticking to her cheek, covering her eyes. She whispered anxiously.

"You won't kill her right?"

Dain put his free hand over his heart. "Would the man you care for do that special one?"

Lily's eyes widened in shock when Ari turned her back on them. Lily wasn't a fool to notice the prince didn't answer the question. She desperately tried to pull her arm free, but it was stuck. Ice crystals began forming on her skin, spreading slowly downwards. She threw her leg out to kick Dain in the thigh. He grunted but refused to release her.

As the cold spread, Lily realized she did not have much time before she would be trapped like Prince Jacy. Only difference was she was human. She didn't have the luxury of immortality or rapid healing. If she remained in the ice for much longer, she'd lose her arm from frostbite. Probably even her life. Desperately, she used her other hand and reached under her gown. She steeled herself when her hands wrapped around an object within her pants pocket.

Thank goodness for pants!

She pulled out her small can of bug spray. With a last-ditch effort, she aimed and sprayed the contents in the prince's face. The prince howled, the stinging liquid burning his eyes. *I guess there was a purpose for bug spray after all.*

Wincing, the prince angrily growled as he rubbed his eyes. "You little!"

A low growl behind her vibrated her bones before a sharp prick traveled down her frozen arm. The ice casing shattered into thousands of sparkling pieces, falling around her in a snowy haze. Her bug spray must have given enough of a distraction. Cabyll had shot a lightning bolt, which broke the ice. Her arm fell to her side, numb, her nerve endings slowly starting to prickle back to life. She hastily rubbed her arm when Cabyll kneeled beside her, his eyes worried.

"You alright?" He joined her efforts to warm up her icy arm, his hands frantic.

Lily nodded, panting. She wiggled her fingers, the biting pain lessening slightly. Cabyll closed his eyes, looking relieved.

"I'm glad you weren't electrocuted."

"Me too...wait what?"

"Mixing of magics isn't science you know," retorted Cabyll.

Lily sputtered, but Randy jumped up to the platform and draped his coat over Lily before she could respond. She shivered when the heat engulfed her. Randy looked at Cabyll, exchanging a wordless glance. Cabyll dropped his hands, standing up, to face Dain. His green eyes were hard and cold.

Dain, healed from the bug spray, tsked. "Oh dear Cabyll, so you have started to care for this insignificant human."

"You shouldn't have hurt her," warned Cabyll.

"Ugh, why is everyone here so dramatic!" Dain scoffed. He shrugged his shoulders, indifferent. "Well, Cabyll, if you're not with me then..." He snapped his fingers.

Dwarves rushed over, surrounding them, their pointed spears inches from Lily's face. Randy clenched his hands, glaring at the dwarves. Cabyll knelt beside her protectively, his arms covering her. He glared at the prince.

Dain walked over to Jacy, pushing him over with a foot. Jacy grunted in pain as he tumbled. Dain looked down at his imprisoned brother with an apathetic gaze. "I honestly do not have time for this. It's time to do what I planned. My special one, are you ready for your destiny?"

Ari nodded shakily, still refusing to look at Lily. Instead, she focused solely on Dain, handing him a variety of items. The prince began arranging various crystals and herbs around the platform. While they worked silently, Cabyll whispered to Lily.

"Look, about what you saw earlier." He began hesitantly.

"When I get feeling back in my arms, I'm going to smack you upside the head so hard you're going to feel it down to your toes mister." She growled, trying to cover her fear and pain. Randy choked down a laugh, noticing Cabyll's ears getting red.

Lily sighed. "But I forgive you. I'm still mad at you but I forgive you Cabyll."

Cabyll let out a soft breath that, to Lily, sounded like relief.

"But!" Lily pointed her icy finger at him. "You owe me a thorough explanation when this is all over got it?"

Cabyll nodded. "More than fair."

Randy interrupted them. "Hate to break the reunion here guys but, what's the royal doin'? Cab if you have any idea since you've been in his circle, now would be a rootin tootin good time to tell us."

Cabyll looked frustrated, his eyes narrowed at the prince. "Not a clue. I was hired to take Ari, but when that fell through, I was to keep Lily away. Dain wanted the sister for something, but I don't know what."

"Be that as it may, I'm afraid we have bigger problems." A familiar voice piped up near them.

"Parr!" Lily squealed excitedly. He was okay! The brownie smiled warmly at her. Ignoring the spears surrounding them and her numb arm, she reached for him and gave him a big hug, practically leaving the little brownie's legs dangling in the air.

Parr yelped, his face going beet red. "Now now Miss Lily. I'm alright. But if you could kindly put me down, I am having difficulty breathing if you please."

Lily immediately dropped him. Parr let out a squeak. Randy laughed softly while the brownie dusted himself off, his face still bright red. Cabyll's frown deepened. Lily swear she heard him mutter,

"...he got a hug?"

Parr ignored the commotion and said briskly. "Look! As soon I was awake it was easy to escape those hulking Neanderthals. Though your new acquaintance, Miss Lily, did help dispatching the two that were still guarding me."

"Spyke? Did you see him? Is he okay?" asked Lily.

"Who's Spyke?" asked Cabyll suspiciously.

Parr and Lily ignored Cabyll. Parr nodded at Lily. "He's fine Miss Lily. He was still tangling with more of the brutes to give me time to arrive here. The dwarves were a chatty lot and we heard some things of the prince's plan that I had to find you straight away."

"He's already started something." Lily motioned up towards the platform.

"Oh no!" Parr said, dismayed. "If he's started then-"

They heard a deep groan.

"That means it won't be long until HE comes." The deep voice coughed.

Prince Jacy, still conscious, had crawled over to them. Lily was amazed. He must have been really strong to make his way towards them. He stared solemnly, his eyes bleak.

"I could tell from the circle he's creating and the herbs. My foolish brother seeks to release something unimaginable. Something that's been imprisoned for eons. One of my sacred duties as Prince of the Forest."Randy's eyes widened in horror, understanding. "Oh, he wouldn't! Is he mad?!"

Jacy nodded sadly. Randy barked something in another language that, to Lily, didn't sound pleasant.

Cabyll raised his eyebrow. "Excuse me, can you provide a clue for those in the room who are not part of the club."

Jacy took a ragged breath. It must have been difficult since he was encased in ice. Lily's heart hurt for him. He spoke in a strained whisper. "Before the Veil was formed, there were beings... very powerful and dangerous beings. They roamed between our world and the human world, destroying everything they touched upon. One such heinous being was imprisoned here shortly after the Veil was formed. My brother seeks to break it out of its confinement. He wants to awaken it. For what purpose, I'm not certain."

Cabyll swore under his breath, running his hand through his hair. He narrowed his eyes at Randy.

"Is it what I think it is?" He asked warily.

Randy nodded grimly. "Yup. Gotta be Uktena...the horned serpent."

Cabyll swore. "*Akma!*"

Randy sighed. "Devil is right Cab."

Lily looked between them worriedly. "Okay...that sounds bad."

"Reaaaal bad darlin'." Randy quipped.

"So, any ideas to stop them from summoning it?" asked Lily.

Jacy's pained gaze glanced up to Dain and Ari. The couple continued setting up the circle, not paying them any attention. "We may be able to, but you must go through the Hecesiiteihii. Honestly, I do not know how you can do this. My Thunderboys were the only warriors that could overcome the dwarves. But they're not here. I sent them on another quest on behalf of my father." His eyes glared up at Dain, full of anger. "I suspect my brother knew of this already. I fear without them, you cannot defeat the Hecesiiteihii."

Lily peered around the clearing, the Hecesiiteihii had moved away from them to spread out amongst the circle of trees. They were on guard, keeping all the guests from leaving. Their backs were to the forest, only focused inward. A strange sense of calm settled over her as she turned back to the prince with a smile.

"Looks like you still have one left your Highness."

Jacy gave her a puzzled frown until one Hecesiiteihii went flying over their heads, smacking against the ground with a loud thud.

Chaos erupted.

Panicked revelers stampeded towards them, all desperate to escape. Fae ran in all directions as bodies continued flying, parting the way. Lily smiled at a familiar gruff figure who emerged from the throngs. The large figure whirled a huge war club, knocking another wailing Hecesiiteihii into a tree with a crash.

Jacy looked dazed, uncertain if what he saw was real. "Shappa?"

Cabyll twisted his thumb towards Spyke, looking at Lily with disbelief. "THIS is Spyke?"

Spyke, twirling the club in his massive hands, bowed his head towards the prince.

"Your Highness, we're here to help."

"We?" asked Jacy. As soon as he asked, an arrow went flying towards the few Hecesiiteihii surrounding the group. The Hecesiiteihii sentries tried to knock off the arrows, but they exploded on contact, disorienting them enough for Spyke to hurl them in several directions.

Lily, grinning from ear to ear, stomped on the closest Hecesi-iteihii's foot, kicking his shin. The dwarf hobbled backward, unbalanced. Lily spun around, using her feet to sweep underneath his feet, which shoved him towards Spyke. Spyke took his massive boot and kicked the dwarf like a football. If he was a football, Lily speculated the dwarf would have given Spyke a touchdown with how far he flew. Spyke glanced down at her with a small smile.

"Nice kick," he said approvingly.

Lily gestured towards the several dwarves lying unconscious around her. "You did pretty good yourself."

Spyke chuckled. "You alright?"

Lily brushed her hands on the sides of her gown, not caring the dirt that smeared the fabric. It was already a torn mess. She looked up at Spyke with a grateful smile. "I'm fine thanks Spyke."

He grunted, giving her a nod. Lily ignored the choked cough Cabyll gave when Spyke elbowed past him. Spyke continued to move forward, reminding Lily of a tank, as he kept plowing through the throng of Hecesiiteihii.

"Whoo!! Good going Spykykeens!" Peri crowed above them. She flew over their heads, kicking a few of the flying dwarves when they whizzed past her. She kicked with such a force they shot into the forest like a rocket.

She landed down on the ground and ran to Lily, hugging her hard.

"Lily sweetie you okay? Spyke had to hold me back when I saw what that awful prince did to my poor sweet human."

Cabyll sputtered, somewhat in a daze. "Wait...*your* sweet human?!"

Peri stuck her tongue out at him, her arms still around Lily. "Stupid Cabyll! Stupid for leaving beautiful, sweet little Lily and oh my gosh! Deceiving her?! How could you be such a-"

Spyke grunted as he wrestled with a massive dwarf. He called over his shoulder. "Not the time Peri!"

Cabyll's eyes widened as he stared incredulously at Lily. "A Peri?! You made friends with a Peri?!"

Lily looked at him, confused. "Is there something wrong?"

Cabyll rubbed his forehead. Randy snorted in laughter, his shoulders shaking. Peri still had her arms around Lily, glaring at the guys. Lily couldn't understand. There was a huge fight, and they were just standing around? Why was Cabyll all worked up about Peri?

Cabyll groaned as he ground out. "Not if you don't mind catastrophes of biblical proportions. Lily, peri fairies are walking natural disasters! They thrive on chaos."

Peri shot her nose up at him, insulted. "And what is wrong with chaos?"

Lily paused as she took in that statement. *Well, the crazy makes a lot more sense now doesn't it?*

She looked at Peri's blinkingly innocent eyes and smiled. What did it matter if she caused tornados or earthquakes. She chuckled and patted Peri's arm in a sisterly fashion. Peri beamed.

Lily smiled at Cabyll. "She's my friend Cabyll. And we need their help."

Cabyll sighed, shaking his head. *"Sunjinhan..."* He pointed his finger at Peri with a glare. "You can help, but no volcanos got it?"

Peri shrugged, her eyes up at the ceiling. "Party pooper."

Spyke, dispatching the last of the Hecesiiteihii near them, yelled over his shoulder.

"Per – a little help with his Highness please?"

She dropped her hug from Lily, clapping her hands. "Oh right! Silly me!!"

Peri dashed towards Jacy, laying her hands over his frozen arms. Her hands glowed, a warm canary yellow light pulsing against the clear ice. Soon, the ice surrounding Jacy's arms began to melt, dripping softly to the ground in small puddles. Parr pulled out a handful of herbs from his pocket to help with the use of his own healing magic. Every spot where the ice revealed Jacy's icy blue skin, Parr quickly covered in green leaves and brown paste.

Peri continued to move from one spot on Jacy's arm to another, the light pulsing and melting. She shouted loudly over the chaos surrounding them. "Someone wanna take care of those two up there? This is gonna take a minute, even when this melts through."

They all looked up towards Dain and Ari. The pair appeared to be nearing the end of their preparation. In the chaos the duo still didn't pay attention to them, but Lily knew that meant time was nearing the end.

Cabyll glanced at Randy and Lily, unsheathing his swords. "Ready?"

Lily's nerves were pulled taunt, but now was not the time to hold back. "I got Ari, can you guys take care of Dain?"

Randy nodded. Cabyll, stoic as ever, raised his eyebrow at her as if to say, *of course silly human.*

With a blink, he jumped, gracefully landing onto the platform. He paused a moment as he straightened his back, fixing his jacket with a slight tug. Lily shook her head. You never would have guessed he was in a hurry. Taking his time, he tilted his head slowly, giving his neck a small crack. He stretched his hands, swords raised. Blue sparks flared out his fingertips, racing down the blades, as he stalked the prince.

Randy smirked, rolling up his sleeves. "Let's get this party started y'all!" Giving her a wink, he disappeared.

It took Lily a moment to realize she was left by herself at the bottom of the platform. With less grace than her fae friends, she clambered up. She tripped as the dress became tangled around her ankles. With a frustrated grunt, she bent down and tore the fabric away from her legs, the spider silk in tatters whispering over her pants. She looked to the sky and blew out.

Grazie al cielo for pants.

She got to the top of the platform and found Ari sprinkling the last bit of herbs onto her portion of the circle. Running up, she knocked the dried weeds from Ari's hands with a loud smack.

"That's enough Ari!"

Ari yelled back. "You're too late!"

Lily watched in dread when the circle began to glow, a faint iridescent light rising up. Dain gave a triumphant cry, yelling out something she couldn't decipher.

Cabyll launched himself at the prince, his sword ready to strike. Dain raised his arm, a red energy shield manifesting to greet Cabyll's sword. The two collided as the circle exploded in a large flash. A brilliant light encircled them until all visibility was gone. Blinded for a moment, the light eased and soon transformed to a mist that rose above them, twisting higher and higher into the sky.

The mist darkened and expanded to engulf the entire glen. Soon murky clouds formed, rising to cover the moon, the swirling darkness converging into a thick black mass. The earth quaked and Lily struggled to maintain her balance. She cried out, ducking as lighting cracked a tree near them. Whether it was from Cabyll or the spell she had no idea. She couldn't see what Cabyll and Dain were doing. All she could hear was screaming chaos. Lily gritted her teeth, keeping her focus on Ari.

"Ari! Do you know what that prince of yours is summoning? That thing will destroy everything!"

Ari looked at her with a gleam in her eye. "You can't understand. The serpent will get rid of all the problems. Then me and Dain will rebuild this place for the better. I will be his queen and he will step into his rightful place. He said we're destined for this Lily!"

Lily couldn't believe what she was hearing. How much did Ari drink from the prince Kool-Aid? It was hard for her to fathom the Ari she knew in the past would be okay with this. She could understand Ari not liking her. But she couldn't imagine Ari being okay with innocent strangers suffering. She tried another tactic.

Getting close to her, she gently grabbed Ari's wrist, speaking in a soothing tone. "Right, you'll be queen. I get it. But do you really need to hurt other people? What would your dad say?" She knew it was hitting way below the belt, but she was running out of options.

Ari paused, her gaze mistrustful, searching for Dain but was unable to find him. Lily could see Ari begin to weaken. She held back, staying silent. She hoped that Ari would come to her senses. For a moment, just a moment, Lily could see the Ari she knew before. Then, as if a curtain shut over her eyes, Ari's gaze shifted.

With cold eyes, Ari said resolutely. "He always said I was a princess. He wants me to be happy. And punish those who are in my way."

Okay...Ari has gone the deep end. Time for plan, well I'm running out of letters.

Lily shook her head, still holding Ari's wrist gently. "Ari, listen to me. Dain doesn't care about you."

"He does!" Ari insisted, wrenching away. She raked her hands in her hair, agitated. "You can't begin to understand what it's like to be special Lily. To have someone so...so amazing be with you. Be in love with you. This is for us to be together. It will all turn alright in the end. Like a fairy tale!"

"That is *not* love," Lily said exasperated. "Can't you see he's using you?"

Ari's furious eyes tore into her. "You're jealous Lily! You always have been."

Lily gritted her teeth, holding back. It would be no good to yell at Ari in the middle of a mini apocalypse. Or so she kept trying to tell herself. Those clouds were only getting darker.

Keep it together girl! She's not in her right mind.

Ari stomped her foot and glared at her as she continued. "Just because you'll be alone forever doesn't mean you have to ruin my chance at happiness!"

Lily's eyes narrowed. *Okay, forget not in her right mind. I kinda want to punch her now.*

Before Lily gave in to her desire to knock Ari out with a swift punch, the earth shook again even harder than before. Both girls fell down hard with a loud thud. The platform cracked in spiderwebs around them. The dark clouds had melded together, forming a spiral that twisted and twirled in a dangerous dervish dance. Ari's eyes gleamed manically. She leaned back on the ground, raising her hands towards the sky.

"He's coming!" She cried with an insane laugh.

TWENTY-SEVEN

The screaming chaos went deathly silent around Lily, similar to the eerie calm when you're in the eye of a storm. Lily watched in growing horror as the vaporous spiral swiftly solidified into a solid writhing mass. Instead of clouds, large dark glossy scales appeared, an iridescent murky green which twisted sinuously above the trees. Lily guessed whatever this thing was had to be bigger than a small mountain. She peered up further, her neck creaking as she remained sitting the broken platform.

Up past its coiling body, beyond the canopy of the trees, sat a vast serpentine head. Two deadly spiked horns graced its' forehead with smaller spikes peppers on its' neck. The creature's long tongue snaked out, tasting the air. It slowly opened its gaping jaw, revealing rows and rows of razor-sharp fangs. Lily gulped.

Oh what big teeth you have...

Large, slitted yellow eyes bright as citrines looked down amongst the frozen group. Those eyes seemed to burn straight into Lily's brain, branding its mark on her, keeping her frozen in place. Her necklace began to burn in tandem, heating her chest. She thought maybe it was her imagination, but was the Uktena grinning at them? It didn't look like a kind smile either. It seemed more like those evil smiles right before the predator swallows their prey whole. Speaking of, as soon as that thought entered Lily's mind, the serpent's massive mouth opened wider. A bright light began to burn within its' maw. The earth trembled beneath her feet. Lily's eyes widened, fear clogging her throat.

Oh...well that can't be good.

Lily desperately tried to get up, her legs failing, but she couldn't find her balance since the ground continued to shift underneath her. She looked around, worried about Ari, but discovered she was alone. Where did Ari go?

Ugh! Fifty bucks says the stupid prince got to her first. Wait...she just left me?!

Lily realized she should put that issue aside for the moment. That wasn't her highest priority while the sky was getting brighter. Yup, seems like her list of high priority problems was growing. She grimaced at the light, or that Lily grimly noticed, was lightning. Lighting that was coming from Uktena. The sparking voltage expanded, exploding towards her in a scorching blast. She scrambled backwards, crab walking on the dirt, desperately trying to find cover. She braced herself, planting herself flat on the ground when she heard someone yell out.

"Lily!"

Another arc of blue lighting hit Uktena's bolt before it could make contact. The blast dispersed above her, breaking into little particles raining down, making soft popping spurts. Lily, her arms trembling above her head, brought her shocked eyes up to find Cabyll staring at her across the glen, his arm outstretched with remnants of blue sparks exiting his fingertips. Breathing heavily, he lowered his arm. His gaze scanned her, searching for any injuries. When he was sure she was fine, he gave her a wink accompanied by a confident smirk. Lily inwardly groaned, warring between thanking and yelling at him.

I'm never going to hear the end of this am I?

She was about to give him a piece of her mind when she saw his eyes widen in alarm. He pointed above her. She drew her gaze upward to find the massive tree which had taken the blast. That tree cracked and splintered. The familiar creak resounded in Lily's ears, the tree beginning to fall down. In her direction! She rolled quickly to get out of the way. A whisper of leaves tickled her ears as the tree smashed into the ground, shaking the earth beneath her, barely missing her. She heard the wailing as another began to fall. Judging from the sound, this tree may be right above her. Before she could roll again, the hard prickle of wood smacked her head, pieces of sequoia raining down on her. The tree had disappeared in a burst of splinters.

"You okay Lily?" A gruff voice asked near her ear.

She shook tree fragments from her hair. Spyke was by her side, brushing off tree chips from his club. He leaned down to help her up, tugging her to her feet as easily as if she was a feather.

Cabyll glared at Spyke from across the glen.

"I had it covered!" Cabyll yelled at them.

Spyke, nonplused, only smacked his club lightly on his hand a few times while staring at Cabyll. Without another word, Spyke nodded to Lily, jumping down to continue his battle with the dwarves.

She turned back to Cabyll while the horrific horned serpent swayed in a deadly dance above him. She cupped her hands to yell out.

"Where's Dain?"

Cabyll shook his head. She scanned the area. Both and Dain and Ari couldn't be found.

"What now?" She yelled over to him, gesturing towards Uktena.

He shrugged his shoulders, not answering her. She blinked. *Wait...really? Just shrugging your shoulders when a forty-foot fanged monster shot lightning bolts at us?*

He must have seen her face as he raised one hand and mouthed, "I'm thinking."

Lily threw up her hands. *He's thinking?! Idiota.* Where was Dain and Ari? If anyone could stop this thing, maybe it was the folks that released it in the first place. She finally found them by the throne. Ari clutched Dain's forearm, staring up at the Horned Serpent. Ari looked at Uktena in fear. Lily scoffed. *Not the happy ending she was hoping for huh?*

She began to yell over to Cabyll but yelped to find he made a massive jump and reached her. *These fae are too fast!* "Where's Randy?"

Cabyll twirled his sword in his hands. "He went to lead the

rest of the fae to safety. Uktena will destroy anything and everyone in its path right now."

"But he's not moving yet, why is that?"

Cabyll looked up, frowning. Uktena was indeed staying relatively still. He was swaying, like a cobra dancing in the breeze. But he wasn't going forward, or backward, or anywhere. Just swaying side to side in a languid motion, eyes darting rapidly.

Cabyll mused. "You make a good point." His gaze flickered down at her. "For a human that is." Lily snorted and rolled her eyes. She took a better look at Uktena, how his eyes followed their every movement. Her brain churning.

"He's looking for something..."

"Or someone." Cabyll interjected.

The serpent twisted its head suddenly at Dain and Ari. Its tongue flicked out, its golden gaze intensely focused on the couple. Lily grabbed Cabyll's arm, pointing towards the throne.

"I think he's found who he's looking for."

Cabyll gazed down at her hand. He nodded, understanding. They decided to take advantage of Uktena's distraction. Quietly, they sneaked towards Dain and Ari when Dain yelled out.

"Great Uktena! I have woken you from your prison."

The serpent hissed at him in a variety of tones. It took Lily a minute to realize that the snake was communicating. Lily could not understand it, but Dain apparently did as he nodded to the serpent.

Dain continued. "Yes, you are correct. The last remnant of the spell is still active. That is why you are unable to leave this space. I was able to awaken you and allow you consciousness, but you cannot move freely...yet."

Uktena's viperous head tilted and motioned towards Ari. A few more hisses echoed in the glen. Dain smiled. A cruel and cold smile. Ari, unaware of Dain, was focused on the serpent, transfixed.

Cabyll's face paled. He grabbed Lily's hand as he whispered urgently.

"We need to get to your sister...NOW."

Dain's cruel smile widened. The prince disengaged his arm from Ari to bow low at the Horned Serpent. Ari stood there, hands open, confused. Ignoring her, Dain called out in a clear voice.

"Of course! She is for you great Uktena. All I ask is that you assist me in my mission."

Ari frowned.

"Dain? What is going on?" she asked, her voice trembling.

Dain smiled at her, his sharp teeth on full display. "Oh, my special one. I am saying Lord Uktena needs you to be free."

Ari twirled a long section of her hair nervously. "Oh! You never mentioned that. How can I help?"

In response, Uktena reared up, opening its mouth wide. Ari paled, her body shaking uncontrollably. Ari slowly backed up but found herself frozen. She tugged her feet, but they refused to move. That was when Lily noticed Ari had a necklace of her own. It was a delicate snowflake that began to glow white, surrounding Ari. It was as if the light held Ari in place, not allowing her to move.

Ari began to panic. "Dain!" She struggled, her eyes widening with fear. "What's going on? I thought he was free."

Dain chuckled lightly. "Not completely dear. You're the final piece to setting Lord Uktena free. Awakening him was only the first part. My 'righteous' father sealed him away, but for one so powerful as the serpent, my father had layers of protection spells wrapped around him. The only way to have Uktena truly be free was taking the life a human girl who came here, on her own free will, who wished to free him."

"But...but you never said about me dying to free him! You...you said I was special Dain. You said we would change things...together!" Ari cried out, tears running down her cheeks. Lily's heart hurt for her. Broken hearts, no matter the reason, are painful.

Dain gave her a pitying look, running his finger lightly down her cheek, freezing her tears. "And you are special my dear. You are the only one to free Lord Uktena. It was entertaining I will admit for the short time we had. Goodbye petit oiseau." His arm fell away from her as he gestured towards the Horned Serpent. "She is yours *Drottinn*." And with that, he walked away without looking back.

Ari screamed. The serpent twisted its coils, lightning flashing behind it in a nightmarish display. Lily probably imagined it, but she swore she heard a deadly chuckle come through the serpent as it hissed. Ari struggled, still glancing over at the direction the prince left. Probably still hoping Dain would come to her rescue, Lily speculated grimly. Lily's heart dropped when the snake reared back, aiming for the distracted Ari. Before she could grasp another thought, her feet moved forward. She was having an out of body experience when she vaguely heard Cabyll cry out.

"Lily wait!"

His fingers brushed faintly on her shoulder, trying to stop her. She ducked out of his grasp, racing towards Ari the same time Uktena dived down. She kept chanting in her head.

Don't look at the man-eating snake. Don't look at the man-eating snake!

With a launch that would have made her football loving grandfather proud, she dove for Ari, tackling her with a force that threw both of them to the ground, throwing them off the platform. A thunderous smash rocked through the glen as Uktena destroyed the throne where Ari was standing. Lily gasped for breath, her lungs burning with exertion. With a shaking hand, she tore the necklace from Ari and tossed it far away. The white light disappeared.

Ari looked up at her, new tears streaming, mixing with the frost-bitten tracks on her cheeks. She gulped, huge sobs wracking her while she trembled against Lily, clutching her with shaking hands.

"Li....Lily!" Ari cried out. She clutched Lily's forearms so tight Lily winced.

Ignoring the pain, Lily wrapped her arms around Ari. She hushed her soothingly, rubbing Ari's back. Debris fell on top of them, biting into her dress and skin, causing Lily to cringe. A random thought of needing two showers to rid all the tree dust made Lily realize she was heading straight to crazy town if she didn't get her act together.

The Horned Serpent must not have noticed Ari had escaped since he was not making another attempt...yet. Lily knew she had only moments to hide Ari. She looked down at her sister, who was covered in dirt and tears.

Lily held her gaze. "I need you to hide. Can you do that?"

Ari, shaking, frantically tried to look around, her eyes unfocused. "Where's Dain?"

Lily mentally rolled her eyes. *Cielo padre – save me from this nonsense when this is over.* She gently reached out and softly smacked Ari's cheek.

"Ari! Focus!"

Ari turned back to her; eyes wide but shining with some clarity. Slowly she nodded to Lily.

"We're going to get up, slowly." Lily explained calmy and quickly. "I will be the distraction. You go hide behind one of the trees got it?"

"But Lil you-"

Lily shook her head. "Do you understand?"

Ari clamped her mouth shut and nodded again. Lily got up, biting back the stinging pain of the various cuts throughout her body, and reached out to help Ari stand. Ari, on shivering legs, hid behind her. The huge body of the serpent slithered next to them, its coils writhing. Lily gulped. The body alone could have crushed them. The coils began moving backward. Uktena obviously realized it didn't have Ari and was reversing course. Lily clenched her hands, taking a calming breath.

"Go!" She said urgently to Ari, refusing to look behind her.

"Thank you Lil," whispered Ari.

She heard Ari's footsteps fade into the forest. Lily closed her eyes and breathed out, feeling strangely at peace. At least she got Ari out. At least they were alive.

For the moment girl...

She groaned at her traitorous thoughts. Why did she have to be so cynical now? A little positivity can go a long way extending ones' life.

"Lily!"

Cabyll yelled over the other side of Uktena's massive coils. He realized his mistake, his eyes widening, when Uktena's serpentine head twisted towards her. The Horned Serpent hissed angrily, its fangs dripping onto the earth, acid smoke drifting upwards. Her nose wrinkled.

Yup...had to be acid. Why not?

It tilted its head, assessing Lily, this new human. Its tongue darted around, tasting the air. It couldn't find Ari, but that didn't matter. It seemed to be okay with the change. The serpent probably thought one human was as good as another. Her chest burned hotter as its yellow gold eyes zeroed in on her, freezing her in place. Her brain was screaming at her.

Okay legs, move! Move for goodness sakes! That thing is going to devour you if you don't get a move on.

Yeah, obviously her body wasn't listening to her brain. It really is true what they say about a snake's gaze hypnotizing you. She couldn't stop staring at Uktena's eyes. On one hand she was afraid if she didn't move, he'd devour her, but on the other hand if she did move and tore her gaze away, he may still strike. She heard Cabyll calling out to her, his voice angry laced with worry.

"Lily move!!"

Lily scrunched up her nose, but her voice was stuck. *I would if I could dang it!*

Blue lightening streaked out, hitting the Horned Serpent with a flourish. The serpent reared back, whipping its head in frustration at Cabyll. It's tail slashed high in the air, coming down with a booming crash. Cabyll jumped deftly in the air, avoiding the hit, making a spear of lightning that he threw towards the snake's head. The bolt hit the serpent's eye with a crack. Uktena shook its head, blinded temporarily. Her frozen state faded away while the serpent's gaze was interrupted.

Cabyll waved as he gritted out in annoyance.

"Any time now!"

Lily barked back. "I'm moving I'm moving!"

She ran towards him, narrowly avoiding the fast-shifting coils as they twined around the platform. Her legs were so tired, but adrenaline kept her moving. Just one more coil and she could grab Cabyll's outstretched hand. Only one problem. She realized the only way was to climb over the coil.

Well lucky ducky me...

She scrambled to grab onto the slithering tail. The scales were smooth and cool, which made it hard for her to get a grip. She struggled as she tried to jump, her nails scraping the scales with no luck. Cabyll lithely climbed onto the tail, reaching down for her.

"Come on, grab my hand!" He called out, his hand outstretched.

Lily stretched out her arm, her fingertips touching his. She strained forward, feeling the burn in her arm but she couldn't stop.

Almost...

Then the earth shook...

A loud roar shook the ground, the coils whipping frantically, effectively pushing them away from each other. Cabyll was knocked off the tail, thrown backwards towards the trees. He did a flip midair, which allowed him to plant his feet on the tree trunk. He pushed forward, landing on the ground with a grunt. Lily would have found that impressive at another time. However, he was too far away from her. She was stuck.

Lily was forced onto her knees while the coils twisted around her, capturing her effectively within its grasp. Her panic rose as Uktena twined around and around her, building a wall of scales above her head. Lightning cracked above her, the storm clouds raging. Sinuous scales continued a horrific dance around her. She knew she'd have nightmares on this for years. Soon, Uktena's head slithered above the scales, looking down at her. It hissed in triumph seeing her trapped.

Lily tried to move, but she was so tired. Flashes of blue light peeked between the coils. Cabyll must be trying to get to her. She blinked back tears. There was no way he could get through. Even if he hacked his way in, he wouldn't make it in time. Uktena knew, its bright eyes reflecting its amusement.

Her chest was on fire. It hurt to breathe. Still Lily tried to gasp in mouthfuls of cold air, reaching for her chest. The heat emanated from her collarbone. She looked down and saw the pendant was burning, a bright crimson light pulsed. She grasped the pendant, clenching her eyes shut as Uktena's head descended towards her.

"Somebody help, please..."

CHAPTER
TWENTY-EIGHT

A light exploded out of her. An overwhelming energy burst forth, surrounding her, vibrating with a radiant light. The light grew until it encompassed Lily in a makeshift bubble. Lily frowned. What was happening? She looked down. The light was not coming from her, rather, it was emanating from the pendant.

Uktena reared back, shaking its head in frustration. It couldn't go beyond the light barrier, Lily realized. She squinted through the glow to find Uktena's slitted eyes widen in shock. The wind kicked up around her in bursts, as something tickled her head. The light dimmed, but not fully diminished, and Lily's eyes widened in awe. Feathers covered her vision. Large feathers.

Above her, two massive wings beat the air with a thunderous roar. Bright reds, golds, and brown gleamed in the starlight as she gazed at the largest eagle she had ever seen. Its talons were larger than Lily's entire body. The eagle stood stoically still, facing the Horned Serpent. Uktena hissed angrily at the eagle, to which the eagle shrieked back. Lily backed up slowly, making sure she was fully underneath the eagle to keep herself shielded from the serpent. Her foot made a loud crunch, stepping on fallen branch. The eagle's head whipped around. It stared down at her, eyes compassionate and wise. It nodded, gesturing her to move backward.

You don't need to tell me twice. Lily quickly ran at the same time the eagle turned back towards Uktena. Screeching at the serpent, the eagle raised its wings high to the sky, bringing them down with a crash. A large thundercrack echoed in the glen, knocking the serpent backwards, trees crashing around them. Lily couldn't tear her gaze away as the two massive creatures began to battle. She jerked when a hand clamped down on her arm.

"Lily!" Cabyll gazed down at her, searching for injuries. Awkwardly, he put his hand on her shoulders, shaking her slightly. He gave a frustrated growl. "Don't ever do that again!"

She patted his hands and replied with a rueful smile. "Believe me...I won't."

They looked up. The eagle rose off the ground, wind whipping around them. It tore into the serpent with its talons the same moment the serpent bit the eagle with its fangs. The sounds were something that Lily would never be able to forget for the rest of her life.

"What is that Cabyll?" She looked up to see him, his hands still on her shoulders, staring at the eagle in awe. He whispered reverently in her ear, as if someone would hear them over the raging battle above.

"That...is Tinmiukpuk. The Thunderbird." He bowed his head respectfully.

Lily's mouth opened in a big o, unable to respond to that. Probably because she had no idea who Tinmiukpuk was. Randy came up to them, panting, his hands on his legs.

"Y'all, remind me to get more cardio activities in the future with you guys. Everyone is clear-" He looked up and whistled low, putting his hand on his heart. "Well, aint that a hoot, it's Tinmiukpuk the ole man himself."

"Will he be okay?" Lily asked, worried. The eagle was screeching in pain, Uktena had slapped it with its tail.

Randy scratched his head and drawled. "Uktena is as crooked as a barrel full of fishhooks. But if anything can take on that old bugger it's Tinmiukpuk. They've fought for eons. Tinmiukpuk helped put that snake in his prison. Made that old geezer madder than a wet hen let me tell you. He's been itching for revenge ever since, hence you see him raising cane."

The 'raising cane' came into full effect as Uktena cried out loudly, opening up for another blast. Tinmiukpuk flew up, raking its talons across golden serpentine eyes. Uktena howled in pain, the blast flying askew, destroying trees in a long-scorched trail down the valley.

Lily ducked as more branches flew overhead. "They're going to destroy the forest at this rate."

Randy shrugged, clearly nonplussed by the chaos surrounding

them. "Such is the way of the ancients. One of the reasons they were put to sleep or put in prison."

Lily smacked his arm, earning a yelp from the fae. "We have to help the Thunderbird."

Randy scoffed. "Help?! You're all hat no cattle girl. What do you plan to do against two ancients? Best stay outta their way. Outta the way and alive is my motto!"

Cabyll gazed at her, then nodded. "I agree with Lily, we need to do something."

Randy rolled his eyes, clearly outnumbered. "Come on Cab! Whatca pitchin' to do? It's Uktena and Tinmiukpuk we're talking about here. They've been fighting for a millennium."

Cabyll raised his eyebrow. "Look at Lily's necklace."

Lily looked down. The pendant was still glowing, bright and warm. Randy cocked his head to the side, peering at the design. He chuckled low.

"Well, I be darned, Tinmiukpuk you sly bird."

"Care to share please." Lily was exasperated. These fae and their cryptic answers.

Cabyll and Randy ignored her, speaking quickly and softly to each other. Lily strained to hear the plan, but she couldn't over the screeching and howling on top of the rumbling thunder. Oh...and not to mention the falling trees, can't forget those.

She began to worry for the Thunderbird. Tinmiukpuk was tiring with Uktena getting the upper hand. They needed to do something. And do it fast. Lily gasped when Uktena's coils started writhing behind Tinmiukpuk. With the ancients surrounded by the forest, the Thunderbird didn't have enough leverage to maneuver; the trees inhibited his ability to fly freely through the sky.

Still staring up at the ancients, she called out over her shoulder. "Uh…guys? Anytime now would be greaaat."

Randy and Cabyll both turned back, wordlessly jumping into action. Randy disappeared into the trees surrounding Uktena. Cabyll ran up to her.

"Listen to me," he said urgently. "That necklace is important. I'm going to work on Uktena's tail to make sure Tinmiukpuk isn't trapped. Randy's got the next part. What I need you to do is whatever you did to release the Thunderbird."

Lily gaped at him. "What I did? I have no idea what I did!"

He shrugged. "Well, you're going to have to figure it out." A thunderous boom made them both wobble on unsteady legs. "And fast."

Cabyll jumped onto the fast-whipping tail with a flourish. He glanced back at her, giving her a wink. "If you don't, we just all die. Got it human?"

And with that parting jab, he started throwing lightning bolts at the tail, forcing it to move the opposite direction from the Thunderbird. Tinmiukpuk glanced over his feathered shoulder at Cabyll with a grateful nod. That distraction proved to be a mistake as Uktena threw itself into the Thunderbird's chest knocking it downward onto the ground.

The Thunderbird was grounded, it's back on the earth, flapping its massive wings frantically creating tremendous gusts to push the Horned Serpent off but to no avail. Lily stood horrified. The serpent towered over Tinmiukpuk, rearing its head back.

Ready to strike. Cabyll shouted, taking his scimitar out and stabbing the tail, hard. Uktena hissed, annoyed by the distraction.

Another huge, warrior cry echoed overhead. Spyke launched himself at the serpent, his club raised high. With a hefty swing, he struck Uktena, knocking a fang off, before falling back towards the tree limbs. Cabyll followed up with another bolt towards Uktena's eyes. The serpent howled in anger. Cabyll yelled down at her, maybe, or in general.

"We can't keep this up!" His eyes were strained as his arms shook with exertion, holding his scimitar in place within the writhing tail.

Lily grabbed the pendant, but nothing happened. Just the same generic warmth she was feeling the entire time. The same soft light glowed steadily, though it began to flicker weakly. She closed her eyes.

Okay...go! She peeked through her lids, nothing. She closed them again. *Um....power up!* Still nothing. She groaned. She was getting desperate enough to say something corny like, open sesame, or whatever words of empowerment could be said.

She clutched the necklace tighter as her friends struggled to keep the serpent at bay. Tinmiukpuk couldn't move, the slithering coils tightened around his wings, pinning him down firmer to the ground. Lily's heart closed when Spyke was smacked with a tail. Cabyll jumped in front of the Thunderbird, using up the last bits of his power to hold Uktena's remaining fangs from piercing the Thunderbird's neck. Desperate, she shook the pendant, staring at it hard, tears pricking her eyes.

No...no no no! Please! Do something! Please save them!

Slowly, the familiar blaze of heat and light rushed over her. It poured out of the stone like fire dust, swirling in trails around her. In a flash, the fire dust snaked out and surrounded the Thunderbird like a cloak, covering the ancient. Tinmiukpuk's eyes began to glow, sparks flying. The dust started to react, creating huge lightning sparks from the wings, soon encompassing the Thunderbird's entire body. Cabyll, exhausted, fell off Tinmiukpuk with a thud to the ground, unmoving.

Uktena reared back in fear as Tinmiukpuk blasted another gale of wind, knocking the serpent back, effectively setting the Thunderbird free. Gaining ground, Tinmiukpuk pumped his wings. He began to hover over the air, energy pulsing around him.

Lily's hair stood up on end, the electric static palpable. The Horned Serpent roared at the Thunderbird in displeasure, thunder crashing. Tinmiukpuk shrieked in response, lightning charged around him like armor. That lightning shot out of his eyes and wings in streaks. They hit the serpent multiple times, slamming it backwards. But instead of falling to the ground, Uktena found itself caught up in webs. Thousands of spider webs were woven within the trees, creating a gossamer net that entrapped the serpent.

Lily watched in amazement, and somewhat in horror, as a large shadow zipped through the trees, more glistening webbing trailing behind it. It was large and bulky, its various limbs moving and pulling threads around Uktena in all directions. The serpent struggled with his bonds, the earth shaking once more around it. Large vines burst forth from the soil to create a second entrapment underneath. Lily heard a grunt behind her. Prince Jacy, propped up by Peri and Parr, gritted his teeth, his arm outstretched with vines surrounding him.

"This..." He gasped, wincing. "Won't...hold him for long."

It is time.

A deep voice whispered in Lily's mind. She frowned, these weren't her thoughts. She didn't conjure up her inner voice to be masculine, deep, and loud. She looked around but everyone was engaged with Uktena.

Look upwards young mortal.

Lily found there was someone looking at her. Tinmiukpuk, paused from the battle, stared down at her, his bottomless eyes capturing hers. The Thunderbird nodded.

Yes young Sentinel. It is time. Use the pendant as it was meant to be, and we shall entrap my enemy once again.

"But how? I'm not magical or anything special. I'm just me." Lily said dejectedly. Watching this epic encounter made Lily realize now, more than ever, how ordinarily ordinary she was.

And that is why you are special. The Thunderbird's mental voice was calming but booming. Tinmiukpuk bent his head down further until they were eye to eye. Lily was overwhelmed. This sheer presence of this ageless creature pressed down on her. If she didn't know any better, she would have sworn the bird smiled, if a beak could smile.

Your mortality makes your special, not weak. Invulnerability can breed hubris and hate. Take Uktena for example. The Thunderbird motioned towards the howling Uktena. *But mortality? Oh...that is a gift. A gift that inspires warriors, poets, and scholars. To know your days are limited brings wisdom to cherish life's everyday miracles.*

Mortals are immortals other halves. It takes both our worlds to exist. Just as I protect you, you too support me and humble me.

Tinmiukpuk turned back as the serpent hissed and howled, tearing the vines and webs frantically. Lily noticed there weren't many bindings left standing. *The binds that hold my nemesis will not hold him much longer. Young Sentinel, we must work together.*

"And do what exactly?" asked Lily warily.

I need to tap into your soul.

"Excuse me?" Someone tapping into your soul didn't sound as easy as asking a neighbor for a cup of milk.

Tinmiukpuk glanced at her, his eyes warm and sparking. *Do what I've seen you do best. Love young mortal. Let your love and kindness seep into your being. With all your heart and soul, put your intention on saving them. We can bind him. Lend me your strength for the task.*

"So...no fire bolts coming from my hands or flashy jump kicks with super strength I take it?" Lily grumbled to herself.

Tinmiukpuk must have heard her for his massive shoulders shook with small laughter. Though that 'small' laughter shook the ground under her feet.

Glad to see I have a Sentinel with a sense of humor. Remember what I said mortal. Even everyday things are miracles. Now – his wings flapped, lightening embedding itself in the gales of wind – *Onward to battle Sentinel!*

The pendant burned hotter, and she winced at the pain. She took her hair ribbon, wrapping it around her hand and the pendant. Taking a deep breath, she squeezed her eyes shut and focused. She thought of her dad, Tabby, and Brandon. Parr, Peri,

Brom, Barlow, Alasdair, Randy, Spyke, and Cabyll. All those people who would be hurt if Uktena would be free. She focused on keeping them safe. But it didn't seem enough. The wind whipped around her face, her hair stinging her cheeks. The shrieks and howls got louder, more dissonant. Just when she thought she was failing, icy fingers wrapped around her free hand. Startled, she opened her eyes. Ari gazed at her, her face dirty and streaked with tears. Ari squeezed her wrapped hand, giving her a small smile.

Clutching Ari's hand in a tight grasp, Lily closed her eyes again. She brought up images of all her family and friends, and Ari. Their hands clasped together, the burning light seeped into the pendant. With an audible blast, the light rushed outwards towards Tinmiukpuk.

Burning crimson flames and ice white lightening swirled around the Thunderbird as the black storm clouds gathered around him. With a bright glow, the ancient raised his wings high to the clouds. Flames and lightning shot outwards, creating brilliant chains. The chains rushed forward, wrapping around Uktena to bind him tightly. The serpent hissed and wailed angrily. The chains glowed and, with a final blow, lighting burst forth from Tinmiukpuk's eyes. The Horned Serpent howled in agony, writhing in pain, unable to break free. The ground rumbled ominously. The sky opened up to make room for a huge lightning bolt that beamed down directly onto the snake with a deafening explosion.

Dust flew all around them, blinding Lily. The wind had knocked her to her knees. An eerie silence rested throughout the glade. Lily opened her eyes, wiping the gritty dust from her eyes.

Uktena was gone. But, Tinmiukpuk also disappeared. Confused, Lily spun around. Everyone stood in silence amongst the fallen trees, the uprooted forest, and the broken earth. You never would have known two ancients were here, except for the massive destruction surrounding them. Lily trembled when someone squeezed her hand. Ari was still there, holding her hand tightly.

"You did it Lily." Ari whispered, a small, sad smile across her face.

Lily squeezed her hand back. "It wasn't just me you know."

Ari ducked her head shyly, then, remembering she still clutched Lily's hand, quickly removed it.

Lily ignored the gesture. She continued to smile at Ari. "I'm glad you're okay Ari."

Ari shuffled from one foot to another, not saying a word. She looked up at Lily guiltily. "Listen Lil I-"

A strong hand slapped her hard on the back, making her wheeze, effectively interrupting Ari. Peri's tinkling laughter tickled her ears.

"Oh my gosh Lily girl that was a-maz-ing!" Peri draped herself on Lily's back, wagging her finger at Ari. "Naughty little human, putting your sweet sister through this. But all's well that ends well I always say. And explosions. Gotta have explosions. Boom!" Peri made a whoosh motion over Lily's head. Lily chuckled.

"Peri, get off the poor girl," grunted Spyke. He lumbered up to them, a cut running down his cheek. Ignoring the blood running down his face, he balanced his club on his shoulder.

Peri sighed loudly, nimbly jumping off Lily. "Ugh! You're no fun Spyke. I mean you got to have ALL the fun while I had to play nurse."

"You had an important job Peri. And I'm sure the prince is grateful," said Lily.

A deep voice replied. "Yes...said prince is grateful."

Prince Jacy approached them, Parr at his side. Lily smiled at the brownie, who beamed up at the group. Limping slightly, the prince paused when he reached the group. He gave them a slight bow, as much as he could allow so he wouldn't fall over.

"On behalf of my territory, I thank you all." Jacy turned to Spyke, reaching out his hand. "Wado dinadanvtli – thank you brother." Spyke clasped the outstretched hand, grunting with a nod.

"Now y'all don't be forgettin' about little ole me!" Randy cackled as he jumped down from the trees carrying Cabyll under his arm. Lily beamed seeing both of them unhurt. Well...relatively unscathed. Cabyll certainly had a grumpy look to him. Lily suspected it probably had to do with being carried.

Cabyll groused. "Put me down old man! I said I needed to catch my breath, not a ride."

With a dramatic sigh, Randy plopped him down on his feet. Cabyll stood upright quickly, brushing off his shoulders.

Ignoring the grumpy Cabyll, Randy outstretched his arms with a flourish. "Prince Jacy, I reckon you owe me a huge thank you right about now."

Cabyll rolled his eyes, giving a hiss. "Can't you not be in the spotlight for two minutes?"

Randy placed his hand over his heart. "You wound me Cab. All

I did was trap Uktena til our little darlin did the final blow. I mean...when I put it that way, you could say I did most of the work."

Cabyll's eyes widened as he growled. "Most of the work?!" Lily didn't think Cabyll had any energy left, but she was wrong when blue sparks flickered to life from his fingertips, his eyes beginning to glow.

Lily jumped in. Time for a distraction. "Wait! I thought there was a spider or something. Randy did you get help?"

Cabyll froze, glancing over at her. He slowly smirked, his arms relaxing as he chuckled out in amusement. "Excellent question human. Go ahead Randy, tell her about the 'spider'."

Randy scratched the back of his head, clearly uncomfortable. "Umm...that's for another time alright? Don't like to web and tell."

Lily inwardly chuckled. Randy would tell her eventually, not that she didn't have an idea to begin with. But it wasn't her story to tell. She was so happy to see everyone and then Ari –

She turned, but Ari wasn't there.

Lily frowned. "Guys? Where's Ari!"

Everyone began looking but were unable to find her. Lily, in her panic, stopped when a slight tug pulled on her leg. She looked down. Parr glanced up sheepishly, his face splotched red.

"Um, Miss Lil," he whispered guiltily. He stopped to hold up a scrap of parchment in his trembling hands. Lily picked the small piece of paper, opening it up hesitantly. Her eyes widened as she skimmed over the words. Quickly, she stuffed the note into her pocket with shaking fingers. Cabyll noticed her shaking. He rushed over, glaring down at the brownie.

"Parr! Explain," he demanded.

Parr clutched his hands together, pulling and breaking them apart. "Well...uh...you see," he began to stammer. "The young lady, she had something to give Miss Lil, but...you know you were talking, and you know it's very impolite to interrupt the natural flow of the conversation-"

Randy groaned. "Simmer down son, let it settle a moment and tell us."

Parr blinked and put his hands on his hips with indignation. "Excuse me! What did I say about the improprieties of interrupting the natural flow of the conversation? Now as I was clearly saying, the young lady was talking to Prince-"

"Parr!" Cabyll barked, startling the brownie. "Get to the point!"

Lily's heart stuttered. She ignored the rest of the argument between the guys. Instead, she walked up to a bewildered Prince Jacy. Lily's eyes caught the prince's startled ones.

"Where's Dain?"

Silence ensured. Jacy's eyes widened, recognition settling in. It came to his attention, along with the rest of the party, that the other prince was nowhere to be seen. Cabyll groaned, giving the brownie a murderous glare. The brownie's face got even more pink as his mouth opened in a big O.

"Oh...I didn't think of that," said Parr.

Jacy pursed his lips, thinking for a moment. "I think I know where he'd go. Follow me."

Jacy raised his hand, gesturing them to follow him. They raced out of the glade, past the large sequoias, past the rolling ferns until Lily could see the faint golden glow of the rising sun cresting over the river. The river sparkled, the dawn light dancing over the water in ripples.

There, by the riverbank, was one of the strangest creatures Lily had ever seen. And that was saying something based on what she'd seen so far. Pale white. As in there was no pigmentation whatsoever. It was as if the creature lacked color rather than white being the actual color. It's extremely long spindly limbs, well almost 90 feet long, were slowly rippling in the water. A wisping fog rose from the creature, surrounding itself and the riverbank in a grey haze, bringing an artic chill to the air. The creature resembled somewhat like a whale, but only somewhat. One thing Lily couldn't get over was its face. It's eerily human face. Lily trembled when spotted at the top of the creature's massive bulbous head two shadows. Dain and Ari. She turned to see her friends had gone pale. Jacy cursed under his breath.

"He brought a Ningen...into MY territory!" The Forest Prince growled, his eyes glowing.

Randy whistled low next to Lily. He shook his head side to side. "That little brother of yours there is broke bad if ever I saw." He nodded towards Jacy. "You fixin' to teach him a lesson?"

Jacy's eyes glowed emerald green. Ferns and vines whipped around them, spearing through the clearing towards Dain. Dain waved a hand, speaking something low to the creature. The ningen raised one of its long lanky hands and batted the vines away, the tendrils turning to ice and shattering when they hit the bank. Lily blinked.

What is it a giant gumby?!

Jacy cursed under his breath. Cabyll resigned, shook his head. He looked over at her regretfully. Lily's panic rose. She turned to Ari, beseeching her with her eyes, hoping that her sister would still come home. Ari refused to look at her. She clasped to Dain's back, burying her face in his shoulder. Dain looked at them with a playful grin, borderline sneering. He called out to the group mockingly.

"While this reunion did not go as planned, I do thank you brother. You've given me much to think about for the future."

Jacy's voice boomed over the river. "Traitor! You are no longer welcome in this territory!"

Dain chuckled. "Fine. Then my petit oiseau and I will be off." He saluted the party, giving a parting wink at Lily. "The fun has only just begun." And with a wave, the ningen sped off through the riverbend, disappearing into the cold fog, taking Ari with it.

CHAPTER
TWENTY-NINE

They say the path returning is exponentially shorter than the path forward. No truer phrase was ever spoken in Lily's mind as she found herself back at the border between the Veil and her home. It seemed it happened in the blink of an eye that she found herself staring at the familiar wall of trees in the ferned forest. Probably was shorter because she was in a daze the entire time, still replaying the last moments where Ari turned her back and walked away.

She seethed, the bitterness still tearing into her stomach. *Walked away with a prince who tried to feed her to a snake! Talk about having relationship issues.*

She recalled when she left Prince Jacy's territory. He had graciously thanked them for everything they had done. Lily would have liked to have remembered how kind and gentlemanly the Forest Prince was...until he dragged the Hecesiiteihii out by vines, tightening them painfully while they pleaded for mercy. The way Jacy was looking at them, devoid of feeling, it seemed like mercy was not going to be granted. Lily vividly recalled the exchange:

"You have abused my generosity for the last time!" Jacy snarled. His hand clasped tighter, the vines squeezing the treacherous dwarves until their breaths came out in wisps.

"Wait! Wait wait wait a minute there princey pie!" Peri called out with a flourish. She flew up, past the prince, to the head Hecesiiteihii. She ran a nail down his cheek softly, slightly cutting skin. "Maybe you could get some information out of these guys."

"The other prince did say that this was only the beginning your Highness," agreed Spyke.

Jacy nodded, his gaze thoughtful. He glanced over at Spyke. "Very true my noble Thunderboy. Shappa, will you consider coming back? The forest could use one of its strongest protectors again."

Spyke's gaze landed on Peri who was juggling knives, where she had hid them Lily couldn't figure out. Spyke gave a shrug. He tilted his head to Jacy, who nodded in silent understanding.

"Very well. Just know that you – all of you," he gestured to everyone there, "have a safe haven when you need it in my forest. Now, Shappa. You and your peri pixie have leave to do what you want with these traitors. Find out what my fool brother is doing."

Peri giggled. "O...M...G...we're going to have soooo much fun!" She snickered, her nail cutting a deeper trail down the dwarf's cheek.

Lily flinched. She forgot that her new friend seemed to thrive on chaos and destruction. The vines pulled the screaming Hecesiiteihii back into the forest away from them. Peri zipped towards her.

"Aww Lily sweetie! I'm going to miss you!!" Peri hugged her, seem-

ingly forgetting what she did to the dwarf a moment ago. Peri turned puppy dog eyes up at Jacy. "Can we go visit her pwease pwease pwease!"

Spyke groaned at Peri but did nod as he addressed the prince. "As a favor your Highness, I too would like to be able to visit Lily."

Lily swore Cabyll growled behind her accompanied by Randy's laugh, but she was too squished in Peri's hug to see anything but Jacy's smile.

The prince chuckled softly. "Of course. She is, after all, a new Sentinel according to the great Thunderbird. It is my pleasure to grant your privilege to visit her."

Peri squealed loudly, hugging her tighter. Large arms surrounded both of them. Spyke gathered them up in a bear crushing hug that lifted her off the ground effortlessly. Peri and Spyke smiled at her warmly before letting her go gently. They both turned and, with a parting wave, vanished into the forest after the dwarves. Lily suspected they were already starting their 'job' to collect information. But she decided she didn't want to dwell on that too much. If this crazy journey taught her anything, it was ignorance in certain situations involving dangerous fae was indeed a good course of action.

Jacy nodded to the rest of the group, his expression solemn.

"It seems due to recent events that a family reunion with my other siblings is in order. I apologize but I will be unable to guide you back to the Gateway. But know this young human." He smiled down warmly at Lily with a deep bow. "While this battle had its wins and losses, you are a true warrior, and I am grateful to you. Your heart is strong young lady, and I am honored to have met you. I can't wait to see where your

journey takes you my butterfly blessed by mystery." He winked. Cabyll yelled out.

"Butterfly?!"

Lily shook herself from her musings, staring at the 'Gateway' as Jacy called it. Randy had taken off, per his norm, saying he had some folks he needed to chat with after these recent developments. He did promise, much to Cabyll's chagrin, that he would stop by for a visit soon. After all, he reminded them again, they were the most interesting story he's seen *in a koon's age.* Whatever that meant. He didn't specify how long a koon's lifespan entailed. Or what a koon was. Lily didn't want to assume he meant a racoon, because who really knew if he meant that or something else entirely.

That wasn't all the unfinished issues she was left with. She still had loads of questions, more than when she started this journey. What was a Sentinel? Was she supposed to be guarding something? Where did Uktena go? What was Dain up to? Where was Ari? Was she safe...ish? And the most important question that lingered on her mind like a nail scraping on a chalkboard...what was she going to tell Tabby and her dad?

She groaned loudly, wishing a hole would swallow her up. Maybe a meteor would hit and poof her into dust. Those all seemed like preferable outcomes than having to tell her parents. *"Oops, sorry! The first time I was sent to watch over my new siblings I lost one to a fae prince who tried to have her killed and she ended up still going with him in the end cause she's smitten by pretty faces!"* Thankfully, she didn't voice her thoughts, but the groan was enough to reach the ears of the rest of her group. Cabyll glanced at her, rolling his eyes.

"You're too young to be whining," he remarked.

"Geez! Look who's talking." Lily retorted icily.

Cabyll shrugged, focusing on the shimmering translucent wall in front of them. He remained silent when Parr scampered up to the gate. Excitement beat from the brownie in waves. Parr turned a wide smile over to them, clapping his hands together in anticipation.

"Alright then! It has been...well...." Parr rocked on his heels, his face trying to remain polite. "It has been an adventure I must say. But I am ready to go home. Just like a pair of nicely worn slippers that you have settled in just right." He turned a tired smile to Lily. "And Miss Lil. I am very much ready to put on my pair of slippers and tuck in tight."

Lily's gaze softened at the brownie's hopeful look.

Parr turned to Cabyll and wagged his finger, his tone stiff.

"And do not think that I forgot about your association with the very individual that put Miss Lil in precariously dangerous situations you...you...ruffian! I will have you know that I plan to report this all in great detail to Mister Brom and Mister Alasdair."

Cabyll smirked. "Are you going to report that in triplicate like a book report? If so, I'd love a copy. Make sure to report my devilishly handsome good looks and amazing skills." He gave the brownie a flirty wink for emphasis.

Parr sputtered, his face red. He jumped through the Gateway with renewed hast. Lily heard him mutter, "of all the rapscallion, insufferable-" In a blink, he was gone.

Lily chuckled. "Devilishly handsome huh?"

Cabyll smirked. "I can only speak the truth."

Lily rolled her eyes. "Be nice to Parr." She gestured to Cabyll's bare neck. "Well now that you're free, can you make sure to forgo drowning in the future please."

"Can't make any promises human."

"Come on! You're not *that* bad," protested Lily.

For a moment, Cabyll's cavalier attitude switched, his gaze serious. He spoke softly, almost hesitant. "Lily...remember. I'm not a good fae."

He stared at her a minute, silent. Waiting to see her response. Lily really had nothing to reply after that. After all, the guy was considered a top assassin. He was right in a sense, but then again, she didn't think it was that blatantly cut and dry. The silence continued. She shuffled her feet awkwardly.

What am I doing? She groused to herself.

Parr was right. It was time to go home. She was about to walk through when a hand tugged her arm. Cabyll looked at the ground, running his free hand through his hair nervously. He cleared his throat, raising his gaze to hers, his expression anxious.

"Hey human, umm...Lily," he corrected when she raised her eyebrow at him. "I just wanted to say. Even though your sister didn't come back like you wanted...you still...well...you..."

She sighed. "You don't have to say it."

Cabyll shook his head. "What you did was one of the bravest things I've seen, and I mean of anyone that I've come across. I wanted you to know. You shouldn't have regrets. You did everything you could have done."

"I'm not giving up on her." Lily pursed her lips, her gaze steely with determination.

Cabyll grinned, the awkwardness surrounding them lightening. "I wouldn't expect anything less from you."

Lily felt her own lip quirk upward. "Thanks for that pep talk if that's what you call it. I hope you give your friends better ones."

Cabyll nervously shifted his hands into his hair again, messing it up. "Well...that is how I talk to my friends."

Lily's mouth dropped. "Wait! Seriously?"

Cabyll's cheeks flushed as he grumbled. "I don't have many friends."

Then in a blink, he gave her dazzling smile, his sea green eyes sparkling. "Of course, only the most adoring of my admirers benefit from my irresistible charm and wit." He gave her a wink for good measure. "And I promise to halt on drowning for now. After all, I think I'd like my doting public to continue idolizing me."

Lily narrowed her eyes at him and grumbled. "Still such an arrogant, pompous-"

Cabyll's warm laughter filled the forest as he grabbed her hand to pull her through the Gate, while she still griped at him.

THIRTY

Lily leaned her head against her arm, listlessly stirring the silver straw in her chocolate milkshake. The kitchen was abuzz with energy. Brom and Parr worked insanely making all kinds of snacks and treats, welcoming the group back with enthusiasm. When Lily and Cabyll had walked into the cottage an hour ago, Brom was so startled he dropped the plates he was holding with a crash. Barlow and Alasdair had yelled with joy, giving Lily hugs all around. Brandon stayed back, his eyes glassy, before finally running up to Lily enveloping her in a fierce hug. Barlow even clapped Cabyll on the back of the head...not too hard this time, his sign of gratitude.

Lily sighed, her head resting on the cold granite tile with a thump. While being back home was wonderful, she still had no idea how to handle her dad and Tabby. By her calculations they would be arriving within the next half hour. She guessed she had about thirty minutes left before her head was going to be on a silver platter rather than on the kitchen table. Maybe it would grace the very platter that currently held an array of very lovely looking cherry goat cheese tartlets.

"Don't look so down Lil." Brandon sat down next to her, handing her a cream puff.

Lily apathetically put the puff back on the platter. She groaned, stretching her arms on the counter limply.

"Dad and Tabby will be here soon. What am I going to tell them?"

Brandon took a deep breath. He scooted closer to her, pausing a minute, unsure what to do. Hesitantly, he wrapped his arm around her shoulders. In a rare display, he spoke seriously. Well, as serious as he could for a teenager.

"You tell them you did everything you could. Lil, I saw what was after you in the mirror and..." He paused, his body shaking softly, remembering the horrific scene. "I mean that thing after you was like crazy scary. And it's not like you have superpowers or anything. Point is, you went to hell and back for her, Lily. And I'll always be grateful for that. I'm just glad I didn't lose both of you."

Lily's eyes welled up. She squeezed Brandon's hand as they sat together. It was one of those moments of familial warmth where a lifetime is packed into one precious second. Lily's heart got stuck in her throat as she choked back both equal parts of happiness and guilt. Because how could she have the right to feel happy when she knew that Ari was gone?

Brandon's voice waivered, his hand slightly trembling over

hers. "We're not giving up on Ari right? We're still going to try to get her back?"

She squeezed his fingers again, reassuring him. "We're not giving up."

Brandon blushed. He clumsily grabbed another tartlet, changing the subject. "At least we won't have to explain the horse to Mom and Tony." He shoved the pastry in his mouth, chewing noisily.

Lily nodded in agreement. Cabyll left a few minutes ago. Now that the collar was gone, he was free to do what he liked. Lily thought he'd run and never look back. However, he told her he'd return since he knew she'd be 'foolish' enough to still try and find Ari by herself. Brom and Parr protested in various polite ways, but of course it did not deter Cabyll. He smiled at Lily and, turning back into his horse form, galloped towards the forest.

He does prance. The memory making her chuckle.

"Apologies for interrupting you Miss Lily, Master Brandon," addressed Brom. "I am happy to report that everything in the home has been swept, polished, dusted, and put away. You should have no extraneous issues that could put you in precarious predicament with your life givers."

Alasdair snorted. "Ack ye daft dandy! Just say the word. Parents! Par-ent-s!"

Brom deliberately ignored Alasdair as he continued. "Please do not hesitate to whisper our names should you need any assistance, but I'm afraid your parents," he glared at Alasdair, "will neither see nor hear us at the present time."

Brandon sighed. "I guess it would have been too easy to ask you guys to pop up to give proof of Lil's story."

Alasdair gave the siblings a sympathetic look. "I'm 'fraid it doesn't work that way lad."

"Just like you can't tell us about Lily being a Sentinel?" Brandon asked.

Brom and Alasdair had the decency to look embarrassed. They had been extremely closed lipped about the whole, "Sentinel" thing. Other than going pale as chalk and Brom practically fainting on the floor when Lily explained what the Thunderbird told her, Lily and Brandon weren't given any more details on the issue.

"It is not our place to speak those secrets, Master Brandon." Brom remarked regretfully.

So many questions answered, and still more questions remained. Lily sighed in frustration. A warm voice whispered to Lily.

Nvtsoasesgvna young Sentinel. Patience, all in due time.

The pendant slightly warmed against her chest as the deep voice of the Thunderbird gently whispered in her mind.

I am here with you. As the water flows over the rocks, solutions will flow over obstacles. Be fluid like the water little one. Go with the river.

All the water allusions in the world aren't going to help when I'm grounded for eternity, groused Lily.

She felt, rather than heard, the Thunderbird's chuckle, his voice fading away, the pendant cooling to the touch. A loud thump of a car door rang throughout the house. Brom and Alasdair winked out of sight as their parents' voices mumbled at the front door.

Tabby yelled, opening the door with a swing. "Hi everyone! We're back!"

Tony was behind her, his arms laden full of packages and suitcases. He stumbled, desperately grasping at the parcels, his arms wailing. Thankfully, he didn't lose any when he regained his footing.

"We got all of you presents!" Tony beamed excitedly at Lily and Brandon. His gaze looked around the kitchen curiously. "Where's Ari?"

A lump built in her throat, her palms sweaty. Brandon shoveled a few more morsels in his mouth, not answering.

Tabby scanned around the cottage as she called out. "Ari?"

"Um, Tabby, Dad? About Ari..." Lily hesitated.

A loud bang shook the cottage. The back door in the kitchen flew wide open.

"Did I hear my name?"

Lily and Brandon sat there, frozen in shock. Brandon's jaw may have dropped down to the floor, if jaws could physically drop that far. There, walking into the house like nothing happened, was Ari. She walked up to the two of them with a bright smile, pushing her sunglasses up and engulfed them in a hug.

Lily sat there, unable to move. She vaguely noticed her hand slowly come up to awkwardly pat Ari on the back.

Ari pulled them in closer, her head in between them. She brought her lips to the shell of their ears and whispered.

"Prince Jacy sends his best. Don't have the brownie banish me again, will you?"

In answer, the cottage's windowpanes flapped open and shut angrily. Ari gave a sly chuckle, winking into the air.

With a quick turn, Ari focused on Tabby and Tony, plastering a brilliant smile on her face. She skipped over to their parents with a soft whistle.

"Mom! I missed you! Can I help you move those packages?"

Tabby blinked. "Oh! Why thank you Ari. That'd be wonderful."

Ari turned around and winked back at them as she herded the parents outside. Lily and Brandon stood there a moment, still stunned. Though that didn't stop Brandon from blurting out. "Hey! You look better this time!"

The Ari glanced backward with a narrowed glare, flipping her sunglasses over her eyes before the door closed shut behind them. The kitchen was quiet for a moment until Brandon sputtered out.

"Was that – is that the...the..."

Lily nodded, resigned. "Looks like the changeling is back. I guess this is Prince Jacy's way of trying to help." Though she wondered if this was his way of 'helping', what did he consider the opposite?

Brandon groaned, putting his face in his hands. "Seriously dude! That's like mega crazy. That thing is insane!"

Lily pursed her lips with a pop. "Yup..."

"We really should tell it to leave."

"Yup..."

"Okay." Brandon paused. "So...who wants to tell it?"

Lily raised her eyebrow at him. "You want to tell your mom and my dad where Ari really is?"

Brandon groaned again. "Yeah, I see your point."

"This actually can work though." Lily motioned Brandon closer to whisper. "If the changeling is here, that buys us some time."

"To do what?" Brandon asked puzzled.

Lily looked down at the scrap of paper she had kept tucked inside her pocket. She unfolded it. It read:

Lil,

Please forgive me. He needs me right now. I'm sorry about before. Tell Brandon and mom I love them. I'll miss you and I hope to see you soon.

Ari

Lily smiled. "No family is perfect, but we stick together. We don't give up on them."

LILY FOUND herself gazing out her windowsill again, staring towards the creek into the forest. This time, she could see the iridescent shimmer of the Veil winking back at her. She could never unsee what she saw the last few days. Thankfully, her father and Tabby were convinced by the changeling's performance. As much as Lily hated to admit it, the fae was a really good actor.

Lily hugged her knees against her chest. She finally understood what her father had told her about family. Ari may be gone for now, but she always will have a place as long as they remembered her, accepted her, and showed her they cared. Lily didn't know what would happen between Ari and Dain. Would he leave Ari again? Would she come to her senses and leave him? If Lily were being honest with herself, she realized it didn't matter. Because no matter what, she had to show Ari there was a place for her with them. She was certain Ari had begun to see that earlier. Ari's note proved that.

After all, a person may be away from their home, but if they are loved, they are never truly alone. Lily jumped down, heading back into her room. She thumbed the newly ingrained wood on her dresser, her finger tracing the outline of the tiger lily she etched that evening. She smiled, her pendant warming. Ari wasn't there, but she still cared about them. And that was hopeful. This wasn't time for goodbyes. This was the time for beginnings.

About the Author

Rachel Hawk is a full-time mom and wife while also working a full-time job. Writing a novel was always on her bucket list, and finally, became a reality.

Rachel enjoys cooking up something new in the kitchen, blaring music on multiple levels of her house ranging from jazz to heavy metal, playing ninjas with her two spirited children, and hiking the woods looking for magic.

She lives in Maryland wine country with her husband, two children, and two cats named Fergus and Bucky who are the epitome of the Odd Couple.

Find her at:
https://authorrachelhawk.com/

www.ingramcontent.com/pod-product-compliance
Lightning Source LLC
Chambersburg PA
CBHW072335020726
47506CB00004B/890